# LEGS

Angela Lam Turpin

iUniverse, Inc.
New York   Bloomington

# Legs

iUniverse books may be ordered through booksellers or by contacting:

iUniverse
1663 Liberty Drive
Bloomington, IN 47403
www.iuniverse.com
1-800-Authors (1-800-288-4677)

ISBN: 978-0-595-53091-5 (pbk)
ISBN: 978-0-595-63147-6 (ebk)

Printed in the United States of America

*For Ed, with love*

# Acknowledgments

I would like to thank the staff at iUniverse for making the publication process as enjoyable as possible.

Many people have influenced my knowledge of real estate and loans over the years. In particular, I would like to thank George F. Adair, George F. Adair II, Tom Torgerson, Ross Liscum, Lee Daniels, Meg Sevrens, and Scott Weiss, who has become my best friend.

To my writing group, I owe a thousand years of gratitude: Jan Ogren, for her constructive criticism, love, support and active encouragement throughout the years; Marjorie Mann, for her feedback and inspiration; and Dianna Grayer, for her example of persistence, daring, and faith as well as her intuitive critiques. Many thanks to the other writers and friends who have offered their time, expertise, and friendship, in particular: Sheridan Gold, who taught me how to live my dreams through the example of living her own dreams; Diane Payne, a fabulous writer and friend who graciously critiqued my novel in a timely manner; Melanie McDonald, who offered her writing expertise, friendship, and support; Bill Rice, who has believed in me since high school; and Melanie Rae Thon, who taught me how to trust my feelings and turn my writing into part of my spiritual practice.

Thanks to Hedgebrook for providing time, space, and emotional nourishment on my writing journey. Thanks to the Vermont Studio Center for the opportunity to work alongside writers and visual artists in a supportive community.

Thanks to my father who learned how to be the loving, compassionate cheerleader I have always wanted. Thanks to my mother for purchasing my first diaries, writing books and magazine subscriptions. I am forever grateful for her suggestion that I study journalism. Thanks to my sisters who continue to inspire me: Cynthia, Elizabeth, and Sylvia, who graciously provided her services as a photographer for the author's photo. Thanks to my in-laws, Don and Sheila, for their love and support. Thanks also to my sister-in-law, Leanne Turpin Refvik, for her artistic advice.

Most of all, I am thankful for my children, Gabriel and Rose, who understand my need to write and for my husband, Ed, who designed the wonderful book cover in record time and who makes everything I do possible.

# CHAPTER 1

▼

"What?" I punch the pause button on the treadmill and slow to a stop, the cell phone pressed against my ear.

"We're getting back together," Diana tells me.

"Umm…congratulations," I say, straining to sound pleased. Damn, I'm going to have to return that Dior purchase. If Diana isn't getting divorced, she won't need that condo we were getting ready to bid on.

"But Jack and I are talking about downsizing," she says, as if to cushion the news. "Maybe after Charlotte graduates."

Their daughter is fifteen. Even if she skips a grade, it'll be another year before they buy anything.

"Okay, great." That's one less sale I can count on.

I hang up and toss the phone on the couch and push the start button on the treadmill. A brisk walk quickly turns into an eager jog. That's the third buyer this week I've lost. And it's only Wednesday. Is real estate the only business where you can work 80 hours a week and still not make a profit?

I wouldn't know. This is all I've ever done. And it's all I've ever wanted to do since I stepped into my first open house when I was eight years old. The saleswoman wore a smart red suit and passed out glossy flyers and gave us a tour of a remodeled ranch-style home the neighbors were selling because the mother was sick.

I pump my arms faster and shorten my stride. A trickle of sweat drips over my nose and lands on my mouth. With the back of my hand, I wipe my face. The cool spring air from the open window rushes in to fill my anxious lungs. Long slants of morning light fall across the room. I increase the speed and adjust the incline. My lungs feel like they could burst. Through short breaths, I smell coffee from the kitchen. Tom must be awake.

Madonna sings, "Express Yourself," my ring tone for work. Not now. I'm almost finished with my three mile run. Okay. I won't answer it. It's probably just another buyer calling to cancel or reschedule a showing appointment. It can go to voice mail.

But what if it's a buyer answering my Craiglist ad?

Before Madonna reaches the chorus for a second time, I punch the pause button and leap from the treadmill. I take a couple of deep breaths so I don't sound like I'm in the middle of having sex. "Trina Kay, T & T Realty, how may I help you?"

"Oh, sorry, wrong number."

What? I gave up the last sixty seconds of my run to answer a wrong number. Two years ago, I wouldn't have cared about the call. I had more buyers than I could handle. And more money than I could spend. But now, with the market as bad as it is, I would give up my morning run entirely if it meant closing a sale and paying off my Visa bill.

I toss the cell phone on the couch and stalk out of the room.

In the kitchen, Tom sits at the table eating a bowl of shredded wheat. He's already dressed in his best Armani suit. He glances up from reading the *San Jose Mercury News* and winks. "Cute outfit. Who has good taste?"

I smile. I am wearing the Elisabetta Rogiani workout wear Tom bought for my birthday last week. I had been eyeing her collection ever since I saw Monica Brant sporting her glitzy gold tank top and boy shorts on the cover of *Oxygen*. That's one of the things I love about Tom. He'll forgo season tickets to the A's game in order to buy me something special. I bend to kiss his forehead. "You do."

I pop two slices of bread into the toaster and pour a cup of coffee. It tastes rancid. I dump it in the sink. God, how I miss Starbucks.

A few moments later, I toss two burnt pieces of toast on a plate and sit down next to Tom. I glimpse the headlines and scowl. "How can you read that? It's all doom and gloom. Subprime market crashes. Foreclosures rise. Home prices are down. Inventory skyrockets. It's depressing."

"Don't worry," Tom says. "I have a plan."

That's another thing I love about Tom. He's always thinking of something bigger and better. Nothing ever gets him down.

"What is it?" I ask, buttering my toast.

Tom winks. "It's a surprise."

"How about a hint?" I ask with a seductive smile.

Tom tilts his head to the side. I love how his mop of golden brown hair flops over his forehead just above his eyes. I dust the crumbs from my hands and reach up to brush the hair away from his forehead.

He reaches under the table and places a hand on my thigh. "It's catchy and dramatic."

"Catchy? Like the Oscar Mayer bologna song."

Tom shakes his head. "My god, that's ancient."

"It's not. My sister and I sang it as kids."

Tom laughs. "That's ancient."

I withdraw my hand. "Gimme a break! I'm not that old."

"Didn't that TV show air a few decades ago?"

Jeez. That's one thing I hate about Tom. He teases me like I'm his younger sister, not his live-in girlfriend. I decide to change the subject. "Is it as dramatic as Val's car accident on *The Young and the Restless*?"

He shakes his head slowly. "I'm not telling."

I try to think of some catchy and dramatic business ideas, but my mind is blank. What's catchy and dramatic about selling real estate?

Tom stands up and gathers his dishes. We no longer have a housekeeper, so he rinses them by hand and places them in the dishwasher for later. I abandon my toast and join him at the sink, pressing the length of my five-foot ten-inch runner's body against his back. Tom's slightly taller than me, at six foot two, and he's built like a basketball player although his sport of choice is golf. I wrap my arms around his waist and trace the muscles in his stomach with one finger until he shivers. "Not now, Trina. I'll be late for cold calling."

I ignore his comment and start playfully licking his earlobe. "Mmm…maybe you should stay home and help me look for qualified buyers."

He tugs my arms apart and turns around to face me. "I don't tell you how to run your half of the business, so don't start telling me how to run mine."

"I was just kidding."

"You don't know how to joke."

"That's not true. Just ask Val."

He laughs. "Your gay guy friend who thinks anyone wearing polyester is funny? That's not what I mean by humor. Just look at you a few seconds ago when I made that comment about your age. You didn't find it funny, did you?"

I cross my arms under my chest and shift my weight to one foot. If my mother wasn't always harping about how I should be getting married and starting a family before it's too late, then maybe I wouldn't be so sensitive about how old I am. "That's not the same."

"As what?" he asks, his voice rising. "As joking about how I should be attracting buyers? That's *your* half of the business, not mine. Maybe you should spend more time door knocking than surfing the Internet for shoes."

"I'm window shopping. It's stress relief. Like you play golf."

"My golfing has led to more sales than you'll ever give me credit for. Your window shopping has only led to more debt than you'll ever be able to pay off."

I flush with anger. "That's not true. I haven't charged anything in months."

"Then I guess your PayPal account doesn't qualify."

"That's linked to our checking account, not a charge card."

"Either way, you spend too much."

I'm going to return the Dior dress today. Hopefully, the charge and the credit will show up on the same statement in case Tom gets to it first.

I think of the other items I've purchased over the last two months:  a shabby chic sweater for my sister, Dee, for making honor roll during her first semester back at college and a new set of golf clubs for Dad so he could better compete against Tom. They were both essential purchases. How can anyone argue with that?

Oh, yes, there was one other thing. A silky baby doll from La Perla. Little good that purchase did me.  If I could, I'd return it and get my money back.  But I've cut the tags off and worn it, so I can't.

That's Tom's fault, not mine. Maybe it's good his libido has weakened since we had to cancel our health insurance. If we spent as much time making love as arguing, then maybe I'd be endangered of jump-starting that family my mother wants so desperately for me.

Tom pushes past me and stalks down the hall and grabs his briefcase. "See you at the office," he says, before slamming the front door.

The 5,000 square foot mansion we live in seems hollow and empty once he's gone. Only the stuttering of my heart threatens the silence.

It didn't used to be this tense between us. We used to agree on everything from where to eat dinner to how to run our business. But living together and working together for two years have created a tangle of confusion. One I really don't want to sort out just now.

The fax machine clicks and whirs in our downstairs office, but I ignore it. All I've done since graduating from college with a business degree and broker's license is work, work, work. Maybe I should take Val up on his offer for a weekend getaway (if only I could afford to hire someone to host an open house).

Instinctively, I reach for the Wednesday ads buried in the center of the paper and start flipping through the glossy pages, daydreaming of all the purchases I would love to make, but can't because it's not in our budget. Like new satin sheets. No, Tom wouldn't appreciate them. Hmm…those Prada purses look good. But I don't need another purse. How about a pair of shoes? You can never have too much footwear.

Madonna sings, "Express Yourself." I drop the ads and scurry down the hall. The rubber soles of my Asics gels squish squash against the marble floor. I snatch up my phone just before it switches to voice mail. My voice is crisp and professional. "Trina Kay, T & T Realty, how may I help you?"

"Do you have the disclosures?" Mr. Wong asks. "I'm leaving for China this evening and won't be back for one week. I want to make sure everything is okay before I go."

I reluctantly pad into the office and grab the pages spooling out of the fax machine. "They're arriving just as we speak," I say. "I'll look them over and forward them to you in just a couple of minutes."

After I hang up, I read over the pages, line by line. Minor electrical repairs. No problem. Shared driveway. No big deal. A death in the house within the last seven years. Okay. Don't panic. Maybe the seller is being overly cautious and wants to include the fatality of his goldfish. But my hands keep shaking as I dial the other agent to get the facts. I know the Chinese are sensitive about death. And I don't want to have to show more houses today when I already am booked with appointments. I swallow, waiting for the seller's agent to answer.

"Hell-o," he says. "Greg Colby, Home Seller's Realty."

My voice quivers with concern. "It's Trina Kay from T & T Realty. I just received the disclosures you faxed on the Saratoga home and I need to know more about the death that's mentioned."

"It's just a rudimentary fact," Greg says. Although I've never met him, I imagine he's a skinny man with a great sense of fashion from his falsetto voice.

"I need to know the details because my client will ask."

"It's not AIDS or the bird flu," he says, trying to reassure me.

I close my eyes. Please, please, please tell me Grandma was visiting when she died. "Then what was it? A heart attack?"

"Not exactly," he says, slowly. He clears his throat. "It was a suicide."

My knees buckle. I grab the back of the chair and sink into it. I know how the Chinese feel about suicide. Bad karma. Someone else's ghost. "I wish you would have disclosed this earlier. My client may cancel the transaction based on this fact."

"It wasn't violent," the agent says, as if that makes a difference. "The woman hung herself from the banister. She was depressed over her divorce."

Oh, god, no. This news can only mean one thing—escrow canceled, home search resumes. And I was counting on this sale closing quickly. I need to make a payment on my Visa card.

I cup my head in my hand, feeling a headache start to bloom at the base of my neck. Maybe I can hire someone to give the house a blessing and help the spirit move to the other side. Then I won't have to start over.

I call Mr. Wong. "I have the disclosures, sir. There's nothing wrong with the house, but the last resident hung herself from the banister. I could schedule a house healing—"

"Why did she kill herself?" Mr. Wong's voice cuts across impatiently.

"She was upset over her divorce."

"Aiya! Broken family, broken house. No good." His voice rises with anger. "Cancel escrow. We'll find another house."

"But I know someone who can give the house a blessing. He comes highly recommended."

"No blessing. I take no chances with my family's welfare. I do not want the dead lingering in my house to fill it with its sadness. I want only happiness and good luck. You find that for me, okay? That's all I ask. Now good day."

By nine-thirty, I have already drawn up and faxed over cancellation papers to Mr. Wong and scheduled appointments to see property during his lunch hour.

Madonna sings, "True Blue." I snatch the phone. "Yes, Tom?"

"Where are you?" he barks.

"At home. Canceling Mr. Wong's purchase. There was a suicide in the house."

"Wong thing to do," Tom teases. "You have a client waiting for you."

"I do?" That can't be right. I never schedule appointments before ten. I sit down at the computer and bring up my Outlook calendar. Nothing is scheduled before noon.

Tom lowers his voice. "Maria is waiting to see condos. You promised you'd take her."

Oh, right. Maria. Tom's client. He found her accidentally when he was cold calling for sellers. I tried to convince him to show her houses since he speaks Spanish, but he made some excuse about how Maria prefers to work with women only.

I'm still in my running clothes. I haven't showered or decided what I'll wear. "Tell her I'll be with her in a half hour. Do you think she'll agree to that?"

"Hold on. I'll ask." The phone line clicks into the advertising melody we purchased last year when we had so much profit our accountant encouraged us to spend thousand of dollars to avoid a steep increase in taxes.

"The twins are getting antsy. So hurry up."

"If the kids can't wait, can she come back at two?"

"Wong time. Her kids take a nap from one to three. Then she goes to work at four."

If I skip a shower and spray perfume on me, I'll save fifteen minutes. And if I wear the dry cleaning I snuck in last night, I won't have to iron. That will shave off another fifteen minutes. "Okay. Tell her I'll be there as soon as possible."

As soon as I hang up, Madonna sings, "Vogue," my ring tone for Val, my best friend who lives two and a half hours north in Guerneville.

I'd love to catch up, exchange celebrity gossip, and complain about our lives, but I let the call go to voice mail.

I've work to do.

# CHAPTER 2

▼

As soon as I'm dressed in a classic black Ralph Lauren dress suit and Tiffany necklace, Madonna sings, "Express Yourself."

Maybe I should let the call go to voice mail. But it could be Maria calling from the office, telling me the twins can't wait any longer.

I slip my feet into my heels and answer my cell phone. "Good morning, Trina Kay—"

"It's Mr. Wong," the caller says. "Can we just write an offer on that home you showed us last week?"

My heart swoops with relief. That will save me a lot of time. "Which home?" I pad downstairs to the office, log onto my computer, and scroll through the list of properties I've shown him.

"That one in Los Gatos. With the pool. My wife really liked that one."

"Do you want to see it again first?"

"No, just write it up. Same terms. Same price."

I find the MLS number and pull up the listing on my computer. "But this home is listed for thirty thousand more."

"I want it for the same price."

I sigh. The listing agent is Dirk Fitzgerald, a man notorious for his inconsistent and sometimes unethical negotiation tactics. I met him once at a broker's open breakfast. I couldn't stand his constant references to my legs and how he would like them wrapped around him. "Are you sure you don't want to look at the homes I had scheduled to show you today?"

"We want this house. As long as no one died in it. Okay?"

How am I going to make this work? I glance at the listing again. The house has been sitting on the market for 186 days. There have been no price reductions. It won't hurt to write it for thirty thousand under, right? It's a buyer's market anyway. I'll find a way to make it work. I always do.

"Okay," I say. "I have an appointment right now, but my admin will fax the offer over for your signatures."

I hang up my cell phone. My temples throb. It's almost ten. Maria's waiting at the office. I stand up and head to the kitchen for a glass of water and two Advil.

It's going to be a long day.

In the living room of the third condo we visit, the three-year old twins cling to my legs like gum. I want to pull them off, but I'm afraid I might rip the nylons. These aren't just any pair of nylons. These are sheer nylons with tiny black bows stitched up the backs of the legs. I bought them on clearance at a specialty boutique that is no longer in business. These nylons have started more conversations and attracted more clients than any paid advertising I have done. I do not want them ruined.

"No, Juan. No, Carlos," Maria pleads. She's a petite brunette with wide brown eyes and coco butter skin who does not look like she's given birth to any child, let alone twins.

I don't know why my mother wants me to have children. Just because I'm thirty-five and have been living with the same guy for two years doesn't mean I want to get married and start a family. If only my sister, Dee, wasn't a flake, then maybe Mom wouldn't pin all her hopes for grandchildren on me.

When the boys won't let go of my legs, I switch to negotiation tactics. "Want a cookie when we get back to the office?"

They both lift their chubby brown faces and smile.

"Okay, then let go of my legs. Now!"

They simultaneously release my legs. I quickly examine my nylons for damage. Nothing. I sigh with relief. The headache I had earlier this morning is starting to return. I grope in my purse for my bottle of Advil.

"So, what do you think?" I ask Maria, when we return to my midnight blue BMW SUV. I prefer driving my silver Mercedes Cabriolet, but it's only a two seater.

"I don't know." She turns her attention to the twins strapped in their car seats and speaks something to them in Spanish. They jabber for a few moments while I check messages on my cell phone.

As soon as we reach San Tomas Expressway, the boy sitting behind me kicks my seat. I glance up in the rearview mirror and narrow my eyes. "Stop that!"

The boy continues kicking.

"You're not getting a cookie when we get back to the office," I tell him.

He starts to cry.

"Oh, no," Maria says, shaking her head.

I wonder if she really has problems with male real estate agents or if the male real estate agents have problems with her kids.

I turn on the stereo, hoping to drown out the boy's crying. His yelling boomerangs like pin balls from the four corners of the SUV. I roll down the window, hoping the wind will carry his hysterical voice away from me. He hollers louder.

I hate Tom. This should have been his client, not mine.

Why won't the boy stop screaming?

I hate Tom. I fucking hate him.

At the next opportunity, I turn onto a side street and park.

"What are you doing?" Maria asks.

"Returning an important phone call," I lie, getting out of the vehicle. Striding a couple of houses down the street, I flip the phone open and dial the office. "It's Trina. Is Tom around?"

"He's in a meeting," Su says.

"Tell him it's an emergency."

A couple of seconds later, Tom asks, "What's wong?"

Not the "wong" jokes again. "Seriously, Tom. It's Maria. I can't stand her children. I'm thinking of firing her unless you want to take her as a client."

He laughs. "You're tough. You can handle anything."

"That's not the point." I rub my forehead. "I know I'm tough. But children don't make sense to me." The phone beeps. Who's calling now? My face flushes with nervous excitement. "Since we're pretty slow, why don't you just take this buyer? I'll do some cold calls and listing presentations for you."

"We won't be slow much longer. The billboard's going to change all of that."

A billboard? So that's the surprise. My head throbs. The Advil is not working.

The phone beeps again. I glance over my shoulder. The boy has stopped crying. Maria has fed him something. It looks like a lollipop with a rubber handle. I hope the sugar won't make him hyper. The phone beeps a third time. "I've got to go," I tell him. Switching to the next call, I say, "Trina Kay—"

"Trina, dear, it's Dirk Fitzgerald." His raspy voice grates against my ear. "I'd love to do a deal with you, but I don't think my sellers will go thirty grand under their asking price unless…" He dramatically pauses. "Unless you're willing to give a little something to me on the side."

"Commissions are not under the table," I tell him.

He lowers his voice, as if he's afraid someone might hear him. "I'm not referring to money."

My lower back tenses. Please don't be thinking what I think you're thinking.

"How about those luscious legs of yours wrapped around me for a half hour?"

I swallow. My voice squeaks with panic. "I could report you to the Board of Realtors and the Department of Real Estate for that comment."

His voice hardens. "I guess your clients will have to pay full price."

"Then I guess you might just lose your license." I hang up before he can argue.

When I get back to the BMW SUV, the boy who was kicking my seat has fallen asleep.

Maria smiles. "I think we'll write an offer on that last condo we saw."

Good. Maybe it will close in thirty days and I will never have to see her or her children again.

By now, it's almost noon. My stomach growls. Lunch will have to wait. I call Su and instruct her to prepare a purchase contract for Maria. When I hang up, I think of Mr. Wong. What am I going to tell him? The sellers won't budge on price. No, that won't do. It's my job to get him what he wants, as long as it is reasonable. I turn onto Highway 101 toward the office. The sun beats through the windshield. I grab my Bolero sunglasses from the console, roll up the windows, and turn on the stereo to a jazzy station. "Do you mind?" I ask Maria.

She shakes her head. "I like it. It makes me feel young again."

My mouth curls into a half-smile. Maybe she's as sick of her kids as I am.

A few minutes later, Madonna sings, "Express Yourself." I fumble with my Blue Tooth. "T & T Realty. This is—"

"Trina, dear." It's Dirk Fitzgerald. My lower back tenses. "I've got a counter offer faxed to your office. Twenty grand under asking. That's the best I can do." He clears his voice, as if to emphasize the point.

I lift my eyebrows in amazement. That was easy, wasn't it? Maybe I should have asked for forty under to get thirty instead. Oh, well. Let's see what Mr. Wong says. "I'll have to consult with my client, but you should have a response within the hour."

The boy is still sleeping. I turn down the volume on the stereo and call Mr. Wong. "Sir, we have a response from the sellers. They've countered back at twenty thousand under asking price."

I hold my breath. Please take it, please, please, please take it.

"That's not what I asked for."

"There's another offer they're considering," I lie. "Only ten thousand under asking. But they liked your other terms and conditions better. They're willing to give you the home if you can accept the price difference." If that's not enough to encourage him, I add, "We could see other properties."

"No time," Mr. Wong says. "Let me call my wife."

In less than three minutes, he calls back. "Okay," he huffs. "E-mail it over. My wife will drop off the deposit check."

Victory! I call Su at the office and give her instructions.

I flip my phone closed and curl both hands on the steering wheel. The throbbing in my head has stopped. Turning up the stereo, I hum along with Duke Ellington. Maria smiles. One boy giggles. The other boy sleeps.

Life is good.

I glance up at the billboards. I can't believe Tom ordered one for our business. I wonder where it will be. There are three of them before the exit to our office. One advertising for AT&T. Another advertising for Snickers. And a blank one. Wait. I lean closer. It's not blank anymore.

A woman's larger-than-life bare legs dangle from the billboard along with our slogan, "Kick Up Your Profits, Choose T & T Realty."

I like the bold red letters. And the slogan was something I came up with. But I don't care for the legs. There's something blatantly sexual about them. I turn off the freeway and loop back around to take another look at our billboard. This time I drive more slowly, squinting through my sunglasses. Those long, bare legs crossed at the knees seem to swing off the billboard. And those toned calves make you want to look twice. Wait. The back of my neck prickles with dread. Those aren't just any woman's legs. My palms sweat and my heart hammers in my chest. Those are—

My legs.

I swerve into the exit lane and brake, nearly missing the car in front of me.

Maria grips the side door handle and curses in Spanish. The boy behind me wakes up, howling. He kicks my seat. The pain in my temples returns.

I hate Tom. I fucking hate him.

# CHAPTER 3

▼

Su thrusts Maria's purchase agreement and a stack of mail into my hand as I arrive at the office.

"Where's Tom?" I ask.

"Taking a listing."

"Get him on the phone."

Su dials his cell phone, then shrugs. "It went to voice mail."

Of course. That's a trick I taught him. Turn off your phone when you're with a client.

"Where's my cookie?" one of the twins asks, tugging on my skirt.

I cringe. "Let go of my skirt."

Su smiles at the boy. "Would you like some water with that cookie?" She gently unwraps his fingers from my skirt and takes his hand. She leads him into the conference room along with his brother and Maria.

Su is a dark-haired, almond-eyed nineteen year old college student who is more polite and professional than most of the people my colleagues hire to manage their offices. I found her on Craigslist when I was searching for an admin. She doesn't have much of a personality, but she speaks fluent Mandarin and types 90 words a minute and loves children and animals. Honestly, I don't know what we would do without her.

I slip into my private office and close the door for a moment to scan through the mail. Bills, bills, bills, ah, the latest issue of *Homes and Gardens*, and what's this? A letter of appreciation from the Dhesi family. They're referring me to their cousins who are moving from Washington. How nice. Oh, there's more. Two tickets to the San Francisco Symphony. I deserve it. After three weeks of searching for homes with a front door that faces true north, not northwest or northeast or slightly off north, I finally found them a townhouse near Evergreen with the perfect layout. They seem genuinely happy from their note. And the gift couldn't be sweeter.

Tossing the bills in my in-box and filing the magazine, thank you note, and tickets in my briefcase, I move the mouse to check any messages on my computer. The screen saver is a picture of the view from Val's hide-away above the Russian River. I've never visited his place, but the redwood trees towering above the water calm my nerves.

A light rapping on the door alerts my attention. "Yes?"

Su pokes her small dark head into the room and frowns. "We're out of cookies."

A shudder of screams erupts from behind the closed conference room door. My shoulders tense. What are the twins doing now? I fumble in my purse and hand Su a twenty. "Go to the nearest corner store and pick something up. Anything."

Ten minutes later, after I try to placate the boys with paper and crayons to no avail, Su returns with a box of Chips Ahoy. I sigh with relief. "How about one for now and one for later?" she says, spreading out napkins on the table. The twins nod their heads and jostle each other for the first cookie. Before Su leaves, I say, "Call Tom again. If you get voice mail, leave an urgent message." Su nods. She never asks questions unless it's to clarify an instruction I've given her. That's another thing I like about her. Across the table, the twins munch on their cookies, wiping their dirty hands on their jeans and gulping cold mouthfuls of water. I turn to Maria and smile. "Let's go over the contract," I say.

At twelve forty-five, after Maria and the twins have left, I return to my private office and close the door. From the top drawer of my desk, I search for my emergency food. I haven't eaten since breakfast, although I had three Chips Ahoy cookies in the conference room. But they don't count as lunch. At the bottom of the drawer, I find a protein bar. It's chewy and stale. The fake caramel sticks to the roof of my mouth. I grab the cup of coffee on my desk. It's cold, but I drink it anyway.

Su's voice travels through the speaker phone. "Call from Dirk Fitzgerald on line one."

I wince. "Send him to voice mail." Scrolling through my inbox, I search for an e-mail from Mr. Wong.

Madonna sings, "Express Yourself."

Without glancing at the caller ID, I flip it open and announce, "Trina Kay—"

Dirk's voice sounds like he's watching a porno and stroking himself. "Oh, baby, I want to kick up my profits."

Anger and embarrassment sting my face. He's seen it. I close my eyes and rub my forehead. The image of my bare legs dangling from the billboard posted high in the sky sticks in my mind. My chest feels tight. I wonder who else has seen it.

"Ummm…" Dirk emits a lusty groan.

My whole body shudders with revulsion. I want to snap my phone shut, but I can't. He's the agent representing the sellers of the home my clients want.

Pretending not to know what he's talking about, I say, "I'm still waiting for my clients' signatures on the counter offer, although I can tell you verbally they've accepted the new price. If you'd like, I could jump ahead and open escrow. The deposit check will be here later today."

My professionalism extinguishes his fantasy. He clears his throat and says, "I'll wait till I get something in writing." Then, almost as if it's an after thought, he adds, "Nice legs."

Placing down my cell phone, I stand up and pace the length of my office. Tears of anger threaten to prick the corners of my eyes. Why did Tom put a picture of my legs on a billboard? And where did he get the picture? It's not like I have a bunch of photos of my legs lying around.

I pick up the office phone and speed dial Tom's number. I'm instantly transferred to voice mail.

Damn. Where is he?

Su knocks on the door, then peeks inside. "Your mom's on line two."

Deep breath. When I'm stressed, I forget to breathe. If I ignore my mother, she is likely to show up unannounced at the most inopportune time. But if I take the call, she'll leave me alone for another couple of days before she calls again. Exhale. I take another deep breath and press line two. "Yes, Mom?"

"Dad and I are wondering if you're going to have one of those dreadful open houses this weekend." My mother doesn't understand why anyone would waste an afternoon driving from house to house when they could be with family or friends doing something more enjoyable. Like eating. "We're trying to make reservations for brunch on Sunday. Will you and Tom make it?"

I exhale with relief. She hasn't seen the billboard. She doesn't know anything about it. I sink into my plush leather executive chair and rub my forehead. "Umm, I'm not sure. I'll have to ask Tom."

"Do you know when that will be?"

"I'm trying to get a hold of him right now."

"All right. Just let me know as soon as possible. Reservations fill up fast." She pauses thoughtfully. "Somehow I just imagined you and Tom would have more time when the market slowed. But you're working more than ever."

My mother should know better. She worked for a real estate brokerage until she retired. Although she mostly did what Su does for us, she has been exposed to all the daily triumphs and tribulations of the business.

Whistling penetrates the closed door. Tom's back. I stand up, suddenly anxious. "Mom, I have to go."

"I know, dear, I know. Business calls."

As soon as I am off the phone, I stride across the room and open the door.

Tom leans against the counter in the reception area and winks at Su. His navy blue jacket is flung over one shoulder and the sleeves of his blue and white pinstriped shirt have been rolled to his elbows. He smells of Orange cologne. When he notices me, he backs away from the counter and frowns. "What's the emergency?"

I grab him by the shirtsleeve. "We need to talk." I usher him into my private office and slam the door. The picture frames rattle against the walls. The room smells of day old coffee. A jumble of paperwork crowds my desk. My computer beeps. An e-mail from Mr. Wong has just arrived, but I'm too preoccupied to open it. I snap the blinds on the window shut. My mouth tightens into a straight line.

"Listen, if this is about flirting with Su again, it's completely harmless."

Tom has a habit of winking at women, touching their elbows or wrists, and joking with them about trivial matters. It bothers me sometimes and I've let him know about it. But today I couldn't care less.

"This has nothing to do with Su or your flirting," I say, clenching my fists. "This is about the billboard."

His eyebrows lift. "It's up already?"

Su buzzes my phone.

"Hold all my calls," I snap.

"But it's Mr. Wong."

"I'll call him back in five minutes."

Tom snickers. "Wong time for wong client to call."

I bat his arm. "No kidding around. This isn't funny."

He continues chuckling. "What did I say wong?"

I shake my head. My cell phone sings, "Express Yourself." I ignore it. "Why did you use a picture of my legs on a billboard?"

Tom gives a nervous laugh. "Don't you like it?"

"*Like* it? Why would I like having my legs on display for the whole world to see?"

"No one knows they're your legs."

"Dirk Fitzgerald knows."

Tom wrinkles his nose. "That creep just assumes they're yours."

"He knows. He already called to taunt me with it." I cross my arms over my chest. "I'm in negotiations with him over a house for Mr. Wong."

"Wong house," Tom laughs. "Wong client. Wong agent."

"Stop it!"

Tom continues laughing.

"Why don't you take this matter seriously?" I ask. "Why is everything a joke with you?"

Tom smiles. "You should see how beautiful you look when you're angry. Your face gets all flushed like it does during sex."

"This isn't about sex." I clench my fists. "This is about business. We sell real estate, not escort services. Our billboard should reflect that."

"It does. Our name is right there on the sign."

I shake my head with indignation. "You don't understand anything I'm saying."

The laughter drains from his face. "I understand you perfectly. You don't like the sign. But I promise you it will increase our profits. Just give it time."

"Take it down."

"I can't." Furrows crease his forehead. "I signed a contract. We've already paid for a year."

"A whole year!" The throbbing in my temples has returned for the third time today. Maybe I should go home and lie down until my next appointment. I search my Outlook calendar. When is my next appointment?

Su knocks on the door.

"We're in a meeting," I shout.

Su opens the door anyway. "I'm leaving for the day, and Mrs. Wong is here to see you."

Damn. I glance at Tom, then at Su. I hate leaving in the middle of an argument. It gives the other person time to think of a rebuttal. But I can't ask Su to stay another hour. We can barely afford to pay her as it is. "Tell her I will be with her in a moment."

"She's in a hurry. She has to pick up her son from kindergarten and take him to T-Ball practice."

Tom strides to the door. "Go home, Su. I'll help her."

"No, you won't," I say, nudging him aside. Leaning close to Su, I whisper, "Please ask her to leave you with the signed counter offer and a deposit check made payable to Simply Title in the amount of five-thousand dollars. Tell her I regret not being able to speak with her in person, but I'm in negotiations and cannot be disturbed."

Su nods.

I close the door. I wish it had a lock.

When I turn around, Tom gazes curiously at me. "You should really help your client."

"I will. After we finish our discussion."

"There's nothing else to talk about. We paid for a billboard for a year. And we're going to keep it for a year. End of discussion."

"*We* didn't pay for anything. You did."

"That's because I'm in charge of finances."

"Maybe you shouldn't be."

"You can't even budget a checkbook."

"I did before I met you."

"And that's why you were in debt and I had to bail you out."

"You did not."

"Did too."

Madonna sings, "Keep It Together," the ring tone for my parents' house. I ignore it. "Why didn't you consult me?"

Tom shrugs. "I shouldn't have to consult you about every business decision I make."

"But we're partners."

"Who handle different aspects of the business." He wipes a mop of golden brown hair off his forehead. His jaw twitches. "I don't tell you how to show property. You don't need to tell me how to market."

"But those are my legs!"

His eyes flash with defiance. "Listen. Your sister gave me that picture. You should be angry with her, not me."

Dee gave him that picture? How did she? A hot wave of humiliation washes over me. Oh, yes, I remember. A class assignment. Body parts as objects of desire. I agreed to model for her because I wanted to show her I was supportive of her decision to leave her job as a paralegal and return to school for her fine arts degree. I never thought anyone except her professor would see my legs.

How could she betray my trust? I'm so mad I could never speak with her again.

The throbbing in my temples has migrated to my left eye. I grope in my briefcase for the bottle of Advil. I shudder as

I gulp down two pills with the rest of the cold coffee. I sink down on the leather executive chair and fold my arms on my desk and bury my face in the dark triangle.

"Are you all right?" Tom asks.

Remember to breathe. In. Out. In. Out. When I glance up, my head feels heavy like a vase full of water on the ledge of a narrow table. "I'm fine," I snap. "Between the billboard, Dirk Fitzgerald, no lunch, a migraine, and your wong jokes, I'm doing just fine."

Tom stares at me blankly.

I can't believe he doesn't understand why I'm so upset.

The office phone rings and rings and rings. Su has already left for the day. She probably thought we would be out of our meeting by now, so she didn't bother switching the phones over to voice mail. Tom reaches over, grabs the receiver, and says, "T & T Realty, Tom Jensen speaking." His face lights up. "Yes, that's us. Let's see. I think I have a two-thirty available. After five?" He scrambles on my desk, searching for a scrap piece of paper and a pen. I reach into my drawer and hand him a notepad and pencil. Without acknowledging the gesture, he continues speaking with the caller. "Six-thirty would be fine. I look forward to meeting you."

As soon as he hangs up, he says, "That was our first billboard call."

The phone rings again. Without waiting for me to respond, he picks it up. "T & T Realty, Tom Jensen speaking." From the twinkling glee in his blue eyes, I can tell it's another billboard caller.

As soon as he hangs up the phone, his whole body beams with triumph. "I told you the billboard was going to pay off. Two appointments in the same day. And it's not even one-thirty."

The phone rings again.

I can't believe people are calling in response to a billboard featuring my legs. I wonder how many calls we would be getting if I posted a picture of Tom's bare chest for the world to see.

"It's for you," Tom says. "Dirk Fitzgerald."

I'm in no mood to talk with anyone. "Tell him I'm not here."

"But it's regarding the contract."

"Put him in voice mail." The screen saver appears on my monitor. Redwood trees, a glistening river. Who am I kidding? My office isn't a glorious mountain get-away. It's a depressing cave. And I feel like a hungry bear who has just woken up from hibernation. I need to get out.

The phone rings and rings and rings.

"Grab line three and four," Tom says. "I'll get line one and two."

I sling my purse over one shoulder, pick up my laptop and briefcase, and squeeze past him to the door.

Tom's face freezes with panic. "Where are you going?"

"Any place but here."

# CHAPTER 4

▼

Twenty minutes later, I pull up into our three car garage and park the BMW SUV next to my silver Mercedes Cabriolet. I stagger into the foyer, my Marc Jacob heels clip-clopping against the marble tiles, and set my briefcase, laptop, and purse down. The house feels like a cool, empty stage set from *Dynasty*. My phone beeps. Oh, yes. Messages. After lunch and a little nap, I'll return everyone's phone call.

From the stainless steel refrigerator, I remove a package of Lean Cuisine and heat it in the microwave. Turning on the flat screen TV in the family room, I flip through the channels. When Val was a regular on *The Young and the Restless*, I used to tape each episode. But since the writers killed him off in an auto accident a year ago, I've stopped watching the show.

When my food is ready, I turn off the TV and stroll onto the deck in the backyard. I kick off my heels, lean back in the chaise lounge, and savor each bite of the Teriyaki chicken. A warm breeze ruffles my hair. Already I feel better. Tom, Dirk, the Wongs, and the billboard are just distant satellites in the warm spring air. Still hungry, I rummage through the freezer and find half a pint of Dreyer's Lite Chocolate Chip ice cream and polish it off. I yawn. All that food has made me sleepy. I glance at my watch. Two-fifteen. I should head back to the office and return phone calls and send over that counter offer for the Wongs. But my eyelids droop and my limbs ache with exhaustion. Maybe I'll lie down for a few minutes. Turning off my cell phone, I climb the stairs to the master suite and collapse on the California king-sized bed and fall into a deep sleep.

Someone shakes my shoulder. I roll over and cover my face with my arm and groan.

"Trina, wake up. I couldn't reach you. Your phone's turned off. And the house phone keeps going to voice mail.

Strong sunlight beats against my eyelids. I blink. Tom perches on the edge of the bed, gazing down at me with concern in his blue eyes. My stomach pitches with anger. I bat his arm. "Go away."

"Are you sick?"

"Of you." I sit up and yawn. Glancing at the clock, I marvel at the time. Four-thirty. I overslept by two hours.

"I had to reschedule a lot of my appointments to cover for you," Tom says. "You owe me big time."

"I owe you?" I laugh. "What about you owing me for destroying my reputation with that billboard?"

"That billboard is generating more phone calls than I can handle."

I sniff with disdain. "I don't care if the Pope or the President call. I'm still unhappy with your decision." A nebulous thought threatens to move forward. Lowering my voice, I add, "I don't know if I want to be business partners anymore."

"What?" Tom stands up and steps back as if I've threatened to punch him. "I can't believe you're willing to throw everything away over a billboard."

"Not everything." I love Tom. But I can't work with him any longer. We just don't think alike when it comes to business. "Just our partnership."

"If you leave our partnership, you leave me." His gaze sweeps around our master suite with the gas fireplace and flat screen TV, the Jacuzzi tub and separate shower, the sitting area and bookcase, and the French doors leading out to a balcony deck. Pictures of us during happier times at the beach and at our parents' houses grace the four walls.

*All or nothing.* It's a tactic he uses whenever he's dealing with an impossible situation at work. I swallow the lump in my throat and feel my eyes sting. "I can't believe you're doing this to me. I'm not an unreasonable client. I'm your girlfriend."

He crosses his arms over his chest. "My soon-to-be ex-girlfriend, if that's what you decide."

A slight thudding knocks against my temples. That damn headache keeps returning. "Well?" he demands.

"You don't understand me." I take a deep breath. "I'm not saying I don't want to be with you anymore. I'm saying I don't want to *work* with you anymore."

"Then it's over." He strides across the room, flings open the walk-in closet, and tosses my Louis Vuitton luggage onto the mattress. "Pack your bags and leave."

I gasp. "You can't make me go. This is my house, too."

"Yes, I can." Tom shoves an armful of my clothing into one of the suitcases. I stagger to my feet and take the clothes out. He shoves them back in again.

"Will you stop?" I ask, yanking on a silk blouse I bought online from Barneys.

He tugs harder.

The blouse starts to slip between my fingers. I grab it with two hands.

His grip tightens.

We pull on the sleeve like two children playing Tug-of-War.

"Let go," I demand.

Tom yanks harder.

The material rips into two jagged pieces.

I gasp.

He releases his half of the blouse. It drops to the floor. My half of the blouse wilts in my hand like a dead flower.

Kneeling down, I gather the other half of the blouse into my hands. The soft fabric rubs against my moist skin. My chest feels tight. I can barely breathe.

The blouse is ruined. Ruined. Just like our relationship.

My eyes sting. Why can't Tom compromise? Why can't he settle for half of what we have instead of forcing me to leave him altogether? My hands shake with anger as I clutch the torn blouse to my chest. Why can't he consider my feelings before he acts?

I glance up. My whole body trembles with panic. I can't believe this is happening. Tom continues walking back and forth from the closet to the suitcases. His purposeful movements remind me of what I adore about him. He is quick to decide, quick to act, quick to take charge of his destiny. And quick to remove me from his life.

My face sags with disappointment. Doesn't Tom love me? Can't he see I'm just angry with his business decision? Why can't he separate our work from our love life? Doesn't he understand they're two separate entities? Or has he fused them together so tightly that any breach will rip them both apart? The throbbing in my head increases. I groan. Maybe I should go to the doctor and get a prescription for something stronger than Advil.

Tom removes my shimmering back-baring Oscar de la Renta slip dress that Val bought me to wear as his date to the Emmys. He wads it up into a ball. My heartbeat thunders in my chest. Standing up, I extend my arms. "I'll do it myself."

Tom silently releases the evening gown.

The purple sequins tumble into my arms. I bend my head to sniff the fragrance of that night when the whole world was buzzing with excitement. I linked my arm through Val's and sidled close to him as we walked the red carpet, smiling and waving at strangers as if they were close friends. Every now and then, Val would stop to chat with a colleague or a reporter. The paparazzi took our picture. The next day the headlines read, "Emmy Award Winning Valentino Ferrari Dates Mystery Woman." That whole night seems like a magical world away. I cradle the purple sequins to my chest. Tears blur my vision. Why can't Tom be like Val? Why can't he respect me?

I lay the evening gown on the mattress and remove the crumpled clothes from the suitcases and fold them neatly. I dump the top drawer of the bureau on the mattress and shift through my bras and underwear, selecting only my favorites. From my shoe closet, I toss in a few of my favorite pairs, including my Asics gels. Finally, I grab my emergency toiletry bag full of makeup samples from Sephora and trial size bottles of toothpaste and hair gel. I don't know where I'm going or how long I'll be there. I just know I need to leave now before I say or do something I regret. When I'm finished packing, I grab a suitcase with each hand. I need to leave before I open my mouth and say something hurtful or sarcastic.

Tom smirks. "You can't make it without me. I'll be your toughest competition."

I turn around at the doorway. My mouth feels cottony and dry. The events of the whole day swirl around me like invisible dust eddies. And in the center of the eddies stands Tom, proud and arrogant as ever. I lift my chin in defiance and steady my voice. "I don't think so."

Tom snickers. "You're wong. Wong, wong, wong."

Damn it. I head down the stairs. I forgot to send over that signed counter offer to Dirk.

In the garage, I open the trunk of my silver Mercedes Cabriolet and toss in the luggage. I go back into the house and retrieve my briefcase, my laptop, my cell phone, and my purse. While waiting for the garage door to lift, I open my laptop on the passenger's seat and wait for it to boot up. I back out of the garage and put down the top. The warm sun beats down on my head. I turn up the stereo. ZZTop plays "Legs." Damn billboard. I snap off the stereo and weave down the street, gripping the steering wheel so tightly my wrists hurt.

At the first stop light, I click through my e-mails and find Mr. Wong's e-mail. Luckily, he attached a copy of the signed counter offer so I don't have to return to the office to fax over the original. I open up a new message and attach the counter offer only to discover I don't have Dirk's e-mail address. The car behind me honks. I switch my attention to the road. I don't know where I'm headed, but I want to avoid 101, not because of traffic, which is always bad at four forty-five in the afternoon on a weekday, but because of the billboard of my larger-than-life bare legs posted for the hundreds of thousands of commuters to see, which is worse.

I turn on my cell phone. Fifteen messages. I try to keep one eye on the road while I scroll through the call log searching for Dirk's office number. Placing the Blue Tooth around my ear, I dial his number and wait.

"Hello, Dirk Fitzgerald's office."

"Mr. Fitzgerald, it's Trina—"

"Ah, yes, the Kick Up Your Profits girl."

I hold my breath and count to five, trying to keep myself calm. "I want to forward the signed counter offer to you, but I don't have your e-mail address."

"Hmm…if you IM it to me, we can chat dirty online."

My spine tightens with disgust. I ease up on the gas, looking for the nearest side street. I don't like driving when I'm distraught. I tend to punch the gas.

The little red Volvo in front of me won't inch forward so I can make a right turn. I tap my fingers on the steering wheel. "I'm not at my desk, so please send an e-mail to Trina@TandTRealty.com and I'll get back to you as soon as I am able."

He growls. "Now you're talking, Long Legs."

I hang up quickly. I don't have to put up with this abuse any longer. I can turn Dirk in for misconduct. I call the Board of Realtors to file a complaint, but the receptionist says I'll have to come into the office to fill out the paperwork so the Grievance Committee can schedule a hearing. "How long will that take?" I ask.

"The paperwork should take thirty minutes, but the wait for a hearing can take up to three months."

Three months. Mr. Wong needs to move within the next forty-five days. If I can't put up with Dirk's lewd comments, then I will have to call Mr. Wong and tell him the truth. I speed dial Mr. Wong's cell phone, but I'm instantly transferred to voice mail. I call his office, but his secretary says he's already left for the airport. I call his house, hoping to catch his wife, but I get the answering machine.

I can't call Tom.

What to do? What to do?

I speed dial Val.

"Hello, sweetie," he says, forever chipper.

My shoulders relax. "Val, you'll never believe what happened."

"The straps on your spaghetti dress snapped."

"No, it's worse."

"You walked out of the restroom with toilet paper stuck on your shoes."

"No, much, much, worse."

"You wore a purple blouse and a yellow skirt."

"It has nothing to do with fashion!"

"Nothing?" Val says, exasperated. "What's worse than a wardrobe malfunction?"

If Val wants to talk about clothes, then I'll tell him about clothes. "Tom ripped the blouse I bought from Barneys and crumpled my Oscar de la Renta dress."

Val gasps like I've just announced his mother has been murdered. "My god...why?"

I lower my voice. "He kicked me out of my own house."

"What happened?"

"I told him I wanted to dissolve our business partnership. It's just not working anymore. You should see the humiliating billboard of my naked legs on Highway 101. It was Tom's idea. I guess he thought it would increase business. It wouldn't be so bad if no one knew it was me, but the agent I'm trying to work with knows. He keeps taunting me with it like I'm advertising for sexual services and it's driving me crazy. And Tom doesn't understand. I love him and I want to keep him as my boyfriend, but he won't have me as his girlfriend anymore if I don't conduct business with him any longer. It's all or nothing with him. So, I'm out."

"What are you going to do?"

The light changes to green. The red Volvo doesn't move. I honk. At this rate, I will have traveled a half block in a half hour. My head throbs. How much Advil can you take in one day before you overdose?

"You still there, KK?" Val's the only one outside my family who calls me by my initials for Katrina Kay. Everyone else knows me by my working name, Trina. Somehow it makes me feel closer to him. Like he's the brother I always wanted but never had.

"Still here."

"Why don't you come north? The fresh air will clear your mind."

For a moment, I seriously consider the offer. "But I have work to do."

"Bring it with you."

I sigh. The light changes to yellow. The red Volvo moves forward. I squeeze past and turn right onto a side street and park against the curb. Staring at the screen of my laptop waiting for Dirk's e-mail, I wonder if Val is right. I need some fresh air. I need to clear my mind.

"Okay," I tell him. "But it's only for one night."

"Yippee! Slumber party!"

A flutter of excitement lifts my spirits. I can't believe I'm leaving in the middle of a work week to spend the night with Val. He's been my best friend for as long as I can remember. We played dress up when other boys and girls were riding bikes and playing flag football. Val knows me better than I know myself, but I haven't seen him since he moved to Guerneville last year. At least when he lived in Southern California, I made the effort to visit him once every three months. On my GPS, I punch in Val's address. I by-pass the instructions detailing Highway 101 and opt for the alternative route. According to the directions, I should be there in two and a half hours. If I leave now, maybe I can make it by nightfall.

# CHAPTER 5

▼

Two hours later, flat pastures stretch for miles along Lakeville Highway giving way to rows and rows of vineyards and the occasional home. I wonder how much these homes cost, how much the land is worth. Trying not to think about real estate, I take the onramp to 101 North and end up in the middle of gridlock. Sonoma County isn't too much different than San Jose.

By seven-thirty, just as the last rays of the sun start to sink below the horizon, I turn off Highway 101 onto River Road. Acres of vineyards stretch endlessly on both sides. I drive past Martinelli's Winery and, a few minutes later, Korbel's Winery and Tasting Room. The last golden bits of light extinguish as soon as the vineyards fall away. My headlights cut into the darkness. Like sentinels, the redwood trees flank the two lane road and stretch up into the sky, blocking out the light. Fragrant forest scents waft over me. My heart contracts with desire, remembering a woodsy, spicy cologne Tom occasionally wears. Soon the redwood trees fall away and buildings sprout up like overgrown mushrooms. I feel like Alice in Wonderland, traveling from one fantastic spot to the next.

At the first light, I turn right and head up Canyon One Road, a steep, windy, dirt and gravel one-lane path that makes my Mercedes shudder. The higher I travel, the more gold, orange, and red light spills across the deepening purple sky. I lean forward and inch the tires around one narrow turn after another searching for Val's address on the side of the clapboard houses. This is not what I was expecting from the pictures Val had e-mailed me. Somehow I had always envisioned a wide paved driveway to a private mansion on a hillside, not a country road littered with shacks on either side.

Dust billows up around me. I sneeze, but it's too late to put up the top. Damn. The Mercedes is going to be filthy. I can already feel the grit clogging my pores.

Just when I start to wish I had a pickup truck, a remodeled summer cottage that looks like the Lincoln Logs we used to play with rises before me. I pull the Mercedes over to the half-moon turnout and park next to Val's dark green Miata. My heart thumps in my chest. I can't believe I made it.

After putting up the top, I tuck my cell phone in my purse and step outside. I wobble as I walk around the Mercedes, running a finger along the side to see how thick the dust is. I wince. The engine's fan hums a frustrated tune. I pop the trunk and lift out the lighter suitcase.

I rap on the door and smile at the pink azaleas in a wicker basket on the sitting porch. So homey. So Val. A moment later, Val whisks the door open and swoops me up into a big bear hug and smothers me with kisses. When he releases me, his wide brown eyes glitter. His dark, wavy hair is cropped short around his ears. The eyeliner and mascara he's wearing make his eyes seem bigger and bolder. The faded Nora Jones T-shirt and sloppy jeans suit him better than the formal wear he sometimes models when he's between acting gigs. "I can't believe you're here, KK," Val says, grabbing my bag.

I momentarily shift into work mode as I survey the inside of Val's home. The wide-open floor plan and open beam cedar ceilings and large windows makes the 400 square foot room seems larger than it really is. In one corner of the living room, a potbelly stove rests on a flagstone perch above the hardwood floors next to a big screen TV which is directly opposite a red velvet sofa adorned with tons of pillows. Val's portfolio graces the black coffee table. On the top shelf of a nearby bookcase Val's Emmy for his work on *The Young and The Restless* gleams like a golden star. Original artwork of vineyards, sunsets, and ocean views line the walls. In the back of the cottage, a garden window above the kitchen sink overlooks the deck. In the opposite corner, a small round table occupies the breakfast nook. Two French doors open to the deck. A warm pine-smelling breeze billows through the screen doors, teasing the candles lit on the bookcase and the coffee table. I feel like I'm in a Tahoe retreat, not in a remodeled summer shack on top of a one-lane road in the middle of nowhere.

"Do you like?" Val asks, spinning around with his expressive hands waving to the immediate surroundings like a game show host pointing out possible prizes.

I nod. "It's very inviting, but if I were going to list it I would use a few feng shui techniques to increase profits. Specifically, I'd add a mirror by the front door and rearrange the furniture to increase the flow of chi through the house."

Val wrinkles his nose like I've said something foul. "You know I hate all that superstition."

"It's not superstition. It's a science. The Chinese use it to increase the good luck in their lives. And I use it to sell houses for more money." I shrug. "It works."

Val nods, weary of my ever-evolving sales techniques. "Whatever happened to burying St. Joseph upside down in the backyard?"

"I still use that, but not everyone's Catholic. Feng shui addresses the huge Asian population in the valley. It gives me a competitive edge."

"So, just imagine for a moment that you're not a Realtor. Tell me again, do you like it?"

"Yes, I do." I say it with authority.

Val claps. "And you haven't even seen the bathroom or my love shack yet." Val winks and takes my hand. "Come outside before the stars come out. I'll start the barbecue. I bet you're starving."

"Tell me again, what happened?"

Val and I are sitting on lounge chairs on the deck beneath a sky dotted with stars. The tiki torches flicker, giving off a slight bug repellant scent. I pat my stomach, full of the barbecue chicken and corn on the cob Val cooked up. A second cosmopolitan in a frosted glass rests on the small round wooden table between us. I take another sip of the sweet, fruity drink before I launch into the whole saga.

"You do have fabulous legs," Val says, trying to sympathize with Tom's decision. "I think they're your second best feature."

I'm still wearing my black Ralph Lauren dress suit. I uncross my legs and stretch them out in front of me, observing them like an outsider would. Most of my five feet, ten inch frame comes from the length of my legs. They're long, lean, muscular, and tan from running. "What's my first?"

"Your fabulous mind."

"Oh, Val." I offer a half-smile.

Val leans forward. "Seriously, sweetie, what are you going to do?" In the glowing light of the tiki torches, his eyes seem large with concern and worry. Didn't Tom's blue eyes look just like that the moment I woke up this afternoon to find him sitting on the mattress beside me? My chest pinches. If I were home right now, we would be eating frozen dinners in our formal dining room, sitting next to each other at the long table. Or if Tom was still at an appointment, I would be curled up on the couch watching the evening news on TV. When Tom would arrive home, he'd sneak up behind me and plant tiny kisses on my shoulder till I turned around and acknowledged him with a deep, open-mouth kiss. I take another sip of my cosmo, trying to drown out the pang of longing I already have for someone I just left a few hours ago. I finish my drink and try to think of other things. But my thoughts keep circling back to Tom. I glance down at my silent cell phone wondering if I should call him.

Val touches my knee. "There's no reception here. If you want to make a call, you'll have to use the land line."

Why call Tom? He doesn't think of me, just himself and the bottom line, which is the only excuse I can give him for using a photograph of my legs to advertise our business. Correct that. Our former business.

I stare at my empty glass.

"Want another?"

I shake my head. My arms and legs feel like they're floating. If I have another drink, I won't be able to drive home tomorrow morning.

I slump back in my seat and gaze up at the sapphire blue sky. Normally when I'm confronted with a dilemma, I run and run and run until I come up with a solution. But I'm too full for a run.

"Listen, if I don't get a call back for that Honda commercial tomorrow, how about a quick trip to the beach? You can borrow my parka. We can pack a picnic and sit on the rocks. It's kind of late for whale watching, but who knows what we'll see."

"I really should leave as early as possible to miss traffic." I can't believe Val still worries about auditions. "Besides, you'll get the call back. You always do."

Val bites his lower lip and glances away.

"You're famous, remember? That's why you left the big Hollywood scene and bought this shack. You wanted privacy."

Val is silent.

"That's why you moved here, right?"

"Okay," Val says, standing up. "Time for a movie." In the darkness, he could be Tom, tall as a basketball player and built like a wrestler. Again my heart pinches with longing. Maybe I should call him. Just let him know I'm okay. That I'm thinking of him.

"How about *The Holiday*?" Val asks. "Jude Law is yummy."

No, if I call Tom, he'll only think he won.

"Or how about *Music and Lyrics*? Hugh Grant is to die for."

Maybe I should call Dee. Demand an explanation.

"How about a classic? *Four Weddings and a Funeral*?"

If I call Dee, then chances are I'll have to talk to my parents. Mom will try to play peacemaker and Dad will ask about Tom. And then I'll have to tell him about the breakup.

"Oh, I know." Val claps his hands. "*Pretty Woman*!"

I chuckle. "You're such a hopeless romantic."

Val bows. "Thank you. Thank you very much. That's why I haven't found The One."

Under my breath, I murmur, "I thought Tom was The One."

I'm glad Val didn't hear me.

I stand up and go inside the cozy cabin and curl up on the red velvet sofa. Val sets up the DVD and snuggles next to me, wrapping his arm around my shoulder. He smells of charcoal and sunscreen.

As the opening scene plays, I think of Tom. When was the last time we went out to a movie? Three months ago? Six months? A year? I can't remember. Val squeezes my shoulder. No wonder I'm tense. All Tom and I ever did was work, work, work. The music starts. Val ruffles my hair just like Tom used to do whenever he was being playful. I try to swallow, but my throat is tight with unshed tears. "The King of Wishful

Thinking" blares through the surround sound speakers as Richard Gere drives down the hill from his mansion just like I drove away from our house today. I sniff. No matter how much I enjoy Val's company, I miss Tom.

I wish I was home.

# CHAPTER 6

▼

I wake the next morning with only one thought: What am I going to do?

Footsteps fall on the squeaky hardwood floors. Moments later, in the kitchen, coffee percolates. The deep, rich aroma wafts through the room.

Yawning, I turn over onto my side and tuck my hands under my cheek and try to fall back to sleep on Val's living room sofa. But my heart thumps with panic, and my head aches with fear. In the back of my mind, I hear my mother ask, "Why can't you think before you act?" Indeed, why can't I? Why did I walk away from the two million dollar home I share with Tom? Why did I suggest severing our business partnership? Did the other agent respond to Maria's offer? And why didn't Dirk e-mail me?

I've got to get back to the office. I glance at my watch. It's almost nine. Ohmigod. It's been several hours since I've checked the messages on my cell phone. I roll onto my back and toss off the covers. At the foot of the red velvet sofa, I find my purse and start rummaging through it, looking for my cell phone.

Val pads into the living room and sips his mug of coffee. "Sleep well?" he asks.

My fingers grasp a tube of lipstick, a set of car keys, a tiny notepad, but no cell phone. Where is it?

Val wrinkles his nose with laughter. "Relax. Stop looking like a hungry man in a dumpster. Remember, we don't have reception."

My head bobs up. "Did you take it?"

Val laughs. "Why would I want your cell phone? It's not like you work for the *National Enquirer*. Your messages are probably bo-or-ing."

Standing up, I shuffle around the room, looking for Val's land line. If I find it, I can at least check messages.

"Why can't you calm down and join me for breakfast before you go all hyper on me?"

Somewhere I hear a phone ring.

"My agent!" Val fumbles with his mug, spilling coffee, as he maneuvers around me to his bedroom. I follow him like an eager child looking for candy. He sets his mug on the night stand beside a silver lamp and a book about how to audition better and stretches across the double bed to the black cordless phone in its cradle on the opposite night stand. "Hello? Thanks for calling me back, Mike. Have you heard from Honda? Oh, really? Okay. Keep me posted."

Val lies down on the mattress, clutching the phone to his chest and staring at the ceiling with a blank expression. I climb on the bed. "What's wrong?" I ask.

His voice is hollow. "They booked someone else."

"So what?" I shrug. "There will be other commercials."

"But this one was national. Do you know what that means? Royalties!"

I eye the phone, wondering how I can get it from him. "Why do you care about royalties? That's why you rented out your beach house in La Jolla. Did Robert Downey, Jr. move out already?"

Val continues to stare silently at the ceiling. Dappled light from the redwood trees outside the French doors flickers over the planes of his cheeks. His brown eyes are as moist as new soil.

Something's not right. I comb my fingers through his dark cloud of curls. "What's wrong, Val? You're never this quiet."

"Here." He blinks rapidly as he hands me the phone. "Go check your messages."

The phone hangs limply in my hand. "There's something you're not telling me," I say.

He sits up and reaches for his mug. "Want to go out for breakfast?"

My thoughts shift back to work, and my stomach flip-flops with panic. What am I doing here? I've got too much going on. I punch in my password and wait for the automated voice. Fifteen messages! That can't be right. I glance around the room, looking for a pen and a piece of paper. Finding none, I walk back into the living room, grab the notepad in my purse, and sink down on the sofa to take messages.

I jot down enough information to jog my memory later. Maria, calling about her offer to purchase that condo we saw yesterday. Did it get accepted? Tamara, calling about homes we saw three months ago. She's ready to buy and wants to know if that cute condo near Santana Row is still available. Mr. Singh, calling about the pest inspection. Did we get a report back yet? Mrs. Nguyen, wanting more information about a property we have listed. Is this the right number to call? My mom, asking about Sunday brunch. Am I coming or not? I go through ten more messages. Not one from Tom.

He didn't even think of calling me.

Why would he? He's the one who threw me out.

I call the office. Su answers, "T & T Realty where we kick up your profits. How may I direct your call?"

"It's Trina," I say. "Is Tom around?"

She hums like she's tapping on the computer searching through our schedule. "He's meeting with Mrs. Wong. Apparently, the counter offer they signed was never faxed back and it expired and someone else put an offer on the house they want to buy."

Shit. Why didn't Dirk e-mail me? Is he trying to antagonize me for not accepting his sexual offers?

I thank Su and immediately call Dirk's office. It rings and rings and rings. I hang up, check the number, and dial again. It rings and rings and rings. I call Tom's cell phone and am instantly transferred to voice mail. How can I get mad at him? He's probably out trying to fix the mess I made of the Wong deal. As I listen to his voice, I wonder if I should leave a message. What would I say? I gulp for air, not realizing I was holding my breath. After the beep, I say, "Tom, it's me. I can't get a hold of Dirk. Please call me about the Wong file." When I hang up, my hands are shaking like they do whenever I've drunk too much coffee. I set the phone on the coffee table and rub my hands over my face.

Val slumps down beside me and wraps his arm around my shoulders. "You look worse than me," he says.

I prop my elbows on my knees and cup my face in my hands. "Remember that offer I told you about last night? With the agent who wants me to wrap my legs around him?"

"Um-hum," Val says, between sips of coffee. "Did he call?"

"No, he didn't. He was supposed to send an e-mail to me so I could forward the counter offer to him, but he didn't. Now there's another offer on the table and my clients may lose the home. Tom's in a meeting with the wife right now, trying to straighten things out."

"Then don't worry," Val says. "Tom can handle it. Why don't we get dressed and go out for breakfast?"

Why did I leave town? Why can't I listen to my mother and learn to think before I act? Why? Why? Why? I stand up to find my suitcase. "If I leave now, I should miss traffic."

"Why bother? By the time you arrive, she'll be gone."

"I don't want to look like a flake."

"You're not a flake. You've suffered a major upset in your life."

"My clients don't know that. They trust me to handle things for them, not screw them up. If this deal falls apart, they will blame me for a lack of due diligence. I could be sued."

"Don't worry. Tom will set things right."

"But I don't want him looking like the hero!"

"Is this about you? Or your clients?"

I spin around. "It's about business."

"You're making it sound personal."

"That's Tom's fault, not mine. He put my legs on a billboard."

"You can't blame Tom for everything. He didn't make you forget the counter offer."

I push my curls off my forehead. "That's Dirk's fault. He should have e-mailed me."

"You could have dropped off the counter offer on your way up here. Or you could have faxed it over from your office."

"If you think you can do a better job, then why aren't you selling houses?"

"I'm only using common sense."

"And your point is?"

"Calm down." Val sets his empty mug on a coaster and grabs my hand. "Go take a cold shower and get dressed. I'm taking you out for breakfast."

I stare down at Val's fingers curled around my fist. For a long moment, I quietly think. Val's right. In my hurry to escape the pain of my breakup with Tom and the humiliation of the billboard, I neglected my responsibilities. I could have faxed over the counter offer or delivered it in person. But I didn't. If I leave now, without showering or changing, I'll arrive around lunch time looking like I overslept. How responsible is that? Maybe Val's right. If I stay a little bit longer, I can at least say I suffered the twenty-four hour flu or had an out of town family emergency, which will make me look a little bit better. It might even alter the appearance of Tom's sudden intervention from a desperate rescue attempt to a clumsy changing of the guard.

"Okay, Val, you win," I say, squeezing his hand. "Where are we going for breakfast?"

"These pastries are sinful," Val says, pointing to a cream-filled puff through the display glass window.

I shift from foot to foot, wondering why Val took us to Michelle Marie's Patisserie, a hole-in-the-wall bakery in the center of a quaint old-fashioned mall unless the food is as good as Sprinkles Cupcakes in Beverly Hills.

"I'm going to have a chocolate cream puff," Val says, ordering.

With one more glance at the display case, I make a decision. "I'll have the lemon tea bread and a cup of coffee."

After Val pays for breakfast, we find a table near the window. It's almost ten, and the parking lot is starting to fill with shoppers. Val grabs the newspaper and glances through the headlines before tossing it back into the magazine basket. He picks up his cream puff off the white china and takes a big bite. A dollop of whipped cream smears above his lips. "Mmm…goo-ood," he says.

I sit back and sip my coffee. The air smells sweet and strong with sugar and coffee. The tiny tables with their marble-tops and spindly black wrought-iron legs create a maze-like pattern on the linoleum. Small children press their faces against the display case while their parents order. Elderly couples lean back and relax with their coffee and pastries. Snippets of conversation float across the room. "I'm going green with a hybrid," one man says. "Don't you think an act of terrorism in San Francisco is as likely as another big earthquake?" a woman asks. Val licks the whipped cream off his long fingers, and I stare down at my lemon tea cake, suddenly not hungry. From my purse, I extract my cell phone, checking to see if I have coverage. I do. Then why hasn't Madonna sang "True Blue"?

"What's wrong?" Val asks.

I shrug. "Part of me feels like I should be on the road by now."

"That's why I let you take your own car and follow me down here. So you wouldn't feel guilty about indulging in a little me time." Val reaches over and breaks the tea cake in half. "Open up, sweetie. This is the closest you'll get to wedding cake, I promise you."

I tuck my chin toward my chest. "What's that supposed to mean?"

Val shoves a piece of tea cake into his mouth. "Mmm… divine." He swallows. "It means you aren't getting married, so why not indulge in the next best thing to wedding cake."

"How do you know I'll never marry?"

Val rolls his eyes. "Really, sweetie. How can you ask? You've been with Tom for two years before calling it quits. The guy before him lasted all of six months, and the rest are ancient history, mere blurbs in the book jacket of your life."

My shoulders tense. He's starting to sound like my mother. In defense, I take the tea cake out of his hands and bite into it. The warm buttery sweet and sour moistness melts against my tongue. It is a juxtaposition: dense like pound cake, light like meringue, and nothing at all like wedding cake. "I'll marry when I find The One."

Val snickers. "I thought Tom was The One."

My face warms with embarrassment. He *did* hear that comment I made last night.

"C'mon." Val dabs his face with a napkin. "Let's go shopping."

I glance at my watch. "It's after ten. I should be going."

"Traffic always picks up around noon. If you leave now, you'll be stuck in lunch-time bumper to bumper." His eyes narrow. "Besides, I thought I'd buy you a little something."

My eyes widen with interest. Val's gifts are always intriguing and delightful. Like the Oscar de la Renta dress for the Emmys. My goodness, it's been two years since he's bought a Just Because gift for me. I gulp down the rest of my coffee and smile. "Let's go."

We walk, arm in arm, across the Sonoma Avenue parking lot, down the outdoor alley between stores and turn left at Chico's.

A new display of summer fashions graces the full-length window of Ann Taylor. I tug Val's arm. "Let's go look."

Val tucks me close beside him. "Not there."

My heels tap dance on the sidewalk to keep up with his brisk pace. "Oh, what about White House, Black Market," I say, pointing to the luxurious white and black slacks and blouses and dresses in the corner closet-sized store.

"Keep walking," Val says.

Oh, where can he be taking me? We turn left again toward the parking lot facing the main street and walk past Sharper Image. Of course, Coldwater Creek. I should have known it would be extra special. "I can't believe it. Shopping *and* a massage."

"No massage," Val says. "And no shopping here. They're overpriced."

Overpriced? "But where are we going?"

Val stops in front of a set of double doors. The black-tinted windows seem to mask the shop from the outside world, but the big bold lettering above the store announces its presence for everyone to see: Ross, Dress for Less.

I gasp. "You're taking me to a discount outlet?"

"It's a treasure hunt." Val opens the door and shoves me inside. "If you're a good shopper, you can find brand names for less than clearance."

The sticky floors and suffocating recycled air nauseate me. I pull away from Val as he moves aggressively toward the handbags. "This is where I found your Calvin Klein handbag for your birthday," Val says proudly.

I can't stand the warehouse-like atmosphere. This place should be a sweat-and-grunt gym, not a department store. I touch Val's elbow. "I should really get going."

"But you haven't picked out anything," he says. "Remember, I'm buying."

I wince. What to do? What to do? I don't want to hurt his feelings, but I never imagined him spending his days rifling through racks looking for bargain basement prices on designer clothes with manufacturer defects. In high school, we always hung out at Nordstrom by the grand piano and the makeup counters, daydreaming about the fabulous makeover we'd get once we were rich or famous. Now that Val is both rich and famous, he decides to downshift and mingle with the little people by patronizing their discount warehouse. Maybe wealth and fame have warped his sense of propriety. Maybe he feels he's lost touch with the general public and this is his way of familiarizing himself with the mainstream. Or maybe he's researching his next role as a wanna-be socialite who can only afford to dress for less.

Val drapes a scarf around my neck and steps back to examine me from all angles. He smiles. "That blue makes your skin look like porcelain."

"Wasn't that a line from a corny love song?"

He whips the scarf off my neck and pouts. "I thought I was being original."

I laugh. "So when are you going to start playing this new role you've been researching?"

"What new role?"

"The one you're researching right now."

A pair of women in their seventies glances up from the jewelry rack and nudges each other. "He looks just like Jerry resurrected from *The Young and the Restless*."

Val beams, stepping around the rack and extending his hand. "It is, the one and only."

The other woman places a wrinkled hand to her chest and gasps. "My daughter won't believe this. May we have your autograph?"

Val giggles like a schoolgirl. He takes their pens and writes on the back of their checkbooks.

"I can't believe the writers killed you from the script," one woman gushes. "My daughter and I petitioned the network to keep you, but our letters and phone calls went unanswered."

I know how she feels. On the drive down to Santa Rosa for breakfast, I returned all the voice mails I received from yesterday. No one answered, so I left messages for everyone, including my parents. By now, I thought I'd have at least one returned call, but it's been quiet. Too quiet. It's like I don't exist.

"I'm acting with the Sixth Street Theater now," Val says. "Our next play is comedy, not soap, but if you love me, you'll love it!"

The women agree to see the play. They wander away, nudging each other and smiling, full of new gossip.

I gape with curiosity. "What was that all about? I thought you moved here to get away from it all, not audition for Honda commercials and star in local theater."

Val's eyebrows shoot up to his forehead in panic. It's like I've opened a secret closet and all the stuffed boxes have come tumbling out, releasing a spray of outdated shirts and socks and holey underwear. "I—got—bored."

Wait a minute. First, he was disappointed over the Honda commercial because of royalties. Then, he walked past Ann Taylor and White House, Black Market, and Coldwater Creek.

Next, he's shopping at Ross. This isn't adding up. I cross my arms under my breasts. "I'm your best friend. I deserve the truth."

Val turns to the display of bath soaps. "Lavender or vanilla?" He shoves the shell-shaped soaps under my nose.

I bat his arms away. "Stop changing the subject."

Val walks toward the clearance rack and starts flipping through the slacks. "You can never have too many black pants."

I take a deep breath, resisting the impulse to slap him into attention. "Are you in some sort of trouble?"

His eyes narrow. "Enough questions. I'm acting in local theater. That's what I've always wanted to do, remember? So leave it alone. I'm fine. Everything's fine. And if you keep bugging me about it, then I'm not buying you anything at all."

"I don't want anything from this store."

"Oh, so you're too good for Ross. Well, then, I guess you can give me back that Calvin Klein handbag. And the Chinese Laundry sling back sandals in blush. And the 1,000 count Vermont goose down comforter."

"This has nothing to do with shopping," I say, stamping my foot like an indignant five-year-old. "This is about you keeping secrets from me."

"You're just like the paparazzi." He pokes my sternum with his index finger. "Mind your own business."

"Fine." I turn on my heels and stalk down the aisle to the store's exit.

"Go back to Tom," Val shouts, loudly. "He's the only one who can support your spending habit."

"I don't have a spending habit," I shout back.

Pushing the door open, I step into the bright spring light. A flood of cool air washes over my hot face. I shiver. My heartbeat thumps in my chest. I glance back, hoping Val is trailing behind me, waving his arms melodramatically, begging me to stop. But he's standing in another aisle rifling through the men's shirts with his back to me.

"Goddamn him." I point my key alarm at the Mercedes and slip inside. Powering down the top, I back out of the parking lot, punching my location into the GPS for the quickest route to San Jose.

As soon as I turn onto Farmers Lane going south to the Highway 12 onramp, Madonna sings, "True Blue," from inside my purse. *Tom.* I pull over to the nearest curb, shift into park, and grab my phone.

"What happened to the Wong deal?" I ask.

"Where are you?" Tom barks.

"You didn't answer my question."

"You answer mine first," he says.

"This is ridiculous." I sigh, first Val, now Tom. "I'm up north."

"Where up north? Milpitas?"

I swallow, wondering why I feel small and insignificant when I should be feeling righteously angry. "Listen," I say, sitting up straight. "Enough questions. I want to know what happened to the Wong's counter offer."

"Trina, you've really disappointed me." He sounds like he's talking to a five-year-old, not another adult. "I know you're upset about the billboard, but that's no reason to flip out."

"I didn't flip out," I yell. "You threw me out of my own house. What was I supposed to do? Beg you to reconsider?"

"You usually take care of business. That's one of the many things I admire about you."

"You admire me? If this is some mind game—"

"I'm not the one who said she wanted to dissolve our partnership."

"It's just the business, not our personal life."

"Well, thanks to your irresponsibility, I'm now too busy fixing your mistakes to take care of any incoming calls. I'm going to have to hire someone to help me."

"It's not all my fault. I asked Dirk to e-mail me. He didn't. I guess he was too upset over not getting any sexual favors from the Kick Up Your Profits pin-up girl."

"Would you stop complaining about the billboard?"

"Only if you tell me what happened to the Wong's deal."

He sighs. "I got them into escrow, but it cost them an extra ten thousand dollars that I agreed we'd pay for since it was our mistake."

I gasp. *Ten thousand dollars.* By the time the transaction closes, we'll be losing money by the hour.

"Are there any other outstanding offers you need to tell me about? I've already gone through everything on your desk and whatever was in the filing cabinet. You're such a slob. It's hard to tell what's new and what's not." His voice lowers. "Are there deals stashed away that I don't know about?"

I try to think. My voice is small and weak. "I wrote an offer on a condo for Maria yesterday."

"And what happened to it?"

I shrug. "I never got a response."

Tom whistles low. "You've really lost it. Just like your hippie sister."

I raise my eyebrows in surprise. "Leave my sister out of this. She didn't flip out. She made an intelligent decision to leave a career that made her very unhappy and return to school for her degree. That's not losing it."

"You're wong. Wong, wong, wong," Tom teases.

"No, you're wrong." I rap my fingertips against the steering wheel. The anger rushes back into my flushed cheeks. "If you were so quick to chip in ten thousand for the Wongs, why don't you cancel the billboard and just pay the cost for the full year?"

"Do you want a lawsuit?"

"Is that what the advertising contract says?" I never saw the contract. I don't know what it says.

"I'm talking about the Wongs. Your mistake could have cost us our licenses."

I rub my forehead. "I know. I'm sorry."

Silence.

"When are you coming into the office?" There is an edge to his voice like I'm some runaway teenager who's dropped out of high school with only two weeks left till graduation.

A Bacardi truck rumbles by. A woman tips a glass of vodka toward her large red lips advertising sex and romance and alcohol. "I don't like advertising my body."

"Nobody knows they're your legs."

"Dirk knows. Why else would he play games with me? Dee knows. You know. I know. Isn't that enough?"

"You should hear how the phone's been ringing. Su's swamped. She's working full-time again. I'm swamped. That's why I haven't called you. It's not that I don't care."

He cares? Let me test him. "I'm not coming back," I say. "I'm taking your advice and starting a new brokerage. But I won't compete with you. I'm bigger than that. I'm starting over." I glance at the GPS. "In Santa Rosa. I want my license back."

Static crackles over the line. "You're being irrational and impulsive," Tom says. "Why don't you come back and help me out with the business. I can't handle everything. Neither can Su. We need you."

Is this some sort of making up plea bargain? If it is, I want my share of the deal. I try to steady my voice. "Only if you take down the billboard and apologize."

"That billboard has generated more calls than all our advertising dollars combined over the last eighteen months. I'm not about to take it down."

My headache is returning. I can feel a slight throb behind my left eye. I take a deep breath. I have to change my tactics. Time for the conciliatory approach. "You're right, Tom. This is all or nothing. As soon as you put my legs up for the whole world to see, you blurred the line between business and personal. And if you're not going to apologize, then it's over. We'll dissolve the partnership, sell the house, and go our separate ways, understand?"

Tom's voice is soft and far away. "Trina, come home. Please."

It's working. He's reconsidering. Time to step it up a notch and guilt him into an apology. "I thought you wanted to end everything. That's why you kicked me out."

"I only kicked you out because I thought you wanted to end things. If it was up to me, we'd be together forever."

I take a deep breath. Time for the closer. "How soon do you think the sign company can remove the billboard?"

"I'm not taking it down," Tom says.

This isn't working.

I'm out of negotiating tactics. I pound my fist on the steering wheel, accidentally blowing the horn. "Listen, I would not be upset with the billboard if you had used the picture on our business cards. But you took a picture of my legs, a picture that wasn't meant for publication, and turned me into a sex object when I'm a professional salesperson."

"Sex sells."

My voice warbles with pain. He's no better than Dirk Fitzgerald. Only he's not interested in sleeping with me, he's interested in profits. He's so wrapped up in money; he can't see clearly. My head aches. I can't continue to argue with him. I have to start over. Now. "I want my license back. I'll contact you with my new address. We can discuss dissolving the partnership and selling the house later."

A pause hums over the line.

"I'll Fed/Ex it to you." Click.

That's it? My fingers tremble. I slump in the leather seat and drop the cell phone in my lap. I take a deep breath and exhale, feeling the rising tide of another headache start at the base of my neck.

It's over. It's really over.

# CHAPTER 7

▼

I toss my phone on the passenger's seat and take Highway 12 to 101, circling back toward Val's cottage. My phone sings, "Keep It Together." I power up the hood and grab my cell. "Trina here," I say, knowing it's my mother or my father or my sister, Dee.

"KK, where are you?" Mom asks. "Your message sounded strange."

"I'm taking a brief vacation," I lie. "I forgot all about it until last night when the hotel called to remind me of my reservation. That's why I won't be making brunch this Sunday."

"But that's not what Tom said." Her voice shakes with urgency and anger. "He said you've lost your mind. You've run off somewhere up north and won't be coming back."

Damn, I hate Tom. Why can't he let me talk to my own parents first?

"Is Dee home?" I ask, ready for a confrontation.

"She's at school, dear."

"Well, I guess Tom neglected to tell you why I've lost my mind," I say with venom. "Go down 101 to the office. You'll see a huge billboard of my bare legs. Dee took the picture. It was supposed to be for a class assignment, not for sale. Tom calls it advertising. I call it prostituting for profits. You take a look and call me back and tell me what you think." Click.

I turn off the phone. There's no one I want to talk to right now. Not Val who's keeping secrets from me. Not Tom who doesn't care about my feelings. Not Mom who's too preoccupied with her happily-ever-after fairy tale to see the real story. Not even Dee who sold me down the river.

The red gas light flickers on the dash. The GPS's electronic female voice directs me to take the Bicentennial Exit west and loop around toward Piner Road. A few blocks later, I pull into the nearest gas station. A guy in a custom-tailored Brioni suit steps out of a rental car in the row next to me. His blond flyaway hair reminds me of dandelions. My heart pinches. I want to make a wish. For my business to get back on track, for Tom to stop using me for profits, for Val to stop hiding things from me, and for my family to understand me. Okay, that's four wishes. Which one would I pick, if I could only choose one?

I reach the double glass doors of the mini-mart at the same time as the guy with the flyaway hair. He's shorter than me, and I almost nudge him aside, but he pulls back the door and waves me ahead.

"Thanks." Tom never opened the door for me. He said it was an anti-feminist tactic used by men to attract women with no brains.

At the counter, I rummage in my purse for my debit card and hand it to the pimple-faced clerk. He refuses to take it. "Sorry, but our machine's broken. Cash only till it's fixed."

I never carry much cash because I tend to spend it too quickly. "Where's the nearest ATM?"

The clerk shrugs.

I plunk my purse on the counter and start searching for some change.

The guy with the flyaway hair hands the clerk one hundred dollars. "Fifty on number six," he says. "And fifty on number three."

Number three? That's me.

"Excuse me," I say, but the guy with the flyaway hair has already bolted from the mini-mart.

I sling my purse over my shoulder and follow him. My heels clip clop on the pavement. The guy with the flyaway hair inserts the pump in his gas tank and glances at his Rolex.

"Sir, I think there's been a mistake."

His brown eyes meet mine. "You're on number three, aren't you?"

"Yes, but you didn't need to pay for my gas. I don't even know you."

He extends a hand. "Zachary."

"KK," I say, taking his warm, firm grasp.

Why did I tell him my nickname?

Zachary glances at the pump, then at his watch.

He seems too busy or preoccupied to wait around for me to go to the nearest ATM and repay him. "Do you have a business card?" I ask. "I'll send you a check."

"Don't worry about it," he says, removing the pump. "I'm sorry, but I'm late for a flight." He slips into the car and starts the engine.

I open my purse, searching for a business card before realizing I don't work at T & T Realty anymore. I tap on Zachary's window. "How can I repay you?"

He rolls down the window. "Just remember, not all guys are assholes."

"What?"

He pulls ahead to the driveway. I run toward him, but he turns into the street. I try to memorize his license plate number before I remember it's a rental car, and I won't be able to trace it back to him.

Oh, well, I shrug. I guess he can afford to be generous with strangers.

If I'm going to stay in Santa Rosa and start a new brokerage, I'm going to need a place to live.

A few blocks from the gas station, a placard advertises: *Luxury Apartments. First Month Free.* I pull into the circular driveway and park in the Reserved for Future Resident space. Swinging my purse from the crook of my elbow, I head up the two steps to the sales office.

A breath of cool air rushes over my face. I smile. Air-conditioning.

A young woman with curly brown hair and black oval shaped glasses peers over the reception desk. "May I help you?" she asks, standing up.

"I'd like to see the apartment for rent."

"One bedroom or two?"

"One, please." I need to be frugal.

She takes a silver key ring from the bulletin board and strides around the barrier to escort me to the apartment. We step outside. My heels clatter on the sidewalk, trying to keep up with her brisk stride.

"My name is Mandy and I'm the general manager." She doesn't look a day over twenty-one in that lacy floral blouse and short black miniskirt. I squint, trying to decipher whether that's foundation or self-bronzing tanner on her face. She stops at a white gated area, sweeping her arm with dramatic flair. "This is a full-service living establishment for professionals," she says. "We have two pools that are heated year round and one sauna. There's a restroom with showers and his and her changing areas complete with towels and toiletries for your convenience. There's no lifeguard on duty, so swim at your own risk. The pool is open from 6 am to 10 pm in the summer, 8 am to 8 pm in the winter. We follow the winter schedule until Memorial Day. Any questions?"

I shake my head.

Mandy's heels click in even strides down the sidewalk. Most of the covered parking slots are empty. Everyone must be at work. The exterior of the buildings gleams with a pearly pink beige hue; a stark contrast to the bold earth tones of the live-work condominiums in San Jose. We arrive at a large building with full-length windows. She unlocks the door and steps inside. The long hallway leads in two directions. We take the hallway to the right. "This is the recreation room. On this side, we have a full gymnasium complete with Nautilus machines and free weights." The room is as big as a cafeteria with wall-to-wall mirrors and tiny TVs anchored to the ceiling. Steel weights gleam on racks beside benches. A row of cardio equipment lines the back wall. Dozens of machines create a maze in the center of the room.

We turn around and head down the other hallway and stop at white double doors. "On this side, we have a kitchen, great room, and movie theater for private parties. We require a $100 deposit and request you arrange for cleanup. Reservations must be made two weeks in advance, first come, first served. Any questions?"

"May I see inside?"

"There's a private party being setup right now. If the room is available when you come back for your key, we can take a peek inside, okay?"

My eyebrows lift. I like her confidence. She assumes the sale.

The apartment for rent is located on the bottom floor and backs to the creek. Mandy unlocks the door and steps inside. My heart sinks. The individual rooms dissolve in a wash of white. It's not bad. It's just dull. And small. I'm used to living in 5,000 square feet of bliss. This place must be only a fifth of that space.

"We've just repainted and replaced the carpets. The stove is gas and so are the washer dryer hookups in the utility room next to the pantry. The living room opens to a concrete patio with a gate to the walking path along the creek. The bedroom has its own full bath with an extra door opening to the living room." Mandy opens the closet doors.

I bite the inside of my lower lip to keep from snapping, *That's smaller than my pantry. The whole bedroom is the size of one of my closets.*

When the tour is over, we return to the office. Mandy steps around the barrier and hands me an application on a clipboard. "Rent is $1,500. Our move-in special waives the first month's rent, so you only have to pay $750 for the security. We only accept cashier's checks or money orders for the initial setup fees. After that, it's direct deposit only." She hands me a black, fine-tipped, ball-point pen. "I'll need to see I.D. and run a credit check."

I start to fill out the application.

Wait. This is the first place I've seen. I need to take a look around, explore the city, and discover the different areas before settling down. Maybe I should contact a Realtor and explain my situation. Just renting for now, but buying in the near future. I could even sign a referral agreement, promising to compensate the agent for the time spent showing me around for one day.

"Actually, I'm running late for an appointment. I'll just take this with me and return it later. There's no rush, is there?"

Mandy pushes the oval glasses up the bridge of her nose and bends to check a list. "We do have a few other potential applicants returning later today, so I can't guarantee the apartment will still be available."

My hands start to shake. I fumble in my purse for my wallet. See? This is why I have to act now. I'll lose out if I don't sign up right away. I hand Mandy my driver's license. If I get my credit checked, I can come back with the deposit later today. I glance at my watch. That gives me five hours to find a Realtor and take a tour of the city.

"While you run credit, I'll go and fill out the application and get the cashier's check," I tell her.

Mandy thrusts my driver's license along with her card into my hand. "Call me before you stop by to make a deposit. The apartment might already be rented and I wouldn't want you to waste your time making a trip."

A good salesperson is a fool for a good sale's pitch. And Mandy is good. Her pitch is dry, but otherwise almost perfect. I reach into my purse and hand her one of my cards.

She studies it with suspicion. "You're a Realtor?"

I nod. "From San Jose.  I'm starting a brokerage here."

She leans forward and lowers her voice. "Are you hiring? I just passed my exam. I'm just waiting for my license to be mailed to me."

I shrug. "I can't open a brokerage if I don't have a place to live first."

She nods conspiratorially. "I'll keep your card.  If any of the other applicants return before you do, then I'll tell them the apartment has been rented, okay?"

I flash a bright smile. Sold! And I even stopped to think. Mom would be proud of me.

It's almost noon. My stomach grumbles. I drive back to the gas station with the mini-mart to purchase a newspaper and ask the pimple-faced clerk for the nearest place to eat something other than fast food. Without a word, the pimple-faced clerk chomps on his wad of gum and points across the street.

The diner reminds me of a smaller version of Denny's with a counter alongside the open kitchen and big booths along the opposite wall. A waitress with a pony tail and a sour expression seats me in a booth. I slide across the vinyl seat and glance at the menu. The chicken sandwich looks good, no fries, and a diet Coke. After placing my order, I unfold *The Press Democrat* and start scanning the classifieds, searching for a Realtor who can show me around town this afternoon.

In the booth in front of me, an older couple discusses their upcoming cruise to Alaska. Behind me, a bald man in a business suit reads a supplemental report to an environmental survey. I shift up on one thigh to get a better look.

He glances over his shoulder. He's much younger than I thought. Maybe my age. His piercing brown eyes strike me with an arrogant intensity and, for a moment, I wonder if he's a trial lawyer instead of a real estate developer. "I'm wearing Obsession," he says, as if women stop him all the time to ask him what cologne he's wearing.

I turn my back as the waitress places my chicken sandwich on the table. I bite into the tender, juicy sandwich and scan the ads. I don't need a self-centered, heartless jerk even if he can help me locate a Realtor.

"Looking for a job?" he asks, glancing over my shoulder.

"Actually, no."

"Then what are you looking for?" he asks. "A new boyfriend?"

I bite my lower lip. Does he think I'm reading the personals? I turn around. "Actually, I'm looking for a place to live, if you must know." Why did I tell him the truth? Val says you need to create a little mystery to keep guys interested. Why do I care if he's interested? I'm not looking for a boyfriend. I just got out of a relationship.

But he doesn't seem to be able to read my thoughts. His hungry brown eyes gaze steadily into mine. My body prickles in response to his desire. How long has it been since I've kissed another man?

What am I thinking? I'm not even interested in him. He's clearly not my type. First, he's too intense. This means he might be a psycho. Second, he's too noisy. This means I'd have no privacy. Third, he's only interested in what he wants. This means he would be selfish.

I take a deep breath and turn back to the newspaper. With a ball-point pen from my purse, I circle an ad that looks promising: Remodeled SFD, 2/1, $1,800 mth. Call Ms. Lashay, Broker. I turn on my cell phone. The little screen glows to life. The bell beeps. Four messages. Without checking voice mail, I punch the numbers into the pad. The bald man watches. I try to scoot down the bench seat to get further away from him, but the cheap vinyl sticks to the backs of my thighs.

Someone answers the phone on the second ring. "Smart Loans, Ms. Lashay speaking."

"Hi, I'm new to the area. I'm looking for a Realtor to show me around. I'm interested in renting for a while, but then buying in the near future."

The bald man studies me. His eyes travel over the length of my body. I avoid eye contact, hoping he'll get a hint and know that I'm not interested.

"I have a rental available. I can meet you at the property at one-thirty or four."

My watch says it's one. Without knowing how far I am from the property, I say, "One-thirty." I take down the address and thank Ms. Lashay for her time. When I turn off the phone, the bald man says, "Call her back. Tell her you've found another agent. I'm a Realtor and I can show you around."

I scoot to face him. My leg rests on the bench seat. He doesn't try to hide the fact that he's staring at it. He's just like Dirk Fitzgerald. "I wasn't interested in what type of cologne you wear. I wanted to know what you were reading, that's all."

"Curiosity killed the cat." He winks. He drapes an elbow over the back of the booth and a gold ring gleams on his finger.

He's married. That makes him even worse than Dirk Fitzgerald.

Without waiting for the waitress to box up my leftovers or offer dessert, I tuck the newspaper under one arm, toss a tip on the table, and stalk up to the register to ask for a receipt.

The bald man strides over to the counter. I can feel his eyes grazing the backs of my legs.

I glance over my shoulder and hiss, "I'm not interested."

"But it's a generous offer. And I have all afternoon to show you around. I even know an excellent place to stay for the night."

I bet. It's probably a pricey hotel with clean sheets and pay-per-view porn. "No, thanks," I say. "I'm already meeting someone."

The waitress waves across the diner. "I'll be with you in a moment."

The bald man leans closer to me. He smells of sourdough bread and greasy fries. "You won't be sorry," he says.

"I already am," I mutter, turning on my heels and stalking out the door.


A freshly painted gray house with maroon trim greets me. I park on the street and walk up the driveway, lifting my sunglasses to get a better look at the condition of the home. It's been recently remodeled. New roof, new gutters, new vinyl windows. I peek into the front window and squint, trying to make out the floor plan.

"You must be the applicant," a woman says. "You were in such a hurry; I didn't get your name. I'm Ms. Lashay."

"Katrina Kay." I turn around and extend my hand downward. Ms. Lashay is a foot shorter than me and at least a few decades older. Her platinum blond hair is swept up like cotton candy. When she smiles, her fresh face crinkles like paper. A faint wisp of baby powder lingers from her firm handshake. She's dressed in a simple black dress suit. No pearls. No gold buttons.

Ms. Lashay holds the front door for me. My heels click against the tile entry. Silvery white light radiates from a solar tube in the high ceiling casting a soft glow throughout the living room with its brick fireplace and taupe walls. My heels sink into the plush carpet the color of crushed stones. I like the circular floor plan moving from living to dining to kitchen to family room. The hallway toward the bedrooms is also lit with a solar tube. It makes the narrow walkway feel wider than it really is. The bathroom is tiny, but nicely done with a shower tub combination, tile floors, granite-topped maple vanity and nickel-colored fixtures.

The first bedroom is small and faces the street. No walk-in closet. The second bedroom is larger and faces the backyard with its neatly mown patch of lawn and recently poured concrete patio. My guess is the house is probably as old as I am, but it's been tastefully refurbished.

"What do you think?" Ms. Lashay asks.

I nod, wondering how much this home would sell for up here.

"You should have seen this place before I got a hold of it. Bad situation. Borrowers were separated. Boyfriend had moved in and wouldn't leave. Beat the poor woman, verbally tortured her kids. Husband didn't have the balls to step in and take charge. The payments slipped. My clients had the second. When they couldn't reinstate the first, I bought the property to save it from foreclosure. I'm planning to sell it and reinvest the profits back into the business, but for now it makes a nice rental. There's even a new furnace."

What type of Realtor is she? I would never bail out my clients. Neither would Tom.

Ms. Lashay looks at her Timex watch. "I know you wanted someone to show you around, and I would love to, but I can't today. An old client called with an emergency. He has a delinquency on his first and he needs a second to make things right. I need to act quickly, so I made an appointment with him at my office in a half hour. If you're done looking inside, I'll lock up. Feel free to spend as much time in the yard as you'd like." She escorts me out of the house and hands me her card. "I'm sorry I have to hurry. Please call if you're interested. We'll talk about details then. If this home doesn't suit your needs, I'd be happy to show you around. But not today. Thanks so much for understanding. Good day." She stalks across the street to a brown Honda Accord. No BMW. No Lexus. No Mercedes. Not even a Cadillac. There's nothing pretentious about her.

I turn around and face the house. It's just like its owner: simple, straightforward, and unembellished. That's not bad. It's just not my style.

I flip through the newspaper on the passenger's seat and place a few calls to some of the big real estate agencies in town. Everyone seems to be too busy to see me today. I rest my head against the seat, gazing up at the cloudless blue sky. I could make an appointment for another day and camp out in a hotel. Or I could call Val and pretend I'm not interested in his little secret. Or I could keep trying to find a real estate agent who can see me today.

Or I could call Mandy.

# Chapter 8

▼

After getting a cashier's check from the bank, I drive over to see Mandy about the luxury apartment.

She stands up and smiles when she sees me strut into the office. "You're back early," she says, handing me the rental agreement and set of keys. "I thought you might return tomorrow."

"I told you I just needed to get the cashier's check." I flash a smile. No one knows I'm here. I haven't returned any calls.

I sign the rental contract and twirl the keys onto my number one Realtor keychain. My new apartment smells as fresh and clean as laundered sheets. I dump my luggage in the living room, push the sweaty curls out of my eyes, and setup my laptop on the kitchen counter to check e-mail and retrieve my attorney's phone number.

My cell phone sings, "Keep It Together."

"Hey," Dee says, as soon as I answer. "Mom said you called."

Her voice sounds so nonchalant. I never sound that way, not even when I'm relaxed. It's hard to believe we share the same parents, because we have absolutely nothing in common.

She's neat. I'm a slob. She doesn't care about fashion. I devour *Vogue*. She's content to live at home. I couldn't wait to get my own place as soon as I turned eighteen. She's never dated. I can't seem to settle down. Even with Tom. Other men always look somewhat interesting. I've never cheated, but the thought crosses my mind more times than I'd like to admit.

"Is something wrong?" she asks innocently.

"Didn't Mom tell you?"

Dee snaps her gum. She must be trying to quit smoking again. "Not really. She just said to call you."

I can't believe Mom hasn't already told her about the billboard. Talking to my mother is like making a public announcement. But I decide not to argue. I just want to understand why my sister betrayed me. I take a deep breath, trying to squelch the anger in my voice. "Why did you sell Tom a picture of my legs?"

"I didn't sell him anything."

How dare she deny the truth! "Then how did he get the photo?"

"Why are you so angry?"

I pound my fist against the kitchen counter. "Because my legs are dangling from a billboard on 101 without my permission."

There is a tense moment of silence.

"I'm sorry." Dee's voice is small and soft. "I gave it to him."

"Why?" My voice booms loudly.

She snaps her gum. "He said he wanted to see my portfolio. When I showed him, he asked if he could have copies of the pictures I took of you. I was too busy with school to develop another set, so after my project was graded, I gave them to him."

"For how much?"

"I didn't charge him."

I shake my head. "I can't believe you sold me down the river—for nothing! Those pictures were supposed to be for school. Not for public display. I only agreed to let you take them because I'm tired of Mom accusing me of not being loving and supportive of you. And now I know why I shouldn't be. You have no common sense or decency."

"It's not my fault Tom decided to parade the photo for the world to see. If you don't like it, then ask him to take it down. Don't yell at me. I'm the one who should be angry. After all, it was my photograph."

"But they're my legs. And Tom won't take them down."

"Why does everything have to be about you?" Dee asks. "Don't you ever think of anyone else?"

"I would if those were *your* legs."

In the distance, my mother yells, "Is something the matter, Dee?"

I tap my fingernails on the kitchen counter. Already another headache tightens across my forehead. I wonder if Mandy has any Advil.

"No, Mom," Dee says, chewing her gum. "Everything's fine."

"Everything is not fine," I hiss. "That's why I'm starting over in Santa Rosa."

"You're what?" Mom asks. She must have picked up the extension.

I take a deep breath. "I'm starting a new real estate brokerage in Santa Rosa. Tom and I have broken up."

"Running's not going to solve your problem," Dee says.

"I'm not running. I'm starting over. There's a difference."

"Yeah, right. Whatever." She chomps on her gum. "Listen, I'm sorry for giving Tom the photo. If I had known, I wouldn't have done it."

"But you did."

"I said I'm sorry."

"I think Dee's right," Mom says. "You should forgive her."

"Have you seen the billboard?"

"Well, actually, no," Mom stutters. "But surely it's not as bad as you're making it out to be."

I shake my head. I can't believe her reasoning. "Go take a look at it first before you go ahead and pass judgment on me. Then call me back."

"I don't care how bad it is. You should forgive Dee."

"It's much worse than you can imagine. An agent I'm working with has started sexually harassing me because of Dee's photo. How can I forgive that?"

"It's not her fault."

"Stop defending her." My phone clicks. "I have another call coming through. I've got to go. Bye." I press the flash button. "Good afternoon, Trina Kay speaking." The phone is hot against my ear.

"I've been doing a lot of thinking," Val says. "Can you talk?"

I don't want to get into another fight. I just want to call my attorney. "Um…I'm kinda busy. I'll call you back later, okay?"

"It's really important," Val says. "But I don't want to talk on the phone. Where are you?"

I don't want to tell him about the apartment. Not yet. It's already bad enough that my family knows I'm here for good. "I'm still in town. Why don't we meet for dinner?"

"Can't. I have rehearsals tonight. How long are you going to be around?"

"I dunno," I say, trying to sound nonchalant like Dee. "But don't worry. We'll work something out. We always do."

As soon as I'm off the phone, I open Microsoft Outlook. Hurry, hurry, hurry. This computer is so slow. My office machine just boots up as soon as I touch the space bar. But maybe that's because Su has everything ready for me before

I arrive. I wonder if Mandy wouldn't mind working for free while I establish myself. Like an internship.

In Outlook, under contacts, I pull up Mr. Leggins's phone number. I slip the Blue Tooth around my ear and dial the number. His paralegal, Paula, answers briskly. "Leggins and O'Brien."

"Mr. Leggins, please. It's Katrina Kay and it's urgent."

"One moment, please."

Vivaldi plays. I yawn. This place is so bare. I'll have to buy everything. Just like I had to after college.

Or I could have Tom ship my things.

"Ms. Kay, how are you?" Mr. Leggins has a cheerful burly voice.

"Not so good. I'm having problems with Tom and I want to dissolve our partnership and sell our house."

"When did this come about? I thought the next time I would hear from you would be about a business expansion or a referral to an attorney who specializes in prenups."

"Long story." I groan. Why does everyone assume Tom and I are the perfect couple? "I'd come in to talk about it, but I'm 100 miles away. Just tell me what I need to do over the phone and I'll start doing it."

Mr. Leggins clears his throat. "Well, there are a few ways we could go about it. If Tom agrees to the dissolution, we could divide the assets and liabilities. But if he objects, we'll have to file a petition in state court, which could take time and be very costly."

"How much time? How costly?"

"At least six months. About $20,000."

"Really?"

"Those are just estimates. Could be less, could be more."

I close my eyes and take a deep breath, but my heart keeps fluttering like bird's wings in my chest. I really need to switch to decaf or just stop drinking coffee.

"You could also offer to sell your portion of the business to him." He lowers his voice in that confidential tone he reserves for his favorite clients. "That's what I would do. Have him pay you one dollar, take your name off all liabilities, and walk away."

*One dollar?* "What about my assets?"

"Are they worth more than $20,000?"

I don't know. I tap my fingers on the counter while QuickBooks loads. Pulling up a balance sheet, I examine the numbers. "It's a little more than that."

"Then I'd have him pay the dollar, and you can walk away."

"Why one dollar?"

"It's the least amount of money needed for it to be legally recorded as a sale, and it's an offer most people can't refuse."

My head throbs. I need to get some Advil. Soon. "What about the house?"

"How do you hold title?"

"Joint tenants."

"Then I would demand the house be sold. If he refuses, I would offer to sell him your half for half of the appraised value. If you held title as tenants in common, you would have a third option of selling your interest to someone else."

Why hadn't I thought of that when we were buying the property? It would be the perfect revenge to sell my half to a complete stranger. How would Tom feel about that?

But I didn't think of it. So it's not an option. "Maybe there's something else, some loophole?" I ask.

Mr. Leggins sounds deflated. "I'm afraid not."

The trip to Walgreens for Advil only takes ten minutes. As soon as I step into the apartment, I call Tom. Amazingly, he answers.

I don't sugar-coat my message. "We need to dissolve our business and sell the house."

"You know, Trina, I was willing to chalk this all up to PMS, but I've had a while to think about it, and I'm mad. You aren't exactly an angel. It's actually been nice to not have you around dropping your clothes on the floor or obsessing over transactions or fluttering from appointment to appointment with an intensity that is hazardous to the health. So if you want to start negotiating with me, I'm not willing. Just tell me where to mail your license. I'm in the process of hiring someone to replace you."

"Replace me?"

"I need help."

The phone beeps. Someone is trying to call me. "Hold on."

I flash over to the incoming line. It's Val. "Do you have a moment?"

"I told you I'd call you. I need to go. I have Tom on the other line."

"Ooo, okay, call me."

I click back to Tom. "I need money." *You could sell your half to him for one dollar and walk away.* "I'm not walking away from my assets. It's my business, too."

"You should have thought about it before you decided to throw it all away."

"I'm having my attorney contact you. I'm suing for dissolution."

"Go ahead. By the time you're done, there won't be anything left to take. And as for the house, I'm not selling in a down market. You're going to have to wait."

I gasp. This is a lot uglier than I thought it would be. "What if we get an appraisal and I agree to sell you my half of the property for half of the appraised value? Appraisals always come in low; you'd be making out nicely."

"You know I don't have that kind of money."

Great, now I have one million in equity that I can't use. I tap my fingers on the counter and bite my lower lip to stop shaking. Think, think, think. "We have an escrow closing soon for Mr. Singh. You have to pay me for my work."

"You took your license. I don't have to pay you anything."

"I'm a broker, not a salesperson. You're legally obligated to pay me at least a referral fee. My name's on all the contracts."

A pause. Is he softening? "Okay, I'll figure out the total and e-mail it to you for your approval. But you don't get any money for the Wong deal or Maria's condo, because you walked out in the middle of those, understand?"

"Sure." The jerk. "I understand." I glance around the bare apartment. "One more thing: I need my things shipped." I give him my new address.

"Are you crazy? If you want your stuff, then you come down and get your stuff. Otherwise, it's staying right where it is."

He wants me to go down to San Jose to retrieve my belongings. How cheap is he? "It can't cost that much."

"I don't have the time or the interest to sort through your stuff. I'm busy. I have appointments booked through eight-thirty every night this week."

Is he serious? Or is he lying? Does he want me to make a trip to San Jose so he can persuade me to get back together with him? Or is he truly overwhelmed with work and totally indifferent toward me? It's hard to tell from the tone of his voice.

Should I go back? I'd have to deal with Tom and my parents and Dee and the billboard. I shudder. No way. "I guess I'll just buy a few things."

He laughs. "You? Buy a few things? Try maxing out your credit card."

I flush. "I don't spend that much."

"You spend more than you think."

"You just want me to come down and see you."

"I don't need to see you. Your picture is everywhere."

"Thanks to you the whole world gets to see my legs."

"Get over it."

"No, I won't. I want it down. Now."

"Too bad. It's staying right where it is. Just like your stuff. I have another phone call. Good-bye."

By the time I get off the phone, I've already tabulated my anticipated income from the Singh sale to compare it with Tom's figures. The same qualities that made him desirable to pair up with are the same qualities that make him formidable to part with.

I try to log into my credit card account to check the balance, but my computer won't connect to the Internet. Who can I call? At work, Su was our onsite IT person.

I phone Mandy at the office and explain my situation to her. "I know I can't pay you anything till I close an escrow, but if you'll work part-time for me, I promise you'll get more in experience than you will anywhere else."

"No problem," she says brightly. "When do I start?"

My computer has completely locked up. I resist the temptation to bang my fists against the keyboard. "Do you know anything about computers?"

"Tons. I have a minor in computer science."

I take a deep breath and release it slowly. "Can you start today?"

"No problem. I'll be right over after I get off work at five-thirty, okay?"

My shoulders relax. "Perfect."

While waiting for Mandy to fix my computer, I take a jog. The path behind the apartments borders a seasonal creek still gushing with water. I feel strangely away in the country although I'm in the heart of town. No one else is out. It's just me and nature. The sun is starting to slant toward the horizon, sending rays of heat across my body. There's something wonderful about the fresh air and the feel of the earth beneath my feet as I press forward.

Half-way through my run, a wash of endorphins powers through me. I get an extra lift to my gait, and my face flushes with a healthy glow. I smile. I'm free.

My phone sings, "Vogue." I carry it along with my keys, ID, Visa check card, a notepad, a pen, and a bottle of mace in a fanny pack around my waist.

I ignore Val's call. But he hangs up and calls again. And again. The pleasure pulsing through my body quickly turns to irritation. I press the answer button and snap, "What do you want?"

"What did Tom say? The suspense is killing me."

A cold prickle of sweat drips down my back. "I thought you had rehearsals tonight," I pant.

"Where are you? You sound out of breath."

"I'm running." I jog in place, remembering our fight this morning. "What are you hiding from me, Val?"

"I'll tell you tomorrow. In the morning. At breakfast. There's a really great down home country cooking restaurant on the corner of Fourth and Farmers in Santa Rosa. It's called Hank's. Just like that guy I dated from Portland for a while. They fill up quickly and don't take reservations. How about I meet you there at nine? That way we'll miss the business crowd."

"Sure." I push the curls off my damp forehead and jot down the time and location in my notepad. "I look forward to it."

My heartbeat settles in my chest, and the smells of new grass sprouting around the creek and exhaust from nearby traffic waft by on a cool breeze. I shiver. I need to start running again. "See you tomorrow."

"Wait! What did Tom say?"

My lips curl into a wry smile. "You'll have to wait until tomorrow to find out."

"Ah, c'mon, KK, just tell me."

I shake my head. "Tomorrow."

# CHAPTER 9

▼

I wake up on Friday morning with a crick in my neck and my shoulders feeling like lead. Rolling up from where I slept on the floor, I stare around at the pool of clothes tossed about from my suitcase. Tom's right. I'm a slob.

Padding to the kitchen, I realize I will have to go shopping. For food. For a coffee maker. For towels. For furniture. After breakfast at Hank's with Val.

I grab my smaller suitcase and head to the gym. After a brisk workout, I shower in their bathroom because they have towels. My eyes look tired. I scrunch gel into my auburn waves and spray them in place. With an expert hand, I whisk eye shadow and mascara and lipstick over my face. When we were in high school, I taught Val how to apply mascara. Now he puts it on better than I do.

Mandy gives me directions to Hank's and the Plaza where Macy's is located. They don't have a Neiman Marcus or a Nordstrom. How provincial.

When I arrive at Hank's fifteen minutes later, Val waves to me. He's sitting in the back by a window overlooking the creek. The smells of fried eggs, sausage, bacon, and maple syrup drip from the warm air. A waitress with a big smile and long fingers takes our order.

"You look stressed," Val says, after she leaves.

I shrug. "Things will get better."

"So what did Tom say?"

I raise my eyebrows. "You go first. Then we'll talk about Tom."

Val leans back against the wooden chair. His cloud of black curls glistens like raindrops have fallen on his head from the wet gel he uses. Expertly applied charcoal eyeliner and ultra-rich mascara make his eyes look big and droopy. His lips quiver, and for a moment, I think he's going to cry.

"I'm a failure, KK."

I cross my arms and place them on the narrow wooden table. "What do you mean?"

He takes a huge breath and holds it before letting it go with a sigh. "It's a long story."

"I have time."

The waitress returns with Val's orange juice and my coffee. I stir cream into my mug, patiently waiting for Val to elaborate.

"It's embarrassing," he says.

"It can't be as bad as having your legs on a billboard."

A crooked smile creases his handsome face. "Okay, but this is worse because it's all my fault. I should have known better." Before I can ask for details, he launches into his story. "When I was working on *The Young and the Restless*, I fell in love with the producer of the show and when we broke up he asked the writers to remove me from the script as quickly as possible." His eyes are moist. "That's why Jerry died in a freak auto accident. It was my fault. I should have never fallen for my boss."

I laugh. Val always falls for someone he works with. He's done that since he played Scrooge in *The Christmas Carol* in seventh grade. Ms. Norman told him to stop ogling Patrick

Lang who played the Ghost of Christmas Past and focus on his lines. I thought he was going to kiss Patrick instead of sob when the Ghost of Christmas Past shows him the hopeful, loving young man Scrooge once was. But he acted right through it. That's when I knew he was going to make it. Only a professional can sob when he wants to kiss someone.

"It's not funny," Val says. "I'm opening up, pouring out my heart to you, telling you my deepest, darkest secrets and you're laughing. You wouldn't be laughing if this was about you."

From my purse, Madonna sings, "A Ray of Light," my ring tone for unknown callers. It's probably a sales call from some company offering office supplies or furniture. I keep forgetting to add my cell number to the Do Not Call List. I reach into my purse and turn off my phone. "Go ahead," I say, trying to look sober.

Val rolls his eyes. "It's not like I was planning on going into debt. It's just that I couldn't stop living the life of the rich and famous." He pauses dramatically. "I sold the condo."

"You what?"

He nods. "I couldn't make payments. The bank was going to foreclose. So I sold it in a short sale. That's why I shop at Ross. If I don't shop there, I don't shop at all."

I sit back and exhale. I never imagined Val was financially troubled. He always seemed to be so together. Like he could not only make money but he could hire someone to manage it well. Isn't that what famous people do? Hire experts to handle their lives.

"And to top it off, I've been blacklisted in Hollywood." He gesticulates with his hands. "The producer said I was a demanding diva. I went four months without auditions before my agent told me the rumor. Then he fired me. That's why I moved here. I sold all my precious belongings, including my great-great-grandfather's antiques and bought the cottage. It was a mess. I gave blowjobs to handymen in exchange for fixing up the place. Sad, but true. Don't lecture me. I know you think it's prostitution. I'm not proud of what I did. But it's the truth. And you deserve the truth."

I swallow and move my arms off the table. The waitress sets the Florentine omelet in front of me and the hotcakes with peaches in front of Val. "Enjoy!" she says.

I stare at the homemade biscuits on my plate. They look better than KFC. But my stomach clenches into a knot. I can't eat. Not now.

"You okay?" Val asks, reaching across to touch my elbow.

"Shell-shocked." The numbness slowly evaporates, leaving a pulsing anger underneath. I clench my fists in my lap. "How can you have lied to me all these months?"

Val shrugs. "I was too embarrassed to tell you or anyone. Thank god my parents aren't around. They'd probably have found out the truth a lot sooner than you did."

Val's parents both died when their private jet plunged into the Pacific Ocean ten years ago. Val doesn't have any brothers or sisters and the rest of his family is so distant they don't even see each other for major holidays. Sometimes he calls me his Rent-a-Sister. It's annoying and endearing all at the same time.

When I don't say anything, he dives into his hotcakes and chews voraciously like he hasn't eaten a hot meal in weeks. Maybe he hasn't. Maybe he's living off welfare for all I know.

"It's not that bad now," Val says. "I get paid for the theater work. It's not much, but it pays the bills. And if I'm desperate I can always give blowjobs." He winks.

"Very funny. Hah-hah-hah," I say sarcastically. My stomach rumbles. I pick up the biscuit and slather it with soft butter. It's moist and flakey and dense and light in all the right places. "The food's good."

Val nods. "I'm sorry I didn't tell you sooner. I just thought you'd hate me for being stupid."

He looks just like he did in sixth grade when he told me he was gay—vulnerable and afraid. He said he didn't tell me sooner because he thought I wouldn't be friends with someone who was different. But how can you stop loving someone when you've loved them all your life? From preschool baby dolls to elementary school dress up and everything in between.

"I forgive you." I reach across the table and squeeze his hand.

Halfway through breakfast, Val asks, "So what's the news about Tom?"

I flush. It's my turn to be fearful. Val likes Tom. He thinks he's better than the losers I usually date:  mostly underemployed, immaculately dressed men who sell jewelry or cars or furniture. Since I met Tom during one of his prospecting adventures, Val has been rooting for us to get married and have children. Just like my mother has.

"It's officially over," I announce. "I'm in the process of dissolving the business partnership. But Tom's fighting it. He doesn't want to buy my half of the business and he doesn't want to sell the house. So I have half a mortgage payment plus rent to pay until my attorney can work something out."

"Rent? In San Jose? You've got to be kidding."

"It's just a tiny hole in the wall," I lie. "And it's not in San Jose. I'm starting a new brokerage here. In Santa Rosa."

Val whistles, soft and low. "You should have told me. Is it too late to change your mind?"

"I signed a lease." I don't tell him it's month-to-month. Although I love Val, I can't live with him again. We shared an apartment after college for three very long and painful months. I'd wake up and find my Donna Karan dress suit missing when I wanted to meet clients. And on nights when I had a hot new date, I'd discover my lingerie stretched out of proportion. I had to charge a whole new wardrobe and keep the clothes in my trunk until I moved out. I'm not going through that again. Ever.

"Can I see your place tomorrow?" Val asks. He glances at his watch. "I have to go. I have an audition for a commercial in the city."

His hurriedness reminds me of that guy with the flyaway hair at the gas station. What was his name? Zane? No. Zachary. Yes, that's it. "Wait. Can I ask you a guy question?"

"Sure," he says with a crooked smile. Val loves when I consider him the expert on all things male.

"I met this guy at the gas station the other day and I didn't have money for gas so he paid for it, but he wouldn't give me any information about himself so I could pay him back. He just wanted me to remember that all guys aren't assholes. What did he mean by doing that?"

Val frowns, mulling over my words. "Maybe he's one of those men who practice random acts of kindness on feminist bitches."

"Really? There are guys like that?"

Val shrugs. "Why not? The men's movement made men too sensitive and the women's movement made women too hard. Why not even the score with a little old fashioned chivalry?"

"I never thought of it like that," I say, remembering how Zachary opened the door and paid for the gas and refused to give me his contact information. Just like a knight in shining armor rescuing a damsel in distress. "Thanks for the explanation."

"Was he cute?" Val asks, leaning closer.

I shake my head. "Not really. Actually, he was strange looking. His hair looked like dandelions."

"Then why are you even thinking of him?"

"I don't know," I lie. He was different than the other men I've met, but I don't want Val to know that I'm thinking of other men when I've just broken up with Tom. It seems a little callous.

"I *really* have to go." Val tosses a twenty on the table and bends to kiss me goodbye. I shove the twenty into his back pocket and return the kiss.

"It's on me," I say.

Val chuckles. "Save your money, honey. I have a job."

Macy's is still Macy's no matter where you go. There are three stories arranged in exactly the same floor plan so an experienced shopper doesn't have to stop the flow by asking for directions. In house wares, I pick up a set of pots and pans on sale for $99.99.

The clerk behind the counter looks like a college student. If he was ten years older and the store manager, I'd ask him on a date. His spiky blond hair gleams like cleats on the top of his head. He's wearing a Men's Warehouse suit with a Calvin Klein shirt he bought here. When he leans forward to grab the box, he smells like he spritzed his wrists with Eternity on his way up to the third floor. His slim guitarist-looking hands turn the box around. "I got this same set at Wal-Mart for $30."

I wrinkle my nose. "I don't shop at Wal-Mart. They treat their employees inhumanely."

He chuckles. "Like Macy's does any better. I almost had to drop a class because management kept changing my schedule even after I gave them the heads up that I had limited hours. But if you still want to pay less and you don't like Wal-Mart, you can try Big Lots." He turns the box upside down and scans the ticket. "One-O-Seven, Ninety-eight. Will that be on your Macy's card?"

He's right. Why pay more for the same thing? I'm on a budget. I have no income until my escrow with Mr. Singh closes and Tom forwards a check. That's if it closes. It happens sometimes, though not often, where a property will fall back on the market for a variety of reasons. Then I'll have nothing but the paltry $500 in my checking account and whatever is left on my credit card. But I don't want to shop at Big Lots.

Maybe I should call Val. He'd go back to Ross with me. But I won't see him until tomorrow and I need a few things today.

What to do? What to do? What to do?

Okay. I'll put back the pots and pans. I don't cook much anyway. I can always buy raw veggies and frozen dinners from Safeway. But I do need a coffee maker and a bed. I can send my clothes to the $1.99 dry cleaners I passed on the way over here so I won't buy a washer and dryer yet. Hmm. What else do I need? A dresser for my lingerie and hangers to store my clothes in the teeny-tiny closet. And linens. Lots of fluffy towels and cotton sheets (the satin ones will have to wait). Ohmigod, I almost forgot furniture and lighting. That's going to add up to more than I want to spend.

Maybe I should go back to San Jose and get my stuff. It would be so much cheaper.

But then I would have to see Tom and my parents and Dee.

And the billboard.

No way. No fucking way.

"Can you show me any cheap coffee makers?"

"What about the pots and pans?"

"Keep them. I'm on a budget."

"You can get the coffee maker at Big Lots, too."

"I know. But if there's anything here that I can't get there, then I'd rather get it here and now with you since you're on commission."

He laughs. "They stopped giving commissions when my older brother worked here ten years ago."

I arch my eyebrow and take out a twenty dollar bill. "What if I paid you to shop at Big Lots for me?"

"What?"

"It would take maybe an hour of your time, right? You probably make $15 per hour here, so if I give you twenty plus gas money you'd make a little profit, right?"

His eyes widen once he sees the twenty. "You're serious."

"Of course, I am. I'm a busy professional woman. I don't have time to go from store to store shopping for a few things."

He glances around as if looking for his supervisor or a security camera. "I get off work at five-thirty today. What do you need and where do I bring it?"

Su has purchased all our company's furniture and office and lunch room supplies so I know how the system works. I write down my shopping list, my address, cell number, and hand him my credit card. "Tell the clerk you're my assistant, if she asks. Give my cell number to call and verify the purchase. Here's twenty now and I'll pay you the rest tonight when I see you."

He smiles. "Cool. This should be fun."

I don't know about fun, since I won't be shopping. But I do know it will be cheaper. A lot cheaper.

I thought Val would appreciate my minimalist decorating style, but the first words out of his mouth are, "How much did you spend?"

I shrug. "Not much. Maybe six or seven hundred dollars. But don't worry. I charged it on my Visa." There is a futon that doubles as my bed, a kitchen table and chair set that doubles as my office, a few lamps, a set of pots and pans, glasses, mugs, and silverware, a coffee maker, some hangers, some bed and bath linens, and a couple of decorative touches like the prints of the ocean hanging on the walls that I found at the Pick of the Litter Salvation Army store down the street. I gave Mike, the clerk from Macy's, forty-five dollars cash for his time. We split a pepperoni pizza and a six-pack of beer before he left last night at nine. "I wasn't going to sleep another night on the floor."

"Why didn't you have Tom ship your things?"

"I asked, but he said it cost too much. He told me to come down and pick it up or else everything I own would stay where it was."

"Actually, that's a good sign." Val sits down on the futon and tosses one of the throw pillows into the air. "He's clinging to hope."

"He's too damn cheap to ship it, that's what it means."

"I'm not looking at just your stuff, KK. I'm looking at the big picture. First, he doesn't want to dissolve the business. Second, he doesn't want to sell the house. Third, he doesn't want to ship your things. Therefore, the grand conclusion is he still has feelings for you."

"Why do you say that?"

"He wants to keep ties with you. He's hoping for reconciliation."

"Whenever I talk to him, he sounds angry."

"I'm an actor. I'm an expert on human nature. He's a guy. Guys like power. When you moved away to start a new life, you took the power away. He wants it back."

I groan. "Maybe I don't want reconciliation."

"Have you filed the petition to dissolve the business with your attorney?"

I cross my arms over my chest and rock back on my heels. "I don't have the money."

"Hah! I'm right!" Val tosses the throw pillow at me. "There's still hope."

The pillow bounces off my arms. I bend and throw it back. "I don't have $5,000 to spend on a retainer fee."

Val catches the pillow and stands up. With one sweeping motion, he waves to the entire apartment. "You had enough money to buy all this."

"This is nowhere near $5,000."

Val narrows his eyes. "What about this apartment? First and last month's rent plus security. Now we're close to $5,000."

"I got a move-in special, so it wasn't even close to that." I sit down on a sleek cappuccino-finished chair that makes the kitchen nook seem elegant and upscale even on my limited budget. No matter what Val says I'm proud of my frugality. I could have spent $5,000 on household furnishings, but I didn't. I do, however, miss my big leather recliner in the entertainment room, the one with the cup holders built into the armrests. But I can't afford to replace it. Yet.

"If you gave all of this a little more thought, you wouldn't have spent anything. You'd be living with me for free. You wouldn't need this futon or a coffee maker or those ridiculous prints on the wall."

"Hey, I *like* those prints."

Val pats the space beside him. I groan and drag my feet over to the futon. He wraps his arm around my shoulders. His voice is soft and low. "Sweetie, I'm sorry if I'm being harsh with you, but it's only because you're my Rent-a-Sister. I don't want you to get in over your head with the spending. Like you did before you met Tom."

Why does everyone I know bring up that bad streak I had? It was only $20,000 on my Visa card and I was still making minimum payments on time so it didn't even affect my credit score. The only reason why Tom paid it off for me was so we could get a better interest rate on the house we purchased. Plus I paid him back with interest during the two years we've been together. So why does anyone mention it?

What they should say is some encouraging words. Like, "KK, I know it's tough, but you're doing the right thing." Or, "Remember you started in the business during the last recession and you made a living. You'll do it again, only better!" Doesn't anyone listen to Dr. Phil anymore?

Maybe I have to be my own cheerleader. I sit up straight and look Val directly in the eyes. "Don't worry," I say, pushing back my shoulders. "My license should arrive on Monday. I'm sure by Friday I'll have some clients. And in a month, I'll have my first commission."

Val doesn't say a word. I don't know if he believes my little pep talk or not.

On Sunday, my mother calls. I've just returned from a run and I'm sweaty and breathless. "Hello?" I say, knowing if I don't pick up she'll just call again.

"It's me," she says. "We just got back from brunch. Tom couldn't make it either. He's been too busy. He thinks he might have to hire two new Realtors and an assistant for Su."

I whistle, wondering if the courts will divide the profits before or after the installation of the billboard.

"On the way home, we drove by the billboard." She lowers her voice. "It is a bit scandalous. If I didn't know any better, I would think you were naked."

Are my ears working correctly? She agrees with me. Finally, I'm being understood.

"Dee's talked to Tom about removing it, but he offered to pay her for the photo instead. She doesn't want the money. She just wants the photo taken down. But Tom's stubborn." She clears her throat. "Dee is thinking about calling Mr. Leggins and seeing if he can help her with some litigation."

"Really?" Dee doesn't like Mr. Leggins, her old employer. She said he was "fusty and musty" and he was one of the main reasons why she quit and returned to school. I can't believe she's considered asking a favor of him.

"I think you should forgive your sister," Mom says. "It's not her fault this happened."

"She's partly to blame. If she hadn't given Tom the photo, then none of this would have happened."

"You're the eldest, KK. You should take the high road and forgive her."

I shake my head and sigh. "Maybe *after* the billboard's taken down."

"You know how I hate it when you two fight."

"Would you stop interfering? If Dee wants forgiveness, she should call me and tell me this herself. Not you."

"Really, I don't think it's necessary to raise your voice to me."

Was I raising my voice? I couldn't tell. I'm sweaty, cold, and pissed off. I yank the T-shirt over my head and press it against my damp forehead. "I need to go take a shower, Mom. We'll talk later in the week, okay?"

"Okay, dear. We miss you."

"Miss you, too," I lie. Sometimes it's better to be 100 miles away. It makes it difficult for her to show up at my doorstep, wanting to talk some more.

On Tuesday, I hang my license with a thumbnail tack in my living room. After breakfast in my own kitchen, I clear the table and set up my office. My laptop and cell phone on one side, my Thomas Brother's map book and list of phone numbers scrubbed against the Do-Not-Call-Registry on the other. I prop a picture of Val on the table for comfort and a postcard of the Versace dress I want for motivation.

At nine o'clock, I start calling.

"May I speak with Don Alberts?" I ask.

"Speaking."

"Mr. Alberts, I'm hoping you can help me. I'm Trina Kay from Kay Realty and—"

"I'm not selling." Click.

*Next.* I smile, hoping the enthusiasm transfers to my voice. "Hello, is this Larry Anderson?"

"What you want?"

"I'm Trina Kay with Kay Realty and I have a buyer who wants—"

"Will your buyer pay a million for my place? I ain't selling for less than a million."

"Well, I haven't seen your place yet. It might be worth more. Is ten or eleven a good time to come by to take a look?"

"Listen, if you know my number, you know where I live. So why don't you just drive-by and send the offer to me in the mail?"

"Sir, it doesn't work that way. My client would like to see the place first."

"Write that into the contract then. Now don't bother me unless you're serious."

I glance at the map to locate the address. Quickly, I pull up some comparables. The last sale on his street went for $595,000.

Why waste my time with an unreasonable seller? *Next.*

After four hours of hang ups, voice mail messages, and just plain rude people, my enthusiasm starts to wither. Not even Val's handsome smile or the chiffon Versace dress can boost my spirits. Years of sales and motivational tapes play back in my mind. Mike Ferry says, "You can't quit cold calling until you have a confirmed appointment."

My stomach grumbles. I take a break for lunch.

At two o'clock, I pick up the phone again. "May I speak with Judy Engle?" I ask.

"Who's calling?"

"I'm hoping you can help me." There's an edge of desperation in my voice like I'm drowning. I try to smile. Can't. "I'm Trina Kay with Kay Realty and I have buyer who wants to live in your neighborhood but the home that's listed is currently in escrow. Have you heard anyone mention they might be selling?"

She pauses. "Actually, my daughter-in-law has mentioned my son might get a job transfer. They live next door at 1505."

"Do you have their number?"

"Of course." She rattles it off from memory. "Don't call until tomorrow, though. He won't know if the transfer is final until tonight."

Finally, an appointment!

# CHAPTER 10

▼

I pull up to the Engle's house on Thursday evening ready to list the property. The house sits in the middle of a busy street. Standing outside, listening to the evening traffic, it sounds more like a freeway onramp than a residential street.

As an appraiser would do, I subtract $25,000 from the suggested list price to account for the noise.

The curb appeal isn't bad. A tiny lawn is rimmed with pebble rocks. I like the new door with the oval window. But that chirping frog that sits beneath the doorbell has got to go.

The door opens. A dark-haired, olive-skinned woman cradles a toddler against her hip.

I thrust my hand forward. "Hello, I'm Trina Kay. We spoke on the phone."

She glances behind my shoulder without smiling. "Where's the buyer?" she asks.

Beads of sweat cling to my collar. Why didn't I ask Mandy to accompany me? Never have I had a seller call my bluff in my sale's pitch. Usually I bring Su with me to the appointment and she criticizes the house to death and we walk out just as Tom arrives with his door-knocking routine. The sellers respond to his warm rescue and the house gets listed with our company anyway. But there is no Su, no Tom. It's just me.

"Uh, the buyer had a heart attack, I'm afraid," I stammer. "But if you'd like, I could still market your home for sale and find you another one within 30 days."

"We'll let my husband decide, okay?" she says, stepping back. "Come in. I'm Margarita Engle. My husband, Troy, is cleaning up the kitchen."

The living room is big with no formal entry, just one boxy room that leads into the kitchen/dining area that steps down into a family room with a sliding glass door leading to the backyard.

The furnishings look dark and dated, but the walls have been recently painted a barely there beige with white ceilings. I take out my yellow legal pad and jot down some notes. New appliances in the kitchen. New linoleum in the bathrooms. Large bedrooms with small closets. Little hall storage space. And an old-fashioned 2-car garage.

"What do you think the buyer will pay for it?" Troy asks. He's as tall as me with broad shoulders and blond hair falling over his green eyes.

Margarita hands him the toddler who looks like a darker version of his dad. "The buyer had a heart attack," she whispers. "But Ms. Kay said she'd find us another one."

"In this market?" Troy asks.

"How long do you have until the move?"

Troy glances up at the ceiling. His mouth silently moves as he calculates the days until his job transfer. The baby bats Troy's face, making Troy lose count. "We move the first week of June," he says.

That gives me nine weeks from start to finish. If there is a 30 day close, then I have exactly 37 days to find a buyer. "Don't worry," I reassure them. "That's plenty of time."

"We can always have the relocation company purchase it," Troy says. "But they're only offering us $550,000. I think the house is worth more, don't you?"

I take a breath and relax my shoulders. "I usually like to do a two-step comparative market analysis, meaning the first visit I take notes on your home, what you owe on it, what improvements you've made and the costs involved. Then I come back and discuss how your home compares to what has recently sold as well as discuss your current competition. But since you're on a tight timeline with the job transfer being approved, if you give me a moment, I'll do my tabulations at the kitchen table and discuss the results with you now."

Troy glances at his wife for her approval. She nods and smiles. "Would you like a glass of water while you work?" she asks me.

"Yes, please," I say, pulling back a chair.

Taking out my calculator, I quickly add and subtract dollar amounts for the best and worst features of the home to arrive at a list price. Then I calculate the costs of the loan payoff and Realtor commissions to arrive at their estimated net. From my briefcase, I pull out copies of the recent sales and current listings and spread them out for them to read along with me. Since I haven't seen these homes except for the few I drove by yesterday, I pretend I'm more knowledgeable than I really am.

"If you want to close escrow and move into your new home within two months like you've just said, then we need to list at $599,000. If you want to chance it and see, we could go as high as $625,000. But that's risky since most qualified buyers see homes in the first two weeks it's listed."

The toddler tugs at Troy's hair. "What do you think, Marg?"

The wife slumps forward, eyeing the numbers. "How about $615,000?"

"If we don't get an offer in two weeks, we'll drop it to $599,000, okay?" I push the paperwork toward them to sign.

"It's a deal," Troy says.

I don't want to go home. I want to celebrate my first listing.

Val is rehearsing at the Sixth Street Theater. I try to call him, but his phone is turned off. I drive downtown and knock on the back door of the theater, but the stage manager won't let me inside. "We're working," he says, shaking his head apologetically. I call Val again and leave a brief message.

The bars are virtually empty for a Thursday night. I don't want to be alone. I drive around until I see a crowd outside Aroma Roasters in Railroad Square. Decaf instead of champagne? Why not? Maybe I'll meet somebody. I pull into the parking lot. A few college-aged students linger on benches drinking coffee out of paper cups and smoking and laughing at jokes only they understand. I pull back the heavy wood door and step into the warm café. The deep aroma of freshly ground coffee beans lingers in the air like a thick mist. A guy with better hair than me takes my order. I stand near the back, waiting for my name to be called. The people here are more colorful than they are in San Jose. Different hair colors, piercings, and tattoos seem to be on everyone. I look like an outcast in my traditional black suit, but my flashy purple blouse makes me feel better.

A young man in a pin-striped suit eyes me. I know he's interested because he's looking at my legs. He's cute with his milky brown eyes and sleek black hair. When he smiles, a dimple creases the corner of one cheek. A phrase that Val always says after he breaks up with someone comes to mind: *It's too early for another relationship, but not too early to get laid.*

"Happy Thursday," the man says. "Nice blouse."

"Thanks, it's Vera Wang."

His eyes glaze over. Good. He doesn't know it's last year's collection.

"May I buy you a coffee?"

"I already ordered, but I'll buy you yours." I wink.

He nervously laughs. Okay, so he likes to take the lead.

The counter clerk calls my name. I wiggle over and cup my liquid Joe. The man follows me. "Do you have time for dinner sometime?"

"Umm…sure," I say, trying to create a little mystery.

"When?" he asks, leaning closer.

I breathe in deeply and try to hold back a little. "I don't have to be anywhere tonight." I sip my coffee, hoping I wasn't too forward. Don't want to scare him away.

He shifts on the balls of his feet. I don't recognize the brand of shoes he's wearing, but I do notice they look scuffed and uncared for.

Maybe I should just go home and soak in the tub and leave dating alone for a while.

"Since you have time, why don't we go to a little place down the street," he says, leaning forward again. "You could follow me in your car or I could drive."

Follow. It's safer. Just in case he turns out to be not so nice.

We end up in a dive that makes Denny's look five-star. The wood floors are badly in need of refinishing. Hunting pictures hang crooked on the walls. The entire place smells of smoke from burned ribs. A scrawny waitress shows us to a booth. The table is sticky with syrup from this morning's breakfast.

Maybe this wasn't such a good idea.

"My name's Derrick." He reaches across the table and takes my hand. My skin prickles. It's been a while since I've been touched by another guy. "I recommend the grilled salmon," he says, rubbing tiny circles on the inside of my palm with his thumb. "But the steak and lobster are good too."

Derrick's pupils are dilating. They almost make his eyes look black, not brown.

The waitress approaches our table to take our order. "We have a special today," she says, squinting at the chalkboard by the register. "Turkey with potato and chives."

I reach for the menu with my free arm and the syrupy table rips from my skin like a bandage. "Ouch!" I tug my hand out of the man's amorous grasp to rub the sore spot. Nothing like a minor flesh wound to ruin the mood.

"Are you all right?" Derrick asks.

I nod feebly. "The table's sticky."

The waitress grimaces like I'm a pathetic baby, not a grown woman. "I can move you to the bar," she suggests.

Why don't you just wipe the table? I wonder.

"No, thanks," I say, making a quick decision. "I'm not hungry."

Derrick lifts his eyebrows. "Are you sure? We could go someplace else."

"Like where?"

He seems to be thinking. "I—don't—know. I only eat here or at my place."

I stand up to leave, not wanting to see the disaster he calls home.

"Wait." He follows me out to the parking lot. "I'm sorry if I scared you. I didn't mean for it to sound like I was suggesting we sleep together. It's just that I don't know where else to go."

I laugh. He's cute, almost endearing, with his bashful, apologetic nature. It's too bad he doesn't know how to impress a woman. I glance at my watch, pretending to check the time. "I'll have to take a rain check." I slip into my car and drive out of the parking lot before he can ask for my number.

"You should have taken me with you when you listed this place," Mandy says at our fifth open house. "I could have told you right then that it's overpriced. The city's widening the road to account for the increased traffic from the new development that's going in just northeast of here. This is the main road and it's only going to get louder and busier. Who wants to live with that?"

I'm standing in the living room with the lights and ceiling fan on, peering out the window to see if any cars are stopping to view the house. I know why my mother thinks open houses are a waste of time, because they are. But they're a great excuse to get out of family obligations. Like Easter brunch with my parents. I didn't have to deal with Mom nagging Dee and I to get along or Dad bragging about his continued friendship with Tom. Lucky me, I got to miss all that.

I turn away from the window. "You're right. The house is overpriced." But what can I do? I've already asked the Engles to lower the price a second time, from $599,000 to $589,000, but they aren't budging. "We'll make sure everyone signs in and when the sellers ask how the open house went, we can tell them it's not attracting any buyers because the price is too high. And if they don't lower it, we won't make their timeline of closing escrow by the end of next month. They'll have two house payments to make and one paycheck to make them with."

"Or they could rent it," Mandy says, matter-of-factly. She pushes her glasses up the bridge of her nose. "I was actually thinking about joining a property management team because this real estate sales business is damn frustrating." She taps her foot against the carpet and frowns at me like it's all my fault. "I've been cold calling on my days off and showing property to strangers who can't make up their mind and I have no money to show for it. Just bills."

"Welcome to Real Estate Sales 101," I say, laughing. "It gets better after your first sale. That's why it's recommended that you have one year's worth of salary in your savings account before you take on this adventure. It's truly a business, not a job. It's a career, not a hobby." I don't tell Mandy I'm in debt from starting over. She doesn't need to know about my Visa bills with the $500 minimum payments or the late fees I've incurred for not paying the March and April payments on time. She doesn't need to know about the money I'm not receiving on the Wong deal or the commission I won't get for selling Maria and her two boys a condo because I walked out in the middle of negotiations. She doesn't need to know I'm two months away from either moving back in with my parents or getting a job.

Mandy strolls into the kitchen and grabs one of the homemade chocolate chip cookies I baked this morning. "Mmm…these are good."

I smile, pretending to be the successful saleswoman. All these years of having an actor for a best friend are starting to pay off.

Five minutes before we begin to close up, a Volkswagen pulls up in the driveway and a family of four enters the house. Mandy gives them the grand tour after I instruct them to sign in. By the end of the tour, the portly man asks, "Are there any offers?"

Mandy and I glance at each other. Her eyes widen with disbelief. My whole body tingles with hope. Discretely, I peer at the register to get the portly man's name. "None so far, Mr. Sanders. Would you like to write one up now or after dinner?"

Mr. Sanders grabs a cookie and pulls back a kitchen chair. With his mouth full, he mutters, "Right now."

# CHAPTER 11

▼

After the buyers have removed all of their contingencies and increased their deposit on the home, I start to count the days till my first commission check. Then I won't have to worry about late fees or collection agents. I'll be able to pay Mandy, taxes, and hopefully, have a little something left over to start saving for that Versace dress before it goes out of style.

It's Memorial Day weekend, but I'm too broke to go camping or rent a house boat, so Val's taking me to Zebulon in Petaluma to listen to live jazz and eat decadent dessert. We've both been so busy we haven't seen much of each other. His show at the Sixth Street Theater just finished a four week run. When not working on my pending sale, I've been prospecting, prospecting, and prospecting. It will be nice to see each other and relax instead of playing telephone tag and e-mailing each other.

I hum a tune while I flip through the clothes in my closet, searching for something fun and appropriate. The late May weather has been exceptionally mild in the evenings, and I'm tempted to wear my low-back cocktail dress just because I haven't been on a date since the failed coffee hookup weeks ago.

In the living room, Madonna sings, "Lucky Star," my ring tone for all Santa Rosa numbers. I pad out in my robe and pick up the phone. "Hello, Trina Kay speaking."

"Ms. Kay, it's Troy." His voice sounds inflated with urgency. Or is it panic? "I have terrible news."

I sit down on the futon and grab a pen and a yellow legal pad from my briefcase, ready to take notes. "Go ahead."

"My manager just informed me today that the location I have been approved for is undergoing layoffs. If I transfer, I'll lose my seniority and possibly my job." He takes a breath. "I discussed this with my wife and we've decided not to transfer. We want to cancel the sale of our home."

"But you signed the release last week removing your contingency," I explain. "You *have* to proceed with the sale of your home or the buyers could sue you for breach of contract."

"What?" Troy's voice rises. "I thought you said we were safe."

I rub my forehead, feeling a slight throbbing. "We wrote in the listing agreement that the sale was contingent upon a successful job transfer, but in the sales contract we negotiated, the buyers asked that you remove that contingency as soon as the buyers confirmed they would proceed with the purchase." I sigh. "You said you understood what you were signing."

"We trusted you and now you've betrayed us," Troy says. "If you don't get us out of this deal, I'll sue you." Click.

By the time Val arrives to pick me up, I'm still not dressed. I've left messages for the buyers to contact me, but they aren't home. It's Memorial Day weekend. They're probably camping like other families, not holed up in their apartment waiting for their Realtor to call with bad news.

"KK, you look like someone died," Val says, rushing into the apartment. He feels my forehead. "You're cold."

I shake my head. "My one real estate transaction is falling apart as we speak."

"What happened?"

I briefly tell him.

"All the more reason to go out," Val says, ushering me into the bedroom. He flings open the closet and selects a silky sapphire blue dress and matching heels. "Too bad you don't have a pearl choker. If I get that role in the *Odd Couple*, I'll buy one for you."

"What role?" I ask, glad to direct the conversation away from me.

He holds up a mint green skirt against his thighs and twirls from side to side, admiring himself in the mirror. "Oh, sweetie, I didn't tell you? I got an audition for a traveling show. Six months on the road for $60,000. You'll never guess what role they asked me to audition for."

I turn my back and slip into the dress. "Felix Unger, the clean-freak."

"Oh, god, no! I got to play Oscar."

"Really?" I giggle, trying to imagine Val playing a slob.

"It was so easy," he explains. "I just thought of you and toned it down a few notches. What fun!"

"Great," I mutter. "Can you help me zip up?"

He hangs the skirt in the closet and tugs the zipper up my back. Placing his hands on my shoulders, he whispers through my curls, "You should be flattered, not upset."

"Why?" I ask, puzzled by the supposed compliment.

He flings his arms out wide and smiles. "Because you're my muse."

Zebulon is dark and crowded by the time we arrive. We make our way to the back by the bar and order two glasses of chardonnay and a slice of their special double chocolate suicide cake. We stand near the wall beside a painting of a fish and wait till a table clears so we can sit down and enjoy the show.

The mosaic table reminds me of the stepping stones Dee and I made for our parents' garden on one of their wedding anniversaries years ago. I wonder how Dee is doing. I haven't heard from her since she called to let me know she wasn't going to sue Tom for using her photograph on the billboard. She said it would be too hard to fight since nothing was in writing. My mother grabbed the extension and pleaded with me to just forgive my sister. But I'm not sure if I can do that yet.

Val takes a bite of the cake. "Mmm-mmm. Absolutely sinful!" He smacks his lips and pushes the plate toward me. "Try some."

I dig into the moist layers and feel the light texture melt against my tongue. "It's good."

Val nods and scoops up another bite.

The local band, which I've never heard of, starts to play a song that reminds me of Duke Ellington. Although the music is good, I can't stop thinking about my conversation with Troy and my inability to contact the buyers. I keep opening and closing my purse, checking the face on my cell phone, hoping it will start to glow with a call. Finally, Val snatches my purse and tucks it under his chair. He offers me another bite of chocolate cake, but I don't want to eat or drink anymore.

"Stop worrying," he shouts over the crowd.

I twirl the stem of my half-full glass of wine and stare at the lead singer of the band. He's tall and lean with long dirty blond hair and rings on his fingers. Val taps my forearm. "Isn't he yummy?" he asks.

I smile. "He's probably married."

"Oh, but that doesn't mean we can't look and daydream, does it?"

I giggle. Val falls in and out of love as quickly as I change clothes. None of his relationships lasts longer than three months. I've stopped asking about them.

We leave a little before midnight. The cool night air feels good against my warm cheeks. A slight breeze blows a strong odor of cow manure in our direction, which is just another reminder that I'm far from San Jose. Val strides ahead, his cowboy boots clip-clopping on the sidewalk. He swings my purse back and forth from the strap dangling on his shoulder. As soon as we're halfway up the block, I say, "I need to check messages."

"No, you don't." He lifts my purse just out of my reach. "You are creating new habits, not continuing with old ones."

"But it could be urgent."

"You're a Realtor, not a paramedic." Val glares at me. "Why check messages? You can't call anyone back tonight."

He's right. But I want to check them anyway. It's worse not knowing.

Val strides ahead of me. His voice carries on the wind. "If I were you, I'd go home, take a long hot bath, and enjoy a peaceful night's sleep. Then, after a refreshing run and a hearty breakfast, I would check my messages and deal with everything then." He stops abruptly and spins around. "But I know you. You can't relax. Just like tonight. You were struck with worry. I could see it in your face. How your eyelids kept twitching. If we could only find a way to harness the power of your worry, we wouldn't have an energy crisis."

I laugh. Val's right. I've got to stop obsessing about work, worrying about other people's problems even when their problems affect me. I've got to start enjoying myself, living a little, not moping in the dark in a room full of strangers while a fabulous band plays.

After a moment of tense silence, Val walks over to me and reluctantly hands over my purse.

I don't open it. I slip it over my shoulder and take Val's arm and walk with him to the car. At the door, I tilt my head up and stare at the wide ebony sky pricked with silver stars. "It's a beautiful night," I whisper.

Val smiles. "Glad you noticed."

# CHAPTER 12

▼

I kept drinking after Val dropped me off at my apartment. First, I poured a gin and tonic for a little night cap, but I must have drank a lot more than just one glass.

In the morning, my head feels like a boulder and my whole body aches like I have the flu.

When Madonna sings, "Lucky Star," I let the call go to voice mail. A few minutes later, when she starts singing again, I roll onto my side and try to sit up. Oh god, it hurts. My head wobbles on my neck, and my arms and legs feel like jelly-covered weights. I squint at the light peeking through the blinds. My watch says it eight.

By the time Madonna sings for the third time, I finally reach the phone on the kitchen counter.

"Trina Kay of Kay Realty. How may I help you?" I manage to say.

"What do you mean the sellers want to back out?" shouts Mr. Sanders. "We've got a moving van scheduled for Friday."

I groan. Why couldn't he have called last night? Before Zebulon. Before the gin and tonic. Before this awful hangover. It's too early to talk business. I haven't had my coffee or read the paper. And I don't think I can keep a coherent thought in my head for long. "Mr. Sanders, may I call you back?"

"Listen. I'm returning your call."

I push a mop of curls off my forehead and sigh. "Okay. Last night I explained to the sellers that the only way they can legally cancel the contract is for you to agree to a cancellation. Otherwise, you are entitled to consult with a real estate attorney about seeking damages."

"Damages? Who cares about damages? I just want the house."

My throat is dry, but my legs are too weak to stride five steps more to the sink to pour a glass of water. I cradle the phone against my shoulder and rub my temples, trying to stop the throbbing orchestra pounding in my head. "How about we write an addendum? You can ask the sellers to pay for any costs associated with postponing your move until you find another home."

"I don't want another home."

I cup my head in one hand while cradling the phone with the other. I really need a few jolts of caffeine. "Can we meet later this morning to discuss this? About ten?"

"There's nothing to discuss. I'm showing up on Friday with the moving van." Click.

I take a deep breath and try to remain calm.

But it's no use. My hands are shaking.

If I brew a pot of coffee, my anxiety will only get worse.

Maybe I'll think clearer if I go for a run.

I gulp two Advil with a glass of water, slip into my tank top and shorts, snap my fanny pack around my waist, and lace up my Asics gels. As I step outside, a cool misty breath of air exhales over me. I jog along the creek side path, pumping my arms and pounding my feet in a steady, increasing rhythm.

Why did I let the sellers remove their contingency? Why didn't I just leave it dependent upon a successful job transfer like it was stated in the listing?

Left, right, left, right. Breathe in, breathe out.

Because the buyers wouldn't accept it. They would have walked away from the deal. And I didn't want the transaction to fall apart. I needed the money.

Breathe in, breathe out. Breathe in—

Now I'm worse off. I can't even enjoy a mindless run anymore.

I run further and further along the creek than I've ever run. The path dips low and turns sharply right, then ascends to the left and dips again. On the second sharp turn, my cell phone sings, "Keep It Together," by Madonna.

Why is my mother calling this early?

Fumbling with the fanny pack's zipper, I trip on a pebble and stumble into the bushes. My cell phone flings out of my hand and tumbles into the creek.

Shit. The top of the phone snaps off and lands on a boulder. A trickle of water slides over it.

Slowly, I maneuver down the rocky slope to retrieve what's left of my battered cell phone. Water slides over my feet, soaking through the canvas and wetting my toes. I shiver. A couple of birds swoop down through the branches, mocking me with their laughing crows. I bend and pluck the damp phone out of the creek. I dial voice mail, hoping the phone works. But I can't even get a signal.

I sit on a rough boulder. My shoulders slump forward. I rest my elbows on my knees and cup my head in my hands.

Can it get any worse?

The apartment office does not open until ten on the weekends, unless it is an emergency. But I can't call the emergency number without a phone.

Why was I too cheap to get a landline? Why did I think I could conduct business on my cell phone? Maybe that's why I don't have as much business as I'd like to. Maybe people would prefer to call a local number that's free.

I can still e-mail, but I decide against it. Who checks e-mails on Memorial Day weekend?

When Mandy arrives a little before ten, I ask to use the office phone. "It's local," I tell her, explaining the whole debacle, including my cell phone disaster.

She gazes at me without a word. Her olive-colored eyes grow large. "I can't believe all that work was for nothing."

"It's not over yet," I tell her. "We can still save the deal."

"How? The sellers aren't moving; the buyers aren't canceling. I don't think some pretty sales pitch will change that, do you?"

I walk around the counter toward the office phone, but Mandy blocks me. "When am I going to get paid?"

"When the transaction closes." I stretch out my arm and pick up the receiver.

She unplugs the jack from the wall, preventing me from making a call. "You aren't jeopardizing my paying job by using the office phone. If you want to make a call, go find a payphone or go buy another cell. The mall opens at eleven."

I drop the receiver and gape at her. "If I can calm down both parties, we may be able to sign loan docs on Tuesday, fund on Wednesday, and close escrow on Thursday so the buyer can move in as planned on Friday. If I wait till Monday, they'll both be so mad, I can almost guarantee that we'll be at a stalemate. And then we'll have to use our E & O insurance to help bail us out, because I'm sure both parties are going to file against us since we represented both of them."

Mandy frowns. "You can't take me down with you. I'm not responsible. I'm just an intern. I haven't even been paid."

"You are responsible. You're licensed. You were at the open house where we met the buyers. You can't use the excuse that you haven't been paid because I haven't been paid either. Realtors never get paid till the job is done. And you're preventing me from doing my job."

The bell rings. Mandy flashes a fake smile at a short man in a cowboy hat. "If you don't mind having a seat, sir, I'll be with you in a moment to give you a tour of our community." Turning back to me, she whispers, "Get out or I'll call security."

I gape at her. "You don't know what you're doing."

She pushes her glasses up the bridge of her nose and speaks in a loud whisper, "I do know what I'm doing. My name and my signature are not on any of the contracts. I can't be held liable for anything."

She's right. I refused to let her sign anything. Not even the contract for her own buyers who decided not to buy anything. I was too concerned with everything being just right that I did it all for her.

"There's nothing holding me back from taking my license and going to work someplace else." She stands up taller, so we're staring at each other eye to eye. "As of this moment, I quit."

After driving around for a half hour searching for an operable payphone, I pull into the parking lot of Coddingtown Mall and enter the World-Wide Wireless store.

Dozens of people mill about the displays. I sign in at the front register and wait for my name to be called. Strolling up and down the aisles, I examine the phones available. Maybe I should splurge and get a BlackBerry so I don't have to lug the laptop with me. Maybe I should buy two phones, one with my current number and one with a new local number. It'll probably be cheaper than canceling my contract early. But that's just one more thing to carry. I should probably just get a landline put in and forward calls to my cell when I'm not around.

"Trina Kay," the salesman says. He has pimples over his freckles, and the suit he's wearing is too short for his legs.

"That's me," I say, glad I'm shopping for a phone and not a man. "Can you tell me more about this BlackBerry? Is it really worth $350?"

His eyes gleam. He must work on commission.

A half-hour later, I walk away having charged another $350 plus tax to my Visa. In the mall courtyard, I sit down on a bench across from See's Candy and call the sellers. After six rings, I am forwarded to voice mail. I leave a brief message, not wanting to upset them any further. "I've spoken with the buyers. Please call me at your earliest convenience." Then I phone the buyers. After two rings, I am forwarded to voice mail. I think about leaving a message, but what would I say? *I called the sellers to inform them of your decision not to cancel, but they're not home so I left a message.* No, that won't do and anything else would be a lie. I hang up, not leaving a message.

I call Val, but he's not home either. I leave a message.

Then I call Mr. Leggins and leave an urgent message on his voice mail to call me first thing on Tuesday morning.

I think about calling Tom. Maybe he would know what to do. He's always handled all of our legal encounters. But if I confess my problem to him, he'll just use it against me. I don't need to be reminded of how bad things have gotten since I left him. I already know.

Maybe I should check my messages to see if anyone called while my phone was out of service. But there are no messages from the buyers or the sellers, only my mother asking me to call her. Oh, well. Why not?

After three rings, Dee answers, "Hey, KK, long time no talk."

"Is Mom around?"

"She's out with Dad for brunch. I decided not to go." She lowers her voice. "Are you still mad at me about the photo?"

I check my feelings. They're jumbled into a knot. I don't know what I feel about anything anymore. "I don't know."

"Well, if it helps, I'm sorry." She pauses, as if waiting for me to accept her apology. When I don't say anything, she continues.

"I tried talking to Tom, but he wouldn't listen. I even sought legal counsel, but suing him would be pointless. I'm not super savvy like you. I didn't get him to sign a contract stating what he could and could not do with the photo once I gave it to him. So I wouldn't have a chance of winning in court."

"But you had me sign a contract."

"That was a pre-printed contract our professor gave us. I didn't have one when I gave the photo to Tom and I didn't think of asking anyone for one. I'm sorry. I really, really am. If I could do it over, I would never have given Tom the photo. I wouldn't even have shown him my portfolio. Honest."

There is some shifting in the background and Dee exclaims, "You're home early." My mother grabs the extension and asks, "KK, when are we going to visit? You missed Easter brunch. You missed Memorial Day weekend. Are you going to miss the Fourth of July too?"

I groan. "I'm too busy."

"Working, I bet. You're probably between appointments right now."

I flush. Do I really work that much? "Actually, I was planning on taking the weekend off, but I had a little business emergency."

"Really? Like what? Your assistant couldn't host your open house?"

I bite my lower lip. I can't tell Mom my assistant just quit. No one who's worked for me in the last thirteen years has quit. If I confess my failure to Mom, she will tell Dad and Dad will tell Tom with whom he still plays golf. Then Tom will have one more reason to gloat.

"Ohmigoodness, my client's early," I lie. "Tell Dad I said hi. Gotta go."

"We miss you," Mom says.

"Good luck," Dee says.

"Thanks." I need it.

# CHAPTER 13

▼

On Sunday, Val calls me back to let me know he got the job as Oscar. "Can you believe they left a message at my home phone ten minutes after the audition? And I didn't bother to check my messages Friday thinking they wouldn't call till sometime this week. Thank goodness, I got a call on Saturday from my agent wondering if I was still alive. I've been making arrangements all weekend. We leave on Tuesday for the grand tour."

"Why so soon?"

"I was the last one cast. Apparently, they were just waiting till they found the right lead before going on the road. And I'm it! I'm packed and I'm ready to leave. If you'd be so kind as to check my P.O. Box and drive-by my house every now and then, I'd be more than appreciative."

My heart sinks. Six months on the road. I'm happy for him, but sad for me. "I'll miss you."

"Oh, no, you won't. You'll be so super-busy you won't even know I'm gone."

I sigh. "You know that sale I told you about?"

"You mean the one the sellers want to cancel?"

"That's the only sale I have." My breath seems caught in my chest. "It's only gotten worse. The buyers don't want to cancel escrow and ask for damages. They want the house. I don't know what to do."

"Have you called Tom?"

Tom? Why would Tom help me? I've avoided his phone calls about the remaining business expenses I racked up before I struck out on my own. I've even created a rule in Outlook to delete his e-mail messages. The only contact I've had with him is the check I received last week for the successful close of the Singh sale.

"You still there?"

I snap out of my reverie. "Yeah, I'm here."

"Call Tom."

"I can't."

"Swallow your pride and call him. He'd know what to do."

"How can I? I've asked Mr. Leggins to file for dissolution."

"So he's been served papers for the business?"

"I sent the check last week."

Val whistles soft and low. "I guess you'll have to contact your attorney."

"I already have."

"Then wait. Don't worry. You're smart. You'll figure it out."

I wish I could be so positive.

The rest of the holiday weekend, I worry. I call the sellers and the buyers. But no one picks up their phone. I even send two e-mails. But I get no response.

On Tuesday morning, at eight-thirty-five, I get a call from my attorney.

"I'd love to help you, Ms. Kay, but your check bounced," Mr. Leggins informs me.

"What?" I spit out a mouthful of coffee. Dabbing the kitchen table with a rag, I wonder what happened. I wrote a check for my half of the mortgage payment and mailed it to Tom on Thursday. I guess he cashed it already. Rent was automatically deducted this morning. I paid the minimum payment due on my Visa. And a few assorted bills. I should have had enough money to cover the check to Mr. Leggins.

I log onto my bank account and check the balance. Yikes! Thirty-seven dollars and fifty two cents in checking and five hundred dollars in savings.

That has to be wrong.

"I'm sorry, sir. It must have arrived before I was able to make my deposit," I lie. As soon as I hang up the phone, I'll call the bank and straighten out the matter. "I'll write you another check and overnight it."

"Make it a certified check," he says, "for $15,000 and overnight it to our office."

"Fifteen thousand?" I knock the mug over and coffee spills on my laptop. *Shit.*

"Assuming the worst, you'll need legal representation immediately. According to your Errors and Omission insurance policy, you are required to pay your deductible up front before I can represent you. That's $5,000 for the sellers' suit and another $5,000 for the buyers' suit. Plus the $5,000 for the suit against Tom. That's $15,000."

But I don't have $15,000. The commission I earned from the Singh sale was only $13,750. And I know I've spent some of it already. Maybe even all of it, if the bank's records are right.

What to do?

Think, think, think.

"I'll have to call you back, Mr. Leggins," I say. I get off the phone and immediately call Val. He's not at home and he's not answering his cell. I leave a brief message, but I need to make a decision. Right now.

Think, think, think.

*You're smart*, Val said. *You'll figure it out.*

I am smart. I will find a solution.

Wiping up the coffee from the laptop, I knock my purse off the table. The contents spill over the linoleum. Bending down, I pick up a tube of lipstick, my wallet, and a card. *Ms. Lashay at Smart Loans.* That's right. The teeny-tiny cotton candy-haired woman who showed me that house she bought before it went into foreclosure. I pick up my BlackBerry and punch in her number. She seemed to know how to get people out of jams. Maybe she'll help me.

# CHAPTER 14

▼

At eleven-thirty, I am sitting across from Ms. Lashay in her plush office. She pushes rhinestone reading glasses up the bridge of her nose and studies my loan application to refinance the house I own with Tom. I lean back in the marshmallow white chair, breathing in, breathing out, wishing I had not passed up the offer for coffee or water so I could do something with my nervous hands. I glance around the cozy office and notice a photograph of a twelve-year old boy on her desk. He shares the same brown eyes and tight smile.

"Is that your grandson?" I ask.

She glances up at the photograph and shakes her head. "No, that's my son, Alex," she says. "He's a lot older now. Around your age, actually. Runs a company in L.A. specializing in commercial lending. I wish he'd work for me, but he won't."

"Don't you have a more recent photo?"

"That's the most recent one I have," she explains. "We haven't spoken much since I divorced his father twenty-something years ago. Occasionally, I'll see him at the California Mortgage Association conferences." Her voice quivers. "He generally won't speak with me, not even if we're sitting at the same table. I've tried to make peace, but the last visit we had ended horribly." She pauses, as if trying to stop the emotions from welling up in her throat.

"What happened?" I ask, intrigued by her family drama.

She sighs. "He blames me for the divorce. Although it was his father who cheated on me."

"Have you explained the situation to him?"

She laughs bitterly. "I've sent letters. They were returned. I try to talk, but he won't listen."

"It sounds like he's been hurt."

She sniffs. "He's just like his father."

"Then why are you trying to make peace with him?"

She pushes her reading glasses up the bridge of her nose and changes the subject. "About your application."

I lean forward, anticipating good news. "Yes?"

From my purse, Madonna sings, "Lucky Star."

Ms. Lashay lowers her glasses. "If you don't mind turning off your phone, we can proceed."

I scrabble in my purse and glance at the caller-ID. "I can't. It's urgent." I stand up and move to the door. "Good morning, Trina Kay of Kay Realty speaking."

"It's Staci from Wine Country Title." Her voice comes across as high-pitched and rushed. "The Engles called instructing me to draw up cancellation papers from the advice of their real estate attorney. Not even a minute later, the Sanders called informing me that their attorney is filing a lis pendens on the property." Her voice cracks. "What's going on?"

This is why no one has called me back. Both parties have been consulting with their attorneys who have instructed them otherwise. I wonder how long it will take before I receive letters from their attorneys.

"Don't panic," I tell Staci, wishing I could follow my own advice. Turning to Ms. Lashay, I say, "Excuse me." Once outside her office, I stalk across the courtyard to the brass table and chairs beside the water fountain for some privacy, but the rushing water is too distracting. Moving toward the elevators, I explain, "Mr. Engle's job transfer was cancelled, so he doesn't want to move. Mr. Sanders wants to close escrow as planned. Neither one wants to negotiate. That's why there are attorneys involved now."

"What should I do?"

"Nothing. You're the neutral third-party. Let me handle it. And if they call back, instruct the receptionist to put them through to voice mail. Every message saved is evidence if this goes to court."

She gulps. "Okay."

I hang up and run a hand through my hair. Why do things have to get so complicated? Maybe I should call Mr. Leggins and let him know what's going on. Wait. I haven't finished my appointment with Ms. Lashay. I stalk across the courtyard. The staccato rhythm of my DKNY heels echoes against the vaulted ceilings. Pushing back the glass door, I try not to do the mental gymnastics I normally do trying to fix things that are seemingly out of my control.

Ms. Lashay glances over the rhinestone rims of her reading glasses. "Are you a real estate agent?" she asks.

"Broker," I say, slumping into the marshmallow chair and crossing my legs.

She frowns at my too short skirt, which I shrunk from drying it at the laundromat. "How long?"

"Thirteen years." I tug the hem down, wishing I could afford dry cleaning, and narrow my eyes. "Why so many questions? Is it going to affect the interest rate of my loan?"

She chuckles. The creases in her face fold back to reveal an enchanting smile. "Oh, no, dear, absolutely not. I was just asking because I thought you would know that I can't offer you a loan based on joint tenancy when you're not applying for joint credit. Your husband will have to come in or you'll have to get him to sign a quitclaim deed to the property in order for us to give you any type of financing."

Why can't things go smoothly for once? I uncross my legs. Air rattles through my chest. I wonder if I'm going to die young from all this stress. "Ms. Lashay, he's not my husband, and he won't sell me his half of anything. He won't even buy my half. And I need $15,000 fast. That's why I'm here."

Ms. Lashay removes her glasses and stares slightly above my head at something on the wall. "I could offer you a job."

A job?

"I already have one," I explain.

"It sounds like you could use another." She tilts her head to the side, and I wonder how much hairspray she uses to keep that thin hair in a beehive. "Private money loans can be very profitable, both for us and the lenders. I've been pretty busy as conventional interest rates have been rising. More and more people are finding they cannot afford their new adjustable rate payments. As a result, they end up in default. Your job would be to help me bail them out. For a price, of course."  She smiles.

Sounds like loan sharking to me.

"Since you're a broker, I could offer you an advance on your commissions. Can you start work today or tomorrow?"

How dare she assume the close?

I stand up and extend my hand. "Thanks for the offer, but I'm going to pass."

She stands up and takes my hand in hers. Her paper-thin skin is cool and smooth. "I understand. This side of the business isn't for everyone." She squeezes my hand before letting it go. "You have to have a tough skin and a good heart to pull it off."

Who does she think I am? A pretty little rag-doll? Or a pit bull?

"If you change your mind, give me a call," she says. "I think you'd be an asset."

When I get home, I check the status of my Visa card. It says I made a $10,000 payment. Really? Oh, yeah, now I remember. I wrote out a check and put it aside anticipating the close of the Engle-Sanders deal. I must have mailed it accidentally. That's how my account was overdrawn. Now I'll have to take out the maximum cash advance and deposit it into my bank account to have a certified check written to pay the attorney's fees for the Engle-Sanders case. I sigh. Dissolving my business partnership with Tom will have to wait.

I open my e-mail program and scroll through 45 new messages. In my bulk folder, I read, "Earn $3,000 in 30 days on eBay." I click the message header to view the details, and then register with eBay. Maybe my business dissolution won't have to wait as long as I think it will.

Picking up my BlackBerry, I call my sister. "Dee, I need your help."

"Does that mean you've forgiven me?" she asks.

"It does, if you can do me this favor." I don't wait for her to ask me what it is. "I need for you to go to my house and take individual photos of anything you think might be worth something. Then e-mail them to me. Or better yet, I'll give you my eBay account information. Maybe you can help me create the postings."

"You're going to sell your things?" She sounds shocked like I just mentioned putting my first child up for adoption. "You love your things."

Maybe I do, but I'm desperate. I do not want to have to get a job. I haven't worked for anyone since college, and even then I was an assistant manager, bossing all the older people around at Delia's Tall and Tame Clothing store. Look at my situation with Tom. I can't even work out a partnership. How can I start taking orders from someone else?

"Please, just do it." When she doesn't say anything, I add, "Think of it as making amends."

"Oh, all right," she says. "But don't get mad at me if you regret it."

"I promise I won't."

# CHAPTER 15

▼

"According to the ratified contract you faxed to me along with all the counter offers, addendums, and contingency releases, it looks like the buyer has the right to force the sellers to complete the sale as long as the buyer can demonstrate he or she was ready, willing, and able to perform on the original date established by the agreement," Mr. Leggins says on Wednesday afternoon when he calls. "But if the case ends up in mediation, the seller might argue that the buyer was aware from the beginning that this sale was dependent upon a job transfer. If the seller can prove his or her company withdrew the job transfer through no fault of the seller, the mediator might side with the seller. The seller will get to keep the house."

I nod, taking notes on my laptop. "What about me? Was I wrong to have lifted the seller's contingency?"

Mr. Leggins clears his throat. "If you had left it in the contract, this would not be an issue. The buyer would have no case except to the return of his or her deposit monies. But since you wrote it in, then took it out as a contingency, it leaves a little gray space for both parties and their attorneys to work with."

"Am I liable?" I rephrase my question. "Can I be sued?"

Static crackles over my BlackBerry. I adjust the Blue Tooth.

"I don't think you neglected your fiduciary duty to either party in your role as dual agent, Ms. Kay. However, that doesn't mean the parties won't try to get you involved in their claims against each other. But if that happens, I would advise you to file a claim against the seller to collect a commission because you produced a buyer who was ready, willing, and able to complete the sale, and the seller's actions prevented the sale from being completed."

I stop typing and rub my forehead.

"To change the topic briefly, Ms. Kay, I was wondering why there was only one check for $10,000. Have you decided to return to business with Mr. Jensen?"

"No, I don't have the money to pay for both cases." My skin flushes with embarrassment. I don't mention to Mr. Leggins I've started having nightmares that I have to move back in with my parents like Dee did. No one needs to know that fear, not even Val. "I've had to prioritize."

Mr. Leggins clears his throat. "I'm sorry to hear about your predicament."

"Thanks." My voice is weak. "If I get any calls, e-mails, or letters from the seller or buyer or their attorneys, what should I do?"

"Call me." He lowers his voice. "I would not lose sleep over this."

That's easy for you to say, I think.

That evening, while I'm eating dinner in my apartment, Madonna sings, "True Blue."

I drop my fork. What's Tom doing calling me? I really should block his calls, but I haven't. Reluctantly, I swallow my chicken salad and answer the phone. "Hello?"

"Stop sending your baby sister to do your dirty work," he snaps.

"What do you mean?"

"You know exactly what I mean, Katrina Kay."

I hate when he uses my full name. It makes me feel three years old, not thirty-five.

I try to steady my voice. "Dee lives in San Jose. The trip for me takes over two hours one way. It only makes sense for her to move my belongings."

"It's not her responsibility. She didn't walk out. You did."

Every muscle in my body tenses. "Why does it matter who picks up my stuff?"

Tom lowers his voice. "Trina, dear, you can't run forever. Sooner or later, you're going to have to face your problems. Why not face them with me?"

Moving from the kitchen table to the living room, I curl up with a throw pillow on the futon. My stomach grumbles, but dinner can wait. *Never eat when you're emotional*, my mother's voice says in my mind.

"I'm not running." I try to speak the words slowly and clearly, but my voice cracks with a sob.

"If you want your stuff, then *you* come pick it up this weekend," Tom orders. "You can bring movers if you need help, but no family. On Monday morning, I'm donating whatever's left, understand?"

"You can't do that," I gasp. "It's not your property."

"Try me."

My hand shakes. Tom's threats are never idle. Once, after showing a client three dozen homes over a period of three weeks, Tom said, "Either write an offer or I'll release you from the buyer-broker agreement." When the client balked, making excuses for why none of the houses would work, Tom escorted the client out of the office.

I log onto my laptop and check what's scheduled for this weekend. I was going to celebrate my first sale with a spa day in Calistoga, but since the sale has been stalled, I've had to cancel those plans. I type, "Trip to San Jose," in my Outlook calendar. I'll rent a U-Haul and ask Dee if she can round up any college students to help with the move.

I snap my laptop shut. "See you this weekend."

The sun is barely cresting over the horizon when I toss my overnight bag in the trunk and slip into my Mercedes. Dee couldn't find any college students to move my belongings on such a short notice, so I went online and hired a moving company. Trying to be frugal, I skipped the Deluxe Moving Package for $800 which included sorting and packing my belongings into cardboard boxes and instead selected the One-Day Move-Only Sunday Sale for $500 and charged it on my Visa. With the $300 I'll be saving, I can stay overnight at a hotel. I logged onto Fairmont.com to book a Presidential Suite for Saturday night, but something must have been wrong with their server since my credit card wasn't accepted. Oh, well…a Jacuzzi tub wasn't available anyway. I guess I'll just find a hotel once I'm down there.

I pull onto Highway 101 going south, sipping coffee from my thermos. It's too cool to put down the top, too early for loud music. By the time brown hills and golden fields turn to strip malls and business high rises, I've finished my coffee, put down the top, and turned on the stereo.

Two hours later, I turn up the street toward the house I used to share with Tom. A van is ahead of me. I speed around it and wind up the last curve to the top where the three-hundred and sixty-degree views of the valley lay below in a smoggy haze. Pulling into the driveway, next to Tom's black Porsche, which is usually parked in the garage, I cut the engine and sit for a moment in silence.

It's only been three months since I've been here, so I shouldn't be surprised the house looks the same. The Zen garden is dry and sandy with too many tiny pebbles. The bay window in the living room has its drapes closed to keep out the hot air. And the double front doors with the brass knocker are still painted a bright red for welcoming, although Tom's always wanted white doors.

My key still fits into the lock. I turn and the door opens.

Padding into the tile foyer, my sneakers make no sound. My breathing is jagged and hollow. My fingers tremble like I'm scared. This is my home, I remind myself. But I still feel like an intruder breaking in.

I stare up the spiral staircase, wondering if Tom's upstairs getting ready for his golf game with my father or downstairs reading in the library. I set my purse on the table in the foyer. Walking from room to room, I take a mental inventory of what is mine. The moving company said the truck can hold up to 1500 lbs which is about the size of a studio apartment. There is so much furniture; I will have to decide what's worth keeping and what stays.

When I get to the entertainment room, I smile at my big leather recliner with the built-in cup holders. I run my hands over its supple back and sink into its luxurious seat, closing my eyes and breathing deeply, relaxing for the first time in weeks.

"Well, look who's here. It's Goldie Locks in Papa Bear's chair."

I sit up abruptly, my heart caught in my throat.

Tom stands in the doorway, all six-feet four of him. His golden brown hair is cropped meticulously around his ears although a small wave falls over his forehead just above his steel blue eyes. He's dressed in a red Polo shirt and khaki shorts. He leans against the doorjamb, crossing his arms over his burly chest, gazing at me like I'm a new fixture in the room.

I swallow. He's as handsome and brutal as a Greek god. My palms rub against the soft leather armrests for comfort and strength. "I'm taking inventory for the movers. They'll be here tomorrow," I say.

His gaze never wavers. "That recliner's mine."

I frown, remembering the Christmas he gave it to me. "No, it's not."

"I bought it with my money. It's mine."

"You gave it to me as a gift. That makes it mine."

"You broke up with me, so I'm taking it back."

"Indian giver!" I stand up, ready for a fight.

"I already moved all of your belongings into the garage," Tom explains. "That's why the Porsche is parked in the driveway. The only things left for you to pack are upstairs in the bedroom. I didn't want to mess with your flotation devices."

"My what?"

"You know, those pads in the bras that work as lifejackets in case you fall into a pool."

My hands clench into fists. "Those are silicone gel inserts, not flotation devices."

He shrugs. A wry smile crosses his lips. "Whatever."

I can't believe he's making fun of my body! First, my legs, now my breasts.

Okay. Calm down. I take a deep breath, but anger quivers through my body. I need to get out of here quickly. "Half of this furniture is mine!" I sweep my arm around the room, indicating the recliner, the leather sofa, the big screen TV, the stereo, the DVD player, the glass-topped coffee table, and the end tables with Tiffany lamps.

Tom uncrosses his arms and steps into the room. He points to each object like a boy at school during Show and Tell. "This sofa was purchased along with the recliner as a Christmas gift to us and our new home. It was paid for by me, therefore, that makes it mine. This TV came from the Gonzales sale, which I arranged because you don't speak Spanish. This stereo and DVD player were gifts from my dad when I helped his friend during that terrible 1031 exchange. The coffee table came from the Hernandez sale, again arranged by me." He stops and fingers the fringe on a Tiffany lamp. "And I think you're right about the lamps and end tables. I think you bought those after you closed that mobile home sale."

I take another deep breath, trying to remain calm. But it doesn't work. My entire body is shaking. "Gift or not, I'm taking my recliner."

He strides around me to sit down on the recliner. He crosses his arms behind his head and stretches his legs out on the ottoman like a dog marking his territory. My temperature flares. I lunge forward, grabbing his arm, trying to pull him off, but he's too big, too strong. He tugs me, and I fall forward into his lap. He tickles my sides, and I squirm, trying to break free.

"Let me go," I scream between giggles. But it's no use, the harder I try, the weaker I become.

He wraps one arm around my waist and holds me close to his chest. My head is buried in the space between his shoulder and neck. I breathe in a whiff of his cologne, and a pang of longing all out of proportion startles me.

"You ready to give up?" His breath is warm against my skin.

I want to kiss him as much as I want to push him away. "Never," I whisper.

He motions to start tickling me again. I cringe. He stops.

"You don't look good," he says, observing me. "You're gaunt and pale. You haven't been eating well or running."

I say nothing.

He moves his hand from my waist to touch my hair, and I feel that longing all over again.

"Please—don't," I say, struggling to sit up.

He lets his fingers brush against my jaw before honoring my request. For a moment that feels like minutes, we stare at each other. My body is soft and warm with desire, but my head is stubborn and resolute. I came to claim my belongings, not let him claim my heart.

I slip off his lap and stand up on wobbly knees. He grasps my hand gently and squeezes. "I've missed you," he says.

I turn away from his sad blue eyes and gaze at the Persian rug beneath the coffee table. I feel my resolve starting to break down. This is why I didn't want to come back, I think. Inspite of all the pain, I still love him.

I slide my hand out of his grasp. "I'm going to the bedroom to pack," I say, half-hoping he might follow me.

Upstairs, in the master suite, late morning sunlight dances against the satin comforter and polished wood floors. I catch my reflection in the mirror above the bureau. Tom's right. I'm thin and pale and gloomy. Like a ghost of my former self.

"I left some extra boxes in the closet," Tom says. He's standing on the landing.

I brush away the thought of making love to him and focus my attention to the mahogany jewelry box shaped like a miniature armoire on the bureau. I pull back the doors and slide out each drawer, checking to see if everything is still there. It is. "Aren't you going to your golf game?"

"I'm not leaving," Tom says. "I thought I'd help you pack, and discuss some things."

"What things?" I place a gold necklace back into the jewelry box and close the doors.

"I want to buy your half of the business for $50,000."

That can't be right. I must have heard him wrong. My half of the business is only worth $25,000. Has the billboard doubled profits in three months? Or is it something else, something personal?

"Why the change of heart?" I ask.

He walks over to me. For a moment, I think he's going to touch my face again, but he shoves his hands into his pockets and glances away. "If I buy you out, it's much easier than starting over. Everything's in place. I just have to remove your name from all the paperwork and I can go on like nothing happened."

Like nothing happened? Like the two years we worked together and lived together don't mean anything. Just like that, I can be erased. When he approaches the next attractive female real estate broker and proposes a partnership, he won't have to mention me. I turn back to the bureau and open up the dresser drawer and stare at the old bras and underwear I left from the first time I packed. "Is that what you want?" I ask.

He places his hands on my shoulders and my whole body warms beneath his touch. Oh, god, not again. I want to feel his hands slide down my arms and cup my waist and spin me around for a deep, long kiss.

"Of course, I don't," he whispers through my hair. "I want you to come back and work with me. I want us to be together again."

I swallow. My throat is tight with emotion. He presses against me, and I can feel his erection. A wave of desire swoops over me. I do not dare look up. My fingers curl around a pair of purple bikini underwear so tightly my knuckles turn white.

He kisses my neck and whispers, "Trina, dear, come home."

Glancing up, I catch our reflection. Tom's golden brown hair flops against my shoulder, hiding his face, while his lips press tiny jolts of electricity into my skin.

"I don't understand," I say. All I can think of is how he smells like the ocean and feels like a warm blanket, and how my body keeps relaxing under his touch until my eyes close and his hands slip under my shirt. His fingers trace the lace outlining the cups of my bra, and a new shiver of desire quakes through my body, making my knees tremble. "You sounded angry on the phone and in your e-mails."

"What was I supposed to feel?" His tongue traces my earlobe while his hand tugs one of my breasts out of the bra. "You just walked out and left me." He gently rolls my nipple between his fingers. My breath catches in my throat. "I've never been left by anyone."

My voice is tiny. "I was hurt." As soon as I say it, I feel it again. A strange, overwhelming hurt, a hurt so huge I haven't felt anything like it in years, not since I was teased in middle school for my gangly arms and spindly legs. *Stilts*, everyone called me, even the gym teacher.

I wriggle away from his touch and step away from the bureau.

Tom's blue eyes are soft and sincere. "I don't want to hurt you anymore."

Oh, no, not now. My eyes smart with tears. I suddenly want to be held and sheltered from the pain of being teased, but I'm afraid to tell Tom why it hurts, because he might not understand. And I couldn't bear to have him make fun of me. Not now.

I wish the movers were coming today, not tomorrow.

I sit down on the edge of the mattress and adjust my bra. I'm torn between bounding down the stairs and not returning until the movers arrive and flinging my arms around Tom's neck and never letting him go.

"Are you okay?" Tom kneels in front of me.

A tear slides down my cheek.

Tom brushes it away with his thumb. I lean forward for a hug, but Tom's mouth meets my quivering lips in a clumsy kiss. His tongue slips into my mouth, stifling my sobs. When he pauses to catch his breath, he stands up and slides me across the satin comforter and climbs up next to me. He tugs off my shirt and unhooks my bra and caresses my breasts. I close my eyes and arch my back, enjoying the delightful sensation of his skillful touch.

An hour later, Tom drapes his arm across my naked body as I lie on my side beneath the satin sheets gazing out the window at the clear blue sky.

Oh, god, what have I done?

"Would you like something to drink?" Tom asks.

I nod.

"You stay here and I'll get us some water."

After he leaves the bedroom, I stand up and make my way to the bathroom. Although my body feels sated, my soul feels uneasy still. I turn on the hot water to run a bath in the Jacuzzi tub. My lavender oil is still beneath the sink. I pour a teaspoon full of its soothing scent into the running water.

"Here you go," Tom says, handing me a glass.

"Thank you." I smile, and take a sip.

"I'll let you take your bath in peace," he says. "We can finish our talk later."

I nod, handing him the glass of water.

His skin still glistens with sweat and his eyes sparkle with satisfaction. "I love you," he says.

I'm silent.

He gazes at me a moment longer, as if waiting for the same words to come out of my mouth, but I can't speak.

Oh, god, what have I done?

Slowly, he steps out of the bathroom and closes the door. I submerge my body into a whirlwind of bubbles and hot water, closing my eyes, trying to think clearly. But my thoughts keep tying themselves into knots.

Should I get back together with Tom. Give him another chance?

Or should I take the money he's offering and invest it in my new brokerage?

What would Madonna do?

Take the money. He's already proven he can break my heart. Why give him another opportunity to break it again?

What would Val do?

Give Tom another chance. The sex is great. The house is great. The business is great.  Everything's great, right?

What would I do?

I don't know.

When I can't stand the heat and the bubbles any longer, I drain the bath and wrap myself in my terrycloth robe. My hair products are still on the marble countertop next to my tooth brush and toothpaste and facial cleansers. It's as if I've never been gone. I pick up my comb and run it through my wet hair, pausing to untangle a few knots.

Why do I feel so bad?

Opening my closet doors, I run my fingers across the remaining blouses, jackets, skirts, slacks, and suits that did not fit into my luggage the first time I left. A slow smile spreads across my face. I seize the sleeve of a velvet jacket and press it against my nose, breathing in the familiar scent. My clothes! I get to keep my clothes. It doesn't matter if I get back together with Tom or I accept the $50,000 buyout. How exciting! I select a green blouse from Bloomingdales and a pair of white cropped jeans from Nordstrom. Once dressed, I twirl around in front of the full length mirror. A rush of happiness floods through my veins. I feel eight years old again, playing dress up in my mother's clothes.

Maybe I shouldn't be so harsh with Tom. After all, he made love to me so tenderly. He said he loves me. Why shouldn't I believe him?

And if I don't believe him, then why don't I just accept his generous buyout offer. I won't have to file a petition with the court and I won't have to pay Mr. Leggins any more money. I can pay Mandy for her time and effort and pay off my Visa and buy that Versace dress before the fall collection arrives. And I can take time off work and enjoy life for once.

But a twinge of uneasiness pinches beneath my breastbone. I don't understand it. Maybe I should go talk with Tom just like I used to back when we were dating. Sometimes would sit for hours just going over possibilities. That's how we ended up merging our businesses. We had been dating for three months, going back and forth from his condo to my apartment, when we decided it was time for one of us to move in. "But I don't want to give up my closet," I said, proud of one feature of my modest abode. "You don't have to," Tom said, snuggling close to me on my leather sofa. "We can buy a house together." I leaned my head against his shoulder and started dreaming of a castle in the clouds just like the ones Val and I used to draw when we were kids in elementary school. "If we buy a house together, why don't we do business together?" I asked. Tom kissed me long and deeply. "You're right," he said. "Why not?" I glance around the bedroom of our castle, feeling a bittersweet tingle from my head to my toes. I could move back in. I could continue with our business partnership. We could pick up from where we left off in our happily-ever-after saga.

Yes! That's what I'll do. Stay.

I pad downstairs, looking for Tom to tell him of my decision. My bare feet do not make a sound on the freshly swept wooden floor in the kitchen or the freshly vacuumed carpet in the family room. I'm just about to return upstairs when Tom's voice drifts down the hall. My feet move silently on the carpet. The office door is ajar.

"Business is great, Dad," Tom says. "That billboard was the best investment of my career."

I stand outside the door, holding my breath, unable to move. My joyful hope is fading away, and underneath I feel a twinge of pain. Tom still has the billboard of my legs posted for the world to see. And he's just told his father it is the best investment of his career.

He continues talking, unaware I am listening. "Actually, she's here. She came to get her stuff, but I think she'll come to her senses and stay."

My body stiffens. He thinks I'm a fool. I try to swallow, but my throat is tight with the threat of tears.

Tom laughs at something his father said. "Sure, next weekend will be great. I look forward to the visit. Maybe we'll play a round of golf with Trina's dad."

A growing indignation sweeps through my body. I thought Tom knew me, but he doesn't. He sees me as a silly girl with a great pair of legs, not a savvy business woman who can manage her life. At least, that's the portrait he's painting for his father and whoever else he talks to about me.

How arrogant of him to assume I am getting back together with him! Sure, he's a great lover. Sure, he's wealthier than I am. But sex and money don't make a life. And no matter how much I adore my clothes, I can live without them if that means I have my dignity intact.

I take a deep, calming breath and knock on the partially closed door before stepping inside. "Business?" I ask, pointing to the receiver pressed against his ear.

He glances over his shoulder and shakes his head. "All right. Got to go, Dad. Love you too. Bye."

"You look lovely." He swivels around on the leather office chair and pats his knee. "Sit down."

I continue standing.

"What wrong?" he asks.

Okay. Stay calm. Ease into it. "I've decided to continue with my original plans and just take my things and go tomorrow." I swallow. "You can keep the $50,000. I want the business dissolved legally through the courts."

Tom's face drops with shock. "But why go through all that expense when we can do it ourselves?"

"Because I want to make sure my interests are protected," I say. "And my attorney has my best interests. Not you."

"How can you say that? Your attorney only cares about his fees." Tom runs his fingers through his hair. "I want what's best for you." His voice warbles. "I love you." His blue eyes glisten like he's about to cry, but for once I don't care.

"Love is not enough."

Tom's face freezes with exasperation. "Then what is?" he asks.

"Respect." My voice booms with emotion. "If you respected me, you would have taken down the billboard of my legs no matter how much money it's bringing in for the company."

His blue eyes harden into steel bits, and his voice tightens with bitterness. "You *need* that money."

"I have plenty of money," I lie.

He laughs. "Is that why you're selling your things on eBay?"

My face grows hot. What else did Dee tell him?

Tom stands up and crosses over to me. His angry, loving, and concerned gaze penetrates me. "Drop the act, Trina. I know how bad it is."

Who told him about my finances?

"It's not that bad," I lie. "I don't know who you spoke with, but if it was my mother, she exaggerates."

Tom lowers his voice, as if he is revealing a secret. "You've been to a lender. She called to see if I would quitclaim the house to you, so you could refinance and pull cash out."

I clench my fists, remembering the disclosures I signed authorizing Ms. Lashay to act on my behalf when I thought I could get a loan.

Tom grasps my arm. "Drop your pride and let me help you."

Help me? Just like he helped me pay off my debt so we could buy this house. "I'm not stupid." I twist away from him. "I'm not some helpless girl you can come back and rescue so I'll love you forever and ever."

"I never said you were."

"Maybe not to my face."

He stares at me with disbelief. "What does that supposed to mean?"

Should I tell him I overheard his conversation with his father? I shake my head. "This is just a game to you. You don't really want to buy my half of the business. It's not even worth as much as you're offering. You just want to convince me to take money from you so you can feel better. Why don't you just admit you were wrong about the billboard and apologize to me? It would make everything so much easier."

Tom lifts his eyebrows. "Is that all you want? An apology?"

I sound like a pouty five year old. "Only if you mean it."

He stares at the floor, exasperated with me. "You're on the verge of bankruptcy and all you want is for me to say I'm sorry? Words aren't going to make it all better. You need money. Don't you see? I still love you, I still care about you, and I want to help you. If you'll just let me." He extends his arms wide, as if he expects me to accept comfort from him.

I turn away. "Thanks for the offer, but it's not help you're offering. It's charity."

# CHAPTER 16

▼

I don't want to spend the night with my family because they're still friendly with Tom and I don't want Tom to know anything about me anymore. But I probably can't afford a room for one night at the Fairmont, although I would just love to soak in a Jacuzzi tub while eating lobster tail dipped in butter delivered on a silver tray by room service. So, after driving a while, I find a Best Western with its distinct pink boxy exterior and white arch entry. It's probably a lot cheaper than the Fairmont and I'm more likely to find a California King bed than I am at Motel 6. That's one downfall of being so tall—my feet dangle off the end of standard mattresses. As soon as I step inside the lobby, a brisk whoosh of air-conditioning blows through my curls. The place smells recently remodeled. My heels sink into plush rosy carpet. Recessed lighting highlights the dark green faux marble counters. And gold diamond-shaped wallpaper gives the lobby a wedding present effect minus the bow. An elderly man dressed in a Hawaiian shirt and Bermuda shorts takes the arm of an elderly woman dressed in a summer pant suit as they step out of the elevator, chatting about shopping at

Eastridge Mall before visiting their grandchildren. Okay. No Armani or Prada. This place should be affordable.

"May I help you?" a guy in his early twenties dressed in a well-worn shirt and slacks asks.

I step up to the counter. "Do you have a single occupancy room with a California King bed?"

He efficiently taps into the keyboard my request. "Yes, we do for $113."

I tap my nails against the counter. Should I go to Motel 6 instead? I could sleep on my side with my knees tucked to my chest and save $50.

"Would you like to book it?" He glances up, expectantly.

How much cash do I have? I spent $60 on gas to get down here and just filled up my tank for another $60. I spent $6 on toll, $15 on lunch, and I had $260 in cash before I left. That leaves me $119. Perfect.

"I'll take it," I say, withdrawing my wallet. I lay out one hundred dollars in twenties, one ten, and three ones.

"The total comes to $122.04 with tax."

I raise my eyebrows in shock.

He counts the bills on the counter. "You're a bit short," he says, as though I haven't noticed. "For your convenience, we accept Visa, MasterCard, and American Express."

Surely, I should have $122.04 left on my Visa. I just made a huge payment, although I did take out another cash advance to pay Mr. Leggins. Still. It's worth a try, isn't it?

I put my bills back into my wallet and remove my battered Visa card. The clerk slides it through the machine and waits while the computer transmits the data for approval. After a while, the clerk frowns and tries swiping the card again. I ignore the hammering in my chest. Maybe the machine is broken. His frown deepens. He punches the numbers into the keyboard and steps back, as if the monitor might explode. I wipe my sweaty palms against my shorts and wonder what's taking so long.

He glances up with an inexpressible look on his face. "I'm sorry, ma'am, but your card has been denied."

"Oh," I say, raising my eyebrows. I must have reached my limit.

"Do you have another means of paying, ma'am?"

I gaze glumly at my wallet. There are a few store cards, but nothing else. I shake my head.

"I'm sorry, ma'am," he says, returning the Visa card.

I tuck the Visa in my wallet. My whole body burns with humiliation. Luckily, no one else is in the lobby. Only the clerk and Visa know of my money problems.

I take a few gulps of air, trying to calm myself. What to do? I sling my purse over my shoulder and stalk out of the lobby without saying goodbye. The glass doors swing open, and a wall of heat crashes against my face. I wince, fighting back tears.

Glancing down the street, I consider staying at Motel 6 for the night. But then a fresh wave of shame hits me. If I use up my remaining cash, I won't be able to pay for anything until I sell my belongings on eBay. And who knows how long that will take.

I sigh. I can't go back to Tom. That will just prove to him that I need his charity.

I can't drive home without my belongings, and the movers aren't coming until tomorrow. That means I have to stay the night. Even if it's in my car.

I unlock the door of the Mercedes and slip inside. Leaning back against the seat, I close my eyes and feel the heat of the sun beating through the windshield. Someone raps on the window. A homeless man with a dirty face and torn clothes peers at me through the glass. "Do you have a dollar, ma'am?" he asks.

With my heart pounding in my chest, I instinctively check to see if the car doors are locked. They are. I shake my head and mouth, "Sorry," hoping the man will walk away. But he lingers at the window a moment longer, staring intently at my Prada purse as if he knows I am lying.

My palms sweat with fear. What if he tries to break in? What if he tries to kill me for a dollar? I rummage in my purse for my BlackBerry and wave the phone at the man, hoping to scare him away. "Police," I mouth, speed dialing my parents' house.

Slowly, the man turns and walks away.

Mom asks, "Is that you, KK?"

"It's me," I say, pressing the BlackBerry to my ear. "I'm in town."

"With Tom?" she asks, her voice high with expectancy.

I shudder at the mention of Tom. "No, I came back to get a few things, but the movers aren't coming until tomorrow."

"Well, come on over," she says, cheerfully. "We'll have dinner."

I smile with relief.

My parents defy statistics. They grew up in the same town, attended the same school, and dated only each other. When most of their friends and acquaintances have changed jobs, changed spouses, and changed houses, they have retired from the only jobs they ever had, celebrated their 40th wedding anniversary, and remained in the same house they raised my sister and me in.

Twenty minutes after speaking with Mom, I pull up to their driveway. Dee is sitting on the porch, smoking.

"I thought you gave them up," I say, walking over to her.

She crushes the butt in a plastic ashtray and shields her eyes with her other hand from the glare of the setting sun behind me. "Where's your stuff?"

"The movers come tomorrow."

"Who's working your business?" She leans back on her elbows. "Do you have another partner lined up?"

"Just an assistant," I lie. "But I'll be hiring sales associates soon."

"Is that why you're selling your stuff?"

I force a smile. "It's a business investment. By the time I'm through, I'll have more than enough money to buy even better things."

Dee narrows her eyes. "Why is everything always so easy for you?"

If only she knew the truth, then she'd be gloating instead of being jealous. "It's called hard work, not hardly working." I step over her and let the screen door slam behind me. My father lifts his head from where he's reading the paper in the living room and smiles. "Hey, KK, long time no see. How's business?"

"Fine," I lie.

"Glad you could come down during summer."

I shrug. "A lot of people are on vacation."

He nods. "I remember. Your mother used to plan her vacations for the week after school was out." My mother managed someone else's brokerage for thirty-seven years until they sold to a big chain for a hefty price of $20 million dollars. She stayed on for a while, hoping to collect some of the new company's benefits, but decided to take early retirement when corporate life proved too stifling.

Dad folds the paper in half and squints at me. "You're looking a little pale. You're not getting out for your runs?"

My father is part Cherokee. You can see it in his cheekbones. And his skin. He tans well like me.

"Busy, Dad."

He goes back to reading. "Mom just vacuumed and dusted your room. She's out shopping for dinner. How's Tom?"

My father likes Tom. Once I overheard my father tell one of his buddies over the phone that Tom was the son he always wanted but never had.

I hate to disappoint him with our breakup. Dad's the only one I've ever tried to impress. It's always thrilling when he takes pride in me. And always a little depressing when he doesn't. "The same."

"He canceled our golf game today. I thought you two might be making up."

"Not likely." I can't see my father's face from behind the paper, but if I could, I'm sure it would be sagging with disappointment.

I turn and head down the hall into my old bedroom. The white wood shutters have been folded back from the window just as I like them to be whenever the sun is out. My childhood furniture sits just where I left it seventeen years ago when I moved out, but the rest of the room has been decorated as a shrine to my competitive running years. My heart clutches with panic. Those were the worst years of my life, full of anxiety and depression. I set my overnight bag on the mattress and tug off the pillow case and cover the trophy I won in middle school for the fastest one mile run. Next, I place the photographs of my unsightly body face down. I remove the ribbons tacked to the walls and the framed certificate for MVP for track and cross country and shove them into the closet. I'll put everything back tomorrow before I leave, but right now, I want to create a welcoming space, full of calm, and that's impossible when the painful success of my youth stares back at me.

"You're here!" My mother steps into the bedroom and wraps her arms around me, squeezing me tight. "Let's eat. There's extra crispy fried chicken, your favorite, and those wonderful biscuits you've always said are better than mine."

"You went to KFC?" I ask. She only buys fast food when she thinks I'm depressed.

"Only the best for my KK." She releases me and smiles. A quick glance around the room and her expression changes.

She peeks her head out the doorway and shouts down the hall, "Greg, what has Dee done to KK's room?"

"I did it, Mom."

She frowns at me. "But I don't understand, dear. I thought you'd be happy to be surrounded by reminders of your previous success. I thought it would cheer you on to greater heights and motivate you to try harder at your new business."

"These aren't happy memories, Mom. How many times do I have to remind you? I was teased."

"They were only jealous, dear. You had Olympic potential, if you had just kept competing through high school." Her voice drips with disappointment, but I don't care. No one ever made fun of her, or if they had, she never mentioned it.

"Let's not get upset, dear. Dinner's ready and you can't eat when you're emotional."

I groan. Maybe I should have spent $50 and stayed at Motel 6.

My parents' kitchen is like a set from a TV sitcom in that it never changes. We each take a seat at the round table beneath the fluorescent lights, Dee on my left, Dad on my right, Mom directly across from me. Mom has placed silverware on the table although almost everything is finger foods. These are the same forks, knives, and spoons we used growing up. I remember hand washing them each night. That's why the tines are not bent and the metal not tarnished. The earthenware plates are fairly new, a gift from Dee during her I-think-I'll-be-a-potter phase of her artistic development.

Without a word, we dig into the food like ravenous wolves. Mom fusses, passing the Styrofoam containers of tasteless mashed potatoes and gelatinous gravy around the table, making sure everyone has seconds and thirds. Mom gabbers, "Isn't this lovely? Our whole family is here for dinner. Just wait till you see what I have for dessert." Dad grunts. Dee scoops another helping of mashed potatoes on her plate, having ignored the fried chicken because she's a vegetarian. "Next time KK visits, can we have something more nutritious?" she asks. I don't say a thing. I'm too busy tugging greasy fried chicken from a drumstick. The skin crunches between my teeth and oil oozes out the corners of my lips. I save the oh-so-bad, but taste oh-so-good biscuits for last. They flake perfectly on my tongue with just a dab of sweet butter. Yum.

But even the fast food with extra fat and extra carbs cannot release enough serotonin into my bloodstream to bring me to a state of bliss. Val always said the dinner table is the best place to try out new skits because if you can fool your family, you can fool anybody. But I'm not fooling anyone. I smile and nod at all the right times, but my family knows the truth. I'm the antithesis of what I used to be. Before I was powerful, successful, and attached. Now I'm helplessly broke and suddenly single.

Toward the end of the meal, Dee wipes her hands on a paper napkin and announces, "I sent a few photos from my portfolio to a contest and won a full tuition scholarship to the NESOP Professional Photography Conference next spring."

I hope the winning photo was not the picture of my legs.

"That's great, dear," Mom says, without looking at her.

Dee can't hide the disappointment in her face. The corners of her mouth turn down, and her fingers fiddle with the paper napkin, twisting it into a long braid. Part of me almost feels sorry for her. She's always had to live in my shadow, even after I moved out of the house.

When Dad hears the news, he lifts his head and shines his full attention on Dee. "Congratulations, honey. How many applicants were there?"

Dee shrugs. "I don't know. Hundreds, maybe thousands. It was a nationwide contest."

"Wow, that's impressive." Dad's entire body beams with pride. "Next thing you know, you'll be charging me to take the annual family photo."

A slight smile spreads across Dee's face.

I flush with new anger. Dad cares more about Dee's future as a photographer than he cares about my future as a Realtor. How fair is that? I bet the only thing that would get his attention away from Dee would be an announcement that Tom and I were getting back together. I consider lying for a moment to steal the spotlight from Dee, but Mom intervenes. "How about some dessert?" she asks, standing up and rummaging in the freezer. She removes a pint of my favorite sherbet from Baskin Robbins, crème de menthe. She fills glass bowls with pale green sherbet and passes them around the table. "Might as well spoil my kids since I don't have any grandchildren." Her gaze is directed at me.

I purse my lips, afraid I'll say something I'll regret if I speak up. I think my biological clock is broken. I haven't heard it ticking, even though a lot of couples my age are getting married and starting families. Maybe someone switched my biological clock with my mother's; that's why *hers* is still ticking.

Feeling empty and full at the same time, I jump up with relief when my BlackBerry sings, "Vogue."

"I have to take this," I say. "It's Val." I excuse myself from the table and shut the door to my bedroom and sit cross-legged on the bed just like I did during high school when Val and I would talk to each other every night. For a moment, I'm transported into another world as he tells me of the wonderful places he's been—Vancouver, British Columbia, Montreal, and how he's going to be back in the states next month.

"Sorry I haven't phoned earlier. It's been crazy. Late nights. Early mornings. Rehearsals. Road trips. Complete pandemonium, but I love it, love it, love it! And the audience loves it too. Our tour has been extended by two months," Val gushes. "But enough about me. How are you?"

I tell him about Tom and the movers, about my parents and their shrine to my athletic years, about Dee and her photographic success, and, lastly, about the dire financial straits I'm in.

"It's that fucking apartment I told you not to get," Val says. "But you never listen to me."

I sink back on the mattress and stare up at the ceiling. "I'm listening now."

He laughs. "That's only because you're on the brink of bankruptcy, sweetie."

Bankruptcy. I shudder with the thought. What would my parents and Dee and Tom say if I had to file for bankruptcy?

"It's not that bad," I lie. "I have some cash."

"Your Visa was denied," Val says. "It can't get worse than that."

I sigh. What to do?

As if reading my mind, Val orders, "Move out of your apartment. Stay at my place. I won't be back till Valentine's Day. That gives you plenty of time to sort things out."

The bedroom door swings open and a bright, blinding light goes off in my face.

"Gotcha!" Dee shouts, waving her camera at me.

I grab the bare pillow and toss it at her. She slams the door, leaving me alone.

I consider Val's offer. It's an option. And, looking at my other options—Tom's handout or my parents' house—it's possibly the best option there is.

# CHAPTER 17

▼

I give my 30 day notice to Mandy on Monday morning. "You don't have to leave on my account," she says, pursing her lips into a straight line. "I'm already leaving in two weeks. I've found a job as a property manager in Rohnert Park."

"Congratulations. But that's not why I'm leaving." I decide to tell her the truth. "I can't afford it. I never could."

She takes out my file and shakes her head with disgust.

I lean on the office counter, wondering how I can rectify things between us. "Listen, Mandy, I'm sorry about what happened. Usually most real estate transactions close. I don't want there to be any hard feelings between us, so why don't I pay you for the time you worked for me."

She glances up, frowning. "How are you going to pay me? You can't even afford your apartment."

The air conditioning vent blows cold air and I shiver, tugging the cashmere wrap over my silk tank top, both luxuries from my previous life. Like the truckload of luxuries stacked up in piles throughout the apartment, waiting to be sold.

"I may not have cash, but I have furniture and artwork and tons of clothes I brought back from San Jose this weekend. You could pick out a few things."

"I don't need more crap," she says, shoving a contract at me. She switches to her calm professional voice. "Your last day will be July 7th. Your security deposit will be mailed to you minus any cleaning or repairs fees. Sign here and fill in a forwarding address if you have it."

I take the ball point pen chained to the counter, sign and date the contract, and fill in Val's P.O. Box for the security deposit check. "What about your contact information? If the Engle-Sanders case gets resolved, I'll have money to pay you."

"And how long will that be? A month? A year?"

"I don't know."

She takes the contract, makes a photocopy for me, and places the original in my file. "I can't wait around for $5,000 that may or may not show up one day."

Think, think, think.

"What if we compromise? I give you my Donna Karan cocktail dress and Tiffany necklace and pay you the other half in cash once the case is closed."

"You're not the only one with money troubles." Her hands smooth dust off the counter. "I have bills, too, you know. And student loans I have to repay."

My first impression of her was right. She's just like me, only younger. "How much cash do you need?"

"The whole five thousand would have been nice," she says, "but I'd settle for twenty five hundred."

"Would you sign a contract agreeing to that?" I ask, just to be sure.

She pushes her glasses up the bridge of her nose. "Do you have one to sign?"

"Yes." A slow smile spreads across my face. "I will."

Sitting at the kitchen table in my apartment, I upload images of my belongings onto eBay with brief descriptions: Prada shoes, hardly worn, paid $139, starting bid at $50, Tiffany lamp, almost new, paid $293, starting bid at $100, 14K gold necklace, paid $350, starting bid at $150.

By the end of the week, I've sold almost everything including the new furniture I bought for the apartment. The total revenue is close to $5,000. Immediately, I go to the bank for a cashier's check in the amount of $500 and Fed/Ex it to Visa, freeing up my credit line. Then I write Tom a check for $1,500, which is my half of the mortgage payment in San Jose. Next I write a check to Mandy for $2,500 and present it to her along with a contract Mr. Leggins drafted for her to sign releasing me from any future compensation. Finally, I write another check for $250 to Mr. Leggins for drafting the contract. That leaves me with a little less than $250 till I either get a job or close another transaction.

But there are no other transactions on the horizon. There haven't been since I moved here. With the mortgage loan crisis in full swing, real estate prices have been dropping further and further, and I have refused to take on any more listings since I know I do not have the money to advertise them. And all of the buyers either Mandy or I have worked with are just waiting to see how low prices can go before they make a purchase. Or the new underwriting restrictions have basically thrown them out of the market (no down payment, no credit history, no loan).

I have to get a job.

Believe me, I've tried avoiding it. The thought of a JOB—Just Over Broke—twists my stomach into a knot. I'm thirty-five. I should be moving up, not starting over. But if I don't do something now, I might end up a guest on the Jerry Springer show confessing how I became a gambler at the River Rock Casino instead of looking for employment.

To begin my new quest, I start a new habit, one that I hope will prepare me for the routine of 9-5 employment. At sunrise, I jog for six miles, shower, change, eat breakfast, then boot up my laptop and start scouring the classifieds. I register with Monster.com and SonomaCountyHelpWanted.com. Over the next week, I manage to e-mail 75 resumes. Twenty-five instant rejections hit my e-mail inbox. Ten queries from human resource managers ask additional questions either about my job skills or my available hours. But instead of those ten interested queries turning into interviews, they end up as kind rejection notices in my e-mail inbox. I dial the first employer, then the second, asking for a reason why I was not granted an interview. The first employer, a woman with a nasally voice, says, "You're under qualified for selling highly accurate timing equipment." The second employer, a man with a gruff voice, says, "You're too specialized. We need someone with more diverse experience. All you've done is real estate." The rest of the potential employers echo the same sentiments, and I begin to wonder if I've plunged myself into a deep hole by not doing a lot of different things first before launching my own business.

At the end of June, when I haven't had any luck on my own, I register with Kelly Temporary Agency, fretting over the timed tests like a student who hasn't studied for an exam. The girl who administers the tests looks as young as Mandy, except she's blond, with no glasses, and she's not friendly. The corners of her mouth seem turned down into a permanent frown. On the employment information sheets, I leave everything as open and as flexible as I can, indicating any wage would be fine, any hours including nights, weekends, and holidays would be fine, hoping it will increase my chances for employment. When I ask how I did on the timed tests and how soon I'll be offered work, the girl snatches my paperwork and snarls, "We'll call you when we find something suitable."

When I don't hear back in three days, I call.

"I told you we'd call you when we find something suitable."

"There has to be something available," I say.

"Can you work in the medical field?" she asks. "We have a need for a part-time phlebotomist."

My shoulders sag. I don't know how to draw blood. That's what phlebotomists do, isn't it?

Maybe I should stick to my field, I think. I could work as a real estate assistant.

There has to be a broker who needs help.

I call through the phone book and ask if any of the brokerages know of any Realtor who needs a full-time, salaried assistant.

"None come to mind," a soft spoken man at Keller Williams says after a pause. "Have you tried Mike Trevoli in Santa Rosa? He has his own sub-brokerage with Century 21."

I call Mike and speak with his assistant, a chipper sounding young woman. "We hire buyer's brokers only who work on a commission split," she says. "No salary, no benefits. Is that all right?"

"But I need money now."

"Sorry, Mike never gives an advance."

When I speak with Val during our weekly telephone call, he says, "Why don't you call that woman who tried to refinance your mortgage?"

I scrunch my nose in disgust. "Ms. Lashay?"

"Yeah, that's her. She offered you a job before, right?"

"Yes, and she humiliated me by telling Tom about my finances."

"She was only trying to help."

I take a deep breath, trying to remain calm. "She's probably the boss from hell. Her son won't even work for her."

"Then I guess you should file for bankruptcy."

Bankruptcy? Never.

The next day, after a strong cup of coffee, I call Smart Loans. Someone else answers the phone, a dour-sounding man. Maybe it's her son. "May I speak with Ms. Lashay, please? It's Trina Kay from Kay Realty."

"One moment."

"Trina, dear, how are you?" Ms. Lashay gushes like I'm an old, dear friend.

My shoulders relax. Already I feel hopeful. "Fine, thanks. And you?"

"Absolutely splendid. How may I help you today? Do you have a client with poor credit who needs a private money loan?"

"Actually, I'm calling to see if you're still interested in hiring someone." I swallow a lump of discomfort in my throat. "I'm looking for a job."

"Oh, darling, I just hired someone two weeks ago." She sounds genuinely disappointed. "But I'll keep you in mind if the person I hired doesn't work out. You still at the same phone and address?"

I give Ms. Lashay my new information and hang up.

I shake my head. Val's right. I should have swallowed my pride and called her first.

When I move into Val's cottage after the Fourth of July, I bring only my clothes, toiletries, laptop, and BlackBerry. It feels a lot like my first visit, only there is no Val to greet me at the front door. Finding a small space in his closet, I roll my luggage inside and shut the door. Although I will be staying for longer than a weekend, I can't bring myself to unpack.

I unlock the French doors and walk onto the deck. Warm sunlight falls against my shoulders. I squint through the redwood branches at the glinting Russian River. It's so beautiful and peaceful up here. So far away from the real world.

I should be happy. Except for my half of the mortgage payment in San Jose, I don't have any major expenses. I don't have to worry about paying for rent, water, garbage, cable, and utilities. Val already promised he would take care of all that. My life is simple.

But a little voice inside of me speaks up. You failed at starting a new brokerage. You can't get your money out of the old brokerage. You don't have a job. Your credit is ruined. And there's only $100 left to your name.

Stop it.

But the voice only gets louder and more insistent.

If you had stayed with Tom, you would be fully stocked with a new wardrobe from the pre-season sale at Macy's, not stuck sporting last year's fashions. You would have a new Mercedes, not your old one. You would be eating muffins at Starbucks every morning, not burnt toast again and again.

I start to pace back and forth along the deck. The old boards creak under my weight.

Okay. Let's not think about it. Let's focus on the future. One day at a time. Isn't that what most people do? Or is that only for alcoholics?

Think of three things you're grateful for. Val, Val's cottage, and…and…

I sink down on a lounge chair and bend my head and cry.

I am not going to give up. I am not going to run home and live with my parents like Dee did. I am going to make it. On my own. Again.

The day after I move into Val's cottage, I expand my online job search to include other sales positions. A pharmaceutical company is seeking a new sales representative for the West Coast division. Even though I don't have medical experience or business to business experience, I convince the human resource manager to grant me a telephone interview. Toward the end of our conversation, she states the job is commission only and involves extensive three out of four weeks a month travel.

"But you have the potential for unlimited income," she says brightly.

Then why aren't you doing the job? I want to ask, but don't.

I try a few technology companies who are seeking a sales rep, but I am told I don't qualify. "We're looking for someone with an engineering background," the gentleman says. I think of the engineers I knew in Silicon Valley. None of them come to mind as a great people person, which is the first requirement for a great salesperson.

Tom calls the second week of July and leaves a message on my cell demanding my half of the mortgage payment. "We can't be late," he says, "or we'll have to pay a late fee."

I call the office to leave him a message, but he picks up the phone. "T & T Realty," he says. "Tom speaking."

"It's Trina," I say, "returning your call."

"Why don't you pick up your phone anymore?"

"I do. Just not when I'm with clients." Why must he always grill me for information? "I just called to let you know I'll pay the late fee when I send my half of the payment."

"When will that be?"

I shrug. "Next week."

Next week comes and goes. Thank goodness Val doesn't get cell reception. On one of the few trips I make down the hill, I pick up my messages. There are thirty of them. Ten of them are Tom's. "Where are you?" he demands. "I called your parents. They haven't heard from you either. Is something wrong? Or are you avoiding me?"

The next five messages are from my mother. "KK, where are you? Tom's worried. We're worried. Are you in some sort of trouble?"

The next three messages are from Dee. "Call us," she says. "I can't stand Mom's worry. Just call us, okay?"

One message is from Mandy letting me know the new office manager mailed my security deposit.

The final message is from Dad who never calls me. "I understand you need help with money," he says. "I gave Tom $1,800 to pay your half of the mortgage and late fee for this month. But I can't keep paying that every month. Please, call me. I love you."

Dad paid my half of the mortgage payment and late fee? Why? I dial my parents' house and leave Val's phone number at the cottage along with a brief message for my father. "Thanks, Dad," I say.

That night, while I'm curled up on the velvet sofa watching Pat O' Brien on *The Insider*, the phone rings.

"Hello?" I say.

"KK," my father says, in his husky voice. "You changed your number."

Should I tell him I've moved to Val's cottage because I can no longer afford my apartment? That would just make matters worse. But it would be the truth. He already knows I'm hurting for money. But I can't disappoint him further. Can I?

"It's the new land line I installed," I lie. "My cell doesn't always get reception when I'm showing property so I miss a lot of calls. I thought I'd install a land line." I make a mental note to change the outgoing message on Val's phone. I hope he doesn't mind.

"Everyone's worried about you. What's going on?"

Part of me wants to tell him everything, but part of me knows if I do, he'll only be more disappointed in me. And Tom will gloat over his victory. And Mom will beg me to move back home. And Dee will finally feel superior. And I'll just feel even worse than I already feel.

"I'm just waiting for my first escrow to close. There was a tiny delay with the lender. The loan went back into underwriting, and the lender was questioning the appraisal because home prices are continuing to fall, but everything looks like it's been straightened out so I should have a check before the end of the month." I hope.

He sighs. "It's not as easy starting over as you thought it would be, is it?"

My heart pinches with sadness when I hear the disappointment in his voice.

"Don't worry, Dad. Tell everyone I'm okay." In a tiny voice, I add, "I'll pay you back as soon as this escrow closes."

"I've been thinking," Dad says. "Maybe you should reconsider Tom's offer."

Tom tells him everything, doesn't he?

I feel my face grow hot with humiliation. What else does my father know? That I've gone to a lender and tried to get a loan? That I've sold all my belongings on eBay? That I'm the foolish girl Tom makes me out to be? I turn off the sound on the TV and start pacing back and forth across the tiny living room. I do not want my father thinking I'm helpless or incompetent. But how can I prove to him otherwise?

"My attorney has advised against accepting Tom's buyout offer," I lie, hoping Dad won't ask Dee to call Mr. Leggins to verify the conversation. "I don't think it's prudent to go against an attorney's advice."

There is a long, thoughtful pause. "Okay," he says. "I love you."

"Love you, too, Dad." I feel my heart breaking. Oh, why can't I just tell him the truth? I'm broke. I have no escrow closing next week. I can't even get a job.

When I hang up the phone, I turn on the volume on the TV and sink down on the sofa and stare transfixed by Brittany's struggle to gain joint custody of her children. At least I wasn't married to Tom. At least we didn't have children.

At least I'm not strung out on drugs or alcohol or prescription medication.

I curl up with a pillow, suddenly comforted by someone else's tragedy.

My life isn't that bad, I think.


A few days later, I receive a check for $750 for my security deposit. I write a check to my father for the amount and mail it along with a note: I'll send the remaining $1,050 as soon as I get it. I call Val and leave him a message, wondering if I can borrow a teeny-tiny bit of money. Val calls me back and leaves me a message, letting me know he's been busy paying back all his debt. "Maybe next month," he says.

But I can't wait till next month. I'll have another mortgage payment due and I'll either have to borrow more money from my father or admit defeat to Tom. Either situation is one I want to avoid.

As it gets closer to August, I start to branch out in my job search to include telemarketing and retail sales. I get an interview to work as a research coordinator, calling people at home to conduct surveys for businesses. The pay is minimum wage with no benefits. After checking in with the receptionist, I take a seat between a girl with flaming pink and purple hair and a nose ring and an elderly man who smells of moth balls. I feel overdressed in my Ralph Lauren dress suit and Nine West heels.

A few minutes later, the recruiter approaches me. "Ms. Kay?" he asks, extending his hand. "Po Garrison," he says, introducing himself. His dark blue gaze zigzags from the crown of my head to the tips of my toes and back up again. He looks like James Bond, tall, dark, and slim with a coquettish smile. His handshake is firm, yet gentle, and I start to relax. Maybe it won't be so bad working for next to nothing if I get to work for him.

Po leads me through a maze of dimly lit cubicles where employees hunch forward, typing into databases and reading from scripts. Their enormous headsets flatten their hair. I flash a false smile. It's just like cold calling, right?

"Entrée," Po says, winking.

I step inside his office, and he closes the door. I take a seat across from his massively organized desk. He leans back in his leather executive swivel chair and taps the end of a pencil against his hand like he's cueing up to conduct an orchestra, not an interview.

"You have a lot of experience on the phone, right?"

I nod, crossing my legs.

"How do you keep a person on a phone for longer than two seconds?"

"I ask for help," I say. "Everyone's secret desire is to save a life. Helping a stranger is possibly the closest they'll ever come to saving a life."

"Interesting," he says, leaning forward. He stretches his arms across the desk and asks, "What would you say to me?"

His eyes are dark, as dark as his midnight blue suit.

My hands flutter like wings in my lap. I uncross and cross my legs again. Closing my eyes, to avoid the distraction of his handsome face, I say, "Good afternoon, I'm Trina Kay from Kay Realty, and I need your help. I have clients who want to move into your neighborhood. Do you know of anyone who might be selling in the next month?" I open my eyes, wondering what he thinks of my routine pitch.

He's staring at my legs like they're familiar.

I uncross them and abruptly stand up.

Does he recognize them from the billboard?

He sits back and folds his hands into a pyramid. Meeting my eyes, he asks, "Is something wrong?"

How can I tell him I feel violated from the way he was gazing at my legs? "I— I—" I take a deep breath and hold it, trying to calm myself down. Of course, he doesn't know you.

He's probably never left this county. That means he's never seen your legs.

My cell phone sings "Lucky Star." I forgot to turn it off.

He stares at the sound coming from my Prada purse. "Go ahead," he says. "I'll wait."

"Excuse me," I say, blushing. The numbers on the glowing dial look familiar. I turn my back to him and answer. "Trina Kay speaking."

"Trina, dear, it's your lucky day," Ms. Lashay says. "The gentleman I hired didn't work out. Can you start today?"

I exhale. If I take the job with Ms. Lashay, I won't have to worry about men looking at my legs. "I'll be over this afternoon." I turn back to Po Garrison and flash an apologetic smile. "The job I really wanted just called back. I'm afraid I'm no longer interested in the position."

"That's too bad," he says, rising from his chair. "You have a pleasant voice. I think people would have responded kindly to your calls."

When I walk out of the office, I turn briefly to close his door. But he's right behind me, with his hand on the knob, his gaze caressing the backs of my legs.

# CHAPTER 18

▼

"The only thing consistent here is change." Ms. Lashay sits behind her desk looking like a Chihuahua on a large pillow. I almost expect her to yap. "Every situation is different. I make up my mind one day and reverse it the next. You almost have to be a little ADD to work here."

"May I ask why the other person is no longer working with you?"

Ms. Lashay pats her beehive hairdo. "My son suggested I stop being a chauvinist and hire a man to assist me. So I did." Her smile tightens. "But he failed. Miserably."

I shift uncomfortably in my seat. Does she have extraordinary expectations?

"I have nothing against men," she says, lowering her voice. "I love them. But it's just that women share a certain sensibility when it comes to business." She frowns, unsure if I understand her. "Let me explain. Most of my lenders are unmarried retired women who have spent their prime in the work force creating their own wealth, often at the sacrifice of their personal lives. My employees and affiliates must treat these women with utmost respect if they want to continue to do business with me. I do not tolerate anyone condescending to my lenders as though they are part of the rich widow club. They're not. These women are savvy professionals. Like us."

I'm glad she thinks so highly of me. I only hope I don't disappoint her, since I know absolutely nothing about the money side of this business.

"Feel free to ask questions and take notes," Ms. Lashay says. "There's so much I take for granted having done this for 44 years that sometimes I just expect people to know as much as I do when they don't.

"As for compensation, I can either offer you a salary of $25 an hour with a bonus for closed loans or a graduated commission split starting at 35% and ending at 60% once you learn everything there is to know. Which shall it be?"

"Salary," I say without hesitation. It is generous compared with the minimum wage Po Garrison was offering.

Ms. Lashay jots down a note. "I tend to work long hours. Will 9 to 5 work for you?"

"Absolutely."

"And you can start?"

"You said earlier that you'd like me to start today."

"Good listening." She extends her hand. "You're hired."

I give my most professional handshake.

Ms. Lashay releases my hand, stands up, and exits her office. I trail behind her, resisting the temptation to touch the top of her beehive. She motions to the desk sitting directly outside her office. There is a computer and a phone. Nothing else. "Feel free to decorate it as you want. It will become your second home."

She gathers employment documents from a filing cabinet and offers me a pen. After I sign them and hand her my broker's license, she says, "Welcome aboard. There's so much to learn, but once you know it, you'll be able to do everything I do. Only you'll do it much better."

The phone rings. Ms. Lashay closes her office door to take the call, and I sink down in the standard office chair and wonder if I'll meet her expectations.

I hobble into Ms. Lashay's office five minutes late for my first full day of work. I smile sweetly at Ms. Lashay through the open blinds of the full-length window that separates her office from the rest of the suite. Although she's talking to someone on the phone, she frowns, pointing to my skirt. Doesn't she realize I would have been twenty minutes late if I had tried to iron something else to wear? It's bad enough I burned a hole through a flimsy Vera Wang blouse and had to find a clean replacement blouse instead. Unfortunately, I shrunk two inches off the hem of this skirt. I didn't realize it until I slipped into the car and saw it rested two inches above my knees instead of two inches below my knees. If I went inside the cottage to find something more suitable to wear, I would have been really, really late.

I wish I could afford dry cleaning again!

I drop my purse under my desk and knock on Ms. Lashay's door before opening it. She ushers me to take a seat while she continues to chat with the caller.

When she is finished, she rests her arms on the table and says, "Trina, dear, you're a very attractive young woman with a fabulous figure. But there is no need to showcase that here at work. In the future, I want you to show less skin."

My face grows hot with embarrassment. "If I could possibly get an advance against my first paycheck, then I can promise you this won't happen anymore."

"Really?" She chuckles. "You sound like some of the borrowers I see. If only you can lend me a few hundred thousand dollars, I'll be able to make my first mortgage payments on time." She slips on her rhinestone reading glasses and peers at a file. "We already set the terms of your work agreement. Therefore, there will be no advance."

Negotiations are never over. That much I learned through real estate sales. I sit up straight and tug my skirt down. "If I had an advance, I could send my clothes to the dry cleaners. You would never have to worry about me coming to work dressed inappropriately again."

She lowers her glasses. "Surely, your mother taught you how to do a load of laundry."

I shake my head. I was too busy with school and sports to bother with learning domestic skills. Like cooking and cleaning.

She laughs. "Oh, dear, what a great opportunity for you to build character," she says. Changing the subject, she hands me a file. "All right, I want you to process this loan file. I showed you how to operate the software yesterday. Let's see what you remember."

I take the file, but I remain seated. "Shouldn't we go through the day and prioritize?" I suggest. "That's what I do to get things done. It prevents a lot of stress and keeps me focused when unexpected things pop up."

Ms. Lashay narrows her eyes. "You work for me now and you will do things my way. You don't need to worry about things getting done or unexpected things popping up. This isn't your business. You just do what I tell you to do and leave the rest to me. Okay?"

I shift uncomfortably in my seat. Leave the rest to her? Not worry about things? Just do what she tells me to do? That sounds like the life of a puppet. Is that how it feels to be an employee?

"Is something the matter, dear?"

I swallow.

"Well, actually, no," I stammer. If I quit this job, I'll have to tell Tom he'll have to assume my half of the mortgage payments and then I'll have to tell my father I'm broke and unemployable. My mother will ask me to come home, and

Dee and I will fight over the bathroom just like we did as kids. And I'll never hear the end of my bad decision to leave Tom.

Already I hate being an employee. I take the file and return to my desk, feeling small and insignificant. I would rather be door knocking than taking orders from a woman old enough to be my grandmother. But I need a paycheck. And this is the only job I've been able to get.

Okay. Deep breath. I log onto the computer and start to type. I don't care how long it takes for me to adjust to this new lifestyle.

I can do it.

"I got a job!" I tell Val. We are finally on the phone at the same time. Between my new work schedule and Val acting on the road, we usually only have time to leave each other messages.

"You sound excited," he says. "Tell me all about it."

"Actually, I hate what I do," I tell him. "It's tough being an employee. Whenever I think of doing something a different way, I have to bite my tongue. And I'm not used to that. And sometimes I don't think I'll ever be." I lean on the kitchen counter and notice the crumbs I forgot to wipe up this morning. Will I ever earn enough for a housekeeper again?

"But you have money," Val says.

He's right. With my first paycheck next week, I'll be able to send Tom my half of the August mortgage payment and late fee. Then I'll slowly start paying back my father. And, finally, I'll start chipping away at my Visa bill.

"So where are you working?"

"For Ms. Lashay at Smart Loans."

"I thought she didn't have any openings."

"Apparently, she fired her other employee. I'm her new Broker Associate which is better than being an assistant. It has much more potential since she's training me to do everything she does. But there's so much to learn. It's like I'm back in school. I'm even getting nightmares like I used to get at the start of a new class. In my dreams, I'm being chased by a ten foot tall Deed of Trust. I wake up just moments away from being smothered by a giant piece of paper. Can you believe it?"

Val laughs. "And I thought the only thing to fear was paper cuts!"

I don't want to spend our few precious minutes dwelling on my new job. "How's acting?" I ask.

"Oh, you know," says Val, trying to keep his voice low and casual. "It's— absolutely—amazing!"

I shiver with delight at the excitement in his voice. I wonder if I'll ever feel that way about work again.

"The funny thing is," says Val, "I never would have done this if I hadn't been laid off *The Young and the Restless*. I always thought I'd end up in movies like Meg Ryan or Marisa Tomei. I'm so glad I ended up in theater. It's so fulfilling. I love the instant feedback from the audience."

I nod, gazing longingly out the garden window at shadows dancing on the deck. "I'm happy for you."

"You don't sound happy."

I shrug. "I kind of miss real estate."

"Do you? Or do you miss Tom?"

"I don't miss Tom." I say it too quickly and with too much emotion, but I don't care what Val thinks. "How can I miss someone who's humiliated me by blabbing about my money problems to my father?"

Val drops his voice. "Love is a strange thing. You still might miss him."

I groan. Why does Val know me better than I know myself? If I admit I still have feelings for Tom, then does that mean I have to admit that I'm wrong for not getting back together with him?

"How can I miss him? I delete his voice mail messages without listening to them. I've even created in rule in Outlook to delete any e-mail he might send me."

Val whistles soft and low. "You really do miss him."

"I do not!"

"Have you put the house on the market?"

"You know I can't without his consent."

"Uh-huh." Val pauses. "And what about your business?"

"I don't know," I say. How am I supposed to save $5,000 for my legal fees when all of my money is going to pay off debt?

Val lowers his voice. "It's okay to miss someone even if you have mixed feelings."

"It's not Tom," I lie. "It's my new job. It's stressful having to learn everything."

A thoughtful pause fills the space between us. Finally, Val says, "Give it time, KK. It's only the first week. I'm sure it will get better."

*Is the trustee the person who lends the money or who has borrowed the money? Is the beneficiary the person who inherits the trust? And who the hell is the trustor?*

I stare at the first page of a Deed of Trust during my third week of work, trying to figure out who I am to call to find out the amount of money needed to bring the first loan current so the second loan that we arranged won't be jeopardized by a foreclosure proceeding. But nothing is making sense.

"Ms. Lashay?" I knock on her door briefly before stepping inside her office. "Can you help me figure out who I am to call?"

She motions for me to sit down. I hand her the file. Slipping her rhinestone reading glasses on, she scans the first few lines. "See this? The beneficiary is the entity who has loaned the money. That's who you want to call."

*The beneficiary.* I write it down in the pocket-sized notebook I've started to carry.

Back at my desk, I pick up the phone and dial the toll free number. Navigating through the maze of voice mail, I finally reach a person. "This is Georgia. Who am I speaking to?"

"Trina Kay with Smart Loans," I say.

"And you represent?"

"The lender for the second deed of trust." I flip through my notebook. "I need a reinstatement amount."

"I don't see an Authority to Release on file."

*Authority to Release?* I flip a few more pages and scroll down my notes. *That's a disclosure the borrower signs giving us permission to give and receive information on his or her behalf.* I find it in the file. "Where do you want me to send it?"

"Fax it to us, then wait ten minutes for it to be entered into our system. We'll be able to help you then."

I want to tell her I don't have time to wait, why can't this process move along more quickly, but I don't. In the three weeks I've been working for Ms. Lashay, I've learned to do as I am told, even if I feel less like a human being with my own will and more like a robot being programmed in a foreign language.

After writing down the number, I run the Authority to Release through the fax machine and wait. Ms. Lashay sashays out of her office, a tiny streak of blue, and grabs her fall coat off the rack by the glass doors. "I'm off to have lunch with Betty Morgan, one of my oldest lenders and dearest friends. Do you have those numbers ready?"

I bite the inside of my lower lip, feeling slow and inadequate in my new role. "I'm still working on it," I say. "They won't give me any information until I fax over the Authority to Release."

"Humph. I thought we already had one on file with them." Ms. Lashay frowns, and I'm not sure if she's upset with them or me. "Oh, never mind. Call me when you have them. Betty wants to bring the account current before the next payment is due."

"I'll call your cell phone," I say. As soon as she leaves, I sink back into my chair and start to dial. I reach voice mail again and patiently punch in the right numbers to deliver me to a person.

"I'm sorry, Ms. Kay," Paul says. "But we don't have an Authority to Release on file."

"I just faxed one fifteen minutes ago," I say, staring at the confirmation receipt stapled across the coversheet. "Georgia said it would take only ten minutes to enter it into the system."

"Georgia said that?" he asks. "Please hold." A dead silence fills the space normally occupied by annoying music.

If I was more adept at my job, I might multi-task during the wait. But I know if I start typing the draft of the prospecting letter Ms. Lashay wants to send, I'll lose track of the purpose of the phone call and end up flubbing through it and getting nowhere again.

What seems like a half hour but must only be a few minutes, Paul returns. "They are just inputting your release into the system. How may I help you?"

I take a deep breath. "I need a reinstatement amount. The second lender wants to bring the first loan current before the next payment is due."

Keys tapping on a keyboard fill the space between us. I switch hands, refusing to use the ungodly headset that makes my head feel like it's in a vise.

"I have to transfer you back to Georgia," Paul says.

A few moments later, Georgia asks, "How may I help you?"

"When is the next payment due on this account?"

"The account number, please."

Don't they have it in the system? What good is a computer network when no one can pull up the same information from one desk to another?

I read off the account number and wait while she confirms it. Another pause. I cradle the phone against my shoulder while I strip off my cardigan, suddenly hot from my mounting frustration.

"The next payment is due on the first," she says.

Just as I thought. "And the reinstatement figure to bring the account current before the first is?"

Georgia says, "I'll have to transfer you to a different department. The figures will be ready in forty-eight to seventy-two hours."

"Business days or calendar days?"

"Business days."

"But that brings us to the end of the month." My voice rises to a dangerous pitch. "That's too late. The next payment will be due and more charges will be incurred. The lender wants to wire the money today."

"I'm sorry, but—"

"Do you want your money or not?" Heat rushes to my face. If she challenges me again, I'll slam my fist against the desk.

Georgia's voice shakes, "Just a moment. I'll go see if I can get those figures." Canned classical music floats over the receiver, and I remind myself to breathe. My fist unclenches. Ms. Lashay struts into the office with a portly gray-haired woman in a floral housedress and nurse's shoes. Ms. Lashay pauses at my desk, and I point to the open file.

"No answer yet?" she snaps. "What's taking you so long? The last wire from the bank goes out in an hour."

I glance up at the clock against the wall. I have been on the phone for over forty-five minutes.

"Trina, this is Betty Morgan."

I stand with the phone against one ear and shake Betty's pudgy hand. "Pleasure to meet you. Ms. Lashay has spoken very highly of you."

Betty chuckles. "Don't believe a word from that old hag."

Ms. Lashay narrows her eyes, ushering Betty into her office. "Bring the reinstatement amount to me as soon as you get it, understand?"

I nod, feeling weak in the knees. I do not want to be fired over this. What would I say to Val the next time he calls? *I got fired after three weeks of work.* How embarrassing is that?

When Georgia returns on the line, her voice warbles. "I have the reinstatement figure good till the end of the month," she says. "Are you ready?"

"Ready." My hand is poised with a pen over a blank sheet of paper.

"Nine thousand, four hundred and fifty six dollars and forty three cents."

I repeat the amount.

"That's it. Anything else I can help you with today?"

"No, thank you." I hang up the phone. I did it! My body quivers with victory. I rap on Ms. Lashay's door before stepping inside, feeling as triumphant as I did when I wrote my first real estate purchase contract.

"Here's the number." I hand Ms. Lashay the sheet of paper.

She lifts her glasses and studies it. "Did you double check with their accounting department to see if there are any additional fees?"

My shoulders sag. I am not getting on the phone again. No, no, no. "That is the full amount needed to reinstate the loan. It's good till the end of the month."

Ms. Lashay eyes me. I don't know whether or not she knows I'm fumbling my way through the system, sidestepping land mines and other possible casualties, often missing my breaks and forgoing my lunch just to keep up. My head aches. And my stomach grumbles. I place my hand over it, hoping the noise isn't too loud. If she asks me to go back on the phone and make another call to this institution, I will scream, *Go fucking do it yourself, bitch*, and walk out.

*Don't be impulsive, KK*, I hear my mother's voice in my mind. *Take a deep breath*. If I walk out of my job, I won't have any money to pay my half of the mortgage payment. I won't be able to give my dad the money back from his loan. And I'll start getting collection calls on my Visa bill. *Exhale*. I will have to move in with my parents. *Deep breath*. Then they'll know I'm a failure. *Exhale*. Okay, I won't walk out. I'll do whatever it takes to get the job done.

Ms. Lashay hands Ms. Morgan the sheet of paper. "Does this look correct to you?"

I feel like a kindergartener in a classroom full of teachers judging my budding penmanship.

Ms. Morgan puckers her lips and nods. "I'll go right now to the bank. Did they say where to send the wire?"

My eyes widen. "I'll have to double check." My heart gallops in my chest. I can't believe I didn't ask anyone where to send the money. I'm going to have to get back on the phone and make another call.

"Hurry," Ms. Lashay says. "Betty has to get to the bank in forty minutes to make the last wire."

I slink out of the office and close the door. Sinking back into my chair, I pick up the phone and dial the number one more time.

The electronic voice mail maze announces the greeting.

*Breathe in*. It's no use. My shoulders tense with panic. I glance at the clock, wondering how long it will take to get a live person. *Breathe out*.

I hate my job.

# CHAPTER 19

▼

After I've been working a month at Smart Loans, my mother calls to suggest a get-together. "Isn't the market slowing down?" she asks.

"Not really," I lie. I'm sitting on the couch, painting my toe nails a lusty red, wishing I had money for a proper pedicure. But I don't. I've had to charge groceries, my cell phone bill, gas, and auto maintenance. I have exactly $42.13 in my checking account after paying Tom my half of the mortgage and my father for his loan. If anything unexpected comes up, I'll have to charge it. And I know I'm very close to my limit again. That's one of the reasons why I can't make a trip to San Jose. I can't afford it.

"We miss you, dear." She pauses, taking long, slow deep breaths. "I just always imagined you'd have more time for your family."

"I would, if I didn't have to start over," I say. "You remember how many hours I worked when I started my brokerage the first time around, don't you?"

She sighs. "Too many to count."

I shift on the couch, trying to get comfortable without smearing polish everywhere. The longer I talk about my imaginary life, the more nervous I become and the guiltier I feel. Maybe if I talk to someone else about anything else, I'll feel better. "Can I speak with Dad?"

"He's out playing golf."

With Tom, I think.

"Is Dee around?"

"She's out taking pictures."

Darn. I guess it's just the two of us. I blow on my toe nails, hoping they'll dry faster.

"Maybe Dad and I can come up for a visit?" Mom asks. "How does next Saturday look?"

Hmm. A visit. I guess I could give them Val's bed and I could sleep on the couch. It might work.

"You can show us your new office," Mom says. "And maybe I can sit with you at an open house. Then we'll go out to dinner. It'll be fun."

Oh, no. My heart leaps in my chest. That won't do. I'll have to confess. And I'm not ready to do that. Mom will be ashamed. Dad will be disappointed. I can already imagine Dee saying something sarcastic like, "So, the secret of your success is keeping your life a secret." No, no, no. I have to stop my mom from showing up.

"I'd love to." My voice rises slightly with nervousness. "But I can't. I'm showing property to an out-of-town couple on a job transfer. I hope you understand."

She takes another long, slow deep breath. "Of course, I do. You have to entertain them. Be the chauffeur and tour guide and hostess all-in-one."

"We'll find some other time to get together," I reassure her.

"How about Thanksgiving?" she asks. "I know it's almost two months away, but I'm afraid with your schedule that it might be the only time we'll get to see you."

"Um, sure," I say, not really wanting to spend the holiday with them. "I'll come down. Any food you'd like me to bring?"

Mom laughs. "We all know you can't cook, KK. So just bring yourself."

Can't cook? Fine. I'll buy something. "Will do," I say, and hang up with relief.

I always dress up on Halloween. Last year, I was a mermaid. Su loved my outfit: hot pink satin shells over my breasts and a glittery green sequined hip-hugging skirt that fanned out around my feet like a tail. I drove around and showed houses and wrote up an offer dressed as the Little Mermaid. One girl wanted to know how I got hair that looks just like Ariel. I smiled sweetly and told her it was my own.

This year I don't have money for a hundred dollar outfit, so I decide to pull something together from my daily wear. I select a short black skirt and pair it with a white poet's blouse and red velvet corset, something Val bought for me on a whim from a Beverly Hills boutique when he worked on *The Young and the Restless*, black fishnet stockings from the Halloween I dressed up as a French maid, and finally black boots I bought last year for the rainy season. But I don't have any accessories. Rummaging through Val's closet, I find a red scarf that I can tie around my head in lieu of a pirate's hat. Now, if I could just find my other gold hoop earring, my outfit will be complete.

By the time I locate the other gold hoop earring at the bottom of my jewelry box, it's a quarter after eight. Shit. I'd better hurry or I'll be late. After a quick shower, I scrunch gel into my wet hair and start dressing. I toss my lunch into my handbag, grab an apple, a cheese stick, and a mug of coffee to drink in my car, and head out of the house. The brisk autumn air stings my face. In the car, I turn on the heater, hoping to dry my hair by the time I arrive at work.

Five minutes after nine, I stride into the office. Ms. Lashay's door is closed but her blinds are open. I smile at her through the window, and her eyebrows tilt together in a frown, but she keeps talking to whoever she's talking to on the phone.

The title company has e-mailed a preliminary title report on the Chavez loan. I print it out and scan through the items, noticing a recorded Notice of Default on the first, which the client didn't bother to tell us about. I phone the title company for a copy of the document. Scanning the appraisal, which the client provided, I notice the parcel number doesn't match the one given in the preliminary title report. By the time Ms. Lashay steps out of her office, I've gathered enough evidence to convince her we should not make this loan.

"Rushed morning?" she asks, touching my damp curls.

I'm getting tired of being silent and submissive. "Not any more rushed than usual," I reply, smiling.

"Your skirt is a little short," she says.

Not as short as you are, I think. My smile tightens. "It's a Halloween costume. I always dress up on Halloween."

She chuckles. "Maybe if you teach kindergarten you do, but this is a professional establishment."

"I'm dressed professionally," I say, standing up, towering over her. "My breasts aren't hanging out and my butt is covered."

She gasps. "Watch your language, young lady."

"No one's here except us." I reach down and hand her the preliminary title report and the appraisal. "I think you'll want to examine these before you meet with your lender at ten-thirty. I've flagged the important pages for your convenience."

She sniffs, taking the paperwork and returning to her office. A few minutes later, she calls, "Trina!"

Obediently, I step into her office and close the door. Sitting on a chair opposite her desk, I cross my legs. My skirt rides up to my crotch. Yikes. Maybe it is a little too short. I tug at the hem. When it doesn't budge, I decide to cross my ankles instead.

For a long moment, she studies me. "You have a good eye for detail," she says, pointing to the appraisal and the preliminary title report. "I'm wondering what you'd do at this point of the loan process." She leans back in her chair and waits.

Without thinking, I say, "Cancel the loan."

Her eyebrows lift. "Why?"

"There are too many inconsistencies," I say. "First, the encumbered property is adjacent to the one cited in the appraisal. Second, the prelim shows a Notice of Default that's headed for publication any day now. Third, the borrower hasn't provided us with any signed disclosures."

Without a word, Ms. Lashay slips on her rhinestone reading glasses to reexamine the file. "I agree the facts don't match with our conversations with the borrower," she says, without looking up. "But if we can get the facts squared away in our favor, would you consider placing the loan?"

"That depends." My left leg starts to fidget with nervousness. I tuck it behind my right leg and flash a tight smile. "There's a question about his character. If we assume all these inconsistencies are mistakes, then he's just another careless borrower who doesn't know how to manage his finances. On the other hand, he could be dishonest. If that's the case, we don't want any of our lenders investing in the property."

"And how do you propose to verify the quality of his character?" Ms. Lashay glances up, removing her reading glasses.

I swallow. How do you prove a person is a crook? Gut instinct, I want to say, but can't. That's not how you make character judgments, is it?

Ms. Lashay lifts her eyebrows in anticipation of my response.

Quick, think. "We could hire a private investigator."

She sits back and laughs. "Really, Trina, would that be timely and cost effective?" She narrows her eyes. "What about a sixth sense?  Do you ever trust your intuition?"

"I—didn't—think—it was a good business tool," I stammer. "My mother's always telling me to think before I act."

"Well, there is something to be said against impulsiveness," she admits, "but I'm talking about good old-fashioned gut-sense. It ranks right up there with common sense, only it's been grossly neglected by big businesses. Don't you agree?"

I nod, although I'm not sure if I agree or disagree.

"Well, what does your gut tell you about our borrower?"

I glance away, trying not to think. But it's there, nagging at me. What if I deny him the loan and he's truly a careless borrower who doesn't know how to manage his money? What if he's so overwhelmed with debt he can't think straight? I've been there, haven't I? Would I want someone denying me a loan based on my state of panic?

"Don't think," Ms. Lashay says. "Off the top of your head, what would you do?"

"I—don't—know."

"Of course you do. You said it once before. Say it again."

"I'd—cancel—the loan."

"Louder and quicker this time."

"I'd cancel the loan."

"Again. With a little more confidence."

I sit up and take a deep breath. "I'd cancel the loan."

She hands me the file. "Call the borrower and cancel," she says. Standing up, she grabs her purse and keys. "I'll call the lender on the way out." She frowns at her son's outdated photo.

"Why don't you call him?" I ask.

She clears her throat. "He's busy."

"So are you."

When her eyes meet mine, she flashes a tense smile. "Get back to work. I'm going out to drum up more business." She pats my shoulder. "I'm leaving you in charge of the rest."

On Saturday morning, a week before Thanksgiving, the phone rings as I'm eating breakfast. I put down my toast to answer the phone, hoping it's not my mother.

"Good morning," I say.

"Morning, sweetie, it's me," say Val.

A smile spreads across my face. I haven't heard from Val all week. "How's my best friend?"

"Fab-u-lous," he says. "We've been on the road, then rehearsing at our new location. It's been so incredibly busy I haven't had time to call. And you?"

I shrug. "Okay. Work's getting better. I'm becoming a full-fledged mortgage broker. Just like Ms. Lashay."

"Do you still miss real estate?"

"Sometimes," I say, trying not to think of Tom. "But with the market the way it is, we've been offering to list our clients' houses if they're in trouble with their current lender and we can't offer them another loan. So I'm doing more real estate than I'd anticipated."

"Good for you," Val says. After we talk about various sundry topics, he asks, "What are you doing for Thanksgiving?"

I sit down at the kitchen table and sip my lukewarm coffee, listening to the first drops of rain on the tin roof. "Not sure. My parents invited me over, but the last visit I had wasn't pleasant. And you?"

"I'll be in Chicago. Eating pizza, of course," he jokes.

My lower back tenses every time I think about Thanksgiving and the lies I've been telling my mother. "I really don't want to go down to my parents, but I really don't want to be alone either," I confess. "I've told my mom my new brokerage is booming, and I don't want to have to continue with the lies. It's exhausting, trying to remember what I've told her."

"Why are you lying to her?"

"Because I'm afraid she'll be disappointed with the truth."

He pauses thoughtfully. "Well, I think you should stop being afraid and just be yourself. If she doesn't understand, then she has a problem. Not you. Right now, you have the problem. You're being dishonest, and that will only come back to hurt you in the end. I'm not lecturing you. I'm being your Rent-a-Brother, and that's my advice to you, sis."

He's right.

"Do you want to rehearse?" Val asks. "I could be your mom, grilling you with questions." He clears his throat. "So, KK, how's the real estate market?" he asks in a falsetto voice. "Any sales lately?"

I giggle in spite of my fears. "No, Mom. Actually, I need to tell you the truth. I got a job."

"Oh, KK, how terrible! I knew you should have never left Tom. You're nothing without him."

I clench the receiver in my fist, flabbergasted at how real it all feels. My heart's stuttering in my chest, and my palms are moist with fear.

"KK?" Val asks, in his normal voice. "You still there?"

"Yes," I say with a quivering voice. "I'm still here. But I can't do this."

"Yes, you can. Just be yourself," he says. "And you'll be fine."

After we hang up, I tell myself, *You'll be fine*. I repeat it like a mantra, hoping the more I say it to myself, the more confidence I will have once the time arrives to tell my parents the truth.

On Monday, I arrive five minutes late for work. My hair is damp because my blow dryer broke, and my blouse is too low because a button fell off. When? I don't know. I searched beneath the driver's seat and couldn't find it.

"Trina, may I see you please?"

I set my purse down on my desk and slink into Ms. Lashay's office. Slumping into a chair, I try to close the gap in my shirt with my hand.

Her gaze scrutinizes me. "Rushed morning?" she asks.

"No, not really," I say, holding my shirt.

She purses her lips and slips on her rhinestone reading glasses. "I've been looking over your files, and I must say I'm impressed." She lowers her glasses and eyes me. "I knew you'd pick up this business fairly quickly, but this is exceptional. I'm going to put you on a commission split with me, because I think you'll earn much more money, and money is what motivates people, isn't it?" She winks.

Commission split? "But I like my salary," I say.

"You could afford to repair your clothes or buy new ones if you're on commission," she says.

New clothes? I flush, holding my shirt together. How can I buy new clothes when I owe Visa, how much? Is it fifteen or twenty thousand? And what about saving money to move out before Val comes back? How can I do that on commission?

"Here's the contract I've had my attorney draw up." She slides a piece of paper across the desk for me to examine.

At a glance, my stomach lurches. No, don't sign it. But I dutifully take it up. I can't be impulsive, right? What would my mother say? *KK, think before you act.* Maybe I should take this home, study it overnight, talk to an attorney, maybe Mr. Leggins, if he won't charge me for it.

"It's very generous," Ms. Lashay explains. "You keep your salary till the end of the month. Then, starting December 1st, you switch over to a graduated commission split. Fifty percent for the first three loans. Sixty percent for the next three loans. After that, it jumps to eighty percent." She smiles. "There are a few additional job responsibilities and a clause or two about company loyalty." She laughs, handing me a pen. "But you would never leave me, would you?"

I frown at the jumble of words. "May I think about it for a few days?"

She purses her lips. "Really, Trina, business decisions must be made in a timely matter."

"Is tomorrow timely enough? I'd really like to talk it over with an attorney."

The phone rings. Instinctively, I stand up to go to my desk to answer it.

She waves for me to sit down as she picks up the receiver. "Smart Loans, Ms. Lashay speaking." She nods, listening to the caller. "Of course, I understand. How about we meet today at my office around noon? Do you like Thai food? There's a new restaurant downtown I've been dying to try. All right, see you then. Ciao." She hangs up the phone. Her gaze lingers a moment too long at the outdated picture of her son on her desk. I wonder what he looks like now and what type of man he grew up to be.

"Why don't you call Alex?" I ask.

She shakes her head, as if clearing her mind. "It didn't go well on our last visit," she says.

"All the more reason to call." I cross my legs, hoping I don't look like a hypocrite. I haven't initiated a phone call with my parents in a long time. But at least I'll be seeing them soon. "You should invite Alex for Thanksgiving."

She bitterly laughs. "I can't imagine he'd accept. He has a girlfriend now anyway. He probably would prefer spending it with her family."

"Have you met his girlfriend?"

"No, but I hear she's absolutely lovely. The Hollywood reporter type."

I think of Lara Spencer on *The Insider*. "I'm sure she'd love to meet you."

"What about you? Are you seeing your family for Thanksgiving?"

"Of course," I say. "I'm bringing a fruit salad."

"I thought you didn't cook."

I smile. "I don't. But Oliver's Market sells everything I need to make me look like I do."

She laughs, and the creases on her face fold back to reveal an enchanting smile. "You never cease to amaze me, dear. Full of ingenuity, you are."

"I'm sure your son has wonderful traits. After all, he had you for a mother."

Her brown eyes narrow. "And persistent, are we?"

The phone rings.

"I have to be," I say, standing up to take the call. "It's my job."

## Chapter 20

─────────  ▼  ─────────

I tuck the contract in the top drawer of my desk and return to work. But every now and then, the same thought pops up in my head: What should I do?

On my lunch, I call Mr. Leggins. I can't get through to him directly, so I decide to send the contract to him as an e-mail attachment.

Ms. Lashay catches me still sitting at my desk when she returns from her lunch appointment. "Do you ever eat?" she asks, raising her eyebrows.

I feel my face grow hot. "I've got a lot of work to do."

"Don't we all?" She offers me a Styrofoam take-out box and a plastic fork and napkin in a shrink-wrapped package. "You may have my leftover coconut walnut salad. I would have brought you something else, but I didn't know you'd still be working."

I stare down at the take-out box. "Thanks, but—"

"No arguments. Eat." She gestures to the double glass doors. "Go outside and enjoy the weather. It won't be long before the sun disappears."

When I continue to sit at my desk, she tugs on my elbow. "That's an order."

I gather the contract, my purse, and the coconut walnut salad and bustle out the door. Crossing the street, I head over to the park and find a shady bench. The autumn sunlight glints off the fallen leaves scattered on the grass, and I take out my sunglasses. A cool breeze lifts the hair off my shoulders and sprays it across my face. I tie my hair into a pony tail and take a bite of the tangy salad.

Who else can I talk to? I'd call my parents, but they have no idea I have a job. And this is definitely not how I want to break the news to them.

If only I could talk to Tom. He would know what to do.

But I can't call him, can I? It's been almost five months since we've spoken. What would I say? I need your help with a contract. He'd laugh and belittle me, right? Remind me of how I'm nothing without him.

No, he wouldn't. He'd be kind and supportive. He'd ask me to e-mail a copy of the contract and he'd go over it with a fine-tooth comb, seeing things I'd missed.

Suddenly, I hear Madonna singing, "Vogue." I scramble in my purse for my BlackBerry. "Val?"

"Guess what?" he asks.

But my mind's still lingering on the contract. "What?"

"Guess."

I take a deep breath and cross my legs. "You've been offered a job on Broadway."

"Guess again."

"You've fallen in love with Chicago and have decided to move there."

"Guess again."

I glance at my watch. "I don't have time for games today. I'm just taking a quick lunch."

"There's a review about me in the *Chicago Tribune*. The reviewer says my performance is better than any he's seen on Broadway."

"Congratulations!" I say, genuinely pleased for him. "Does that mean you get a raise?"

He chuckles. "No, darling, it means I'm being taken seriously. Ser-i-ous-ly. Don't you know how good it feels to be considered a serious actor and not some washed up soap star?"

"We've always known you had more talent than opportunity."

"Yes, but now the world will know." He drops his voice. "Or at least everyone who reads the *Tribune* will know."

"That's terrific." I glance at a squirrel climbing up an oak tree. If only life were that simple.

"Enough about me," Val says. "What's new with you?"

I tell him about my new contract.

"Read it to me," he says.

I read it through twice.

"Hmm…" Val says. "What does your gut tell you to do?"

"I don't trust my gut. I've made so many poor decisions this past year."

"So you want to abdicate to me?"

"Not just you," I sigh. "I've already e-mailed Mr. Leggins."

"Your attorney can't make life decisions for you. And neither can I or anyone else you know." He lowers his voice. "Really, KK, your self-confidence has been in the crapper ever since that damn billboard Tom put up. You need to get over it. Move on. Take some risks."

"That's easy for you to say. You're getting glowing reviews in Chicago."

"And a year ago I was unemployed. But I didn't sob to anyone about my plight. I just moved forward." He pauses to catch his breath. "I love you and I love helping you, but I'm not going to be the person you pin your bad decisions to."

"I should change your ring tone to 'Crucify My Love'," I joke.

"Good one." He laughs. "What would Madonna do?"

I smile. "Probably consult her manager."

"If you had a manager, you wouldn't listen to him," Val says. "You always do what you're going to do. So why ask for advice when you're not going to take it?"

I uncross my legs and stand up to stretch. "I really need to be heading back to the office."

"Don't change the subject."

I glance at my watch. "I really do need to go."

"Okay," he says, with hesitancy. "I worry about you."

"Don't worry. I'll be fine," I lie.

He chuckles. "At least we know you won't go shopping."

"Not till Visa lifts the ban on me," I say. Yes, I've reached my limit. Again. "Or I close a bunch of deals."

"Sounds like this new contract might work out for your wardrobe."

"That's what Ms. Lashay was referring to. I can't believe I'm wearing the same old clothes since March. I feel like a bag lady."

"You probably look like one," he jokes.

"Ha-ha."

"I thought you had to go back to work."

"I do. But I could talk with you all day." I smile wryly. "I miss you."

"Miss you, too." And he blows an air-kiss goodbye.

At a quarter to five, I get an e-mail from Mr. Leggins. "It looks legally sound," he writes. "So it's up to you. Do you like this position?"

That's it?

I pull the contract out of my purse and read it again. It looks harmless. There's the standard tiered commission split and list of job responsibilities and some verbiage about no compensation owed if one's job is voluntarily abandoned. Mr. Leggins says it's legally sound, which leaves the decision back in my court where I don't want it to be.

Ms. Lashay opens her door and glances at the contract in my hands. "Still pondering it?"

I nod. "My attorney just gave me the green light. But I wanted to look over it again to be sure."

"And?" She stands by my desk, waiting.

Why not? I pick up a pen, sign and date it. Handing it back to her, I say, "I accept."

A slow smile spreads across her face. "You won't regret this. I promise."

The next day, Ms. Lashay bustles into the office, her face flushed with excitement. She pauses at my desk. "You won't believe what I have done," she says.

I set my work aside and lean back in my chair to appraise her. "You're giving me the rest of the week off."

She chuckles. "Guess again."

I tap my pen on the edge of the desk. "You've found a lender for the winery in Kenwood."

"Wrong again." She smiles. "I asked Alex and his girlfriend over for Thanksgiving. And they accepted. They're arriving tomorrow afternoon. You'll get to meet them."

I stand up and throw my arms around her. "I'm so happy for you!"

She pushes away, straightening her jacket, as if uncomfortable with my sudden burst of affection. "I'm nervous," she says. "I've never had a good visit with my son."

"Well, can you imagine it being any different this time?"

She stares at her old shoes. "No, I cannot."

"Let me help you." I lead her into her office and shut the door. "Have a seat and close your eyes."

Oh, this is fun. This is something Val and I used to do when he started acting in middle school. We'd make up different stories about our classmates' lives. I sit down. "Okay. Imagine you have just met your son and his girlfriend. You decide to take them to lunch at some new restaurant you've been dying to try. At the restaurant, he offers to place the order for everyone. When he tells the waiter to order two of the same thing, you both look at each other and laugh, realizing you are more alike than you ever realized. His girlfriend asks about your business. She's genuinely friendly and outspoken and cares a lot about your son. Your son doesn't mention the past or any hard feelings between you. He focuses on the present, enjoying your company. And you do the same. By the end of lunch, you feel as if you have started over. You both vow to keep in touch." I smile. "And you do."

Ms. Lashay opens her eyes. "So one good visit would lead to another good visit?"

"Of course," I say. "Don't you deserve a happy ending?"

"What about you?"

Me? Why is she turning this conversation around? I don't want to talk about myself.

"Didn't you break up with your boyfriend?"

"That was months ago. I hardly think of him anymore," I lie.

"Have you started dating again?"

I shrug. "There's more to life than men."

"Do you have friends?"

"Of course."

"And you're close to your family?"

"I have a wonderful father and a doting mother and a younger sister, too."

"I bet you're a great role model for her."

I strain to keep the smile on my face.

The phone rings.

Thank goodness! I jump up to answer it.

Ms. Lashay follows me to my desk. She waits for me to finish with the caller. When I hang up the phone, she places her smooth, cool hand on my wrist. "Thank you for encouraging me, dear. I never would have called Alex if you hadn't kept pestering me about it." Her forehead wrinkles with thought. "I only hope it goes as well as you say it will."

I squeeze her hand. "Don't worry. It will."

The next day, when I return to the office after lunch, I hear Ms. Lashay's bright laughter spilling from her office. The door opens briskly and a short man with flyaway hair as fine as dandelions steps out followed by Ms. Lashay. "I'd like you to meet—"

It's the guy from the gas station. "Zachary."

The man glances up and his brown eyes widen with recognition. "KK?"

"You both must be mistaken," Ms. Lashay says. "This is Alex, my son. And this is Trina, my associate."

Ms. Lashay's son is the Random Acts of Kindness guy? That can't be right.

"Actually, Mom, everyone knows me as Zachary Alexander Lashay II."

Pretentious, are we?

"And KK is my nickname. It's short for Katrina Kay."

Ms. Lashay's forehead wrinkles with astonishment. "You two know each other?"

I nod. "We met briefly at a gas station. Zachary was kind enough to loan me fifty dollars for gas." I grab my purse from underneath my desk and rummage around for my pocketbook.

The glass doors swing open. I glance up. Oh. My. God. That tall, svelte twenty-something woman is wearing the latest Emilio Pucci psychedelic print dress I would love to own. My hands fumble with excitement, and my purse falls from my desk. The contents spill over Zachary's shiny black Cole Haan shoes. He kneels down to gather the items: pen, notebook, lipstick, pocketbook, condom. Zikes! I grab the condom out of his hand and shove it into the zippered pocket of my purse. My face flushes with embarrassment. I haven't even used a condom since I've lived with Tom. But I have it just in case. I'd rather be safe than sorry. But how do you explain that to someone you've only met twice?

Quickly, I remove a fifty for the gas and another ten for interest from my pocketbook and hand them to Zachary. "For the gas," I say.

He stares at the bills in confusion and tries to give them back to me. "I said there was no need to pay me back."

The woman in the Emilio Pucci dress steps between us. "What's going on?"

Zachary places a hand on the woman's lower back and smiles. "I'd like you to meet my girlfriend, Candie."

His girlfriend? I feel the blood drain from my face. But, of course, he has a girlfriend. What nice guy doesn't have a beautiful, stylish girlfriend?

Candie extends her hand. Her grip is firm and dry. "You must be Zachary's mom's assistant."

"She's my *associate*," Ms. Lashay says, meaningfully. "She does everything I do only better."

Candie's bronze face pinches into a frown.

"Well," Ms. Lashay says, stepping between us. "If you don't mind watching the phones, dear, I'll step out for an hour." She turns to Candie. "How does coffee sound?"

"Wonderful," Candie says, flashing her bleached teeth.

"My treat," Zachary says, folding the bills in his hand.

Why can't I come?

Oh, that's right. It's my job to answer phones, not chat with Ms. Lashay's estranged son and his snooty girlfriend.

I sit down and move my mouse around to wake up my monitor.

Zachary opens the glass door and ushers the women into the lobby. "I'll be just a moment," he says.

He strides over to my desk and lays the folded bills next to my purse. I flush, remembering the contents of my purse at his feet. How he just picked everything up without a word. I wish I had that type of grace.

I glance over at the money, then up into his gentle brown eyes. This isn't the hard, unforgiving man Ms. Lashay has spoken about. This is a man who is full of love and generosity.

Without removing my eyes from his gaze, I grab the money and try to hand it to him. He shakes his head slowly. I stammer, "Why? Why won't you let me pay you back?"

His fingers close against my hand. My whole body tingles from the unexpected touch.

"You already have," he says, squeezing my fist once before letting it go.

What?

He quickly turns and strides toward the glass doors.

"Wait!" I stand up.

But he keeps moving. Once he steps outside, Ms. Lashay leads him toward the stairwell. He places a hand on Candie's lower back and guides her forward.

I gaze out at them, but don't move.

Damn. What's up with his riddles?

"How did your visit go?" I ask Ms. Lashay when she returns alone.

"I don't particularly like his girlfriend. She seems too nosey."

I don't like her either, but for different reasons. She seems too perfect. "What about Alex? Did you two get along this time?"

She puckers her lips, considering my question. "We didn't fight. But I think that's because Candie was there."

"Well, it's a start."

"We'll see how it goes tomorrow at Ms. Morgan's house. All four of us will be cooking dinner. It should be—interesting." She turns to me and smiles. "So, have you picked up your fruit salad?"

I blush. "After I finish this loan file."

She slides her rhinestone reading glasses up the bridge of her nose and takes a peek at the lender-borrower disclosure packet. "The government is going to change the way we do loans, because of the subprime market scare. I wouldn't take on any more second deeds of trust, if I was you. And I would be very careful with owner-occupied homes. It will be a lot harder to earn money off them." She removes her glasses. "Alex was saying the commercial lending business hasn't been affected by any of this. I'm thinking maybe we should refocus our business after the first of the year."

"But that would eliminate the majority of our clients—"

"I know. But Alex thinks it's best."

How dare he? He doesn't know anything about what we do. He's in a different segment of the industry. If Ms. Lashay follows his advice, it will ruin her business. "I really don't think that's a wise decision," I say, carefully choosing my words. "He also suggested you hire a man. And that didn't work out. What makes you think this will?"

Her eyes soften. "It's always been my dream to work with my son and build an empire. Leave a legacy."

What? This powerful woman who helps strangers out of their most dire financial situations wants to merge her business with her son's business. What a mistake! "I tried that with my ex-boyfriend and it didn't work. Just because you love someone doesn't mean you can do business with them."

The phone rings. But I'm too upset to answer it.

Ms. Lashay glances at me, then at the phone.

I close the file and stand up. "I've been waiting a long time to use the restroom."

Before I reach the glass door, I hear Ms. Lashay say, "You should have gone before we left."

Without glancing back, I reply, "And you should stick to doing what you do best. You shouldn't cave into some fantasy just because your son decides to visit and be civil with you. You can't change to make someone like you. Either they like you or they don't."

On Thanksgiving, I arrive at my parents' house a little after five, hoping to spend as little time with them as possible. I considered staying overnight at a hotel, but I need to save my paycheck in case I don't close as many loans in December as I'm anticipating. *One night won't hurt*, I tell myself. *I'll leave tomorrow morning after a hearty breakfast.*

Dee greets me at the door. Her long hair is swept back into a pony tail and her crinkly dress looks freshly washed. Her skin smells of cigarette smoke when I hug her. I wonder if I'd start smoking if I lived with my parents. Nah. More likely, I'd start drinking.

Mom frowns at the fruit salad I brought. "I know money's tight with you starting over, so I told you not to bring anything. But you don't listen, do you?" She grabs the salad and shoves it into the refrigerator, muttering, "I hope this is store bought." When she turns around, she tosses a bag of buns at me. "Help me with the rolls."

I obediently move about the kitchen, searching for the baking tray from the abundance of drawers and cabinets.

Dad sneaks up behind me and pecks my cheek. "Good to see you. There's a bit of sun on your face. Running again?"

My lips part in a broad, proud smile. "Yes, I am. Every morning before work."

"How's business?" Dee asks.

"Good," I lie. I think about my old real estate business. The last time I spoke with Mr. Leggins two weeks ago, he said the Engles and the Sanders couldn't decide on a mediation date. He told me it could take months, maybe even as long as a year, to resolve.

Mom hands me a baking tray. "Sell anything lately?"

I arrange the buns in neat little rows and hand the tray back to my mother. *You can do this*, I remind myself. When my heart continues to stammer in my chest, I repeat the mantra over and over again in my mind until my shirt stops visibly moving. Why continue to lie to them? I'll only hate myself. Who cares if the whole world knows I'm a failure? It's my life, not theirs. I take a deep breath and exhale. "I got a job."

"A job?" Mom drops the tray. Buns spill across the linoleum.

Dee stoops and gathers them up.

"You can't hold a job," Mom says, wiping her brow with a dish towel. "You can't take orders from anyone."

"I just took orders from you," I say, grabbing a glass from the cupboard. "You asked me to take care of the buns. And I did." Turning to Dad, I wink.

He chuckles softly, taking my glass and filling it with water. "I have some sodas in the garage, but I take it your diet's pretty clean, right?"

When I was competitively running, I would only drink water. But I haven't competitively run in years. Why can't my parents see me as I am today, not as I was years ago?

Without a word, I take the glass of water and gulp it down.

The doorbell rings.

"Who's that?" I ask. It can't be a delivery person or a door-to-door salesperson. I wonder if Jehovah's Witnesses solicit on Thanksgiving.

Dad answers it. Low male voices fill the foyer. Dad steps into the kitchen followed by Tom. His blue eyes meet mine.

I'm overcome with both the desire to bolt into the garage and the desire to throw my arms around his neck and kiss him long and hard.

*Deep breath. Exhale.* I calmly set my empty glass on the counter, but my voice quakes. "What's *he* doing here?"

Dad's smile droops. Mom turns her back to us, stirring the gravy on the stove. Dee snaps her camera. Bright lights flash like silver fireworks. I snatch the camera out of her hands and smash it against the door to the garage. Bits and pieces scatter over the floor.

She gasps. "My camera!"

I stalk across the kitchen, pushing past my father and Tom. In the foyer, I grab my jacket and my purse and step outside, slamming the door. The brisk air feels refreshingly cool against my hot, angry skin.

The door opens and someone rushes outside. Footfalls pad up to me and a hand closes over my shoulder. "Trina." I don't have to turn around to know it's Tom.

I stop, holding my jacket and purse against my chest. My voice is soft but firm. "Why did you come?"

"Your parents invited me. I didn't know you'd be here. They said you were spending the holiday with Val."

"Val's in Chicago acting. He won't be back till sometime next year."

"I didn't know."

I turn around, and from the shocked look in his blue eyes, I believe him.

I hate my parents.

"Look, I'll go. You stay." Tom motions to move past me, but I reach out to stop him.

He glances down at my hand against his coat. My nails are chipped and short from typing. My skin is dry. I must look terrible.

"Listen, Trina. I don't want to hurt you any more than I already have. If your parents are playing games, trying to get us back together, I don't want to be a part of it, understand?"

I swallow. I want to believe him, but I don't.

"I got a job." I don't know why I tell him. Maybe I want him to know I can take care of myself without his charity.

His eyebrows lift in surprise. "Really? Doing what?"

"Selling trust deeds."

He smiles. "Do you like it?"

I shrug. I want to tell him, *I miss us working together, being with each other every night. I miss our house. I miss our life. I miss you.*

But I can't.

He wraps his arm around me before I realize I'm shivering. "Want to go for a drive?"

Why not? It's not like it's a date or anything. It's just a way to get out of the cold without being at my parents' house.

"Sure," I say, opening the passenger's door to his Porsche.

# CHAPTER 21

▼

As soon as we are strapped into the black leather seats, Tom starts the engine and turns on the heat. Soft jazz plays through the speakers. He drives down the street, around the neighborhood I grew up in, before turning down Montague Expressway.

I don't say anything at first. I close my eyes and listen to the straining rhythms of the big brass band, feeling the familiar comfort of leather molded against my back. But curiosity eventually rises to the surface, and I ask, "How's work?"

"It was busy all through summer, but now it's starting to slow down," Tom says. "Since you've been gone, I hired two agents to replace you along with a part-time assistant for Su. The agents were good, not great. They couldn't handle the same volume as you could, so I was working more than ever. I ended up canceling our season tickets to the opera and missing a lot of Rotary meetings and playing less and less golf with your dad."

"How's Su?" I glance at his profile, sleek and professional in the twilight behind his Bolero sunglasses.

"The same. Efficient, quiet, dependable."

"And her assistant?"

"Chatty and sloppy, but amazingly good with people." His mouth tilts into a crooked smile. "Reminds me of you."

I blush, wondering if that was a compliment or an indication that he has a crush.

Tom glances at me. "I guess I should ask whether or not you've read any of the e-mails I've sent over the past couple of months."

I twist my hands into knots in my lap, embarrassed. How do you tell someone you've created a rule in Outlook that deletes their e-mail as soon as it's received?

"Um…actually, not all of it. I've been quite busy."

He chuckles. "You aren't using that as an excuse to avoid me, are you?"

"Not really." I stare down at my hands in my lap, hoping he won't catch my lie.

If he does know the truth, he doesn't let on. "Well, you'll be happy to know the Wongs closed escrow on their home and we made a small commission, which I used to pay off your open house ads." He glances over at me. "I hope you don't mind."

I shake my head. "No, of course not." I wonder if he offered to pay me first, but I never responded to his e-mail so he spent the money on bills instead.

"And Dirk Fitzgerald…"

"Yes?" I shift in my seat and press my hands against the cool leather, completely focused on the name.

"He was brought to disciplinary action by the Board. Apparently, a woman who attended one of his open houses filed a sexual harassment complaint."

"Really?" I sit back, contemplating Tom's words. Sexual harassment. Maybe Tom believes my comments now. About the billboard of my legs. And Dirk's insistent phone calls and e-mails. Maybe I should have stayed and filed the complaint. Then the poor woman would not have had to experience what I had. But it's too late now to think of what I should have done. I'm only glad someone finally brought the man to justice.

"I'm sorry I didn't take your complaint against Dirk more seriously," Tom says. "I just thought you were being overly sensitive. Like you are about your legs."

I wince. Don't mention the billboard, please.

He doesn't. Instead, he points to the glove compartment. "There's something in there for you."

Cautiously, I pull the compartment open and reach for an envelope. I rip it open and a check made payable to me in the amount of $5,000 falls into my lap.

"What's this for?"

Tom smiles. "Maria closed escrow on that condo you found for her. I felt bad for not sharing the profits with you. So that's your half of the commission."

I finger the check. I can finally start paying off some of my bills without waiting for my first commission check, now that I've made that agreement with Ms. Lashay to split profits in lieu of a regular paycheck.

"Thank you." I reach over and peck his cheek.

"You're welcome." He pats my knee. "You're the best Realtor I've ever worked with. I guess it took your absence to make me recognize how good you really are."

We talk for an hour, as Tom drives aimlessly through the city. When it becomes dark, Tom removes his sunglasses. I settle against the leather seat and drink in the sound of his voice. Despite how bad I feel about my parents setting us up for Thanksgiving dinner, I feel wonderful talking about my everyday life with Tom. This is what I've missed.

"How's your new job?" he asks.

What to tell him? There's just so much to it, I don't know where to start. "It's interesting. I never knew what happened when we referred a client to a lender. And I never cared to know. Now I'm right in the middle of it, organizing trust deed sales for new and existing loans."

"And you deal with foreclosures?" Tom asks.

"We deal with everything. Ms. Lashay prides herself on helping others in times of need."

He nods. "Sounds like she's a very *charitable* person."

The edge in his voice startles me. I thought we were getting along so well. Why the sarcasm? "She doesn't go around trying to save the world."

"Just her clients."

"And her lenders. She bought back a trust deed from Ms. Morgan when the borrowers stopped making payments and filed for bankruptcy. She said her friendship was more important than $30,000."

Tom is silent.

I stare out the window, at the ebony sky, and notice we're on 101, taking the same route that leads to our office. My lower back tenses when I see the billboards flash by. Why is he taking me this way? Does he secretly want to torture me?

"I think we should be getting back to my parents' house. I'm getting hungry." I squirm, feeling trapped in the Porsche. The billboards keep coming. I can't help but look, knowing a larger-than-life image of my legs will soon flash by.

"KFC is closed," he says. "But we can stop at Taco Bell."

Fast food? On Thanksgiving?

"Sure, why not," I say, anything to get him off the freeway. "Can we take the next exit?"

But it's too late. We've just passed the last exit before the off ramp to our office. My hands clench into anxious fists, and beads of sweat gather under my arms. Where is the billboard? Did I miss it?

Wait. What's this? A large yellow billboard with black letters reads, "Your Ad Could Be Here," along with a toll-free number. A few moments later, we turn off the exit to our office. That last billboard must have been where our old ad was. The one with my bare legs crossed at the knees, one foot swinging beside our slogan, "Kick Up Your Profits." My lower back relaxes.

The ad is gone.

"What happened to the billboard?" I ask, just to make sure I didn't miss it.

Without taking his eyes off the road, Tom simply says, "I took it down."

I stare at my hands in my lap. *He took it down*, I think. *For me.*

# Chapter 22

At Taco Bell, Tom and I find a booth and sit across from each other. We remove the paper from our tacos and burritos and sip from extra large soft drinks in the brightly lit dining room. A homeless man cowers in a corner drinking coffee and muttering to himself. A few teenagers yell over heavy metal at the drive-thru window. Tom reaches across the table and dabs a smear of sour cream from my lips. I smile. "Want a bite?" Tom nods, and I hand him the burrito. He takes a huge bite and offers me his taco. The crispy shell breaks off and falls against my shirt. He snickers. It's like old times.

After dinner, we drive up the hill to our old home. Tom parks in the driveway. I step out into the chilly night and gaze out at the twinkling city lights. Tom wraps his arm around my shoulders and tugs me close. "I've missed you," he whispers through my curly hair. I tilt my head back and gaze into his moonlit eyes and see the love I have for him reflected in his stare. My body feels full and warm. "I've missed you too," I say.

Hand in hand, we walk up the steps to the front door. Tom turns the lock and pushes the door open. Bending, he swoops me into his arms and carries me to the alarm panel in the foyer. I laugh. "Try turning it off with one hand," I joke. He swivels me around to the panel. "You turn it off," he says.

"But I don't know the code."

"I haven't changed it."

He hasn't changed it. Does that mean he was expecting me to come back?

The alarm beeps every five seconds. I punch in the code from memory. The beeping stops. The house is silent except for the expectant beating of my heart. Slowly, Tom carries me up the stairs to our bedroom. The room is dark except for the moonlight. Tom bends down and places me on the satin comforter I bought but he never liked. I'm surprised he hasn't changed it for something more practical, something more to his taste. Does that mean he kept it because of me? He slips off my shoes and socks and massages my ankles. Tingling circles of pleasure radiate up my legs until my whole pelvis pulses with warmth. Mmm. It's been so long I almost forgot how delicious his touch feels. I sit half-way up and tug him down to me. His body is heavy and firm against my breasts. I gently part his lips and he slips his tongue into my mouth. He tastes of beans and hot sauce. When we stop kissing, he tugs off my bulky sweater, and I claw at the buttons on his shirt. Hurry, hurry, hurry. Before I change my mind. But the buttons don't come apart fast enough. A thought lodges in my mind. Why are we doing this? We aren't a couple. We broke up, remember? This isn't making up sex. This is just sex.

I drop my hands and scoot back on the bed. Tom continues seductively unbuttoning his shirt, one button at a time. I reach for my sweater. He nudges it aside and lowers me back down to the bed. The satin sticks to my sweaty back. "Why are you doing this?" I whisper.

"Because I love you," he says, before pressing tiny kisses against my neck.

My whole body shivers with anticipation. If this is wrong, it feels so right.

"I didn't know how much I love you until you were away," he says, his hands cupping my bare breasts. He places his mouth over a nipple and gently flicks his tongue against it until I arch my back with darts of pleasure.

My hands travel down his back and cup his butt through the fabric of his pants. He kneels, unbuckles the belt, and removes his pants and underwear with one fluid motion. In the moonlight, his body glows like one big exclamation point.

I close my eyes as he lifts up my hips and slips off my pants. My legs quiver. Slowly, he presses kisses up my right leg while his hands massage my thighs. His tongue traces the crease of my groin in a wide arch that continues to narrow until his tongue slips between the folds of my labia, and I gasp with delight.

My fingers curl against his hair as his head continues to move in steady rhythm with his dancing tongue.

"I want you," I say.

"How badly?" he asks, slightly rising.

I sit up just as he lies down. Kneeling before him, I repeat the same pleasure course of kisses up his legs that he just showered on me. As I lower my mouth on his penis, he gasps, "That badly, huh?"

"Mmm-hmm," I mumble with his shaft in my mouth.

I glance up at him and meet his glistening eyes in the semi-darkness.

"Do you want me?" he asks.

"Mmm-hmm," I reply, running the tips of my fingers over his balls.

Slowly, he lifts me by my shoulders until I hover above him. Gently, he nudges me down until I feel my wetness on the tip of his erection. I tilt my head back as my hips rock against his hips with a passion I haven't experienced since we first started dating almost three years ago.


In the morning, I blink several times before realizing I am here, in my old home, in my old bed, naked under my old satin sheets. Tom rustles beside me.

"Good morning, sunshine."

Tom reaches across the pillow and strokes the fuzzy auburn curls away from my face. His palm lingers against my cheek. "It's so good to wake up and see you again," he says. "I know you have a new job and you're house-sitting for Val, but if you could make other arrangements, would you move back in with me?"

Move back in? I want to close my eyes and tug the covers up to my chin and roll over and go back to sleep. It's too early to think about getting back together.

But he continues talking. "I miss you. And I'm sorry I hurt your feelings with the billboard. I've realized my mistake and I'm asking you to forgive me and come home. To us. To our business. To our whole lives together."

Get back together. Is that what this is all about? I guess Val was right. Tom wouldn't buy my half of our business because he didn't want to let go of me. He was hoping I would give up my attempt to start over and come back to our old life. And when I didn't, he decided to remove the billboard. To see if it would be the magic that would bring us back together.

It's not, is it?

"For a long time, I was angry with you," Tom says. "I didn't understand why you took off like that. I still don't. But I do know I hurt you and I've never meant to hurt you. Please think about it. You don't have to decide anything today. Or tomorrow. I just want you to know I'm sorry and I want us to be together again."

He slides his hand underneath the sheets and caresses the side of my body closest to him. Tiny goose bumps rise up from my thigh to my shoulder.

I wriggle away from him. If I consent to more lovemaking, am I consenting to getting back together with him? Should I tell him to stop touching me because it's scrambling my brainwaves into a jumble of confusion?

Tom playfully rolls over and parts my legs with his knees. I reach up and press my hands against his chest. "Please, don't," I say. "It's making me want to do things I'm not sure I want to do."

"Like what?"

"Like get back together with you."

"Is that a bad thing?"

I shrug.

He hovers above me just like I hovered above him last night. The memory brings a smile to my lips. If we got back together, I could go to bed each night with a terrific orgasm and wake up in bliss. So what if I have to drive two and a half hours once or twice a month to check on Val's cottage and pick up the mail at the post office? Tom and I can make a weekend of it. Maybe stop by a few wineries and indulge in a little chardonnay. What else do I have going for me up north? Just a little litigation I can come back for and a job I can quit. I'll be courteous and give Ms. Lashay two weeks notice. It's the least I can do to show my appreciation for her generosity and confidence in me.

"Okay," I say. "I'll get back together with you. But it won't be right away. I have a few things I need to do first."

Tom's face beams with satisfaction. "Do whatever you need to do. I'm just happy we'll be together again soon."

"Me, too." I reach up and kiss him, feeling the gritty early morning residue in both our mouths and not caring one bit.

"Want a repeat performance?" Tom asks, as soon as our lips part.

My smile broadens. "Definitely," I say, tracing tiny circles on his chest.

# CHAPTER 23

▼

Tom and I spend the day after Thanksgiving lounging around in bed until mid-afternoon before heading over to Valley Fair to window shop. At six-thirty throngs of people still push and shove through the boutiques hunting for the perfect bargain. Tom links his arm through mine and smiles benevolently at me. "Want a little something?" he asks.

I haven't purchased anything for myself in what seems like ages. Not even bubble bath.

But is there a price?

Nothing, after all, is free. Is it?

I shrug, trying to hide my indecision. "Not really."

Tom frowns. "Has moving up north made you—frugal?" He spits out the last word like he's choking up a hairball.

How can he suggest that when he knows I don't have money? Or does he think I'm doing quite well now that I have a job as an associate broker for a mortgage company? Maybe he thinks I've partnered up with someone successful. Like himself.

My gaze catches our reflection in the storefront window of Tiffany and Co. Tom's broad shoulders seem to dwarf me.

I've never felt so small, so dainty, so much like a little ballerina in a child's jewelry box.

"Would you like to go in?" Tom suggests, leading me to the door.

"Um, not really." I don't particularly like stopping to look when I know I can't afford to buy anything.

Tom doesn't seem to hear me. He pushes open the door and there's a little ping to alert the staff that a shopper has entered.

I look down at my feet. Maybe if I avoid eye contact no one will bother to help us.

Tom leads me past the display of watches and necklaces. We settle in front of the engagement rings. "Which one would you choose?" Tom asks.

I glimpse the price tag on a one carat emerald cut diamond with tapered baguettes for $6,000. Six thousand dollars! I could pay off a huge portion of my Visa. My gaze finds another bauble for $24,000. Twenty-four thousand dollars? Really, if I had that kind of pocket change, I wouldn't need a job.

Tom nudges me. "Pick one out. Just for fun."

Just for fun. Hmm. Like you sky dive just for fun. Or bungee jump just for fun. Or race a Formula 1 car just for fun. You pick out a twenty-four thousand dollar engagement ring just for fun.

"Why are we playing this game?" I ask, laughing to hide my nervousness.

Tom shrugs. "Don't all girls like playing dress up?" He waves a young blond clerk wearing a trendy Valentino suit over to the glass counter. "May we try the emerald cut diamond, please?"

The clerk smiles sweetly. "Of course, you may." Her gaze lingers a bit too long, and Tom encourages her by winking.

Ugh. That flirting hasn't stopped.

The clerk holds up the emerald cut diamond engagement ring like she's getting ready to hand-feed a piece of shrimp to Tom. "Would you like to try it on your fiancé?" she asks.

Fiancé? Really, this is ridiculous. I'm not ready for marriage. I don't even want children.

Before Tom can slip the ring onto my finger, I cross my arms over my chest. "We've just gotten back together. Isn't this a little premature?"

He laughs. "If I was Val, you'd have tried on half the case already."

Yes, I agree. But with Val I know the difference between real and make-believe. With Tom, I don't.

"Listen, Trina, if it's going to make you upset, we won't try anything on, okay?" He turns to the clerk and hands her the ring like he's proposing to her. "I'm sorry," he says.

The clerk flashes a pitying glance in my direction before she places the ring back in the display case. She must think I'm a fool to be waltzing around Tiffany and Co. with a drop-dead gorgeous hunk on my arm and refusing to try on twenty-four thousand dollar engagement rings.

A chill sweeps up my back, and I step outside, away from the sparkling glitter of happily-ever-after to face my thoughts in the comfort of the shopping crowd.

Something's wrong with me. Maybe I'm the Runaway Bride. Commit-phobic. Maybe that's why my best friend is a gay man, and I spend all my money on frivolous things. Because I can't stand the thought of being barefoot and pregnant in the kitchen baking pie for my husband and chasing after my disobedient kids.

Okay. Maybe that's a bit melodramatic. Married women nowadays aren't barefoot and pregnant in the kitchen. They're stylishly dressed and working their careers. They hire full-time nannies and part-time chefs and take spa vacations every six months. They aren't Desperate Housewives, looking for a cheap thrill just to keep their blood moving. Are they?

Silently, Tom steps beside me. "You all right?" he asks.

I turn to face him. "No, I'm not. It's not fair to put that kind of pressure on me."

"It was just a game."

"*Everything* with you is just a game." I throw my arms up in exasperation. "And I'm tired of playing."

Tom's face sags with hurt and disappointment. "I thought it would be fun. I know how much you love shopping."

My chest feels tight with fear. "I don't know if I love it so much anymore," I say.

Tom stares at me with disbelief. "What do you like doing nowadays?"

I shrug. "Running."

He smirks. "You've always run."

"*Outside*." When I was living with Tom, I would only run on my treadmill.

"Really?" He tilts his head, studying me with interest. "What else are you doing?"

"Following orders from a woman old enough to be my grandmother."

He chuckles. "Really?"

I nod, trying to suppress a smile. But I can't help it. I'm so different than I used to be. It's like the old me is a caricature.

"So, no more dress up?"

I shrug. "Not since I can't afford it."

"Ah, yes, money problems," Tom says, opening his arms to me. "Well, once you move back and we start working together again, all that will be history."

I hope.


On Saturday night, Tom drops me off at my parents' house to pick up my Mercedes. It's parked in the driveway just like I left it three days ago. The house is dark except for the porch light.

"Want to stop in and tell them the news?" Tom asks. "I'm sure they'll be excited." My stomach clenches, remembering Thanksgiving night. How I felt setup by my parents and betrayed by Dee. I can't believe I broke her camera. I never did say I'm sorry. I just stormed out like I always do, avoiding the situation. Now I'm standing in the driveway beneath roiling clouds. A brisk wind sweeps my curls across my face. I shiver, not from the cold, but from a deep nagging sense that something's not quite right.

If I step inside that house and announce our getting-back-together, my parents will flush with pride. See, they'll think, we knew what was best for you even when you didn't know it. And Dee will smugly say, I told you so. And then I'll feel worse. About Thanksgiving. About breaking Dee's camera. About running away from everything in the first place.

I shake my head and open my car door. "Not now," I say to Tom. "You can tell them after I've left, but I don't want to see or talk to them."

"Why not?" Tom frowns. "They'll be happy for us."

I gaze down at my feet, knowing he's right. That's the problem. They'll think it was their little Thanksgiving Day setup that led to our reunion, and I'll forever hear about it.

But I'm not back together with Tom because of them, am I? I decided on my own, after I discovered he had taken down the billboard. If I tell them that, they'll argue with me, trying to prove they're right. They'll say I never would have known Tom had removed the billboard if they hadn't invited him to dinner because I've been avoiding his phone calls, e-mails, and snail mail letters. And I'll just get angry again and probably break up with Tom just to prove my point—I'm a grown woman who can make good decisions without the help of anyone else.

"C'mon, it'll just take a minute," Tom says, reaching for my hand.

I tug my fingers out of his grasp. "Please, not now. Why can't you tell them after I'm gone?"

"What's going on? You're not making sense to me anymore. First, you throw a fit while shopping. Now, you're ready to have a tantrum over telling your parents good news." He studies me for a long moment. "It is good news that we're back together, isn't it?"

I take a deep breath and glance up into his moonlit eyes. "Of course it is," I say, feeling my chest expand with hope. "I just can't talk to them right now."

Out of the corner of my eyes, I think I see the curtains rustle in the window overlooking the front yard. Quickly, I slip inside the Mercedes and start the engine.

Inside the house, a light flicks on.

Tom glances over his shoulder.

My mother's face peers out the window. She squeals and my father's face appears beside her. Then they're gone.

Hurry, hurry, hurry. I don't want to talk to them. With one swift tug, the door slams shut. Tom taps at the window. I roll it down and lean out to kiss him goodbye.

He parts his lips and tries to wedge his tongue into my mouth. I jerk away.

"Will I see you back at the house?"

I shake my head. A few droplets splash against the windshield. I hate driving in the rain, but I don't want to risk staying another night.

"When will you be back?" Tom asks.

The front door clicks open.

I hold my breath, my chest thudding with panic. "Soon."

Tom's eyebrows knit together with worry. "You can't keep running."

"I'm not running!"

But he doesn't look convinced as I back out of the driveway and speed away.

# CHAPTER 24

▼

Ting-ting-ting. A steady rain pelts the tin roof. I roll over in the stiff bed and cover my head with designer-look-a-like sheets and groan. Maybe I should have stayed another night in San Jose. The bed would be warm and soft and comfortable. And I'd be in Tom's arms.

When I can't stand the sound of rain any longer, I get up and shove my big feet into a pair of fuzzy slippers and start the fire in the living room. Flipping through Val's CD collection, I select something jazzy and play it loud enough to drown out the rain. I sip a mug of coffee and contemplate whether or not I should go for a run when the phone rings.

"Hey, KK, how was your Thanksgiving?" Val asks.

Should I tell him? I smile sweetly. "You'll never guess."

"Hmm…you ate too much pumpkin pie and bought the Best of '80's Rock from an infomercial."

Oh, he'll never guess. "Try again."

"Oh, that's right. You're maxed out on your credit card. Hmm…you watched the Macy's Thanksgiving Day parade and drank bourbon with your father."

This could go on forever. "Give up?" I pause dramatically. "Tom showed up."

"Really? Who invited him?"

"My parents did."

"And?"

Should I tell him everything? Or can I edit out the bad parts? A little editing never hurt anyone. "Well, at first I was angry and I stormed out and Tom followed me. We went for a drive and that's when I discovered he took down the billboard."

"He took it down?"

"You heard me right the first time." I proceed to shower Val with details of my wonderful time together with Tom, leaving out the trip to Tiffany's and the unexpected getaway at my parents' house. Better to keep it light and simple.

"Are you really back together?" Val asks. "Or was this just a once-for-old-time's-sake-fling?"

I giggle like a school girl and blush. "After I put in my two weeks notice, I'm moving back to San Jose."

"Finally!" Val shouts. "You've seen the light!" And he starts singing Madonna's "Ray of Light."

I dance a jig while Val sings. The rain has stopped and sunlight streams through the branches, casting a golden glow in the tiny kitchen. Suddenly I wish Val was dancing next to me. We could bump hips and giggle over the turn of events, talking them over and over like a scene from a favorite movie. But I'm here, and Val's thousands of miles away.

Cheer up. What's a little loneliness? Just think. In two weeks, I'll be home again. With Tom. And I'll never be lonely again.


On Monday morning, Ms. Lashay greets me sternly. "Hurried morning?" she asks.

I go through a quick mental checklist. Dry hair? Check. Modest make-up? Check. Skirt the right length? Check. On time? I glance at the clock against the wall. Check. Then why is she complaining?

Ms. Lashay gazes briefly at my legs. Oh, yes, that's it. In my excitement, I strode into the office a little too briskly. That, coupled with my long legs, must have given her the impression that I was rushed.

I slow down my gait and place my purse on my desk. "How was your Thanksgiving?" I ask.

Ms. Lashay gathers papers from the copier. "Very good. Alex and Candie were delightful. I didn't know my son could cook so well. And you?"

"Actually, I have some news," I tell her, not wanting to delay the inevitable. "Tom and I are getting back together. I'm putting in my two weeks notice."

Ms. Lashay's eyebrows knit together. "Honestly, dear, do you think that's a good idea? After all, you told me just because you love someone doesn't mean you can work together."

"It will be different this time." I tilt my chin with confidence. "Tom took the billboard down and apologized."

"What billboard?"

I guess I never told her the circumstances of our breakup. "Tom was using a picture of my bare legs to advertise our business. It was embarrassing to drive down 101 and see my legs next to our slogan, 'Kick Up Your Profits, Choose T & T Realty.' That's why I left. But he took it down."

"Because he decided it made good business sense or because he was convinced it was the only way you'd come back?"

I stare blankly at her. "I—don't—know." I never bothered to ask Tom why. I was just so relieved that he did. That's all that seemed to matter.

Ms. Lashay touches my elbow. "May I see you in my office?"

Reluctantly, I follow her. I choose the seat closest to the door and cross my ankles, knowing she hates the way my skirt rides up to my thighs when I cross my legs.

Ms. Lashay sits on her plush chair and clasps her hands on her desk. "I hope you're not leaving because of me. I know I can be demanding and critical, but I expect the best from you. And I know you can deliver it. You just need some coaxing sometimes."

"I'm not leaving because of you. I'm leaving because of Tom."

"Tell me more about him. What makes him so wonderful?" She leans forward expectantly. She smells of baby powder and hair spray.

I smile, remembering our weekend together. "My family adores him. He's the son my father never had. And he's a good business man. When we agree, things run smoothly."

"And when you don't?"

I flush. "I end up leaving."

"Like you're leaving me?" she asks.

"Yes, I mean, no." I sigh. "You've been wonderful to me. I really appreciate everything you've taught me. Not many employers would have taken the time."

"You're right. They wouldn't." She leans back and studies me. "But my interest in you wasn't completely selfless. I'm getting old, and I'd like to retire someday. I was hoping I could train you to take over my business, but I guess I was wrong."

Take over her business? Why hadn't she mentioned it before?

"You seem surprised, Trina. Don't be. A woman of your caliber doesn't come around every day."

"But what about your son? Aren't you going to start commercial lending with him next year?"

"I changed my mind. Because of you."

Me?

"Alex and I are getting along better, but it would be foolish of me to hand over my business to him when I have already trained you. Everyone loves you. The borrowers, the lenders, the title companies, even the couriers adore you. Why would I risk losing all of that because of my desire to have a relationship with my son?"

My chest pinches with guilt. How can I leave when she's invested so much in me?

"Don't look so conflicted, dear. It's only business." She slips on her rhinestone reading glasses and grabs the Johansen file on her desk.

"You're not going to stop me?"

She glances up, perplexed. "Why should I? It's your life."

I take a deep breath and exhale with relief.

"I assume you don't want the commission on these loans," she says, indicating the pile of files on her desk.

Those are my loan files. I've worked hard on them. "Of course, I want the commission."

"Then I guess you'll be staying until they close."

"But the Johansen file isn't scheduled to fund until after Christmas."

"Then I guess you'll be spending Christmas here." She gazes over the rims of her glasses. "You did read the contract you signed, didn't you?"

Quite frankly, I don't remember what it said.

"You checked with your attorney about it, right?"

I nod slowly. "I did."

"And he agreed it was legally sound?"

Oh, god, why can't I remember what my contract said? I spent so much time pondering it.

"Trina?"

I nod.

"Shall I count on you staying for two weeks or five weeks?"

Oh, god, I feel faint.

Without waiting for a response, Ms. Lashay taps out the figures on her calculator. "If you stay, you'll earn $15,000 in commission."

Fifteen-thousand. After taxes, that would leave me about seven thousand five hundred dollars. I could pay off my Visa. Without Tom's help.

"Let me think about it," I say, feeling an itch at the back of my throat.

"No thinking," Ms. Lashay says, tapping her nails on the desk. "The best business decisions are made instinctively. That's what's wrong with big businesses today. People spend too much time in meetings debating about the obvious. Either you stay and earn your full commission or you leave without it."

Is this some sort of test?

She lifts her eyebrows and points to the clock on the wall beside her. "You have thirty seconds."

Thirty-seconds?

"Why can't I talk with my boyfriend first?" I ask.

Instantly, I realize my mistake. Ms. Lashay, proud defender of single working women everywhere, would not understand my need to consult with my boyfriend over a business decision. Even if my boyfriend was…and will be… my business partner.

She leans forward conspiratorially and asks, "Do you want me to believe that a competent professional woman such as yourself is really, underneath it all, a whimpering pansy?"

My heart thuds in my chest. What's she thinking? That I can't be strong *and* rely on a man? For his opinion, that's all. Not for my life direction. And definitely not because I'm a whimpering pansy.

I should quit. Right now.

Wait. That would just validate her opinion of me.

Okay. That's it. I'll stay. Just to prove a point.

But whose point?

"Ten seconds, dear." Her eyes narrow with interest.

Why not stay a few more weeks for fifteen thousand dollars? Then I can also leave with dignity in Ms. Lashay's eyes.

But why should Ms. Lashay's opinion matter to me?

My throat thickens with fear. What about my life? I can't put it on hold forever.

The second hand sweeps past the six on the clock.

"Your decision, dear."

I swallow. The tightness in my chest competes with the churning in my stomach.

What to do, what to do? "I'll stay until my last loan closes."

A slow smile spreads across Ms. Lashay's face.

I hope Tom understands.

# CHAPTER 25

▼

Five more weeks, not two. Okay. I can do this.

I sit down at my desk and start phoning lenders in my database, hoping to place the Baker file this week. Carlson is closing next week. And Zonderman will close the week before Christmas. Then I'll only have the Johansen file outstanding.

In the middle of a call, my BlackBerry blurts "True Blue" by Madonna. Ms. Lashay stalks out of her office. As she passes my desk, I quickly put the lender I am speaking with on hold and reach down into my purse, trying to silence Madonna.

"Really, dear, you should turn off your cell phone while at work," Ms. Lashay says.

"I thought it was turned off," I reply.

Ms. Lashay hovers by my desk like a bee ready to stab at the heart of a flower. I want to knock her over, but I smile sweetly before taking the lender off hold and continuing with my sales pitch.

After a moment, she returns to her office and shuts her door.

Only five more weeks, I remind myself. Just 25 working days to go.

ೞ    ೞ    ೞ

"I only have a minute," I tell Tom.

A toilet flushes in the stall next to me.

"Where are you?" he asks.

"The restroom," I whisper. "It's the only place I could get some privacy."

He laughs.

"It's not funny," I hiss. "Ms. Lashay put me on the spot when I told her I was quitting. I have to stay till all my loans are closed. That means till New Year's Eve."

There is an awkward silence.

"Why can't she handle your loans?" Tom asks. "You could pay her a referral fee."

I shake my head, feeling worse. "I renegotiated our work agreement when I thought I was staying. Now I've got to keep my end of the agreement or lose my commissions." And my dignity, I think.

"If it's money, I can help."

Something Ms. Lashay said creeps back into my mind. About the billboard and good business sense. I can't help but wonder if Tom really has the money or if he's just trying to get me to come home sooner.

The restroom door swings open and rubber soles scuff along the tiles. I recognize the squishy-squashy sound. Ms. Lashay. She steps into the stall next to me. I fake a cough and flush the toilet, moving quickly out of the restroom. In the corridor, I say, "I've got to go, Tom."

"I wish you were here." His voice sounds wistful.

"Me, too." My legs quiver, remembering the morning after Thanksgiving. I want to curl up naked against him, not return to the office and process loans.

"I guess I shouldn't complain." He sighs. "I've lived seven lonely months without you. At least, you're taking my calls now. I guess that will have to tide me over for the next five weeks."

By the time Ms. Lashay returns from the restroom, I really do need to go. But I can't leave now. I have an appointment in five minutes with Ms. Morgan. She's signing a Substitution of Trustee for the foreclosure we're handling, and then she's going out to lunch with Ms. Lashay. Maybe once they're both gone I can sneak out and take a real break.

The glass door pushes open and Ms. Morgan, dressed in another billowing floral housedress, shuffles inside. Rising, I greet her with a firm handshake. "Let's have a seat in the conference room, shall we?"

Ms. Morgan shuffles into the conference room and sits down across from me at the long narrow table.

"How was your Thanksgiving?" I ask, trying to be friendly.

"Hmph. Would have been better without Alex and Candie."

I frown. "Ms. Lashay said it went well."

"There's more to getting along than keeping the peace."

"What happened?" I hand Ms. Morgan a black fine-tipped ball-point pen and the document for her signature.

"It was fine until Candie started asking questions she had no right to ask, and Alex defended her instead of his mother." Ms. Morgan shakes her head sadly. "Poor Ms. Lashay got all shook up. She was having chest pains." Ms. Morgan pauses to study the document. "This needs to be notarized," she says, handing it back to me. "Are you a notary?"

Oh, shit. I forgot all about that. Now I have to either send for a mobile notary or suggest she take it to her bank.

"Hi Betty," Ms. Lashay says, poking her beehive into the conference room.

Ms. Morgan glances up. "Have you made an appointment with a doctor?"

"I'm fine," Ms. Lashay says. Turning to me, she asks, "Any problems?"

I smile sweetly. "I forgot to send for a notary."

Ms. Lashay scrunches her face for a moment before she smiles with a solution. "Don't worry, dear. Betty and I will pop into the bank after lunch." She touches Ms. Morgan's shoulder. "Oh, that reminds me. I wanted to talk to you about possibly investing in a bed and breakfast in Glen Ellen."

Betty lifts her shoulders like she's carrying the weight of the world on them. "No more loans. If I keep shelling out money for this foreclosure, I'll have to dip into my home equity line."

"I offered to buy your interest before the default," Ms. Lashay says, sitting down next to her.

Ms. Morgan bows her head in thought. "I guess I should have listened to you."

Ms. Lashay pats her hands. "Now dear, about that bed and breakfast in Glen Ellen." In the other room, my BlackBerry rings "Keep It Together" by Madonna. Ms. Lashay glances up and meets my gaze, meaningfully. My face flushes a deep red, and I motion to leave.

"Trina, dear, can you take care of the file on my desk for me while I'm at lunch?"

I feel like Cinderella when she is bossed around by her evil stepmother after she's been told she can go to the ball if she gets her housework completed on time.

"What needs to be done?" I ask.

Ms. Lashay stands up and ushers Ms. Morgan to the double glass doors. My BlackBerry beeps with a message. I ignore it, focusing on the two women before me.

"Just a GFE and a Reg Z," she says lightly. "I've left a write up in the folder."

"No problem." Why can't she process her own files? Doesn't she know I have tons of my own work to do?

As soon as they've left, I snatch my BlackBerry from my purse to check my message.

"KK," gushes my mom. "Tom just told us the news. How wonderful! You two are just perfect for each other." She lowers her voice. "Just don't mess it up this time, okay? Oh, and could you talk to Dee? She's really broken up about her camera. Apparently, it costs a fortune to fix."

Great. My mom is as happy as ever, and my sister probably wants to kill me.

The office phone rings. From the caller ID, I know it's Ms. Lashay. "Smart Loans, Trina Kay speaking," I say, in my most professional voice.

Madonna sings, "Vogue," from the BlackBerry on my desk. I hold down the shut off button, but it's too late.

"If you don't turn off that cell phone, I will confiscate it from you," Ms. Lashay says. "Now, about that file on my desk—"

When I call Mr. Leggins' office the next day to cancel my litigation with Tom, his paralegal puts me on hold.

I glance up at the clock on the wall in the office and listen to my heart thudding faster than the Mozart playing on the phone. I hope Ms. Lashay doesn't arrive until after I finish this phone call. If I hadn't been so busy at the office, I would have stayed home to make this call. But, unfortunately, it seems like everyone wants money before the holidays. And private loans are the only way to go for quick cash if you have equity in a property.

I place the call on speaker phone and start organizing my messy desk. Filing is something I always left Su to do. Now Ms. Lashay seems to think it's part of my job description.

A few moments later, Mr. Leggins picks up the line. "Ms. Kay," his throaty voice booms. "So glad you called. I was meaning to discuss the mediation with you. The date has been set for the second week in January. I'll e-mail you the details."

That means I'll have to come back. Oh, well. At least Val's cottage will be vacant till Valentine's Day. That means I'll have a place to stay if the mediation drags on and on and on.

Squish-squash. Squish-squash.

Quickly, I snatch the phone up and place it against my ear just as the squishy sounds in the corridor approach the double glass doors. Ms. Lashay, dressed in an old ebony raincoat and wearing black and white checkered galoshes, pulls back the glass door and squish-squashes over to my desk.

"You're in early today," she says, without regard for the phone pressed against my ear.

"Excuse me, sir," I tell Mr. Leggins. "But I have to put you on hold for a second."

After I press the red hold button and place the receiver back in the cradle, Ms. Lashay lifts her eyebrows in astonishment. "You didn't need to do that, dear. I just made a comment, not a demand."

I sit back in my chair. "I prefer talking to one person at a time. That way, there's less likelihood of a misunderstanding or a mistake," I say.

Ms. Lashay straightens her spine. "I took a listing last night. I'll need you to hold it open this weekend. Both Saturday and Sunday. Ms. Morgan and I have an out-of-town engagement with a lender in Malibu."

I rock forward in my chair. "But I have plans this weekend."

"Your boyfriend can come up and visit you," she says, as if reading my mind. "Won't hurt him to put in a little effort. To show he cares." She adds with a smile.

Is this what my contract says? I reach into my top desk drawer and pull it out.

The red light beeps. I have to finish this call. Or tell Mr. Leggins I will call him back. Beads of sweat gather beneath my collar. Of course, Mr. Leggins doesn't mind the wait. But I do. He gets paid by the minute. I don't.

Ms. Lashay taps the desk with her chipped nails. "No need to check your contract." She points to the clause in the second to the last paragraph titled, "Additional responsibilities." I quickly scan the line. She's right. It's listed.

"Ciao." She saunters into her office and closes the door.

My face flushes, hot with anger and humiliation. I grab the receiver and in my best professional voice say, "Mr. Leggins, thank you for holding."

"My pleasure, Ms. Kay. As I was saying, the mediation is set. Now what's this about you and Tom?"

"We're back together," I say, glancing over my shoulder to make sure Ms. Lashay's blinds are closed. I hate when she opens them up to stare at me like I'm some fish in an aquarium, working for her amusement.

"So you don't want to dissolve your business?"

I swallow. "Yes, I don't."

"You do understand there will be a bill."

"But you didn't file any paperwork. Did you?"

"No, but there is a minimum consultation fee I must charge."

I sigh. "How small?"

"Five hundred dollars."

I tap my fingers on the desk, a habit I picked up from Ms. Lashay. More money. More reason for me to stay. To collect these damn commissions. None of which will go toward a new Vera Wang dress. Or Marc Jacob shoes. Or even a down payment for a new Mercedes. "Of course," I say, thinking of all the things I cannot buy. "I understand." But, of course, I don't.

"I can't come up this weekend," Tom says, when I finally reach him.

I'm sitting at my desk, eating a cold turkey sandwich from the deli across the street, hoping to finish my personal business while Ms. Lashay entertains another lender during her lunch hour.

"I have tickets for the Niner's game on Sunday," Tom says. "It was supposed to be a surprise."

"What about Saturday?"

"My father's coming up. We were all going to your parents' house for dinner. Now I guess I'll have to cancel dinner. But my father's not going to cancel his trip. He's already on the road."

My parents' house for dinner? Why didn't he tell me that before? I glance at the tons of e-mail on my laptop and wonder if my parents or Dee or even Tom sent a little notice. I've been too busy to check even my voice mail.

"Can't the two of you come up? We can go out to dinner and maybe a movie," I say, feeling a little lift in my chest. "And we can go out to breakfast before the game. There's a quaint little shack above the river that serves the best homemade biscuits."

"I'll ask, but I can't promise," Tom says. "My father's going to be exhausted from driving. And I don't know if he'll want to spend another two and a half hours in a car just for dinner and a movie."

"And breakfast," I remind him.

He chuckles lightly. "And breakfast." Then, in a low, serious voice, he says, "I miss you."

"I miss you, too," I say.

Squish-squash. Squish-squash.

Damn, she's back early. A terrible heaviness settles in my chest, making it hard to breathe. "I have to go, Tom," I say, and hang up without waiting for his good-bye.

The glass door swings back. Ms. Lashay squish-squashes over to my desk and squints at my laptop monitor.

Quickly, I snap it shut.

"Love notes to your boyfriend?" she asks.

"Why does my personal life interest you?" I ask. I'm tired of her parading around like the evil stepmother in Cinderella, shoving more work on my desk when she knows I just want to quit and walk away from it all.

"Just a bit of advice, dear. Men come and men go, but your career is forever."

This isn't my career. It's a JOB. Just-Over-Broke. Remember?

But I can't tell Ms. Lashay that, can I?

I smile sweetly. "Is that why you haven't heard from your son?"

She stiffens, and the grin on her face falls away. "Please, don't talk about Alex."

Ah-ha. Just as I suspected. They haven't spoken since Thanksgiving. He's probably upset with her for not switching her business to commercial loans. And she's probably miffed because he only thinks of her in relation to business. I sit back and decide to use this bit of information to my advantage. "Then, please, don't mention Tom."

Our gazes meet, and for a moment, I wonder which one of us will speak first. But we're both silent. It's as if there is finally an understanding between us.

# CHAPTER 26

▼

"When you're not running away from things, you're closed off," Tom says on the phone, during our Saturday night conversation.

I kick off my heels and tuck myself into Val's comfy couch in front of the fire and turn down the volume of the weekend edition of *Entertainment Tonight*. Tom just got back with his father from dinner at my parents' house and I just got back from hosting an open house an hour away in Glen Ellen. Only three groups of people came through—a family with two small kids, an elderly couple with nothing better to do, and three college students looking for a rental. That's it. I was so disappointed I stopped at a tiny restaurant and ordered dinner and a glass of chardonnay and stared at the rows and rows of vineyards until the sky turned black, as black as I've been feeling lately, before driving home.

"I'm not closed off," I tell him. "I'm trapped."

"Only if you think you are."

I sigh. Tom hasn't had a job since he started his brokerage after receiving his master's degree ten years ago. What does he know about being an employee with a crappy contract? Nothing.

"Your parents invited me over for brunch next weekend," Tom says. "I think you should join me."

"Only if this house goes into escrow."

"Can't Ms. Lashay host her own open house?"

"She's busy. Charity balls, visits to her lenders in convalescent homes, even a trip to the county jail to bail out a borrower for drunk driving so he could sign papers on his condo purchase."

"Sounds like she doesn't have a life."

"She does. It's just not about her family."

"She's alone?"

"Yes." I stretch out on the couch and wiggle my toes. I wish Tom was here to massage them. "She has a son, but he's grown up, in L.A. They tried to reconcile over Thanksgiving, but they're not speaking with each other again."

"Sounds like you and your parents."

"Not fair," I say, sitting up. "I'm *nothing* like my boss. Sure, I haven't responded to my mother's voice mails or my father's snail-mail letters or Dee's e-mails, but it's only because I've been busy."

Tom sighs. "You're more like her than you think you are."

My face flushes with fury. "How dare you compare me to my employer? I'm not some control-freak who lords my power over other people and consoles myself with donating my love and generosity to strangers."

"Okay, you're right," Tom says. "You don't give your love or generosity to strangers."

I sink back onto the couch and feel my shoulders relax. "Thank you."

"You save them up for a rainy day and donate them back to yourself."

"What?" My fist clenches the receiver so tightly my wrist hurts.

He tries to chuckle. "When you closed the Ingrid deal a year ago what did you do with the proceeds?"

Think, think, think. Oh, yes, that couple who bought the condo through the referral network of their church. Only they misdialed the number on the directory and ended up with me, and I played along with them, pretending to be part of their church. I promised to donate 10% of my commission back to their church. And I bought a Gucci handbag instead.

"But that was just once," I cry, trying to defend myself.

"Well, what about the Lowe deal? Or the Choi deal? You wouldn't cut your commission to fix the roof or clear the pest, and you would have lost the commission if I hadn't rescued you by hiring my handyman to do the work." He pauses thoughtfully. "You never did pay me back for those favors."

I guess from Tom's perspective I'm a selfish woman consumed by possessions. But he just doesn't understand. When I had money, I'd indulge in shopping sprees and spa dates to soothe over any bad feelings I had. Now that I don't have money, I dodge them. Or bury them under a mound of work. And blame my damn contract. Oh, god.

Maybe he's right. I'm running away from my problems when I should be confronting them directly like any grown up would do. That's why I haven't spoken with my family yet. I would have to admit my fault in the situation, and that seems—distasteful—right now. Okay, distasteful is a bit of an understatement. Repugnant is more like it. But isn't that childish and immature? After all, I'm thirty-five, not thirteen. Maybe I should call them right now. Apologize to Dee. Maybe even offer to pay for a new camera. Yes, that's what I'll do.

"I've got to go," I tell Tom.

"Did I say something wrong?"

"No." I take a deep breath. "I'm going to call my parents."

"You are?"

"Yes." I stand up and turn off the TV. "Wish me luck, okay?"

"You'll do fine," he says. "I love you."

"Love you, too."

After our brief goodbye, I dial my parents' number and wait. My heart thumps louder than the crackling fire in the woodstove. What if Dee answers and when she hears my voice she hangs up on me? What if my father answers and wants to know why I left on Thanksgiving? What if my mother nags me about when I'm moving back to San Jose? Stop it. Think of something else. Dee will be happy to hear from me. My father will only want to talk about golf. And my mother will ask me what I want for Christmas.

On the third ring, before anyone can answer, I hang up.

A week before Christmas, it starts to rain again. Lots and lots of rain. The roof sounds like a death metal song on repeat, all hard edges with no end in sight. It's getting harder and harder to run up and down the hill in the mornings, and the roads are starting to flood. But I can still make it to the office.

I've closed all of the loans except for the Johansen file, and I've finally received an accepted offer on Ms. Lashay's listing, which means I can go to San Jose this weekend and stay a few days for Christmas. When Tom discovered I flaked on my phone call to my parents, he suggested I talk to them at Christmas dinner with him by my side. "For courage," he said. I really don't want to go, but I agreed to it anyway. I have to talk to them eventually, right? They're my family, and I owe them an explanation.

But some part of me is dreading the holiday visit.

On the day before I leave, Ms. Lashay stops by my desk. "You've done good work," she says, eyeing the closed files on my desk. "Too bad I'm losing you at the end of the year.

You've learned so much in so little time. Just like I knew you would."

I lean back in my chair and glance up at her. Her eyes sparkle with tears. I'm surprised. She's always nitpicking me about everything. I didn't know she cared that much.

"You know I didn't expect you to take orders forever." She sniffs. "I just wanted to teach you a level of humility that prepares you for the larger things in business and life. Like how to be compassionate."

My face contorts with suppressed laughter.

"What's so funny?" she snaps.

Should I tell her? Why not? In a few more days, I'll never see her again. "You haven't been compassionate toward me at all. You've tied me to a contract that's kept me from moving on with my life."

"You mean your move back to San Jose?" Her steady gaze criticizes me, but her lips quiver with emotion. "That's not real life." She glances away.

I follow her gaze through her office window to the picture of a twelve-year-old tow-headed boy smiling in a photograph on her desk. "You miss your son," I say, instinctively.

She shakes her head, as if to deny it. "It's too late for me," she admits. "I've made too many mistakes there. But you—" She takes a deep breath and holds it. "You seem to have found someone who cares about you, no matter how crazy your career is, and that's more precious than any loan I'll ever make." She bends down to embrace me, and I smell her sticky hair spray and baby powder skin against my cheek. "Take care, Trina. I will miss you greatly. You are the daughter I've always wanted but never had."

Really? Is this how she treats family? No wonder her son doesn't speak with her.

But I decide to be kind. "Thank you, Ms. Lashay." I turn my head and kiss her cheek. "It's been quite an experience working for you."

"Drive safely," she says, stepping back and dabbing her eyes with a handkerchief.

"I will."

I wake up the next morning to the blaring beep-beep-beep of the Emergency Broadcast System on Val's clock radio. "Emergency crews have closed off the Sonoma Marin line due to flooding," the announcer says. "Please keep your radio turned to our station for further notice."

I lean back against the pillows and sigh with secret relief. I won't have to face my parents or Dee after all. I get to spend the holiday alone. Without leaving the bed, I reach for my laptop on the night table and dash off a quick e-mail to Tom, letting him know I won't be down this weekend because the roads are closed. "Please, let my parents know," I add.

Within minutes, I get a response. "Why don't you call or e-mail them? I'm sure they'd love to hear from you. Love, Tom."

I contemplate writing my mom an e-mail since my dad doesn't use a computer. I don't want to write Dee. Not yet, anyway. And I don't want to repeat the jittery nervous failed phone call fiasco.

"Dear Mom," I type. "I know I should have called or written earlier, but I've been incredibly busy with work, as Tom probably already told you. Still, that's no excuse. I was meaning to talk to you on Christmas, but since the roads are closed and the storms are supposed to continue until New Year's, I don't think I'll be at Christmas dinner as I had originally planned."

So far, so good. I reread what I've written and contemplate whether or not I should add some details about work and Ms. Lashay to spice up the "busy with work." But I decide against it. Too dramatic, as Val would say.

I move the mouse over to the SEND button when the phone rings.

Sitting back against the pillows, I listen for the answering machine to start.

"KK," says my mother. "Are you there? KK? Please answer. Tom says you're rained in and won't be here for Christmas. Are you okay?"

Damn, I can't bear the pain in her voice. But I can't move my legs out of the warm, comfy bed either.

"KK, it's your mother. I'm concerned. Please call."

Click.

I consider the e-mail I'm about to send. Should I add an addendum? How about, "I was in the shower when you called. Sorry to miss you. I would call you back, but—" But what? I can't think of a clever excuse. What's the use? She didn't sound mad, only concerned. If I don't respond, she'll only get sick with worry and then Tom will call wanting to know why I'm such a coward when it comes to my family. Sheesh.

Finally, after much deliberation, I delete my previous message and simply type, "I'm fine."

Okay. I can do this. I take a deep breath and click the SEND button.

An hour later, I get a response. I'm sitting at the kitchen table debating between adding more kindling to the wood stove or microwaving a bag of popcorn when the message arrives in my inbox.

"Glad you're okay. Please call when you can. Love, Mom."

I stare out the window at the silver rain slashing through the gloomy afternoon sky. When I moved into Val's cottage, I didn't think about winter. I didn't care that he lived in a flood zone. Now I wonder if I should have given this whole thing a lot more thought.

Turning back to my laptop, I reread my mother's message. Is she pretending everything is all right between us or is everything all right between us because she's already forgiven me? I can't tell. And I'm too afraid to ask.

On Christmas Day, the power goes off. The phone is down and my BlackBerry doesn't get reception. With trembling hands, I suit up in a yellow rain slicker and head out into the street. How bad is it? I tuck my head toward my chin and dodge to the neighbor's house. Rapping on their front door, I anxiously wait. No one answers. They must have left before the storm. I go down to the next house. Gray rain pelts against my head and shoulders and slides off the jacket to the heavy boots on my feet. I rap on the front door and wait. Again there is no answer. I trudge further down the hill. My foot slips in the mud, and I stumble. Leaning against a rusty car in a turnout, I squint through the redwood trees and the torrential downpour. My heart thumps loudly in my ears. At the bottom of the hill, yellow tape ropes off the street from the main road.

I'm trapped.

Scrambling up the hill to the cottage, I take off the rain slicker and hang it against the back of the front door and unlace the heavy boots. Sinking to my knees in front of the wood stove, I take a few deep breaths.

Okay. Don't panic. It's probably just a precautionary measure, nothing to be concerned about.

Maybe I should take a long hot bath and relax a little.

But as I lie in the tub beneath a cloud of bubbles, my mind loops around and around to the same thing: I'm stuck in the cottage with only a few days worth of food and water.

And I have to get to work tomorrow to wire funds on the Johansen loan.

I get out of the tub and decide to dress up. A little makeup and perfume always makes me feel better. But no matter how many silk dresses I slip on or how many spurts of Euphoria I spray on my ankles, behind my knees, between my breasts, and on my wrists, I still can't stop thinking the same thing: I'm a prisoner in Val's cottage.

And I need to get to work tomorrow.

Padding out of the bedroom, I pause at the round table in the kitchen nook where my laptop lays. Ah-ha! Maybe I'll check the news and see how bad it really is. Logging on, I surf the web. "Russian River Floods, Five People Missing." That can't be good, I think, scanning the article. Oh, but the photos are worse. A man and his daughter clutch a sofa as it rushes down the muddy river to the Pacific Ocean. I feel the wooden planks beneath my feet and wonder if the house will slip off its foundation and slide down the hill to the main road and float down the river.

Stop it. That's no way to think. Especially on Christmas.

I decide to dash off a quick mass e-mail to everyone in my address book, letting them know I'm alive and well, in spite of what the media is reporting.

Twenty minutes later, Tom e-mails a response. "Happy holidays!" he writes. "Leaving for your parents' house right now. I'll tell them you're okay. Hugs." A tiny icon with a smiley face and big arms move out to embrace me. I smile. How cute.

One hour later, Val writes, "The can opener—regular, not electric—is in the right hand cabinet behind the fire extinguisher. You can cook on the wood burning stove. Use that metal pad I use when I heat tea, okay? I've got tons of emergency food in the basement along with lots of bottled water and a case of wine. Enjoy!"

Always practical, my Val.

My mother e-mails next. "Glad to hear you're okay, dear. Your father says hello. Wish you could have made it. Tom brought his famous mashed potatoes. Yum!"

My father doesn't use a computer. He says it's the invention of the devil. He doesn't even own a cell phone. I guess it doesn't really matter. Whatever I tell to either one of them, the other one finds out about eventually. It's like they took their wedding vows a little too seriously; they're one person sometimes.

Dee is the last one to write. "What's your problem? Still afraid to face us? My camera cost $250 to fix. Too expensive to buy a new one. Sometimes you can be so selfish. Tom deserves someone better. Dee."

Geez, I love you, too, sis.

Before turning off my computer to conserve the battery, I check the status of the roads. Nothing will be opened until emergency crews are able to clear the fallen trees from the main road. I guess I'd better send Ms. Lashay an e-mail. "Dear Ms. Lashay," I write, "I'm trapped in a cottage above the Russian River until the roads open. I never even made it to San Jose. If I'm not at work tomorrow, could you please make sure the funds get wired on the Johansen loan? We're scheduled to close before New Year's. Thanks, T."

I shut off my laptop and stare out the window through the weeping redwood trees. Somehow the rain sounds louder, more menacing than it did just two hours ago.

I open up a can of beans and a bottle of Merlot. Although I'm warm from the fire and full from the food and wine, I feel cold and empty. Staring at the flickering shadows from the candles lit up all over the tiny room, I wonder if Dee's right. Am I selfish?

Two days after Christmas, I'm still trapped in the house. The power is still down. So are the phones. The rains have only gotten worse, creating a slide at the bottom of the hill that the emergency crews hope to fix by the end of the week, if the rain stops.  It has to stop, right?

Trying to conserve my slowly dying battery, I log onto my computer e-mail account only twice a day to check messages. Tom and Val have both written to see if I'm all right. Mr. Leggins has sent a reminder about the mediation date in two weeks. I scan through the messages one more time, hoping for news about the Johansen loan. But there's nothing. I frown. Ms. Lashay is usually so prompt and professional, but I haven't heard from her. She hasn't even responded to the first e-mail I sent on Christmas.

Maybe she's rained in, too, and the battery on her laptop has died.

I'm getting sick of canned food and wine. I'm getting sick of these four walls. I'm getting sick of my own company.

I want to get out and run, run, run.

Being trapped in a house by myself gives me plenty of time to think. Too much time, in fact. I'm starting to review the last year of my life and wonder if everything I've said and done and felt was all a bit too impulsive and child-like. Like moving to Sonoma County when Tom put up the billboard. And starting a new business when the one I already had was on the brink of success. And selling all my beautiful belongings to pay the bills I didn't need to accrue if I had just stayed in San Jose. And making enemies with Dee. Over her photos. I know I shouldn't have thrown her camera, but I was angry. I normally don't throw anything. That's two year old tantrum behavior, isn't it? I should have at least offered to pay for the repair, right? Or e-mailed her back and said, I'm sorry. That's what I would have wanted, right? Maybe she's right. I am selfish.

"Please, stop raining," I beg whoever's listening. I can't stay inside much longer. I'm starting to hate myself.

# Chapter 27

▼

Two days after the New Year begins, the roads open. I haven't heard from Ms. Lashay. I feel bad for missing five days of work. That's not how I wanted to end my employment.

I decide to go to the office and collect my belongings before calling Tom to let him know I'll be coming home tonight. I park in the huge rear lot of the office building we share with a few other companies. The back door is open. Winding my way around the brass tables and chairs lining the fountain, I forego the ultra-slow elevator for the stairs.

A strong odor of Red Door wafts down the stairwell. I glance up. A tall, model-thin woman in her mid-twenties with dark hair and bronze skin dressed in a Dolce and Gabbana suit I would have killed to have owned rushes around the corner with a cell phone plastered against her ear. Candie? What's she doing here? Did Ms. Lashay invite her and Alex for Christmas? I stop to greet her, but she's yelling into her phone. "Are you stupid or deaf? I told you to get me Jessica Simpson, not her assistant. I need a quote by noon." Candie nudges past me, and our shoulders crash. Ouch! I rub the sore spot, wondering if I'm out of shape or if Candie is made of steel. Either way, I feel like I'm going to bruise.

Candie shoots me a venomous look, but keeps talking to the person on the other end of the phone. "I don't care if you have to lie to get her. Get her for me now." She bounds down the stairs and turns the corner.

I continue upstairs. The office is brightly lit. I push open the glass door. A man in his mid to late thirties is hovering over my desk like a giant bee above a flower.

"Alex?"

He glances up. "It's Zachary."

Alex. Zachary. It's all the same to me. I set my purse on the desk. "It's good to see you again, Zachary. Are you visiting for the holidays?" Maybe that's why Ms. Lashay hasn't responded to my e-mails. She's been busy entertaining.

His face looks pinched like I've suggested something offensive. "Actually, I'm here on business. My mother's had a stroke."

I gasp. "Is she going to be all right?"

He shrugs. "Maybe. Maybe not." He waves his hand over my desk. "These files are a mess."

I blush, suddenly embarrassed.

A glass doors fly open and a breeze smelling of Red Door billows up from behind me. I turn. Candie is yelling at someone on the phone. As soon as she sees us, she barks goodbye and snaps her phone shut. "What's going on?" she demands.

Whatever happened to manners?

I turn toward Zachary and ask, "Did funds ever get wired for the Johansen loan?"

He scrunches up his forehead in thought. "Yes, I believe I took care of that. There's a check for you in your top desk drawer."

Candie sidles up to Zachary and asks, "How long is this going to take?"

He shrugs. "I don't know. Let me ask KK."

God, why did I ever give him my nickname? "I prefer Trina," I say. "Only my family calls me KK."

Although Zachary is six inches shorter than me, he maintains my steady gaze as if we were the same height. "Okay, Trina. If you don't mind going over a few things with me—"

"Actually, I've already put in my notice. I just came to get my check."

"You aren't staying?"

"Technically, I don't work here anymore."

I remove the check from the top desk drawer and key in the numbers on the calculator, making sure I did not get shorted on my commissions. But the numbers are correct. I sigh with relief. "Thank you," I say to Zachary, tucking the check in my purse. "What hospital is your mom at? I'd like to say goodbye."

The phone rings. Zachary picks it up. "Smart Loans, Mr. Lashay speaking." He looks like a bobble head doll when he nods. "Of course, just one moment." He hands the phone to me. "It's Betty from the Dead Husbands Society."

I frown, feeling the hairs at the back of my neck bristle. How dare he refer to Ms. Morgan, Ms. Lashay's oldest and dearest lender and friend, as a member of the Dead Husbands Society. She was never even engaged.

Sinking into my chair with the eyes of an audience surrounding me, I say as brightly as I can, "Trina speaking."

"Oh, thank goodness you're back," Ms. Morgan gushes. "I told the doctor not to call Alex, but he has power of attorney."

"How is Ms. Lashay?"

"She's conscious, but she's having a hard time talking." She drops her voice. "Alex and Candie haven't been too kind."

"When can I see her?" I stare at the mound of paperwork littered over my desk and wonder if it's always been this messy, or if I'm just starting to notice it now that I no longer have to deal with it. "I want to say goodbye."

"You aren't moving back to San Jose, are you?"

"Yes, I am. I've already fulfilled the terms of my contract."

"Please, dear, I'm begging you to reconsider," Ms. Morgan says. "I don't trust Alex and Candie. You're the only one who knows how she runs her business. Without you around, I don't know what will happen."

I think about my promise to Tom. To get back together. In life and in business. It's a promise I made over a month ago. A promise I've postponed for one reason or another. I know I can't put it off much longer and expect Tom to sympathize. I need to get back to San Jose as soon as possible. Preferably today. "I'm flattered you think so highly of me, Ms. Morgan, but I have other obligations. To my boyfriend and our business."

"Not that insensitive chauvinist who put your legs on a billboard?"

I cringe. Does everyone know? I should have never confided in Ms. Lashay. Should I deny it? No, there's no use in lying. "Yes, but he apologized." At least, I can try to make Tom look better than he is.

"I would have burned him at the stake."

I flush, remembering how indignant I was when I first saw the billboard.

"Dear, if you stay, I'm sure Ms. Lashay will compensate you handsomely," Ms. Morgan bargains. "Once she gets better."

"It's not about money. It's about love."

"Love?" she grumbles. "When did love do anything but injure people? Look at Ms. Lashay. She's loved her son his whole life and he's bent on destroying her."

I glance up at Zachery Alexander Lashay II and his girlfriend. "It's doesn't always end badly."

"Name one person it ended nicely for."

I don't have to think. "My parents. They've been married almost 40 years and they're still happy."

Ms. Morgan sighs. "Well, dear, if there's no reason left in you, then you might as well go. I'll be by at noon to take you to the hospital. Just be quick about your goodbye. I don't want you to break the old woman's heart."

I glance down at my feet. "Don't worry. I won't."

Ms. Morgan offers to drive to the hospital. I slip into her old Toyota Camry. It smells of baby powder and hairspray. The scent reminds me of Ms. Lashay, and my heart contracts with worry. "How did she have a stroke?"

Ms. Morgan waits till we reach a stop light before she says anything. "She was having Christmas dinner at my house when she mentioned her arm had fallen asleep. Then it was her leg. I knew something was wrong, so I called 9-1-1." She shakes her head sadly. "This wouldn't have happened if she had gone to the doctor like I told her to, but she wouldn't listen to me. She thinks she knows better. But she doesn't. She's in denial. About her health. And her son. She thinks she can trust him, but he's a no good bastard just like his father was."

"Isn't that a little harsh? After all, he did come up to help out."

"He's only interested in her business." Ms. Morgan purses her lips. "On Thanksgiving, he asked if she would consider a joint venture in commercial loans. She kindly turned him down. That's the last time they've spoken with each other." She pulls into a parking slot and turns off the engine. "Honestly, dear, I think you should stay. At least until she's better."

I stare at my hands twisted in my lap. "I can't. I've already promised Tom."

"If he's as good a man as you say he is, he'll understand."

Maybe. Maybe not.

The hospital is bright and clean with wide hallways. It smells of Pine Sol. In a private room, tucked at the end of the hall, a tiny woman as withered as a blanched raisin lies beneath a crisp white sheet with an IV taped to one arm. Oh. My. God. Is that Ms. Lashay? As if reading my thoughts, the woman struggles to turn her head. A thick blue vein pulses above her right eyelid.

My chest contracts with fear and pity. How can I say goodbye?

Ms. Morgan nudges me. "Make it quick."

I step next to the bed but don't sit down. "How are you doing?" I ask, although Ms. Morgan has warned me she cannot talk yet.

Ms. Lashay's brown eyes glow with recognition. She opens her mouth, but nothing comes out.

I can't help but think of my parents slowly approaching their seventies. They could have a stroke. They could end up in a hospital like this. And I might not even know it. A prickle of apprehension inches up my spine. I shiver, wondering if Tom would be at my parents' sides long before I would if something happened to them. I know Dee wouldn't call unless it was to gloat about being the better daughter.

Ms. Lashay looks so old and helpless in the middle of the white hospital bed. Wrinkles crease her face. The muscles in her arms are ropey knots. I grab her hand and squeeze. Miraculously, she squeezes back.

"Is there anything I can do before I go?" I ask. "Squeeze once for yes, two for no."

She squeezes once. I wait, but she doesn't squeeze again.

Oh, why did I ask? I try to imagine what she might need. "Do you want me to take care of business till you get better?"

She squeezes twice.

I glance at the pitcher of water by the bed. "Are you thirsty?"

She squeezes twice again.

I turn to Ms. Morgan, wondering what Ms. Lashay might need. Ms. Morgan's hazel eyes fill with tears, but she doesn't say a word.

I take a seat on the edge of the bed and stroke the papery crinkles of Ms. Lashay's hand. What could she want? She has a friend who cares for her like family. And in spite of Ms. Morgan's fears, I know Alex, I mean Zachary, can handle business. If his bitchy girlfriend stays out of it.

Ms. Lashay moves her mouth again, and this time there is a faint sound. "Alex," she says.

I lift my eyebrows. "You want me to take care of Alex?"

She squeezes my hand once.

Yes.

After Ms. Morgan drops me off at the office, I drive back to Val's cottage. Although it is the middle of winter, I drive with the top down. Cold wind brushes against my cheeks. I think of Ms. Lashay squeezing my hand to let me know she wants me to take care of her son. She can't be serious. She knows I can't take care of my own finances. How can she expect me to take care of another human being?

Inside the cottage, I drop my purse on the coffee table and hurry into the bedroom to pack. Although it is cold, I refuse to light a fire. I'll only be here a few more minutes anyway. The stillness of the cottage leaves me only with my thoughts which keep circling back to work and Ms. Lashay and her son, Zachery or Alex or whoever he is.

Music. That's what I need. I stroll through the living room and turn on the portable stereo on the bookshelf next to Val's Emmy. Lilting jazz tumbles into the room. I return to the bedroom. In my haste to leave, I forgot to make the bed. The white sheets remind me of Ms. Lashay lying on the hospital bed with her brown eyes staring up at me. Damn. Why won't that woman leave me alone? She's miles away but she's here, haunting me with her odd request. Take care of my son. Hell, I can't even take care of myself.

The phone rings.

I reach over the bed and grab the extension. "Hello?"

"It's me."

I suck in my breath. *Tom*. He's probably calling to see when he can expect me.

"I'm packing," I tell him. For some reason, I start to sniffle. I really didn't want him to call. I was going to wait until I was just miles from our house before letting him know I was in town. I didn't want him to worry about me, and I didn't want to have to discuss Ms. Lashay on the phone.

"What's wrong?" he asks, sensing the tears in my voice.

What's the use of lying? I'm terrible at it anyway. I sink down on the mattress and toss my La Perla bras into the suitcase. "My boss had a stroke," I say. "Her son came up from Southern California to help, but he's more a thorn in the side than anything else." Should I mention Ms. Lashay wants me to take care of him? Would he laugh? I wanted to laugh when I heard her say his name. How can I reconcile them to each other when they haven't been able to for years? I'm an outsider.

"I'm sorry to hear that," Tom says. "Are you feeling guilty for leaving?"

"No, it's not that." Should I tell him? Why shouldn't I? It's not like he's going to tell my parents, is it? And, even if he did, why would they care? They already hate everything I've done in the last year. Or so it seems.

"She wants me to get involved in her personal business. I've never been asked to do something like that."

He laughs. "What does she want you to do? Shampoo her dog?"

I wish it was that simple. "She wants me to take care of her son."

"I thought her son was grown. Did she adopt a child?"

"No, she only has one son. And he definitely doesn't need to be taken care of. Or if he does, he has a girlfriend who's capable of it. I feel really uncomfortable being asked to interfere."

Tom clears his throat. "Maybe you misunderstood her wishes. She's sick, right? A lot of people don't think clearly when they aren't well." He pauses. When I don't say anything, he continues. "I wouldn't worry about it. She's your former boss. You already stayed past your notice. You aren't obligated to her for anything."

Ms. Lashay may only be my former boss, but she's so much more to so many other people. Her clients bring her homemade cookies for no reason. Her lenders come by to take her out to lunch. Her entire business is run like one extended family, not a corporation. How do I know where one obligation ends and another begins in an environment like that?

"If you feel bad about it, then stay a couple of days to make sure her son knows how to run her business," Tom says. "But don't do anything else."

"You want me—to stay?"

"Well, that's up to you. If I was all alone and Su had just quit and I was laid up in the hospital, I'd be thrilled if she took care of things until I was able to."

I finger the lace fringe of my favorite teddy. I was hoping to wear it tonight during my reunion with Tom. How selfish is that? Even Tom would expect his former employee to stay. But for how long? I toss the teddy aside. One week? Two? Surely, not more than a month, right?

"Okay, I'll stay for a little while."

"Cheer up," Tom says. "I'm only a phone call away."

But that's not the same as wrapping my arms around his broad back and kissing that tender spot between his neck and shoulder until he can't stand it any longer and he scoops me up and carries me to our bedroom.

I get off the phone feeling worse, not better.

Padding into the living room, I light a fire.

It's going to be a long night.

# CHAPTER 28

▼

"What type of idiot are you?" Candie yells at Alex, as soon as I walk into the office the next morning. "I told you to get me a decaf, non-fat, double cappuccino, light foam. You brought me a decaf, non-fat, double latte with nothing but foam."

I contemplate turning around and exiting through the double glass doors, taking a ten minute break while they finish their discussion, but Alex's eyes widen with surprise when he notices me. "You're back?"

I shrug. "I've decided to stay a little while longer and help out. If you need me."

"Of course, I do." He motions for me to enter Ms. Lashay's office. I stand awkwardly in the doorway. Candie tilts her cup of Starbucks dangerously above Alex's fine blond hair. Will she do it? I wonder. Will she dump the coffee on his head?

Alex scoots the chair away from his girlfriend and reaches over to hand me a sheet of paper. "We have a potential client arriving around noon. If you don't mind talking to them, I'd appreciate it. Candie and I have another appointment."

I take the sheet of paper and leave the office, closing the door discretely behind me. Sitting at my desk, I read over the brief notes: couple with baby needs to refinance for medical reasons. Need quick close. Surgery in two weeks. Ask about income, assets. Pull credit. Call appraiser or pull comps. Compute LTV. Discuss possible loan scenarios.

The door swings open and Candie yells, "I have a telephone interview with Cher at eleven. If it runs late, don't order for me. I don't trust your judgment, you idiot." I hold my breath, pretending to check e-mail. She stalks through the office, her hips swaying beneath her tight DKNY pencil skirt. When the glass doors close behind her, I exhale.

I hear Ms. Lashay's voice in my head, *Take care of my son.*

I ignore it. My job isn't to voice my opinion about rage-addicted girlfriends. It's to obtain and close loans.

Alex appears beside my desk. He places his palms beside my keyboard. I stop typing.

"I'm sorry for the disturbance," he says. "I hope it didn't upset you."

*He's* sorry. For *her* disturbance. Why is he apologizing for her behavior?

Mind your own business.

"Um, no problem." I wish he would go back into Ms. Lashay's office and close the door. Then I can pretend I am alone and work without my conscience screaming, *Tell him to tell her off!*

He rubs his hands on the desk, as if checking for dust. His fingers are long and thin and pale. I wish he would stop touching my desk. All that movement is distracting.

"Do you mind helping me with these files?" he asks, pointing to the stack of green folders on the filing cabinet.

I glance up. "Those are closed. I haven't filed them yet."

"Why don't you file them now?"

Who does he think he is? The boss? I swivel in my chair. "Filing is not a top priority. I need to finish this investment opportunity package so I can find a lender to fund the

$180,000 first we promised the Kleins before they get antsy and go with one of our competitors."

He continues to trace mini-crop circles on my desk.

"Please, stop touching my desk." I take a deep breath, trying to stop my knee from jiggling. "It's making me nervous."

Alex removes his hands from my desk and drops them to his sides.

"Thank you." I swivel back to face the monitor.

"KK?"

I stop typing. "Call me Trina, please."

"Trina, do you have the password to QuickBooks?"

"Why?"

"I need to pay the bills and run the business till my mother gets better."

"We have a part-time bookkeeper that takes care of that. Ms. Lashay takes care of the mundane day-to-day tasks just like me. So, if you want to help, you can start inputting that 1003 into Calyx." I hand him a new loan application from the messy piles on my desk.

He stares at it like I've pulled a grenade out of my pocket and offered it to him. Very slowly, he says, "I don't do paperwork. I have a loan processor for that."

I drop the file back on my desk. This guy is annoying even without the fidgeting hand maneuvers. "Have you visited Ms. Lashay today?"

"It's upsetting. She can't communicate."

"She can squeeze a hand once for yes and twice for no."

He lifts his eyebrows. "You're kidding?"

"Why would I joke about her condition? It's heart-breaking. That's why I'm staying till she gets better."

"What if she doesn't get better? Are you going to stay then?"

"I'll stay as long as I'm needed."

"I appreciate it. I really don't want to have to hire someone. I won't be here forever. I have my own business to run. I'm hoping I can get things squared away in the next two weeks." He clasps his hands and rocks back on his heels. "Unless she dies, of course. Then I'll stay for the funeral. But I can settle her estate in L.A." He flashes a crooked smile. "Aren't attorneys wonderful?"

The glass doors part and Candie waltzes into the office with the cell phone against her ear. "Can I quote you on that?" she asks, smiling at the caller.

She stalks past us into Ms. Lashay's office and closes the door.

I stare at Alex. He drops his gaze.

"How is your relationship with your mother?" I ask.

He shrugs.

I think of Ms. Lashay lying on the hospital bed, staring up at her son, unable to say what's on her mind. "You do know that she loves you."

He laughs bitterly. "How would you know? You're just an employee."

"I'm also her friend. She tells me things."

His wary gaze penetrates me. "Like what?"

I sit back and cross my legs at the knees. Alex continues to stare into my eyes, patiently waiting for my answer. What should I tell him? There's so little that I know. Maybe it's best if I keep it vague. Let him think I know more than I actually do. Maybe then he'll go visit his mother and try to make amends, and when Ms. Lashay gets better, I can go home with a clean heart, knowing I tried my best to get them to communicate with each other. I clear my throat. "She divorced your father years ago, and she wishes she had a better relationship with you."

"Then why did she disappear? She never visited or called. I didn't even get a birthday card from her every year like some kids do."

"She did write." My shoulders tense. "But the letters were returned."

"Prove it."

I can't. I have no evidence. Just Ms. Lashay's word. That's good enough for me. But not for Alex.

Candie's voice rises through the closed door. "Zachary! Can you get me a glass of water?"

Without a word, Alex hustles into the break area and returns with a paper cup. Slipping into the office, he deposits the cup and returns, closing the door quietly behind him. He catches me watching him. "She's a really nice girl," he says. "And a top notch reporter. She didn't want to come, but I asked her to. She's really supportive."

I nod, pretending to agree.

Alex takes a seat in the reception area and flips through an old magazine.

"Aren't you going to help me with these files?" I ask, pointing to the stack on my desk.

Without glancing up, he says, "That's your job."

"Oh, that's right," I say, smacking the edge of the desk. "You don't handle paperwork. You might get a paper cut."

He glowers at me.

I can't believe this is the same man I met months ago at a gas station. "Are you only helpful to strangers?"

"What are you talking about?"

"You paid for my gas. And you wouldn't let me pay you back. But you won't file and you won't input any loan applications and you probably won't call any lenders. Why are you here if there's nothing you can or will do?"

His mouth twitches. "I was in a hurry and I couldn't wait for you to sort through your change. And from what my mother's said about you, you can't afford to pay me back."

Oh, really? "And this is coming from the man who told me to remember that not all men are assholes."

Alex's voice is cold and steady. "Are you calling me an asshole?"

I shrug. "If the description fits."

Candie storms out of the office. "Are you ready to go?" she asks.

Alex flings the magazine aside and stands up, his gaze never leaving my face.

Candie follows his stare. "What's going on?" She narrows her eyes at me.

I pretend not to notice.

Alex clears his throat. "Let's go," he says, smoothing his slacks. He offers Candie his arm, as if he's trying to show me his kindness extends beyond strangers. Candie curls her fingers against his sleeve and tosses her dark hair over her shoulder. "Ciao," she says, flashing her teeth.

"Goodbye," I say with a false smile. Good riddance.

A little before noon, a young man and woman enter through the glass doors with a blanket draped over an infant carrier. The man's woolly eyebrows practically hide his black eyes. The woman looks like the Mona Lisa, only sad.

I stand up and extend my hand. "Trina Kay. You must be?"

"Jack and Joanie Ivy," the man says. "And that's little Iris, sleeping."

Iris Ivy. What a horrible name for a little girl, I think. What are they trying to do? Set her up for a lifetime of teasing?

*Stay out of it*, I tell myself. Deep breath. Focus. *It's none of my business.*

I lead them into the conference room and gently shut the door.

Once they're settled in the big chairs, Mr. Ivy clasps his hands on the table. "We're tried three other lenders and we've been turned away. We saw your ad in the *Press Democrat* and thought you might be able to help."

Mrs. Ivy removes a crumpled piece of newsprint from the baby's diaper bag and slides it across the table.

I've seen the ad more times than I can count. *No credit, bad credit, no job, no problem, we can help.*

I start asking questions, filling in their answers on the loan application. They need $25,000. A small second. It shouldn't be a problem, I think.

While I step out of the office to run a credit report, I leave them with a bunch of disclosures to sign. Glancing at their negative score summary, I pick out a few medical collections and a couple of thirty day lates on their first mortgage. That's it. But that's enough to ruin anyone's credit.

Mrs. Ivy holds the baby in her arms when I return. The blanket covers the baby's head and back so I can't see her face or body.

I take my seat, mentally calculating the loan-to-value ratio. Even without pulling comps or ordering an appraisal, it doesn't look good. Their income is low, their credit is poor, their recent history is spotty. None of which would be problems, if the amount owed on their first mortgage wasn't so high. Maybe I should kindly turn them down.

Mr. Ivy hands me the signed disclosures. "After Iris was born, we both took a lot of time off work because of her health problems. She had to have heart surgery. I know we've missed a few payments here and there and had more bills than we could afford to pay from what the insurance wouldn't cover. But we've got some assistance with a few charitable donations from our church and a referral to a wonderful children's medical network from a friend who works at the American Heart Association. I'm back to work now. Joanie will return once this last surgery is complete.

"The problem we're having is that this last surgery isn't medically necessary. The insurance company considers it cosmetic, but we feel it's absolutely vital in order for our daughter to lead a normal life. That's why we're here. We thought we could take out a second on our home. It's our last hope. The surgery is scheduled in two weeks, and we don't want to have to wait till she gets older."

The baby starts to cry, and Mrs. Ivy takes her off her shoulder. The blanket falls away from her face. That's when I see it: a flesh-colored cauliflower-shaped tumor growing out of a cleft lip.

My chest contracts with a spasm of pain and my eyes fill with sudden tears. Oh, what hateful names the children will call her! Cauliflower-face, tumor baby, and worse. So much worse!

"May I hold her?" I ask.

"She's hungry," Mrs. Ivy explains, removing a bottle from the diaper bag. "If you'll let me get her started, then I can hand her to you."

I don't know why I asked to hold her. I don't know anything about babies. I've never even baby-sat.

Once the baby snuffles against the nipple and the milk starts to flow, Mrs. Ivy walks around the conference table and places the baby in the crook of my elbow, instructing me on the best way to cradle her so she won't fuss.

I stare down at little Iris Ivy. She has her father's woolly eyebrows, her mother's little nose, and that horribly misshapen mouth. Suddenly, I don't care about the terrible loan-to-value ratio or their poor credit rating. I want to help them help their daughter.

I don't care what I have to do. I'm getting them a loan.

# CHAPTER 29

▼

"You're in the middle of a soap opera," Val says, when he calls that night. "Forget *The Young and the Restless*, I want to know what happens at *Days at Smart Loans*."

"Hah-hah. Very funny, Val." I've told him about Ms. Lashay's stroke, her annoying son from Southern California who happened to be the Random Acts of Kindness guy I met at a gas station months ago, and his rude girlfriend. "I'm working on a loan for a couple with a baby who needs cosmetic surgery. You should see this kid. It's heart-breaking."

"You should see my co-star. He's heart-breaking." Val sighs. "I think I'm falling for him."

I groan. Val promised to never date another actor ever again. "It's too messy and complicated," he once said. "Someone has to leave the set, and it's always me." I try to gently remind him of his promise.

"It's not like I planned this," Val argues. "Antonio and I are great friends. He plays a stern Felix. And he's brilliantly funny. He has a streak of improv in him that I envy. We get along like you and I. It was completely harmless."

"Was? What happened?"

Val sighs. "I don't know exactly when or where it happened, but we've started getting a little too close for comfort. I mean I've told him all my secrets and he's told me all of his. And the next thing you know I'm thinking of him differently. He's no longer, Antonio, my pal, he's Antonio and he's hot."

"You've slept with him?"

"Oh, no, sweetie. You know once I sleep with someone I'm hooked. It's like a drug. I can't get enough of the person and I self-implode with desire. And then I get fired and sent home."

"That's why you promised never to date another actor ever again."

"We're not dating. That's just it. We hang out together. We talk. We share our likes and dislikes, the funny and sorrowful stories of our lives. This zinger of attraction is a complete surprise. I tried ignoring it, but that didn't work. I kissed him or he kissed me or we kissed each other. And I've never felt anything like it. Never." Val lowers his voice. "I think I'm in love."

*In love.* And I thought I had problems.

For the next couple of days, I push most of my work aside, focusing on my pet project, the Ivy Loan. I call through the database of lenders, but quickly learn that a bank full of independent-minded women with hearts of dollars and cents doesn't translate well with a maternal sob story. "That loan to value ratio is way too high," one lender says. "What if the surgery isn't successful or they find something else wrong and they need more cash? What if they drown all their money in this kid and neglect all their other financial obligations? They could end up in foreclosure or bankruptcy or, at the very least, delinquent. And you know how much money it will cost me to cure that?"

I can't deny their arguments. They're all sound. But they're all wrong, too.

In the middle of my phone marathon, Tom calls. "How much longer are you going to stay?" he asks.

Wasn't staying his idea? Then why the pressure to move? I sigh. With so many files piling up on my desk and so little help from Ms. Lashay's son and his pesky girlfriend, it looks like I'll be staying until Ms. Lashay returns to work. But I don't know when that will be. "Not much longer," I tell him. "I have a loan I need to fund. For a little girl who needs surgery."

"I thought you were just going to give her son a few pointers and then leave," Tom says. "Are you having second thoughts about us?"

I sit up, startled by his question. "I know I haven't called much, but I've been buried."

"Did you lie to me when you said we were getting back together?"

I flush with anger and spit, "Of course, not."

"Then why do you attract all these helpless people? First Ms. Lashay has a stroke. Now a girl needs surgery."

Why is he blaming me for other people's tragedies? It's not my fault. I can't pretend to be God and make everything better. And neither can he. "It's life," I tell him. "Things happen. You roll with the punches and make the best of it." I glance at the calendar on the wall next to my desk. "This loan needs to close next Friday. As soon as it does, I'll come down for a weekend visit. We can discuss everything then, okay?"

Tom's steady breathing barrels down the phone line. "I guess that will have to do." I imagine the vein twitching in his forehead, and the frown lines creasing his thin lips. It makes me want to hang up, jump in my Mercedes, and speed back to San Jose to cup his face in my hands and gaze up into his eyes and reassure him things are going to be all right between us.

But I can't. I have a loan to fund.

On my lunch break, I visit Ms. Lashay at the hospital. Ms. Morgan sits on a hospital chair next to the bed, reading aloud from Robert Kiyosaki's *Rich Dad's Prophecy*. Ms. Lashay blinks when she sees me. Ms. Morgan stops reading. They look like a couple. I think of Tom and wonder if he would stick by me through thick and thin or blame me for getting sick just like he blamed me for Ms. Lashay's stroke and Iris Ivy's disfigurement. After Thanksgiving and the removal of the billboard, I thought Tom and I could resume our old life together. But maybe I'm wrong. I've been wrong about so many things lately.

I sit on the edge of the bed and clasp Ms. Lashay's cool hand. "Are you feeling well enough to talk?"

She squeezes, yes.

Ms. Morgan gathers her book and purse. Her gray hair falls above her sparkling hazel eyes, and I glimpse the fire in them that keeps her alive. And even though she wears baggy housedresses and sensible shoes, she doesn't seem as frumpy as I first thought of her when we met months ago. She looks comfortable in her own skin and confident with her own style. "I'll leave you both alone," she says, touching my arm and smiling.

After she leaves, Ms. Lashay says, "Good to see you." Her voice is hollow and slurred and difficult to follow.

I lean forward, wondering where to start. "I'm doing well with the loans we have and the loans we're getting except for one." I pause, unsure of why I'm afraid to proceed when I know she will understand. "There's this couple with a baby who was born with some medical problems. Although the life-threatening issues have been resolved, they want a cash-out refi of $25,000. I told them I could get it for them before the surgery next week, but no one will fund the loan. It's 70% LTV." I take a deep breath and wait.

Ms. Lashay squeezes my hand. "I have money in my pension fund. Get Alex to sign."

Oh, great. One more impossible job for me to do.

"Can't you sign?"

She lets her hand slip out of my grasp. It dangles from her wrist like a broken hinge. "Can't write yet. Soon."

But will it be soon enough?

"If it's that important to you why don't you use your own funds?" Ms. Morgan asks, when I step outside the hospital room.

I lift my eyebrows, surprised she was listening. "I don't have any money. That's why I took this job in the first place. I was headed for bankruptcy."

Ms. Morgan purses her lips. "I think you've gotten yourself in over your head with this loan. Maybe you should call them up and tell them it's been cancelled."

I can't do that. I can't disappoint them. Not after how much work they've already gone through to get their daughter the care she needs.

No matter how much respect I have for Ms. Morgan and her devotion to Ms. Lashay, I understand she is different, much different than Ms. Lashay. Her compassion only extends to those she knows and loves. It is not reserved for strangers.

Turning on my heels, I stomp down the hall. I need to get back to the office. I need to talk to Alex.

"It's a poor business decision," Alex says, pacing back and forth in Ms. Lashay's private office.

I sit down on the chair opposite Ms. Lashay's plush executive chair, crossing and uncrossing my legs. I knew he wouldn't go for it. Why did I think to ask?

"It's her wishes," I tell him.

His brown eyes flash with determination. "I'm not letting her invest her money foolishly. If she dies, I'll be in charge of her estate. I don't want to have to go bailing irresponsible dimwits out of their own troubles."

I stand up, ready to fight. "These parents are hardworking individuals. They have no immediate family nearby to help.

He's returned to work and she's returning to work as soon as this surgery is done. They're a little behind in their payments, but that's understandable in a tragedy."

"Exactly," he spits. "Tragedies are born from fatal flaws."

He sounds like Tom. "The baby couldn't help being born with a cleft lip. It's no different than you being born with your mother's flyaway hair or me being born with my mother's skinny legs. It's not the parents' fault either. So don't punish them with your financial self-righteousness. Your mother wants to invest her capital in them, not their house. She knows sometimes the best business decisions aren't the ones with high yield interest rates. That's what makes her different than the competition. That's why she's been in business so long. She prides herself on helping people who can't get help anywhere else."

Alex stares at me. "You're crying."

I reach up to touch my cheeks. He's right. I'm crying.

He hands me a tissue from the desk. "I know you think you know my mother because you work with her, but you don't," he says, matter-of-factly. "She may masquerade as the touchy-feely business woman, but she's dark and conniving. She left my father and me penniless when I was just seven. The courts never enforced the palimony or child support payments owed to us. I'm here to collect my debts. When she dies, this company will be mine."

I can't believe him! He's here to destroy her, not nurse her back to health. "Your mother's getting better. Ms. Morgan said once she gains strength to stand up they're going to move her to a convalescent home. She'll be released before you know it. And back to work functioning like she's never been gone." I don't know if all of this is true or not, but I need a convincing argument and this sounds good.

The door flies open and Candie bustles in. She glances from Alex to me and back again. Her forehead creases. "What's going on?"

"Just a boring business discussion, dear," he says, reaching on his toes to kiss her. "If you're ready, we'll go to lunch." Turning to me, he adds, "I'd invite you to join us, but I believe you have a loan to cancel."

They walk out, arm in arm, through the double glass doors. When they are gone, I sink into Ms. Lashay's plush overstuffed chair and tilt my head back, staring at the ceiling. I think of Iris Ivy growing up with a cleft lip and a tumor on her face. I imagine all the pain and humiliation she will have to endure. And the tears well up beneath my lids and slide down my cheeks again. I sit up, grab a tissue, and dab the tears away. I don't know how I'm going to ever reconcile with my parents and my sister. I don't know if or when I'll be moving back to San Jose. I don't know if Val and Anthony will live happily-ever-after or if Val will be fired from yet another acting job. I don't know how long Alex and Candie plan to stay in Santa Rosa. Or if they'll kill each other first. I don't even know what's going to happen to Ms. Lashay.

There's only one thing I know for sure: I am not canceling this loan.

# CHAPTER 30

▼

The next day, I can't focus. I try working on other files, but my thoughts keep circling back to the Ivy loan. My stomach grumbles. My head aches. I glance at the clock on the wall. It's almost two. Grabbing my purse, umbrella, and raincoat, I head across the street to the deli for a sandwich.

In the warm deli, I pace back and forth in front of the display case, unable to decide. The smells of good old fashioned home cooking fill the air, and I think of my mother and the Thanksgiving dinner I missed. "I'll have the spinach quiche," I say, at last. After paying, I grab the tray and select a spot next to the window overlooking the business park with its wide walkways, pond and fountain, and huge parking lot. Dirty rain slants across the sky, splattering drops against the already too wet world.

Biting into the soft, dense, rich quiche, I think back over my most recent discussion with Alex. A wave of shame and disbelief washes over me. I've never cried during a business discussion. Never. No wonder he doesn't respect my position. I was acting like a whiny two-year-old, not a mature and disciplined equal.

Maybe he's right. Maybe Ms. Morgan's right, too. This is a poor business decision. I should let go of it. Call the borrowers and cancel their loan before the surgery next week.

But Ms. Lashay thinks it's a good investment. I respect Ms. Lashay. She's taught me so much in so little time that I can practically run the business without her.

I push the tray aside, prop my elbows on the table, and cup my head in my hands. I think of my dad, how I'd love to call and ask for his advice. But I can't. We'd have to talk about my absence on Thanksgiving and I really don't want to get into that right now. I have too much to deal with already.

In my mind, I scroll through all the possibilities, making sure I haven't missed anything that might make this loan possible. A glimmer of hope twinkles when I discover one more possibility that just might work.

I get up and return to the office. The brightly lit rooms are empty. I hang up my coat, tuck my umbrella beside my desk, and bring my purse into Ms. Lashay's office and close the door. I leave the office phone directed to voice mail. Sinking into the overstuffed chair, I notice the bottom desk drawer partially open. Someone must have been snooping, since Ms. Lashay usually keeps those drawers locked. A few papers stick up. Damn, that Alex or Candie. I reach down and shove the papers back into their confidential manila folders. I try to close the drawer, but it's jammed. Oh, god, something must have fallen from one of the other drawers when the lock was jimmied. I yank on the handle, and the drawer comes off the runner. Kneeling down, I reach into the cavity and pull out a crumpled wad of envelopes. I sit back on my heels, smoothing the envelopes against my thighs. They're addressed to Z. Alexander Lashay II and they're postmarked on various dates: 1981, 1984, 1987, 1989, 1990. Each one has also been stamped Return to Sender.

My fingers tremble. Should I open them?

I turn the first envelope over and place my finger against the seal. What am I doing? This is private property. What if Ms. Lashay discovered I had read her letters to her son? Would she ever forgive me? Could I ever forgive myself? After much deliberation, I remove my finger from the seal and set the envelopes on the desk. Placing the drawer on its runner, I slide it closed. I'm through with trying to get to the bottom of the mother-son mystery.

I've got work to do.

I take out my BlackBerry and call Tom.

"Hey, Trina, I was just thinking of you. I'm sorry I was a little harsh when I called yesterday. I just wish you were home."

*Home.* That elusive place where everybody loves and welcomes you. I haven't felt at home in so long, I can barely remember what it feels like. The sound of Tom's voice makes my heart ache. I want to wrap my arms around him, but I can only wrap my mind around his voice. What started as a small favor for Ms. Lashay has mushroomed into a mission to accomplish. "Tom, I need your help." I launch into my sales pitch. "Remember that girl I told you about yesterday, the one who needs surgery?"

"Yes," he says, slowly, cautiously, as if waiting for a trap.

"Well, I called everyone in Ms. Lashay's database and no one will take on the loan. They say the loan-to-value ratio is too high. But I know these people. They care about their daughter. They wouldn't do anything to hurt her, and that includes letting their payments slide because that would mean they would lose their home."

"And your point is?"

My skin bristles with irritation. Why can't he let me finish my story? Why must he insist I be as direct as he is? But if I continue to tell him all the good reasons why I want to help these people, he won't listen. So I need to get to the punch line without stumbling over my thoughts. I sit back and close my eyes, trying to focus on a few key words that will convince him to help me. "I want to fund the loan. But I need money. Can you loan me $25,000 from our business?"

Why is he pausing? Doesn't he know I've swallowed my pride to ask him for this favor? Why won't he just say, yes, and get the painful moment out of the way?

"But I thought we were back together," he says.

"I'm not asking you to buy my half of the business," I explain. "I'm just asking you to pull a little equity out of our business and invest it in this loan with me."

"What type of investment are we making?"

Why does he have to ask so many questions? Can't he be happy with the fact that I'm allowing him to help me? That I've finally broken down to accept his charity?

I take a deep breath. My legs jiggle with nervousness. I cross them, hoping to stop the distraction. "We'll be yielding eleven percent."

"That's pretty high in this market. There has to be a lot of risk if you can't find an investor."

"They're securing the loan with a second deed of trust on their primary residence," I explain.

"What's their credit score?"

I sigh. "Let me get the file."

"Don't bother," Tom says. "It doesn't sound safe."

"But it is. Completely."

"Then why can't you find anyone to invest their money?"

"Because they're only looking at the numbers, not the baby." My voice breaks. Why am I getting so emotional over this baby? She's not even my child. I take another deep breath before I continue. "She was born with a tumor and cleft lip. You should see it, Tom. It's horrible. She has to get it fixed before she starts preschool. I'm sure there are people who are already stopping and staring and making comments." I stop to wipe the tears streaking down my cheeks. Why am I crying? Am I having a nervous breakdown?

"When did you become a charitable organization?"

"It's not charity, Tom. It's a loan."

"Then why can't someone else come up with the funds?"

"Because the market is bad, just as you know. Everyone's scared of foreclosures. But I don't think there's anything to worry about. The father's returned to work and the mother will, too, after the surgery." I sniffle. "Please, Tom. You were going to buy the business before, but I was too proud to accept your help. I'm dropping my pride and asking you to help me now."

"Trina, I understand it's taken a lot for you to come and approach me like this, but I don't understand why now? Why this?"

"I don't understand it either, Tom. But something happened when I saw that little girl. And I just *have* to help her."

"You don't even like babies," he says.

He's right. I don't.

Outside the closed office door, I hear voices rising. I stand up and walk over to the blinds and peer through the window. Candie and Alex stand in front of my desk, arguing over something.

"Trina?"

What are they fighting about now?

"Trina, are you there?"

I sniff. "Yeah, I'm here. But I need to get back to work."

"You need to finish telling me why I should help you now."

I step back from the window and face the desk. I wish Ms. Lashay was here. I wish she could just fund the loan by herself without Alex's signature. Then I wouldn't be here on the phone with my boyfriend begging for money.

"If you don't tell me, Trina, I won't help you."

My temperature flares. "Stop being a bully, Tom. You're just like the kids on the playground picking on the smaller kids who can't defend themselves. You'd probably make fun of this little girl, calling her Cauliflower Face or Tumor Baby. And it's not fair. She can't help it. Just like I couldn't help having my mother's long skinny legs. But that didn't stop people from calling me, Stilts, even when I ran the fastest mile."

The voices outside are getting louder. I go to the window to investigate. Candie raises her arm and throws her cell phone. Alex ducks, and the phone hits the closed office door. The panel of glass beside the door reverberates. I jump back, startled, unable to believe what I just witnessed.

"I have to go, Tom." I don't wait for him to continue arguing or to say goodbye. I hang up and open the door.

"Why can't you both behave like adults?" I ask.

Candie places a tiny hand on the waistband of her Ralph Lauren suit and shouts, "Stay out of our business."

"Then get out of the office," I tell her. "I was on a business call. It's not very professional to hear people screaming and throwing things in the background. This isn't a daycare center."

Candie scrunches up her pretty face and stalks over to me to retrieve her phone from the floor. "This isn't even *your* office," she hisses.

When she's gone, I turn to Alex. "Do you have a moment?"

He nods.

We step inside Ms. Lashay's office. I shut the door. I motion for him to take a seat on one of the two chairs facing Ms. Lashay's overstuffed chair. He hikes up his slacks and sits on the edge of the chair by the window. I sit on the chair by the door.

"I really don't like interfering," I say, "but your girlfriend is beyond mean-spirited. She's abusive. I wouldn't put up with that, and neither should you."

My BlackBerry sings, "True Blue." I try to ignore it.

"Aren't you going to take the call?" he asks, when Madonna continues to sing.

I glance at the number. It's Tom. I let him go to voice mail. As soon as my BlackBerry stops ringing, I turn it off. "I don't take personal calls when conducting business."

He snickers. "I didn't know you had a personal life. I thought you were part of the Never Had a Boyfriend Club."

I flush with anger. He really knows how to irritate someone. Still, that's no excuse for Candie's behavior. "If you must know, that was my boyfriend calling."

His eyebrows lift. "You have a boyfriend?"

"Kind of. We broke up and then we got back together. I was going to move back to San Jose when your mother had her stroke. I decided to stay and help her till she gets better, but you and your psycho girlfriend are only making matters worse. If I didn't have this loan to fund, I would have walked out a long time ago."

He snickers. "So I was only slightly off. You're part of the Yo-Yo Boyfriend Club."

"I'm not part of any club," I say, trying to keep my voice even. "Just because you can't stand up for yourself with your girlfriend, does not give you permission to take out your anger and frustration on me." I stand up and open the door. "I'm sorry for interfering in your personal business. I promise I won't get between you two love birds again. Even if she's wielding a knife."

He crosses his legs and studies me. Why is he still sitting? Can't he tell from the open door that it's time to leave? I need to get back to work.

"Why did you break up with your boyfriend?" he asks.

Is he genuinely interested or trying to make small talk? "He put a picture of my legs up on a billboard to advertise our slogan, Kick Up Your Profits."

"Your slogan?"

"I co-own a real estate brokerage in San Jose. I was on the phone trying to get Tom to loan me some money so I can fund that impossible loan you want me to cancel when I was rudely interrupted." I wave my hand, motioning him to leave the office. "I have work to do. So if you don't mind leaving, I'd greatly appreciate it."

He slowly stands up. He's much taller than Ms. Lashay, but still shorter than me. His brown eyes look softer. He touches my elbow, and I'm surprised by the tingling warmth traveling up my arm. "I'm sorry for the disturbance."

"I accept your apology, but I won't let you apologize for her behavior. She needs to do that."

His lips tilt into a crooked smile. "You don't know Candie. She'll never apologize."

I nod, believing him. My glance catches the envelopes piled on the desk. I reach over and hand them to him. "I found these in Ms. Lashay's drawer. I think they're addressed to you."

He gazes down at the envelopes like I'm offering a poisonous snake.

Maybe this is a bad idea.

"On the other hand, it's probably nothing." I clutch the envelopes to my chest.

Alex slowly extends his hand. "I'll take them."

My shoulders tense. Oh, god. Why did I even mention the envelopes? What if Ms. Lashay wrote things she doesn't want anyone to see? Am I violating her privacy?

Alex continues to stand in front of me. I can't tell him I've changed my mind, can I? Reluctantly, I place the envelopes in his hand. His fingers brush against mine as they curl around the paper. My skin prickles with a slight jolt of electricity. Why is my body so sensitive around this man?

Alex places the envelopes in the inside pocket of his suit jacket. "So you're going to fund that loan, after all." He looks impressed.

I shrug. "Tom didn't say he would loan me the money. We got into an argument. He thinks it's a silly loan for a silly reason. But I just can't let that little girl go through life being picked on and teased for something that can be fixed." I whisper to myself, "I feel like the only one who understands what it feels like to be treated poorly for something beyond your control. Like your looks."

He frowns. "What's wrong with your looks?"

"My legs." I point to them like they're offensive and ugly. "People called me Stilts. It still hurts. I can't stand my legs. That's part of the reason why I run. To get away from it."

"How can you get away from something that's attached to you?" he asks.

I laugh. He's right. I've been running for most of my life, figuratively and literally, and no matter where I go, my problems still follow me.

"But I understand about the teasing," he says. "I was called Shorty. I'm still short for a man, but I know what you mean. It never goes away, even when you think it shouldn't affect you anymore. It's like a scar."

*A scar.* I wonder if that cosmetic surgery will leave a scar on Iris Ivy's face. But, it doesn't matter. Right now, I don't even know if I can fund the loan.

Alex squeezes my elbow. "I'll let you get back to work. Thanks for the talk." He releases my arm and walks across the office, stopping to gather his coat and umbrella before heading out the double glass doors.

"You're welcome," I say, although there is no one around to hear it.

# CHAPTER 31

*Beep-beep-beep.* I roll over in Val's bed and glance at my BlackBerry on the nightstand. Why is it beeping at me? It's Monday morning. I don't have to be to work until nine. It's only six-thirty.

When the sound doesn't stop, I reach over and grab the device, punching buttons until the beeping stops. The glowing reminder on the screen says, *Mediation.* I roll onto my back and groan. Why today?

On Friday, after Alex left, I spent the rest of the afternoon and evening catching up. With three other private money loans funded and closed, I had tons of paperwork to process: Department of Real Estate sheets to fill out, checks to deposit, servicing agreements to start, and files to be stacked away in the cabinets where they belonged. I didn't return Tom's call until I left the office at seven. His phone was off, so I left a message with all of my numbers. He called once over the weekend, but I was running down the hill and the call went directly to voice mail. By the time I called him back, he was unavailable. I tried sending a text message on Saturday. No response. I sent an e-mail on Sunday. Nothing.

I stumble out of bed and tiptoe through the kitchen to check Val's answering machine in case I slept through a call.

Nada. A headache starts to bloom at the base of my neck. What if Tom won't lend me the money, then what will the Ivys do?

I gulp down two Advil with a glass of water. My thoughts swirl in a whirlpool of emotions. How am I going to find the money? Who else can I call? What else can I do?

Okay. Don't panic. I slip into my T-shirt and running shorts and lace up my Asics gels. A brisk run is what I need. A gust of rain splatters my face as I step outside. My feet hit the muddy road, and air squeezes into my lungs. Pumping my arms back and forth, my feet find a rhythm. Soon my heartbeat pulses in my ears, drowning out the negative thoughts.

After I return from the run, soaked and exhilarated, I quickly shower and dress in my best suit. Standing at the kitchen counter, sipping coffee and nibbling on toast, I call each one of Tom's numbers from Val's land line. When the last recorded message stops, I say, "It's urgent you call me back as soon as possible. The borrowers need to sign today if the loan is going to proceed because I'm up against a three day right of rescission." As soon as I hang up, the phone rings. My heart leaps into my throat. "Tom?"

"Oh, goodness, no," say Ms. Morgan. "It's Betty, dear. Sorry to disappoint you."

I slump against the counter and pour a cup of coffee. "How's Ms. Lashay?"

"She's being released at the end of the week," she says. "Not because she's any better. Her insurance won't cover the hospital stay beyond that. I need to speak with Alex and ask him to release the funds to transfer her to a convalescent home, but I can't reach him."

*How convenient*, I think. Then I remember how I've conveniently been unavailable to my own family. In fact, it's been almost two months since I've spoken to Dad or Mom or Dee, other than that e-mail over Christmas letting them know I was okay.

"Can you talk to him, dear? Maybe he'll listen to you."

Me? Why me? But I smile and say, "Of course. I need to call him anyway."

After I hang up with Ms. Morgan, I call Alex's cell phone and leave a message for him to call me about his mother's care and a reminder that I'll be out of the office today on appointments. That's all he needs to know.

Before I leave, I spin around and admire my reflection in the full-length mirror behind Val's bedroom door. For a moment, I think of the times I used to dress up with Val, both of us jostling for the first glimpse of ourselves in the full-length mirror, pretending to be people we were not. Today I feel like someone else, someone I used to be, someone I no longer am.

The rain has stopped for once. Although it's cold and cloudy, I tie a wool scarf around my head and put down the hood. I drive down the windy lane, letting the damp after rain smells soak into my lungs. The dense redwoods standing like sentinels along River Road give way to valleys of vineyards glistening with moisture from the rain. So much green! I feel like I'm a part of nature, part of this beautiful paradise.

The mediation is taking place in an attorney's suite in downtown Santa Rosa. I punch the address into my GPS and follow the directions. I park in the rear lot beside Mr. Leggins' black BMW. Although we've spoken more on the phone in the last few months than the entire time I've known him, I haven't seen him since I left San Jose.

A cheerful young man greets me in the reception area, offering me coffee or water. I politely decline. A much older overweight man in a gray suit that matches the swath of gray hair pulled over his crown glances up from the magazine he is reading. Standing up, his gray eyes twinkle and his thin lips part in a smile. "Ms. Kay, it's a pleasure to see you again." He pulls me close and whispers. "You're looking well, I must say."

I step back and flash a tight smile. Mr. Leggins is my father's age and has been a widower for a number of years. Dee has always said he has an affinity for younger women, only I have no affinity for older men. It's a tightrope act to keep things friendly and professional between us. "Thank you, Mr. Leggins. You're looking good yourself, I must say." I shake his pudgy hand and take a seat next to him, setting my briefcase down between us.

"I really think you should press for your commission," Mr. Leggins says, leaning over to whisper into a tangle of my hair. "You have a good chance of winning it, if the mediator sides with the buyer, which I think he will."

"Sure, whatever you say." I trust Mr. Leggins' professional opinion.

Ten minutes later, the young man in the reception area leads us back into a conference room with a long table and several chairs lined up on both sides. I take a seat next to Mr. Leggins across from the Engles and their attorney. The Engles have brought their son who is playing with a toy truck on the table. He makes rumbling sounds, pretending to crash against his mother's arm. She frowns and quietly scolds him. I wonder why they couldn't get a sitter.

Mr. Sanders and his attorney arrive, both looking dapper in new suits. A couple of minutes later, the mediator arrives. His name is Bob. I don't catch his last name. Bob is a tall, willowy man with a faraway look in his eyes. When he speaks, his voice sounds as softly lulling as a jazz singer. I try hard to concentrate on his words, not his voice, or else I might fall asleep.

"We're going to go around the room and each party will have a chance to discuss their case without interruptions for ten minutes. I will write down the party's suggestion for a resolution on the white board. Once everyone's spoken, we will break up into caucuses and brainstorm alternative resolutions. I will meet with each party in their separate rooms to facilitate the discussion and take notes and ask questions. Then, after a short break, we will reconvene in the conference room and I will present the alternatives each caucus discussed before coming to a decision."

Mr. Sanders presents his case first. After eight minutes of discussing his move to the area and the number of homes he and his family had seen before writing an offer on the Engle's home, he says, "I went into the purchase agreement believing I was buying a house. I want the sellers to agree to specific performance." He leans back in his chair and smiles smugly at his attorney who nods in agreement.

Instead of having the sellers present their case next, the mediator points to us, indicating we are going clockwise around the table. Mr. Leggins clears his throat and speaks on my behalf, carefully crafting a brilliant, though dry presentation of the facts, noting the proper disclosures about my dual agency had been signed by both parties and pointing out the listing agreement and MLS printout indicated the sale was contingent upon the seller's job transfer, but also emphasizing the sellers had removed that contingency in writing a week before they called the title company demanding cancellation papers be drawn up. "My client found a willing and able buyer to complete the transaction," he says, folding his hands over his papers. "She is entitled to her full commission."

The mediator writes COMMISSION on the white board under SPECIFIC PERFORMANCE. He nods for the Engles to present their case.

Mr. Engle's long, pale hands fumble with his papers. Mrs. Engle pushes her black hair off her olive-skinned forehead and shifts their antsy son in her lap. Their attorney, a young man with rectangular-shaped glasses, stands up to address the room. "My clients were under the impression that the sale would not be completed if they could not successfully transfer jobs. Since it was no fault on their behalf that the job transfer did not go through due to a company reorganization which included layoffs, they feel they are entitled to cancel the transaction and return the earnest money deposit to the buyer with no further obligation to either the buyer or their dual agent."

It is by far the weakest argument. What attorney goes around talking about their clients' impressions or feelings? I glance over at Mr. Leggins, but his gray eyes are fixed on the white board where the mediator has written, CANCEL SALE.

We are given instructions on how to proceed with our caucuses and then dismissed into separate rooms. I file out behind the Engles. Their son turns around at the doorway and runs up to me, wrapping his plump brown arms around my legs. He rubs his hands back and forth against my nylons and smiles. "Nice," he says. I glance down at the black-haired boy, not knowing what to do. Mrs. Engle bends down to scold him. "Not nice," she hisses. "That's the lady who's trying to kick us out of our house. Don't touch her." She snatches him up into her arms and stalks down the hall following their attorney into a room. The boy smiles and waves his truck at me from where he bobs against his mother's shoulder. The door closes behind them. Mr. Leggins clears his throat. "Ms. Kay?"

I glance over at him. "Yes?"

"Don't let your maternal instinct sway you," he warns.

I'm not thinking of the boy. I'm thinking of his mother. *That's the lady who's trying to kick us out of our house.* I shudder. That's not how I want to be remembered.

Mr. Leggins and I make chit-chat in the tiny room while we're waiting for Bob to arrive and discuss the issue with us.

"So, how's it going with Tom?" Mr. Leggins asks.

"Fine."

"How's your business?"

"I don't know."

"What do you mean, you don't know?"

I fumble with a button on my suit jacket. "I haven't been back to San Jose yet. I'm still working my old job."

"The one with the contract you had me look over?"

"Yes, that's it."

He shifts uncomfortably in his chair. "How can you possibly manage a job *and* your business?"

Good question. I turn toward the window. Cars stop and go at the signal light with more direction than I have given to my own life.

Mr. Leggins coughs. "Well, if things don't work out with the job or Tom, there's an excellent opportunity for you to switch careers since your sister's left our office to pursue her education."

"Are you offering me her old job?" I ask.

"It would give you a chance to get your feet wet in the legal arena. Who knows? If you like it, I could possibly arrange a scholarship for you to get your education. It would be nice to have a smart woman on our legal team."

I smile, flattered by the offer. But I don't want to fill my sister's former job. I cross my legs and let my heel dangle out of my shoe. "Thanks, but I think I have my hands full already."

Bob raps on the door before he opens it. Smiling, he sits down between us on a vinyl chair and props his yellow legal pad against his knee. "I have some good news. The buyer is considering a remedy at law rather than specific performance. If the seller agrees, would you be willing to reduce your commission?"

I glance at Mr. Leggins for interpretation and guidance. He sits up, places his hands on his knees, and leans forward to engage Bob's attention. "My client would be willing to negotiate with the buyers and sellers if the compensation given to her is fair and equitable."

"Fifty percent of what she is asking," Bob says, looking up from his notes.

"Ms. Kay?" Mr. Leggins studies me.

Fifty percent is a little over $17,000. That's almost as much as I need to fund the Ivy Loan. "When would the settlement be complete?" I ask.

"As soon as everyone agrees. It could be today."

My heart flutters with hope. "That would be fine."

Bob leaves.

Mr. Leggins reaches over and pats my hand. "Good job. You're still ahead."

A few minutes later, Bob returns. He sinks into the chair and taps the end of his pen against the legal pad. "The sellers won't agree to pay the amount of money the buyers are asking, but they don't want to relinquish their home either."

Mr. Leggins chuckles. "They're young and stubborn and green just like their attorney."

I sigh. If we don't reach an agreement, the case will be transferred to binding arbitration. More time, more money spent. More sleepless nights worrying. "How much do the buyers want?"

"Twenty four thousand dollars for damages. If you include their initial and increased deposits, the total comes to $42,000."

That's a lot of money. But it's a great solution if the sellers don't want to lose their home. I uncross my legs. "How much are the sellers willing to pay?"

"Thirty thousand, tops."

That's a twelve thousand dollar difference. I wonder if there is a way to bridge the gap.

Mr. Leggins clears his throat. "Have you spoken to the buyers?"

Bob nods. "They will take the case to arbitration if the sellers don't agree to $42,000."

Mr. Leggins sits back and folds his hands over his stomach. "Let it go to arbitration. We've already offered a compromise on the commission."

Bob stands to leave.

"Wait." I stand up and walk briskly to the door. Leaning forward, I whisper, "Throw in my commission."

"Excuse me, sir, but my client doesn't know what she's agreeing to." Mr. Leggins meets us at the door. His gaze is stern. "We'll go to arbitration." He grabs my upper arm and leads me away from the door. His breath is hot against my ear. "It won't cost you any more money, if that's what you're concerned about. And it might be a chance to get your full commission."

I yank my arm free. "That's not my concern." Turning around, I walk back up to Bob and repeat my request, "Throw in my commission."

Bob hesitates for a moment, glancing from me to Mr. Leggins and back again. "Okay," he nods. "Let's go back to the conference room and I'll announce the decision."

Mr. Leggins bristles beside me. "That barely covers your legal fees. Why are you walking away with nothing?"

I don't answer his question. I sit down at the conference table across from the Engles. Their son has fallen asleep. Mr. Engle holds him against his shoulder. Mrs. Engle narrows her gaze at me. I sit up, tall and proud. Mr. Sanders and his attorney stride into the room and take a seat beside us.

Bob stands up to speak. "I'm happy to announce we've arrived at a solution." Very carefully, he erases the white board and writes down the decision. "Mr. Sanders has agreed to give up his request for specific performance in exchange for a settlement at law totaling $42,000. The Engles have agreed to return the buyer's initial and increased deposits and to pay for damages totally up to but not exceeding $30,000. The Engles have also agreed to pay $17,970 to the agent, which is half the requested commission."

I glance at Mr. Sanders, who seems concerned, and Mr. and Mrs. Engle, whose stony faces mask all emotion.

Bob continues speaking. "The agent, Ms. Kay, has agreed to contribute her commission to make up the remaining balance of $42,000 the buyer is requesting, leaving her with $5,970 in commission. I will have my secretary type up the agreement for your signatures and will file the decision with the court. Case dismissed."

Mr. Sanders stands up and shakes his attorney's hand.

Mr. and Mrs. Engle's expressions do not change. I'm disappointed they do not acknowledge the fact that I've saved them time and money and possibly their house by avoiding arbitration. But if I hadn't been so concerned about salvaging the transaction in the first place, I would have never removed the seller's contingency, and the case would never have proceeded to mediation. The buyer's initial and increased deposits would have been returned, and the transaction would have been canceled, costing the sellers nothing. This entire ordeal has been born out of my selfishness.

Mr. Leggins notices me staring at the Engles. He whispers, "I warned you against letting your maternal instinct sway you. What good has it done? They don't even appreciate your generosity."

I take a deep breath and sigh. He's right about the Engles, but I do not regret my decision. "Why are you so concerned?" I ask. "It's not your money."

"No, but it's my reputation. I pride myself on getting my clients more than they deserve."

"Then your reputation has not been hurt," I assure him. "Because, frankly, I deserve nothing."

# Chapter 32

After I leave the mediation, I walk across the street to grab some lunch. While sitting in a booth by the window, I turn on my BlackBerry and pick up a message from Tom. "Sorry we keep missing each other. Both of my buyer's agents quit. I'm stuck working everything right now. If I get a moment this afternoon, I'll call."

*Is he playing games or is he really working?* I wonder. I stare at the calendar on my BlackBerry. If I don't get the money soon, it doesn't matter. I won't be able to close the loan by Friday and that poor little girl will have to go without the surgery.

I finish my tuna sandwich and dial my old office to speak with Su.

"He's not here," she says. "May I forward you to his cell?"

"Yes, please," I say. I have a better chance of him picking up if he thinks it's business.

It rings. My palm is moist with nervousness. I sit up, trying to remember to be firm, not emotional. On the third ring, it clicks over to voice mail. My shoulders sag. "Tom," I say, slowly and clearly. "I want to believe you when you say you're busy, but I can't wait any longer for you decide whether or not you want to loan me $25,000 from our business." My voice cracks into a sob. I hang up without saying goodbye or leaving a list of numbers where I can be reached. I take a deep breath and call Val.

Amazingly, he answers. "Oh, KK, I'm so glad you called. I'm shopping for your pearl choker. What's your neck size?"

I almost choke on a sip of water. I'm scrambling to come up with $25,000 and he's blissfully browsing jewelry counters. "I don't know my neck size. I just got out of mediation. And I'm still trying to call Tom. But I think I'm going to have to cancel the loan and I don't know how to tell the clients the bad news."

"Well, I'd send you money, but I don't think I have enough. How much do you need again?"

"Twenty-five thousand."

He whistles long and low. "Girlfriend, these pearls are real, but they don't cost nearly that much."

I laugh. I know if Val had the money, he'd loan it to me to loan it to the Ivys. "I didn't call asking you for money. I called to talk to my best friend."

"Hold on a sec." Soft voices mumble in the background. "Still there?"

"Still here." I smile.

"Good. I'm leaving Antonio to browse for me, if you don't mind. Okay, I'm outside. Geez, it's chilly. Talk."

"I feel like a failure."

"Oh, KK, you're the best. I'm sure if you just explain to your clients that no one wants to take the risk, they'll understand."

"But they've been turned down three times already. I don't want to be the fourth one to turn them away. It feels so wrong."

Val laughs. "Listen to you. It *feels* wrong. When did you start feeling when it comes to business?"

"Sometime after I started working for Ms. Lashay."

"How is she doing?"

"A little better. But it's going to be a long road to recovery. They're releasing her on Friday because her insurance won't cover any expenses beyond that. And her son can't be reached to release any money to help her."

"The bastard. He makes Tom look like a saint."

"He's pretty black and white. He told me he wants revenge against his mother for abandoning him and his father. Tom, on the other hand, will tell you whatever you want to hear as long as it will get him whatever he wants. That's manipulative, not saintly."

"I'd take Tom any day. He's at least good looking."

"You haven't even seen Alex."

"If he looks anything like you've described his mother to be, he's short, blond, and intimidating. Not my type."

I giggle. "So intimidating he lets his girlfriend throw things at him."

"Really? Oh, why didn't you tell me that first? This is good."

"Not really. She's abusive. And he takes it."

"Mmm…not good. A real man wouldn't put up with that."

"No one should put up with that."

"Speaking of abusive, I need to get inside. It's freezing out here."

I grip the BlackBerry tighter. "What should I do?"

"Oh, KK," Val says, softly. "It doesn't matter what I tell you to do. You're going to do what you're going to do anyway. You're wonderfully impulsive. Now, if you don't mind, I'm going back to shopping with my Antonio."

"You're a couple? Does anyone in the cast know?"

"Not yet. And we're not really a couple. We're really good friends." He lowers his voice. I can barely hear him through the crowd of the mall. "I haven't slept with him yet."

I smile. "You still feeling in love?"

"More than ever," he says, brightly.

On the way back to the office, I decide to stop by the hospital and see Ms. Lashay. Maybe she'll be able to offer kind words of wisdom on how to let the clients down gently.

I walk down the hall, hearing my heels click-clack against the linoleum. Why didn't I wear some flats or rubber soles? I don't want to wake Ms. Lashay if she's sleeping. Leaning against the wall, I take off my shoes and pad silently on the cool floor. The door to Ms. Lashay's room is open. People are talking. I recognize their voices. I pause in the doorway, afraid to enter. Alex bends to embrace his mother. She closes her eyes, draping her arms over his back. There is a smile on her face. "I love you," she says, in her gruff, unsteady voice.

I back away from the door, feeling like an intruder. Finding a chair in the wide hallway, I take a seat. I'll just wait till he leaves, then I'll speak with her. I cross and uncross my legs. The longer I wait, the more uncomfortable I become. I can't get over Ms. Lashay's face, so radiant with love, with hope, with reconciliation. Maybe I'm reading too much into her expression. For all I know, she could be one of those hopelessly desperate mothers who love their children no matter if they're convicted murderers on death row. I glance up at the clock on the wall and sigh. It's been twenty minutes.

Maybe I should go back to the office. I'm just postponing the inevitable.

Standing up, I yawn and stretch. A doctor strides down the hall and flashes me a smile, his eyes traveling down the length of my body and back up again. It's a familiar glance, but it still rattles my nerves. I can't help but wonder what it is these strangers see in me and my legs. Am I really that beautiful? Or am I just different? All those years wearing braces to straighten my legs from becoming bow-legged only made people stop and stare and ask questions. The children's taunts still echo in my mind, "Here comes Stilts!" The name stuck even after I stopped wearing the braces in middle school. No matter how much running I do or where I go or who I'm with, the memories linger in the shadows of my mind, threatening to destroy whatever happiness I have managed to pluck from the tree of life.

"Sticks and stones may break your bones, but words will never hurt you," my mother always said.

Then why do the bruises disappear, but the words reappear whenever I least expect them to?

I walk briskly down the hall toward the elevator. Once inside, I lean against the rail. The doors close. "You're closed off," Tom said. Tiny lights blink as the elevator descends. Just because my parents and my sister and my boyfriend don't understand me doesn't mean they don't care. If I keep excluding them from my life, I'll end up like the women lenders in our database who have built profitable careers but have no family or friends to share it with. I'll end up alone.

The doors open. I step out into the lobby. A new mother cradles a baby in her arms while a nurse pushes her in a wheelchair to the waiting car outside. I think of Iris Ivy and her parents. My heart sinks. I do not want to have to make that call.

Who would know what to say to a parent of a disfigured child?

I need to call my father.

When I was growing up, my father adored me. I was his favorite. I could do no wrong. He would shelter me, spoiling me with whatever I wanted to make me feel better whenever the students or teachers or strangers teased me about my legs. My mother, on the other hand, hated the special attention he gave me. She said if I was a strong young lady, I would learn to tolerate the taunts at school because the other children were only jealous of my leg braces, at first, then later, of my ability to run the fastest mile. My father used to intervene whenever my mother would push my feelings so far aside that I would wake up with a stomachache. He would take her into their bedroom, shut the door, and calmly speak with her. I never knew what he said, but whatever it was, it kept her mouth shut for at least a few weeks.

In the car, I dial my parents' number. No one is home. I lose my courage and hang up without leaving a message. I rationalize my decision. If Dee got home before either of my parents, she might delete the message. I'll think my father is holding a grudge against me, when he might be completely unaware of my call.

Oh, why can't I just make the phone call to the Ivys and get it over with?

When I get to the office, the glass doors are locked. The sign says, "CLOSED." I wonder if anyone has been into the office today. Alex must still be at the hospital. I don't care where Candie is. Sometimes I wish she'd pack up her little designer bags and board the next jet plane. I set my purse under my desk, transfer the phones off voice mail, and write down three messages I'll return later. I go into Ms. Lashay's office and close the door.

Sinking into the big, overstuffed chair, I take out a pad of paper and a pen to compose a script. "I'm sorry to have to disappoint you, but I cannot find a lender who will fund your loan. I'm going to have to cancel your application. Good luck." I stare at the words before ripping the sheet of paper from the pad and crumbling it into a ball and tossing it into the garbage can beneath the desk. I lean back, close my eyes, and visualize the Ivys at home, taking care of their daughter. Actually, Mr. Ivy would probably be at work. Mrs. Ivy might be folding laundry while Iris sleeps. If I call, she'll jump for the phone, anxious not to wake the baby. Her voice will be soft and eager, straining to hear the good news.

My eyes snap open. I cannot do this!

I call home again, hoping to reach my father.

Dee picks up the phone. "Hello?"

"It's me," I say.

Her tone changes. "What the fuck do you want?"

"Is Dad there?"

"No, he's out with Mom."

I hold my breath, thinking of Ms. Lashay and Ms. Morgan. I do not want to grow old without my sister beside me. "Dee, I'm sorry."

Silence.

I exhale. The words rush out of my mouth, unplanned. "I'm sorry for blaming you for the billboard. I'm sorry for breaking your camera. I'm sorry for acting like a selfish, spoiled brat. Please forgive me. I want to be your friend again."

The glass doors part. Candie stalks into the office cursing at her cell phone. I stand up and close the door, standing by the window, staring out the blinds at her.

Dee finally says, "What's come over you? You never apologize for anything."

I don't have time to tell her about Ms. Lashay. "When I was flooded in, I had a lot of time to think. I realized I missed you and Mom and Dad and Tom. I didn't want to spend the rest of my life disconnected from the ones I love."

"Apology accepted," Dee says.

The glass doors part again, and Alex strides into the office. His golden hair, as fine as spun sugar, sticks up around his face like a nimbus. Candie rushes up to him, yelling, "Why is your cell phone off, you fucking idiot?"

Dee asks, "Where are you?"

"At work."

"Sounds like someone's fighting."

"My boss's son is here to help. That's his girlfriend you hear in the background."

"Sounds like you." She giggles.

"I'm not *that* bad," I laugh.

"No, you're worse."

We both laugh. It feels good to joke around with my sister again, even when I'm the butt of the joke.

"When are you coming down?" she asks. "I have a portfolio of new photos to show you."

"Why don't you come up? I'm staying at Val's cottage. There's so much to photograph here. Vineyards, rivers, forests, sunsets, historic buildings."

She thinks about it. "Maybe next weekend. This weekend I'm going to a photographer's conference."

I promise to call her back later next week to firm up our visit. Hanging up the phone, I turn back to the window.

"I was trying to get a hold of you." Candie raises her cell phone in her fist. Is she going to hit him this time? She shakes the phone in his face. "I shouldn't have to leave a message. Where were you?"

"Please, stop yelling. I can hear you just fine," Alex says, calmly. He sets down his briefcase beside my desk. "My cell phone was turned off because I was at the hospital visiting my mother."

Candie lowers her fist. Her eyes shine with hope. "Are we selling the business and going home?"

Alex shakes his head. "I've changed my mind."

She lifts her fists and starts pounding him. But he's stronger than her. He grips her wrists. "Please, stop hitting me," he says, firmly. "I don't deserve it. I never have." Releasing her, he steps away. "It's over. Go back to L.A. I never want to see you again."

The phone rings. I reach across Ms. Lashay's desk to answer it. "Smart Loans. This is Trina Kay."

The door flies open. Candie stalks up to me. "It's all your fault, bitch!"

I cup my hand over the receiver. "I'm on the phone with a client."

"You're screwing him, aren't you?"

Alex stalks inside and grabs Candie by the shoulders. "I'm not sleeping with her or anyone else. I should have broken up with you months ago, but I was afraid of you."

I release my hand from the receiver. "I'm sorry for the disturbance. May I help you?"

The caller says, "It's Joanie Ivy. I called the title company to see when we could sign papers but the escrow officer told me to contact you for loan documents. Is there a problem?"

Madonna sings, "True Blue." I glance at my BlackBerry with hope.

"That's the lender right now. Can I call you back?" I hang up the phone and reach for my BlackBerry, but Candie snatches it first.

"Give that to me," I say, feeling panic pump through my veins. "That's an important phone call. I can't miss it."

Alex tries to grab the BlackBerry out of Candie's hand, but she darts around him. I lunge across the desk and seize a handful of her hair. She yelps. With my other hand, I pry the BlackBerry out of her fist. "Tom?"

"Ah-ha! I win phone tag. What's the grand prize? A kiss from you?"

I don't have time for his jokes. "Are you going to loan me the money or not?"

His voice drops. "I can't. Most of our assets aren't liquid."

"But you were going to buy me out a few months ago. What happened to the money?"

"It's been slow since I've taken the billboard down. I've been using savings to pay the utilities and the lease. There's just enough left for a couple months of payroll. I'm struggling."

Shit! That means I have to call Mrs. Ivy back and tell her the bad news.

Candie reaches across the desk and claws my arm with her nails.

Damn! The sleeve of my best suit rips. I lower the BlackBerry from my ear and slap her face.

She raises her hand, ready to strike back.

Alex steps between us. "Stop it. Both of you."

Candie's chest heaves with each breath. I step toward the open door, ready to escape.

"Trina? Are you there?" Tom asks.

"I'm here," I say with a flat voice. "How should I tell the Ivys I can't fund the loan?"

"Be diplomatic," Tom says. "Make sure you let them know how you were willing to put up your own money only you ran out of time."

I shake my head. No matter what I tell them it's going to sound bad and feel worse.

"Hang in there," Tom says. "If by some miracle, I find some cash lying around, I'll call you."

"Thanks." I hang up. Turning to face Alex and Candie, I say, "You two can go back to your love making, I quit."

Alex extends his arm toward me. "Don't leave."

I stride over to my desk. I grab my purse and toss my BlackBerry in it. Without glancing up, I say, "You can sell the business. I'll take my license and go back to San Jose. I have a family and a boyfriend waiting for me."

Candie stands smugly in the doorway watching us.

Alex turns to her. "If you don't leave immediately, I'll call the police and file a restraining order."

Candie crosses her arms over her chest and continues to linger.

Alex picks up the phone on my desk and starts punching numbers.

Candie stalks over, grabs the receiver out of his hand, and slams it down in the cradle. She hisses, "I'll be out of the hotel in an hour, then out of your life for good."

After she leaves, Alex turns to me and says, "She doesn't know I checked us both out this morning. Her luggage is being stored in the lobby along with a prepaid one-way ticket from SFO to LAX for seven this evening."

I stare at him curiously.

He bends to pick up his briefcase beside my desk. Opening it up, he says, "I'm not selling the business. I read those letters you gave me the other day. And I've spoken with my mother. She's going to fund the Ivy loan. I've signed the documents and sent them off to the pension company before coming back here to tell you. The funds will be at title tomorrow morning. The loan will close on time."

What? Did I hear him correctly? Or am I hallucinating?

"I've been mistaken about a lot of things," he says. He shifts from foot to foot, glancing up at me with a tentative look in his brown eyes. "I owe you an apology for my behavior the other day. You were right. I was an asshole."

I swallow. He's apologizing. He wants me to forgive him. But is it real?

He seems to sense my reservation. "I've been thinking about a lot of things." His brown eyes are moist. "I should have never got you involved with my family problems. But I'm glad I did. If I hadn't, then I would never have known that my mother tried to contact me for years, but my father wouldn't let her. He refused to relinquish custody in family court or even grant her visiting rights. All these years I thought her acts of kindness were manipulative ploys to get at me because she hated my father. But she was genuinely interested in getting to know me." His lips quiver. "It was very kind of you to give me those letters. I want to thank you."

"You're welcome," I whisper. "Apology accepted."

Alex glances at the clock. "We're running out of time," he says. "Why don't I call the title company while you prepare loan docs?"

He wants to help me.

"Sure." I sit down and pull up the loan document software on the computer. Alex sets the signed pension fund documents on the desk next to me and picks up the phone. I glance over at his signature. It's real. My whole body floods with relief.

Iris Ivy will get her surgery.

# CHAPTER 33

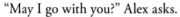

"May I go with you?" Alex asks.

I pause at the double glass doors with my briefcase full of loan documents in hand. He looks small and concerned, more like his mother than he ever has, except without her firm confidence. "Of course," I say, and let him get the door. "I'll drive."

The sky has cleared, and the wind has died down. Alex slides into the passenger's seat and turns off the stereo. "I really appreciate the way you've helped my mother," he says. "It's really hard to understand her speech still, but from what I did understand, you've been instrumental to her success."

I laugh. "I think you must have misunderstood her. I've only been with the company for a little while. She's been spending most of her time training me more than anything else."

He turns to gaze out the side window. I wonder if I've hurt his feelings or offended him in some way. He's so quiet.

"Your mother, though, has been instrumental in my life," I say. "She offered me a job before I had to file for bankruptcy."

He swivels toward me with sudden interest. "But you have a business in San Jose, right?"

"A business from which I am getting no cash flow. And a house I can't refinance because I'm not the only one on title. And a stack of bills from starting over. Sometimes I think my impulsive decision to relocate was a big mistake. But other times I think it's just exactly what I needed." I flash him a smile. "Before I met your mother, I only thought of the bottom line, the win. But your mother showed me it's not closing the deal that's important; it's who you help along the way."

"We talked about that," he says. "She mentioned that a few years after her divorce, she realized she was lonely. She had accumulated all sorts of wealth but at the cost of her family. That's when she decided to refocus her business. She started helping out people who needed help." He sighs. "She's not the same person I imagined her to be."

I pull into a parking spot outside the title company. Alex gets out and walks around the car to open my door. It's so nice having a gentleman around.

The lobby is cool and quiet. The receptionist, a small woman with a cap of black hair, ushers us into the conference room where Suzie, the escrow officer, and the Ivys sit waiting for us. I introduce them to Zachary Alexander Lashay II. "Call me Alex," he says, shaking their hands.

Iris is sleeping in the baby carrier with a blanket draped over her. I hope she wakes up. I want to see her.

During the signing, a tiny hiccup rises from the baby carrier. Mrs. Ivy bends to lift the blanket. She unfastens the belts and lifts Iris into her lap. I smile and wave at her. Iris smiles back, and the tumor on her mouth lifts up to press against the bottom of her nose. I wonder if it's hard for her to breathe with it covering one nostril.

Alex's hand brushes against my arm. I glance over at him. "What is it?"

But he's not looking at me. He's looking at Iris.

೮১   ೮১   ೮১

With the loan documents signed, I feel a huge wave of relief. "I can't wait to go home and relax with a glass of syrah," I say, and toss my briefcase in the trunk.

"How about dinner?" Alex suggests. "My treat."

I don't know. Haven't I seen enough of him for one day?

He seems to sense my resistance. "That's all right. Why don't you drop me off at the office? I think I'll head over to the hospital before visiting hours are over."

On the other hand, seeing Ms. Lashay might be good. I'd like to thank her for funding the Ivy loan. "Why don't we both visit Ms. Lashay?" I slip inside and start the engine.

"Then dinner?" he asks.

Where did he get that streak of persistence?

"We'll see." I don't want to make any promises I don't intend to keep.

At the hospital, we walk side-by-side down the wide hallway. Alex opens the door to his mother's room, holding it for me to enter. Ms. Lashay sleeps. Light snores rattle from her half open mouth.

Ms. Morgan sits on the chair next to the bed watching TV. "Hi Betty." Alex bends to kiss her cheek. "How's Mom doing?"

"Better." Ms. Morgan folds her hands in her lap. "She's getting stronger in her arms and legs. But she's not ready to go home. I'm glad you've released those extra funds."

"And I'm glad you've let me stay in your home," Alex says, smiling. He motions for me to sit beside him. "I'll be back and forth every couple of weeks to check on things, but you can call me anytime."

"When are you leaving, Trina?" Ms. Morgan asks, turning to me.

"I don't know," I say. "I've been so consumed with the Ivy loan that I haven't thought about it."

"Didn't you cancel that loan?" Ms Morgan asks.

"No, I didn't." I smile and take a seat beside Alex on the bed. "It will close on Friday."

"Really?" Ms. Morgan's eyebrows lift with surprise. She studies me closely as if trying to figure me out. "Well, dear, that *is* impressive. You really wanted that one."

I did. More than I've wanted anything for anyone else in my life.

Ms. Lashay stirs. Her eyes flutter open. She smiles when she recognizes Alex. "Son," she says, and reaches to touch his hand.

He grasps her fingers in his palm and brings her hand to his lips, kissing it. "Betty says you're getting better."

"Bit by bit." She chuckles until she coughs.

I stand up and pour a cup of water from the pitcher on the swivel tray that has been pushed against the window. Alex and Ms. Morgan help Ms. Lashay sit up. I bend to hand Ms. Lashay the plastic cup. Like a child, Ms. Lashay wraps her weak hands around my hands and sips.

Alex talks with her about Friday's move to the convalescent home and setting up a joint bank account with Ms. Morgan. "So you don't have to call me in L.A. every time you need something." He winks.

Twenty minutes later, when it's time to go, I bend over and hug Ms. Lashay. "Thank you for funding the Ivy loan."

She grips me closer. "No. Thank *you*."

"I was just doing what you would have done."

"Only better. Just like I knew you would."

And, for the first time in months, I feel the rush of success I've always felt whenever I've made my father proud.

The sky has darkened into a purple bruise. Dark clouds scuttle across the face of the moon, threatening more rain. I hug my jacket over my chest, wondering how much longer winter will last.

In the hospital parking lot, I unlock my car with the remote control on my number one Realtor keychain. Alex opens my door. "Thank you," I say, slipping inside.

After he straps the seatbelt across his waist, he asks, "Shall we go to dinner?"

"I don't know. I'm tired."

"I promise to bring you home early."

I laugh. "You aren't driving. I am."

"Then I guess I'm at your mercy." He shrugs and turns his palms up in mock surrender.

I smile, backing out of the parking slot.

When we get to the light, Alex asks, "Mexican or Italian?"

"What?"

"Food." Alex points to the west. "There's a great little Mexican restaurant on the corner of Stony Point and Sebastopol Road. But if you prefer Italian, we can go to the Italian Affair."

I laugh. "You eat out a lot, don't you?"

"What else are you going to do when you live in a hotel? When I'm home, I cook. My best dish is orange roughy and red potatoes with a tossed apple walnut salad."

"Sounds yummy."

"If you prefer, we could stop at the store and pick up the ingredients. I could cook you up a meal at your place."

It's been a long day. I'm not up to entertaining. But a home cooked meal by someone who professes to know how to cook. "That sounds wonderful."

# CHAPTER 34

▼

After grocery shopping, I drop Alex off at the office so he can follow me to Val's cottage in his rental car. Rain drops start to splatter against the windshield. I turn on the high beams on the two lane road that cuts through the forest. Glancing up into the rearview mirror, I double check to see if Alex is keeping up. He drives just like I do, fast and aggressive. Not bad for a guy who took punches from his girlfriend.

Driving up the windy road to the cottage, I park in the turnout, leaving room for Alex's rental car. When he gets out, he pops the trunk and grabs the bag of groceries. "I never would have guessed you liked living out in the boonies."

"It's not my place." I unlock the front door. "I'm house sitting." It sounds better than saying I'm homeless.

"Whose house?"

"My best friend, Val. He's on a six-month cross-country tour of the *Odd Couple*. He plays Oscar." I turn on the lights. My clothes are scattered on the floor and over the furniture from getting dressed in front of the wood burning stove this morning. I scramble to pick up my underwear off the sofa. How embarrassing.

"Don't bother," Alex says. "My house looks worse."

"Really?" I clutch the dirty clothes to my chest.

He treks across the hardwood floor to the kitchen and sets the bag of groceries on the table. "My cleaning lady quit because I never picked up." He walks over to the French doors leading to the deck and places his hands on his waist. Moonlight glitters on the river between the redwood trees. "What a view."

I don't care if he's messier than me. I want to clean up a bit. I toss my clothes on Val's bed and glimpse myself in the full-length mirror. What a fright. My hair is frizzy. My mascara has smeared, giving me raccoon eyes, and my suit is torn and wrinkled. "Do you mind if I change into jeans?"

"Sure, but you aren't helping me cook. You're having that glass of syrah."

I smile. He remembers everything, doesn't he?

I close the door to the bedroom and slip out of my suit and into faded jeans and a soft sweater. With a moist makeup removal towel, I scrub off the raccoon eyes. I sprits styling gel into my hair and scrunch my hair into spiral curls. I pick up a bottle of perfume, and then place it down. I'm not on a date. I just want to look decent. When I enter the kitchen, Alex lifts his head from the pot of potatoes on the stove. He flashes a crooked smile. "Nice outfit. Nice hair. Nice eyes." It's nice he notices.

I pour two glasses of syrah and set them on the counter. Alex won't let me help him chop, dice, or baste. "I like orange roughy because it doesn't stink like other fish," he says, holding up the white fillets for me to sniff. He's right. There's no odor. He rubs each fillet with a pat of butter, then sprinkles lemon pepper on both sides. He sets the fish on a tray and places it into the oven to bake for twenty minutes. With the salad prepared and the baby red potatoes boiling on the stove, Alex raises his glass for a toast. "To the Ivy loan."

Our glasses click. The wine feels good and warm going down my throat. My shoulders start to relax. Alex places his hand on the small of my back and leads me to the sofa. I think about lighting the candles I've left all over the room but decide against it. This isn't a date. This is a business dinner. Right?

"Are you cold?" I ask. "I could start a fire."

"Sure. Would you like me to help?"

Although he's loosened his striped yellow and blue tie and removed his navy blue jacket, he's still wearing his suit. "No, thanks. I think I'll manage. It's the least I can do since you cooked dinner."

I place some logs and kindling into the stove and light a match. The bright flame ignites, and soon a crackling fire radiates warmth throughout the room.

Alex takes the matches I've left on the coffee table and lights the candles. A sweet vanilla scent mingles with the smoke from the fire and the aroma of vinegar from the kitchen. We sit together on the sofa, and Alex drapes his arm behind my head and accidentally tousles my curls. A zip of electricity shocks the back of my neck, and I involuntarily scoot away.

"I'm sorry," he says, removing his arm.

"Don't apologize. You do too much of it."

He sets his glass of syrah on a coaster and picks up the photo album.

"Those aren't my pictures," I warn him.

But he's already looking through it. I don't stop him from pointing to the tanned red head standing next to the dark-haired guy wearing mascara and eyeliner. "Is that you?"

I nod. In the photo I'm wearing Mickey Mouse ears and Val is holding up a peace sign behind my head. It was taken during one of my visits to L.A. while he was working on *The Young and the Restless.*

"Your hair's gotten darker."

"It always lightens up in the summer. It looks brighter against my skin because I tan well like my father."

"How long have you and Val known each other?"

I shrug. "Seems like forever. He calls me his Rent-a-Sister."

Alex laughs. "I wish I had siblings. But Dad never remarried and neither did Mom. It was a lonely childhood." He closes the photo album, sets it down, and retrieves his half-empty glass of wine. Taking a sip, he stares across the room. The candlelight flickers in his dark pupils. I wonder what he's thinking, but I'm too afraid to ask. For a man, he strikes me as fragile, and I don't want my words to break him.

The timer buzzes. I stand up too abruptly and startle him. "Sorry," I say, and move toward the kitchen to set the table.

"I thought you said not to apologize."

"I was referring to you, not me. I don't do it enough."

"What could you possibly do that would warrant an apology?" He removes the fish from the oven.

I fold the napkins and place the silverware on them. "Why so many questions? Tell me about you. I hardly know anything except what your mother's told me."

"What has she said?"

"You don't want to run her business. You're a lot like her only you don't know it. Some of that is true, but most of it is not. You don't strike me as part of the Dead Girlfriend Society."

He chuckles. "Not even with Candie gone?"

It's the first time we've spoken her name since the blowup. I feel a prickle of uneasiness, but decide to press onward. "How did you meet her?"

"At the airport," he says. "I was catching a flight to Colorado to go skiing with some friends and she was going to interview Robert Redford who, as you know, hasn't been interviewed in years. We started chatting and exchanged numbers. The interview didn't go well, and she ended up calling me. We spent the rest of the weekend together. By the time we came back to L.A., we were inseparable. She was young, bright, and aggressive. Just what I thought I needed to get out of the slump I'd been in with my business and my non-existent personal life. She spiced things up at first, but tore me down in the process."

I nod.

"Looking back, I think we moved too fast. I was so desperate for a relationship, I wasn't very discriminatory. I think I'd be a lot more cautious now." He sets two plates full of fish and potatoes on the table, then brings over the apple walnut salad. We sit down and he bows his head to silently pray. His mouth moves but no words come out. When he glances up, I lift up the bottle of wine. "Another glass?"

He shakes his head. "I'm driving. But you go ahead."

I pour half a glass and begin to eat. The orange roughy is delicate and buttery. The potatoes are perfect. The apple walnut salad is crunchy and tangy and sweet. "You're a great cook."

"I'm glad you enjoy it. Candie never liked me cooking. She said it took too much time away from her. She preferred going out."

And bossing other people around, I think.

After dinner, Alex loads the dishwasher and I wipe down the table and sweep the floor. "I'd better go," Alex says, grabbing his jacket.

I can't believe the clock on the stove. Ten-thirty. It feels so much earlier.

"Wait." My heart hammers against my ribs. If he walks out the door, I may never see him this way again. So small and tender in his dark suit.

He shrugs into his jacket and turns around. "Yes?"

I gulp. What's wrong with me? I have a boyfriend. But I want Alex to stay. Not just a few minutes longer. But all night. In my arms. Naked.

As if reading my thoughts, Alex walks over to me and gathers my hands. My skin tingles, alive from his delicate touch. I tip my head forward anticipating a kiss, but he steps back, still holding my hands, gazing at me with his soft brown eyes like I'm the last wonder of the world. My body feels warm and moist all over. "Thanks for inviting me over," he says. "I enjoyed our time together."

"You're welcome. Thank you for cooking. It was delicious." *As delicious as your skin probably tastes.*

Oh, my god. What am I thinking? What would Tom say if he knew? Sweat smears my forehead and under my arms and between my legs like I'm in the middle of a long distance run. But I'm standing in the living room of Val's tiny cottage holding hands with my boss's son, wondering what his skin tastes like and feeling guilty about it.

Just when I think I should pull away, Alex raises my hands to his lips and kisses each knuckle. I shiver with unexpected pleasure.

"Sleep well." He lowers my hands and squeezes them briefly before releasing them. "See you tomorrow."

*Tomorrow.* The word sounds like a whole universe away.

# CHAPTER 35

▼

On Friday morning, after the Ivy loan closes, I get a call from Tom. "I'm lost," he says.

I'm sitting at my desk in the office, sorting the mail. I try to imagine Tom in an existential crisis, but I know he's not the type of guy to agonize over the meaning of life. "What do you mean, you're lost?"

"I've walked around this building twice and I can't find your suite."

A stack of bills flutters from my hands. Tom is in the building? "What are you doing here? I thought I'd see you tomorrow."

"I couldn't wait any longer, so I've come to see you." He pauses. "Oh, here you are."

The glass doors part and Tom strides into the office. His broad chest and powerful shoulders shift beneath his black Armani suit. The muscles in his legs are hidden beneath freshly pressed slacks. He removes the Blue Tooth glowing in his right ear and slips it into his jacket pocket. I recognize the briefcase in his other hand—it was a gift from his father for listing his first property for sale. A golden brown wave of hair falls over his blue eyes, and something catches in my throat. My whole body quivers with desire. Val's right. He's handsome. Terribly handsome.

I place the phone in the cradle and stand up. My knees wobble, and I grasp the ledge of the desk. Why did he come here? Didn't he read his e-mail? I don't need him to help me fund the loan anymore. The deal is closed.

I suddenly wish Alex was here. But he's helping his mother move into the convalescent home. I'm alone with Tom in the office, and I don't like it one little bit. There is no one to help me, and no place to run. I feel cornered like a caged animal, and some part of me wonders if that's how I'll always feel when I try to confront a problem head on, instead of skirting around it or ignoring it, hoping it will magically go away.

Tom flashes me a disarming smile, and my knees buckle with the conflicting impulse to pull him close and push him away. Too weak to stand, I sink back into the chair. Why did he come? To confuse me? I thought we were through playing games with each other.

"I couldn't wait till you move back to San Jose." Tom sets the briefcase down and kneels beside the desk, placing a firm hand on my knee. "I know it's too late for the Ivy loan, but I know it's not too late for us." He removes a tiny blue and white box from his inside breast pocket and hands it to me.

The air squeezes out of my chest. It's not what I think it is, is it?

"Open it," he commands.

My fingers tug at the white ribbon. It falls away. I remove the blue box top and pull out another box. It opens like a clam's mouth, revealing a sparkling one carat princess cut diamond ring in a white gold setting. I gulp for air. This is not happening, is it?

"Katrina Kay, will you marry me?"

This *is* happening. Tom Jensen has asked me to marry him.

I guess I take too long to answer, because Tom asks, "What's wrong?"

My mind fills with doubt. "Is this another one of your games?"

"What are you talking about?" Tiny furrows crease his forehead. "You're supposed to throw your arms around my neck and shout, *Yes*!"

There he goes, assuming the close. My whole body tenses with anger and disappointment. "You knew how important funding that loan was to me, and you couldn't come up with the money." I thrust the ring in his face. "How much did this cost?"

His hand slips from my knee. He whispers, "Most women would kill for anything from Tiffany's."

I gulp for air, not realizing I was holding my breath. "Why now?" I ask.

"Why not?" he answers. "I thought you were moving back to San Jose and we'd live happily-ever-after. But I guess I should have known something was wrong because you kept pushing the move date back with one excuse after another."

"*You* told me to stay and help Ms. Lashay."

"And now you're done helping her." Tom stares at me intently. "So why won't you marry me?"

The ring catches the fluorescent lights, and the diamond winks. I know my parents would want me to accept this proposal. They already treat Tom like the son they've always wanted and never had. Dee likes him. Val does, too. It seems like I'm the only one with an ounce of doubt.

Why is that?

Maybe Tom was right. I was running. I kept running because I didn't want to be vulnerable and insecure, although I am. Over my legs. The same legs Tom put up on a billboard. The billboard that ignited this whole new path for me. And even though the billboard is down, I can't go back. I just can't.

I'm not the same person anymore. I've started caring for other things, other people.

I snap the box shut and hand it to him. "I don't know why. I just know I can't."

He studies me for a long moment. "Who is he?"

"It's not a he. It's a she. Iris Ivy. That baby I told you about."

His mouth drops open, perplexed. "You're leaving me over a baby?"

My eyes feel moist with sudden tears. "I don't know how to explain it so you'll understand. But when I saw that little face, something changed in me. I had to help her. And I did. I funded the loan."

Tom studies my face, as if searching for a different answer. But there is none. Slowly, he stands up and tucks the box into his pocket. His face is drawn out, almost sad. I want to stand up and embrace him, but I don't want to give him any false hope. And I definitely don't want to be tempted to touch him any further. Like I did on Thanksgiving.

He frowns, stacking some files into a corner on my desk. I stand up, reaching to remove the stack, knowing how much he's always hated my messiness. But he waves me away. "No, don't. I just want to sit for second." He perches on the edge of the desk, facing me. Beads of sweat dot his forehead. I frown, wondering what he's nervous about. When he speaks, his voice quivers. "I'm sorry. About everything. I knew you were upset about the billboard, but I never knew why. You were so closed off, you never told me you were teased about your legs. They're gorgeous. I guess I just saw you as you are now, not as you were then. If I had known, I never would have done it. Can you forgive me?" He folds his hands and gazes at the floor. Is he crying? His eyelashes blink rapidly. A silver trail cruises down his cheek and cups his chin. He *is* crying.

I can't take it anymore. "Yes, I can forgive you, but I can't get back together with you." I reach up and touch his moist chin. "I'd like to stay friends, if you're comfortable with that. Everyone I know loves you. My parents would be heartbroken if you just went away. Even I would." I take a breath, feeling my heart expand. "I still love you. I think I always will. But I can't marry you. I just can't. I hope you understand."

Tom lifts his gaze, and his blue eyes glitter. Something hard lodges in my throat. If I could just wish away our history, maybe we could start over. Maybe we could make it work. But then I think of Iris and the money and the ring, and I know I'm kidding myself. We aren't bad people. We just have different values now. And it's those conflicting values that would eventually tear us apart.

Tom stands up and wipes his cheeks with the back of his hand. From his briefcase, he removes a set of papers and lays them on the desk. "I do understand," he says, and hands me a pen. "These have to be notarized, but the others don't."

My mouth opens in disbelief. He brought the dissolution papers for our business. I separate the pages that need to be notarized from the ones that don't. Our fingers brush against each other when I reach for the pen. And there's no sizzle. No irresistible pull to wrap my arms around him and pull him close. I don't feel anything but a sense of loss, of something that once meant so much, falling away.

Tom forces a smile, but I imagine he feels just as terrible as I do. It's never easy ending something, even when it is what you want to do. With a trembling hand, I sign. I can never go back to T & T Realty. It no longer exists.

There's only one thing left to tell him. I take a deep breath and square my shoulders. "I'm not moving to San Jose."

Tom shifts into business mode. His face washes clean of emotion, revealing a polished, professional veneer. "We should make a decision about our home." His voice is solid. "I suggest we can keep it as an investment and rent it out until prices start to rise. Then we'll sell and divide the proceeds."

I nod. "That sounds good."

I stand up and make copies of all the documents before returning the originals to him. From my number one Realtor keychain, I remove the keys to our former office and our old home and place them in the palm of his hand.

Our whole life together no longer exists.

Ten minutes after Tom leaves, my BlackBerry sings, "Keep It Together." My parents. My hand slightly shakes as I pick up the BlackBerry, wondering if Tom already told them the news.

"Hello?" I say. "Trina Kay speaking."

"KK," Mom says. Her voice sounds far away, as if she is trapped in a tunnel. Ugh. Great. Speaker phone. I wonder who else is listening.

"We just heard the news," Dad says. "You're staying in Sonoma County, right?"

Shit. Why didn't I think of calling them? Actually I had thought of it, but the office phone kept ringing.

"Yes, I am. But I really can't talk. I'm manning the phones at the office," I tell them.

My mother sniffs. "Tom said he proposed. Why didn't you accept?"

Tension snakes through my upper back. I feel stiff. Why can I talk to lenders and clients and attorneys but not my parents? Why must I always feel five-years old trying to justify why I wouldn't play with the other girls or boys on the playground?

"Don't listen to them," Dee says. "We know it wouldn't last."

Dee's home? Why isn't she at school? I don't know her schedule anymore.

My mother's sniffles overwhelm the phone line. I shift in my chair, crossing and uncrossing my legs. I try to will the office phone to ring or someone to enter through the glass doors, but the phone is silent and I am alone.

"I know you're disappointed, but Tom and I just don't share the same values anymore. It's not that I don't care about him. I do. But he's not the one I want to share the rest of my life with. You can still invite him over for brunch and holidays, and Dad can still play golf with him. We're still friends. We're just no longer a couple. So, don't think of it as losing a son, think of it as having both of us, together, separately."

"Your mumbo-jumbo doesn't fool me," Mom says. "You're foolish. You'll never meet a man as good as Tom. He's hardworking and dependable."

Hardworking? Yes, I agree. Dependable? Well, it depends.

"And good looking," Dee says.

Definitely good looking, I agree.

A moment of silence fills the space between us, and I consider mentioning Thanksgiving, how I ran out on them before dinner without a phone call or an apology. It's been almost two months since the event, but neither my parents nor I have spoken of it. It's like an invisible cord caught between us, tangling our arms and legs, making it awkward to be together.

My mother breaks the silence. "You should be grateful for what you have. But you're never happy. You hate us, and I don't know why. You didn't stay for Thanksgiving. You didn't send gifts on Christmas. And you didn't remember my birthday. You're incredibly selfish. Tom is lucky you said no. He would have been miserable living with someone as self-centered as you are."

I am stunned. My mother's voice stings like venom. She's right about some of it. I forgot her birthday. It was New Year's Day. How could I forget? But am I selfish? I don't think so. "Mom, I'm sorry about your birthday. I was rained in and preoccupied. The phones were down. But I could have sent an e-card and I didn't. I hope you can forgive me. As for Christmas, I didn't have money to send gifts to anyone. I was on the verge of filing for bankruptcy." My hands are cold with fear. I uncross my legs and stand up, hoping to pump blood through my body by pacing in front of my desk. "You're right about Thanksgiving. I behaved badly. I'm sorry. Just because I was angry with you and Dad for inviting Tom to dinner didn't give me the right to pitch a fit and walk out. That was selfish and childlike of me. I've already apologized to Dee for breaking her camera, and she's forgiven me. I hope you can forgive me, too."

My father is the first to speak. "That's fine, dear. Apology accepted. Don't worry about not marrying Tom. I just want you to be happy." I can almost hear him smile.

But my mother is a different story. "You aren't getting any younger. Aren't you ever going to settle down?"

I laugh, thinking of baby Iris and how I want nothing more than to have someone small to hold and take care of and nurture. But not with Tom. And not right now. I want to grow a little more first. "How can I be a good parent if I'm as selfish as you say I am? Aren't parents supposed to be generous and loving and supportive?"

My father clears his throat. Dee is silent. My mother sniffs.

Alex steps into the office. I mouth, *My parents*, and point to the BlackBerry pressed against my ear. He nods and disappears into Ms. Lashay's office, closing the door. I want to tell my parents about him, but I think it's too early to tell anyone anything. It's not like he's my boyfriend. But it's not like he's just my boss's son either.

"Tom isn't the last person I'll love, Mom. And I am not ruling out marriage or children either. I'm just trying to get through my life as best as I can without causing a lot of collateral damage to the ones I love. Like you and Dad and Dee." I pause, trying to clear the itch in my throat. I glance at my desk, looking for my cup so I can get some water, but it's buried somewhere in all the paperwork. Geez, I'm such a slob. One more thing to work on. I can't exactly tell my kid to pick up his or her room when my room looks like a hurricane hit it.

"She's trying," Dee says to my mother. "Give her credit for that."

My mother sniffs again. I imagine her dabbing her eyes with a tissue in a melodramatic move that would make even Val laugh. She seems to think my life is over when I feel like it's just begun.

"I don't know," my mother says. "I just don't know."

"What if I tell you about the little girl that made my heart break?" I perch on the edge of my desk and dangle my heel out of my shoe. I tell them about Iris Ivy and her disfigurement, about the teasing I endured over my legs, about Tom's ignorance over the whole situation because I never told him, and about Alex and Ms. Lashay and their family feud. "And when Alex changed his mind, I was absolutely stunned. You know how doubtful and mistrusting I am, Dee. If he hadn't shown me the documents, I never would have believed he had signed for his mother. But he did! It was real. I almost fainted. You can't believe how happy I was. It felt better than a long distance run." My voice rises with excitement and my cheeks hurt from smiling too much. "Did I mention he cooked dinner for me afterward? I know you're a great cook, Mom, so please don't take offense, but I didn't know fish could taste so delicate and flakey and buttery good. It was absolutely amazing! And Dad, you'll never guess what happened afterward. No, he didn't make a pass at me. He said he had to go home to get up early for work the next morning. And he kissed my hand when he said good night. Isn't that adorable? I mean, how many men do you know who still kiss hands and open doors for women? He's such a gentleman. And then—"

"Honey, stop crying," my father says to my mother. "Can't you see she can't marry Tom no matter how much you want her to? She's in love with Alex."

I am? If I'm in love, I certainly don't feel like it. Doesn't falling in love supposed to feel like unwrapping a gift? You tear into it with anticipation, shredding the paper, discarding the bow, sometimes even ignoring the card that's attached so you can get inside and see what you've got. But then I think of Val and Antonio. How they started out as co-stars, then became friends, before becoming so much more. Is that how love happens?

My mother's sniffling stops. "That explains everything," she says, matter-of-factly. "When can we meet Alex? Is he as good looking as Tom?"

I flush, turning to the window in Ms. Lashay's office, trying to peer through the blinds. The door opens and Alex strides out. When he sees me on the BlackBerry, he mouths, *Are you okay?* I shrug. How do I tell him my father just informed me I am in love? *Water?* he mouths. I nod. He rummages through the papers on my desk and finds my cup. How did he do that? I couldn't find it and I looked a lot harder than he did. He never ceases to amaze me. Moments later, he returns. I smile with gratitude and sip from the cup. The cool water rushes down my parched throat. He mouths, *Anything else?* How thoughtful of him to ask. I shake my head and place the cup beside me.

I tell my parents to hold for a second. "When are you coming back?" I ask Alex.

His eyebrows lift. "I haven't left."

"But you will on Sunday, and my parents want to meet you."

"Already?" He chuckles. "I didn't know we were going together."

I flush, embarrassed by his comment. How could I have just blurted that out? I should have worded things more carefully. After all, I'm a salesperson. I'm supposed to be tactfully suggestive, not in-your-face blunt. "It's not like that,"

I say, hoping to back pedal without looking defensive. "They like to meet my new friends."

He laughs again. "It's okay. Tell them I'll be back in two weeks."

I wait for him to leave, but he stands in front of me, unmoving. What is he waiting for? Doesn't he have work to do? Phone calls to make? A business to run? When he doesn't leave, I lift the BlackBerry to my ear. "If you're free in two weeks, you can come up and meet him. He's helping his mother with the business till she gets better."

"Mark it on our calendar, dear," my mother says to my father. "I want to meet this Alex guy. See if he's better than Tom."

My father grunts like he's searching for a scrap of paper and a pen to write with.

"I have to go," I tell them, gazing at Alex who is gazing at me.

"Love you," Mom says.

"Love you too." I hang up. The crook of my arm feels stiff from holding the BlackBerry to my ear for so long.

Alex flashes a crooked smile. "So, your parents want to meet me?"

"Why not?" I tell him.

"There's something else." He shakes his head. "What are you hiding from me?"

I take a deep breath and tell him about Tom. "He came to the office and proposed," I explain. "And I turned him down. My parents didn't know why. And I guess I didn't really know why either till now."

"What's different now?"

I trace the rim of my cup with my index finger, wishing I was tracing circles in the palm of Alex's hand. I stare at my big feet, and I suddenly feel shy. I've never felt shy around a guy before. Maybe that's because I've never been the first to say what I'm about to say right now. "I love you." I glance up to gauge his reaction. There are tiny lines in the corners of his brown eyes when he smiles. He takes my cold hands in his warm hands and pulls me to him. My heart stutters in my chest, and my knees wobble. We are standing only millimeters apart. I can smell the coffee on his breath.

"I love you, too," he says, tilting his head up for a kiss.

# CHAPTER 36

▼

At five-thirty, Alex grabs his jacket from the coat rack by the double glass doors. He slips his arms through the sleeves and adjusts the lapels. Although he smiles when I catch his eyes, there is a hint of disappointment in the dip of his shoulders. "I thought we'd go out and have a romantic dinner tonight, but Betty says Mom is lonely at the convalescent home." He turns up his palms like he is offering up an apology. "Would you mind having dinner there? The food might be terrible, but the company might be great."

I walk over to him and wrap my arms around his shoulders. "I don't mind as long as I am with you."

He smiles and steps back to get the door.

We take separate cars. I follow him through evening traffic through the Valley of the Moon. It is too cold to put down the hood, but I am warmed by the beauty of the lush green hills and the rows and rows of old grape vines amidst enchanting chateaus turned into tasting rooms. Maybe Alex, my parents, and I can go wine tasting. Wouldn't that be fun?

Before I lose cell reception, my BlackBerry sings, "Lucky Star." I snatch it up. "Hello?"

"Is this Trina Kay?" the caller asks.

"It is."

"It's Joanie Ivy."

I smile. I've been waiting to hear from the Ivys all day, but I've been too cautious to call, afraid I might be intruding. I decided to send flowers and Alex delivered a homemade casserole to their neighbor's home since they were at the hospital when he arrived. "Joanie, how are you? Did the surgery go well?"

"Absolutely. Iris is doing well. We'll bring her by next week for a visit. We're calling to thank you for the lovely flowers and the delicious casserole. And for the loan, of course. We couldn't have done this without your help."

"My pleasure," I say, beaming with happiness. "I look forward to your visit next week. Would you mind me taking your family out to lunch? Maybe Portofino or Checkers?"

"Checkers would be great. My husband loves their Greek salad."

"Then it's a date. I'm driving, so I can't check my calendar, but I'll call you on Monday to arrange things. Have a great weekend and please kiss Iris for me."

"I will." I can hear her smile through her voice.

God, I've never felt so good.

The convalescent home is a one-story stucco building painted buttercup yellow and surrounded by green gardens and a big parking lot. I pull into a slot and turn off the engine and rush out of my Mercedes waving my hands at Alex. I pounce on him as soon as he steps outside. "You'll never guess who called."

"The Ivys."

I frown. It was supposed to be a surprise. "How did you know?"

"They called me first to thank me for helping them fund the loan and to reassure me that their daughter is going to be all right. They wanted to get together next week, but I told them I'd be in L.A. and I asked them to call you. I thought you'd be happy to hear from them. And from the looks of it, you were."

They called him first? I can't believe it.

"Don't look so sad." He grabs my hand. "I already feel bad about coming here. I mean, it's not exactly the best way to end the week."

I shrug. "I'm not thinking about that. I'm wondering why the Ivys called you before they called me."

"That's because I gave them my number just in case they ran into any glitches. Like extra fees that weren't calculated into the costs of the surgery. I told them to have the doctors call me. But apparently, everything went as planned, and so they called to thank me."

Our feet match each other's stride. Why am I surprised he offered them extra cash in case they needed it? That type of generosity transcended anything Ms. Lashay would have done. She never extended credit without adequate security, even if that security was in jeopardy.

The automatic doors slide open. A gust of warm air smelling like antiseptic whips around us. Alex steers us toward the reception area and asks the nurse behind the counter where the dining hall is. "Over to the left and down the hall to the right," she says, checking the clock against the wall. "Dinner starts in ten minutes."

Alex gazes intently at me. "Are you sure you're okay with coming here for dinner?"

I grin and squeeze his hand. "It's okay," I reassure him. It doesn't matter where we go. He could have taken me to the seediest restaurant in town, and I wouldn't order from the menu, but I would feast on the movement of his mouth as he spoke to me. He could have taken me to the dirtiest theater in town where the soles of your shoes stick to the syrupy floors and you can't see over the person's head in front of you, but I would tilt my head till it touched his shoulder and close my eyes and dream.

Alex laughs. "You're the first girl I've known who would say something like that and mean it." He pauses, as if thinking. "That is unless you're fooling me and I'll get pummeled with your purse later when we walk back to our cars."

My grin broadens, though a nervous quiver rushes through my arms. Do women really treat him that badly? "No, I wouldn't do that. Why would you be with anyone who would?"

His face darkens. "I've never had too much luck with women," he explains. "I seem to fall for all the glitz and glitter. Guess that comes with living in L.A." When I frown, he continues to explain. "I put up with a lot of stuff most men wouldn't put up with for the glamour of being with a starlet or a very young woman who looks like a starlet. Like Candie. They always leave for men with more money or power so it's doomed to fail from the start, but that doesn't stop me from trying." He steps toward the wall of windows and pulls me toward him. "It was a happy accident to meet you." He kisses my nose, then my lips. I open my mouth and push my tongue between his teeth. My whole body feels soft and warm like a content kitten curled up in a patch of sunlight.

"Oh, my," Ms. Morgan says, when she sees us.

I reluctantly stop kissing Alex. He pulls away and smiles sheepishly at Ms. Morgan. "Sorry," he says.

"No apologies," I say, playfully shaking my finger at him. Turning to face Ms. Morgan, I say, "He's an excellent kisser. Only topped by his excellent cooking."

"Really?" Ms. Morgan lifts her eyebrows. "Is that why you were up early this morning baking?"

"That was for someone else," he says.

"So, you're suddenly the ladies' man, I see." She tilts her chin and narrows her eyes. "I have great respect for Ms. Kay, and if I ever get wind that you're cheating on her like your father cheated on your mother, I will personally hurt you."

Alex blushes, as if embarrassed. "I don't think you have anything to worry about." Alex glances from Ms. Morgan to me. "I'm not that much like my father."

"From the looks of your last girlfriend, you are," Ms. Morgan says, sternly.

I step aside, hoping to dodge the bullets between them. But Alex reaches for my hand. His voice rises. "I'm more honorable than my father. I broke up with Candie before asking Trina out."

Ms. Morgan glances at me, as if for reassurance.

"It's true," I say. "He did."

Ms. Morgan studies us carefully before she turns on her heels. "Your mother is waiting."

We follow Ms. Morgan into the dining hall where residents in wheel chairs and walkers sit at square tables waiting to be served. A few attendants bring out trays full of meatloaf and mashed potatoes and green beans with glasses of milk and tiny bowls of red gelatin. Ms. Lashay sits in the far corner, frowning. When Ms. Morgan approaches, her face cracks into a smile. When she notices Alex, the smile broadens and her eyes gleam. When she notices me, her eyebrows lift, as if she's surprised to see me.

"Trina?" Her voice is getting better. "Shouldn't you be in San Jose?"

Should I tell her? I guess I should. "I'm not moving. So, if you don't mind, I'd like my old job back. That is, if it's still available."

"Of course you may have it," Ms. Lashay says. "But why come all the way out here to ask for it?"

"She's my date," Alex explains, his hand on the small of my back.

"Your date?" Ms. Lashay's forehead furrows.

Ms. Morgan clears her throat. "I saw them kissing in the hallway like two exhibitionists."

Exhibitionists? Isn't that a bit too strong? It's not like we were naked and groping each other. But I don't protest. I look to Alex to rescue us from this situation.

"Trina has a lot to celebrate, don't you?" he says, eyeing me.

I take a seat across from Ms. Lashay. Ms. Morgan sits across from Alex who is sitting next to me. "I signed dissolution papers for my business in San Jose and gave my ex-boyfriend the keys to our old home. We're officially through with each other."

"And Candie, as you know, is out of the picture," Alex reminds everyone. "So we're both free to see each other now."

"You're a couple?" Ms. Lashay asks.

Alex gazes at me. I smile and return the gaze. "I guess you could call us that," he says. "We haven't really discussed it."

"Some things don't need to be discussed," Ms. Lashay says. "You just know."

An attendant in a black and white uniform delivers two trays of food. Ms. Morgan helps Ms. Lashay tuck a napkin in the collar of her blouse. "What do you want first? The meatloaf or the mashed potatoes?"

"They both look awful." Although her speech is getting better, Ms. Lashay's hands are pretty useless still. She gropes for her silverware and sends her spoon tumbling to the floor. I bend to retrieve it.

Ms. Morgan uses her utensils to spoon the mashed potatoes. She presses it against Ms. Lashay's closed mouth. "You have to eat," she scolds her. "Or they'll give you an IV." Reluctantly, Ms. Lashay's lips part. Her mouth puckers as she chews.

"I'll bring you dinner tomorrow in your room before I go," Alex says, staring at the two additional trays of food that are being placed in front of us.

"He's a wonderful cook," I say.

"Must be from his father. I couldn't boil water."

We eat in silence, poking our forks through the mushy, tasteless food.

Toward the end of dinner, Alex leans across the table and asks, "Do you approve of Trina and I being together?" His face looks young with concern like he's eight years old asking for permission to play with the girl next door.

Ms. Lashay studies us. "I'm surprised, that's all." Her brown eyes seem to penetrate me. "That's not exactly what I expected when I asked her to take care of you."

"What did you expect?" I ask, full of curiosity.

Her eyes moisten. "I don't know," she mumbles. "I just hope it works out for you two. I'd like to see everyone happy for once."

Ms. Morgan lifts her glass of milk. "To happiness," she says.

We lift our glasses, except for Ms. Lashay who lets Ms. Morgan raise hers. The glasses click and we sip our milk like one extended family.

After dinner, Alex walks me to my car. He holds me close and kisses me. Again I am warmed by his touch.

"Would you like to come to the cottage?" I ask, hinting at a romantic interlude.

He shakes his head. "Not tonight. It's late. And I'm tired."

I try to mask my disappointment. "Well, what about doing something tomorrow?"

"Like what?"

I shrug. "Wine tasting?"

For a moment, he's silent. "How about driving to the coast? I miss the ocean."

I think of the bitter chill and shudder. "This isn't L.A. The water's cold."

"We can stay in the car and keep each other warm." He smiles.

"Then it's a date?"

"I'll pick you up at eleven. If you're free, we can spend the afternoon together."

"Just the afternoon?"

"I have to make dinner for my mother tomorrow night. I promised."

I groan. Will I always be in competition for his time and attention? Does he love his mother more than he loves me? Maybe I'm just being selfish, I think. Goodness knows I wish I could erase that part of me. Along with my impulsive streak.

I kiss him one last time. He cups my head in his hands and gazes at me with eyes full of moonlight and magic. I do not expect him to say something, but he does.

"Thanks for coming with me tonight," he whispers. "It meant a lot to me to have you here. I may be getting along better with my mom, but I still have a long way to go to get to a place of feeling completely comfortable around her like I feel when I'm with you."

"You're welcome."

He opens the driver's door of my Mercedes for me. I slip inside and he shuts it. Part of me doesn't want to drive away. I want to spend the night with him. Why doesn't he want to spend the night with me?

I start the car and glance at the clock on the dash. Only fifteen hours till we meet again.

# CHAPTER 37

▼

When I arrive at Val's cottage, it is almost ten o'clock. As soon as I unlock the front door, I hear the phone ring.

I flick on the lights and stride across the room, wondering who could be calling at such a late hour. My pulse quickens. Maybe Alex changed his mind and wants to come over and spend the night.

"Hello?" I say, bright and hopeful.

"KK, it's me," Val says.

"Oh." I don't hide the disappointment in my voice.

"Ohmigod, what's happened to you? You used to be excited to hear from me."

"I was just hoping you were someone else."

"Who would you rather hear from than me?" he jokes.

"Alex."

"Ms. Lashay's evil son?"

I wince. "So much has happened since we've last spoken; I don't know where to start."

"Then let me go first," Val says. "Antonio and I are moving in together after the tour ends in February. You'll never guess where we're moving."

I play along, hoping to hide my disappointment. "Chicago?"

"Guess again."

This could take a while. "New York." I grab a sponge and wipe the kitchen counter.

"Wrong."

Outside, the wind howls. Oh, please, not another storm. I toss the sponge in the sink and grab a book of matches from the counter and tuck them into my pant's pocket just in case the power goes out. It's so annoying trying to find matches in the dark.

"C'mon, KK. It's not that hard. Where else would an actor live?"

"Hollywood."

"Ding-ding-ding! She finally gets it! Antonio has a condo in West Hollywood. I haven't seen it, but it sounds absolutely gorgeous. You'll have to come down and visit."

The lights flicker with another gust of wind. Then the room goes dark.

My heart sinks. Why is everyone leaving? First, Alex. Now, Val. I prop my elbows on the blue tiles of the kitchen counter. Through the window, long shadows from the redwood trees flit across the floor like dancing couples. I feel lonely although I have my best friend on the phone.

"KK? You still there, sweetie?"

"Yeah, I'm here." I strike a match and the yellow flame flickers against a candle wink, blinking to life.

Val pouts, "Aren't you happy for me?" After a long moment of silence, he finally asks, "What's wrong?"

"I'm not moving back to San Jose." Then, before he can ask why, I add, "Tom and I aren't getting back together. I turned down his marriage proposal and sold my half of the business to him."

"Oh, sweetie," Val says, with that honey drenched voice. "I'm so sorry. Listen to me, rattling on and on about the love of my life, and you've just lost yours."

"I don't think Tom was the love of my life." A vision of Alex pops into my head. I try to push the thought of unbuttoning his shirt out of my mind. "That's not what I'm sad about."

"Well, look at the bright side. You don't have to look for a place to live. Of course, I'll have to charge you rent, but it won't be much."

I involuntarily half-smile. "Thanks, Val."

I tell him about the other events since we've last spoken, about Tom being unable to fund the loan, about Alex's breakup with Candie, and about Alex and I becoming a couple. "And when you called I was hoping he had changed his mind and wanted to come over and spend the night. That's why I was disappointed. It's like he's avoiding me."

"He won't have sex with you because he just broke up with Psycho Cell-Phone-Throwing Candie. What makes him think you won't hack at his balls with your BlackBerry?"

I had not thought about that.

"Don't worry," Val tries to reassure me. "If you love him like you say you do, then it won't matter if you have to wait. It will be worth it."

I groan. "I don't know how to wait for anything."

Val dramatically sighs, playing up my frustration. "Maybe this is the universe's way of making you learn."

"I think I'll self-destruct from hormonal overdrive first."

Val chuckles. "Go take a cold shower and go to bed. Staying up and thinking of him will only make it worse."

I agree. I thank Val and congratulate him on his growing relationship with Antonio. I even try to joke, "Next call I'll get, you'll be telling me you're moving out of state and getting married." He jokes back, "Only with a prenup. Never want the spouse taking all the goods if things go wrong." We say goodnight, and I hang up the phone feeling a little better. Maybe Val's right. Maybe I should learn to be patient.

But as I lay in bed after my cold shower staring at the ceiling, I can't help but wonder, *Does Alex make love as good as he cooks?* My skin tingles with the thought. *Mmm...I sure hope he does.*

I wake up to rain pattering on the tin roof. I stumble out of bed, cinch a robe around my waist, and shove my feet into soft wool slippers. Padding to the French doors, I pull back the curtains. Gray clouds scuttle across an equally gray sky. The redwoods seem to droop with all that moisture. I've seen too much rain these last few weeks. When, oh, when, will it stop?

I shower, change into my most sensual cashmere sweater in berry red and black wool slacks and hiking boots, just in case Alex wants to walk along the too cold beach. I scrunch gel into my curls and apply a thick layer of mascara to my too short lashes. With a quick spritz, I add a scent of freesia to my wrist and rub them together until the scent dissipates into a faint whiff. The clock on the dresser says ten-thirty. I pace back and forth, resisting the temptation to call and beg him to come earlier. Instead, I sit down on the couch and flip through old newspapers, reading the comics though nothing seems particularly funny.

At ten fifty-five, Alex arrives. "Good morning, gorgeous!" He stands beneath his black umbrella, grinning at me. His brown eyes twinkle. I want to pull him inside and shut the door and rip his jacket off him, but I take a deep breath and grab my purse and keys and follow him outside to the waiting rental car. Slipping into the passenger's seat, I tug the seatbelt across my waist as Alex shuts my door.

He shakes the water out of the umbrella before tossing it into the back seat. A drop of moisture clings to his forehead like a baptismal kiss. I reach up and touch it. His eyebrows slant together in curiosity, and I bring my palm to the freshly shaven plane of his cheek and let it soak up the warmth of his skin.

"I want to kiss you and make love to you all day," I whisper.

He takes my hand, gently kisses it, then returns it to my lap. Starting the engine, he backs out of the turnout and heads down the windy hill without saying a word. Water slashes against the windshield, making the wipers work overtime. The drive to the coast cuts through redwood groves, skirts around a golf course, and flows along pastures where cows graze. At the juncture where River Road dips into Highway 1, the rain stops. Alex turns left and travels along the edge of the mountainous coast. Below us, rollicking waves crash against boulders. The sky is full of fleecy, white clouds that trap the sunlight in tiny pockets of translucent yellows.

"It's beautiful," I say.

"You should come to Southern California," Alex says. "The sunsets are to die for."

"I probably will be there more than I care to," I say. "Val called last night. He's moving to West Hollywood to be with his lover."

"Really? Does that mean you are indefinitely house-sitting?"

I laugh. Why not tell him the truth? "I have no where else to go."

"I'm sure my mother could find you a great deal."

I grin. "She already tried to. That's how we met. She showed me a rental she purchased to save from foreclosure."

We park in a turnout and Alex opens the door, braving the cold and the wind. He opens my door and offers me his hand. "Want to walk?"

"Not really. It's too cold."

He smiles. "I'll warm you up."

I interlock my fingers with his cool hand. He tugs me close and I start to wonder if he'll let go of my hand and wrap his arm around my waist, but he won't bridge the distance. With my free hand, I tug my coat close against me and follow his lead toward the edge of the turnout where the panoramic views of the Pacific Ocean seem to stretch for hundreds of miles. The salty air sears through my nostrils, stinging my lungs till I feel like I've run too long and too hard. Alex points north to a craggy cliff that looks like an old woman's crooked finger pointing toward the sky. "That's Goat Rock," he says, proudly. "Before we moved to L.A., my father and I used to watch sleeper waves crash against the shore from here."

"What's a sleeper wave?"

"It's a wave that starts out like a ripple and ends like a tsunami. It's infamous for swallowing up unsuspecting people and animals." He eyes me. "It's the dangerous side of nature. That's what my father loved." He glances out at the ocean. "He died a few years ago."

I squeeze Alex's hand. "It sounds like you miss him."

He nods while staring at the waves. The bitter wind slaps against my cheeks. After a while, my face starts to feel numb. I release his hand and rub my nose. Alex wraps his arm around my waist and pulls me close. I bury my freezing nose against his shoulder. "Are you all right?"

"I'm becoming a popsicle."

"Let's go back to the car."

Inside, Alex turns on the heater and lets the engine idle. He stares out at the waves in silence while I briskly rub my hands in front of the vents, trying to revive the circulation. From my purse, I remove a tube of moisturizer and smear it onto my face.

"Want to get some clam chowder?" he asks.

"Sure, as long as they serve it indoors."

He chuckles. "Sorry about making you freeze. There's something hypnotic about the ocean for me. It's where I go when I'm confused and want to think."

"What are you confused about?" I ask.

"You."

"Me?" I touch my chest and raise my eyebrows in disbelief. "Why would I confuse anyone?"

He shakes his head. "I should have phrased that differently. It's the way I feel about you. I've never felt this way before." He gazes out at the waves as if for strength. His voice sounds far away and dreamy. "Part of me wants to take care of you and protect you although I know you're perfectly capable of taking care of yourself. That same part of me doesn't want to leave tomorrow. I'm afraid if I'm gone too long, you'll forget about me. It's like I want you to need me so you'll never let me go."

I reach over and take his hand. "I'm not going anywhere," I reassure him. "I want to jump your bones, can't you tell?"

"Having sex and needing someone are very different things."

I think about it. Okay, maybe he's right. "But what's so different about them?"

"Sex is about desire. Need is about survival."

"Are you saying you can't live without me?" What a romantic gesture.

"I don't know what I'm saying." He drops my hand and shifts the car into reverse. We drive south along the coast in silence. I want to ask him more about his confusing thoughts, but decide to give him space. When he's ready, he'll talk, right?

A few minutes later, we pull into the parking lot of The Tides Wharf and Restaurant. "Alfred Hitchcock filmed *The Birds* here," Alex says, opening my door.

I shiver. "I hated that movie. I was seven when I saw it on TV. I can't believe my parents let me watch it. I wouldn't go outside for a week, I was so scared."

He chuckles. "Me, too."

Inside, the open beamed ceilings and wood floors offer an inviting shelter from the bitter cold. I snuggle up against Alex as he stands in line to order from the walk up counter. While we wait for our number to be called, we find a table by the big windows overlooking the ocean. A sea gull hops along the deck, pecking for crumbs. He looks so lonely.

Alex points behind me. "In the main dining area, they have photos from the movie lining the walls."

"We'll look later, if I'm not too scared," I say, hoping to be playful.

Our clam chowders arrive in bread bowls. The chewy clams and the thick cream soup and chunks of potatoes taste good. I finish everything, even the bread bowl. Leaning back, I rub my stomach. "God, I'm full."

Alex laughs. "You look like a guy who's drunk too much beer."

I giggle. "I'm definitely not one of those self-conscious, have-to-be-perfect girls who are afraid of eating too much."

"You're definitely nothing like Candie."

I feel her shadow between us. I sit up and prop my elbows on the table. "Do you miss her?"

He shakes his head, but does not meet my gaze. "I only wish I would have broken up with her sooner." He pushes his empty bread bowl aside and crosses his arms on the table.

I reach over and touch his wrist. "Why don't we go back to the cottage?" I suggest.

He glances at his watch. "It's only three. Why the rush?"

Should I tell him? "I want to make love to you."

He stares at me like I'm one of those man-eating birds hovering above him. Am I too forward? Is he still afraid I'm going to hack at him with my BlackBerry?

"What's wrong?" I ask, hoping I didn't just stick my foot into my mouth.

He reaches across the table and laces his fingers through my hands. "If you don't mind, I'd like to wait. We're just starting to get to know each other, and if we just fall into bed, we might never get very far, understand?"

I shake my head and withdraw my hands. I feel ugly from head to toe. "You don't want me."

"I never said that." He tries to smile. "You're beautiful inside and out. If I didn't love you, then I could go to bed with you and leave tomorrow without any regrets. But I don't want a one night stand or a casual fling. I want something meaningful and real. That's why I want to wait." He chuckles, trying to relieve the pressure mounting between us. "Don't you know by now I'm old fashioned?"

I think of chastity belts and virgins. "I don't want to wait till we're married."

He leans back and laughs till his eyes glitter with tears.

"It's not funny," I say, crossing my arms under my breasts. "It's painful. It feels like you're rejecting me."

"Quite the opposite." He wipes his eyes with a napkin. "You're very attractive. I absolutely adore you. I'm just not going to risk blowing it." His lips tilt into a crooked smile. "Pun intended."

I stand up and grab my purse. "I can't believe you're joking about this."

He follows me out to the parking lot. I keep walking past the rental car. He grabs my hand before I get to the cusp of the highway and tugs me to him. He kisses me long and hard. When he releases me, I gasp.

"What was that for?" I ask.

"To show you that I want you just as much as you want me. Maybe even more."

I stare at him, and feel my knees wobble. I'm afraid to move; I might collapse.

"Let's go. You're shivering." With his hand on the small of my back, he guides me to the car and opens the door. I feel a prickle of anticipation as I slide against the leather seat. As soon as we crest onto the highway, I place my hand on his knee. He keeps his eyes on the road, but his jaw twitches. I inch my fingers up his thigh. He brusquely removes my hand, tossing it aside like a dead fish. "I thought I made myself clear. But I guess you don't understand." Without looking at me, he slams his foot into the accelerator, and I involuntarily grip the Oh Shit handle above the door. My heart flops around in my chest, but it's not from sexual excitement. It's from fear.

"What's going on?"

His knuckles gleam like white stones against the steering wheel. "If a guy makes a move too early, he's accused of thinking only of sex. If a guy wants to wait, he gets accused of not finding the girl attractive." He eases up on the accelerator to turn onto River Road, then picks up speed again. "Damned if I do; damned if I don't. Either way, I lose."

I reach toward him.

He flinches. "Please don't touch me."

I retract my hand, tucking it against my side like an injured wing. I remember what Val said last night. Maybe he's right. Maybe Alex is afraid of having sex with me. Because of Candie, not because of me. My voice sounds hollow when I speak. "I didn't mean to upset you." I swallow some discomfort, unaccustomed to having my desires take the back seat. But I don't want to pressure him into anything if that means I'll never see him again. I sigh. "If you want, we can wait."

"You don't sound too thrilled," he says. But he slows down to the speed limit.

I release my grip on the handle and hug myself around my waist to keep from feeling like I'm falling apart.

For a few minutes, neither one of us speaks.

By the time Alex pulls into the turnout in front of Val's cottage, I'm ready to cry. How did I mess up so badly with him? Why didn't I just keep my mouth shut instead of telling him how much I wanted to have sex with him? But the conversation is over, and there is no way we can go back and start over. I sniff, feeling shaky. I don't know what to do. I've never waited for anything or anyone. And now I'm being asked to do something I've never done before, something I don't even know if I'm capable of doing.

I open the door for myself and fit my key into the lock. Alex stands behind me. Soft sprinkles of rain dot my hair and shoulders. I do not turn around. I push the door open and flick on the lights to relieve the cavernous pressure of the closet-sized cottage.

"May I come inside?" he asks.

"Sure." I toss my purse on the coffee table along with my keys and sit on the couch to unlace my hiking boots. Alex closes the front door and perches on the arm of the sofa, clasping his hands together.

"I'm sorry," he says.

"You apologize too much," I tell him. "And I apologize too little."

"Maybe we'll balance each other," he says, forcing a smile. When I don't respond, he continues. "I didn't mean to go off like that. I was just angry. I promised myself I wasn't going to get into another relationship where I'm not taking turns in the driver's seat. It's not fun being bossed around all the time and not having a say in anything. I don't want to spend my life conceding to someone else. I want my needs heard and respected too."

I nod. His request is reasonable. But that doesn't negate how I feel. "I'm just not used to waiting," I tell him. "I have sex as soon as possible. It's like closing the deal. In this day and age, why wait? There's no need to, from what I can see."

"I think that's why most relationships fail. No one gives it time to mature into something substantial. They take the easy route instead."

"Is that what you did with Candie?" I ask, gazing at him.

He purses his lips and nods. "It was convenient."

I extend my hand. He takes it this time and brings it to his lips.

And although I still want to rip off his jacket and unbuckle his pants, I restrain the urge as best as I can. I scoot over on the sofa, making room for him to join me. He removes his jacket and snuggles close. I scoot down and lean my head against his chest and close my eyes and listen to him breathe. His skin smells like the ocean. After a while, the restlessness disappears. It's kind of nice to just sit here with no expectations. It's almost like prayer.

Many minutes later, when I'm almost asleep, Alex shifts to glance at his watch. "I have to leave soon to start cooking for my mother."

I lift my head and blink. "Will I see you before your flight?"

He shakes his head. "Not likely. I leave for the airport at six."

"What would make you stay?" I ask, sitting up and tucking my feet under my hips.

He smiles, caressing my face with his fingers. "I'm not out of the picture. I'm just in the periphery. I'll be back in two weeks. You'll hardly notice I've been gone."

I pout. "Long distance relationships are tough."

Alex laughs. "It's better than the one I just got out of."

I agree.

He leans over and kisses my lips softly. "I already miss you," he says.

My eyes fill with sudden tears. I feel so full of his tenderness; I'm overflowing.

That night, I can't sleep. I lay in bed and toss and turn, twisting the sheets. My whole body feels on fire. I've already taken two cold showers, trying to erase the memory of his delicate fingers against my skin, but as soon as I emerge, my nerves explode with desire.

I undress and lie on top of the sheets and move my hands over my body, pretending to be Alex. I slip my fingers into the wetness between my thighs and arch my lower back and utter a low growl. God, I want him.

The phone rings. I wipe my hand with a tissue from the night stand and squint at the clock. Five-thirty. Who calls this early in the morning?

The phone keeps ringing.

I sit up and grab the extension. "Hello?"

"Good morning, sunshine."

A slow smile spreads across my face. "Alex."

"I couldn't wait to call you. Just wanted you to know I've booked a return flight for this Friday night. I was thinking we could have that romantic dinner before your parents arrive the following weekend."

I twist a lock of hair and tuck it behind my ear. "How sweet. Will you be staying with Ms. Morgan?"

There is a pause on the other end of the line. I wonder if the connection has died, but then I hear his voice, tentative with nervousness. "I was thinking maybe I could stay at your place."

My smile broadens. "Absolutely."

# About the Author

Angela Lam Turpin has worked in the real estate industry for over 15 years. Her book-length memoir, *Red Eggs and Good Luck*, won the Mary Tanenbaum Award for Creative Nonfiction. Her essay, "Strange and Wonderful," appeared in *Wild Child: Girlhoods in the Counterculture* (Seal Press). *Legs* is her first novel.

Printed in the United States
127075LV00001B/4-81/P

9 780595 530915